HOME

HOME

THE PORTAL SERIES, BOOK 3

RICHARD BOWKER

Book design by eBook Prep
www.ebookprep.com

Cover design by Jim McManus
www.complexstories.com

April, 2019
ISBN: 978-1-64457-042-5

ePublishing Works!
644 Shrewsbury Commons Ave
Ste 249
Shrewsbury PA 17361
United States of America

www.epublishingworks.com
Phone: 866-846-5123

For Joe and Paula

PROLOGUE

Lamathe

L amathe heard the news first from Samos, who pounded on his door in the early morning, desperate for admittance. Surely what Samos told him couldn't be true, Lamathe thought. Perhaps he was still asleep, and this was a particularly bad dream. Perhaps Samos was mistaken; he was young and a bit of a hothead—maybe he'd gotten the story wrong.

But Samos had not gotten the story wrong. One priest after another showed up at Lamathe's house, in a small castella not far from the center of Urbis. All were distraught, disbelieving, horrified. All told the same story.

Urbis—the holy city of the Roman empire and the site of Via, its most sacred object—had been invaded during the night. The invaders had raided the armamentarium and obtained its gants, and with those powerful weapons they could destroy anyone and anything. The soldiers' barracks and the palatium were ablaze; people were fleeing the city in panic. The pontifex's palace had been taken, and that meant Tirelius and his associates were dead or in the invaders' hands.

And the temple of Via itself?

Yes, it too was theirs. No one had returned from the sunrise service at the temple. Those who had attended the service were likely dead or prisoners as well.

Who were the invaders? How had this happened?

And what was to be done now?

The priests looked to Lamathe for wisdom and guidance. And Samos was the one to ask him the obvious question: "Is Affron responsible for this?"

For months the priests had talked of little besides the struggle between Tirelius and Affron for the soul of Urbis. Tirelius had finally arrested Affron and sentenced him to death. But on the eve of his execution he had been freed from his jail cell in the palatium and, along with others, escaped from the city. He had not been seen since.

Lamathe had supported Affron, but he was not a rebel. He had tried to make peace between Affron and Tirelius, to no avail. And now this. "It is not Affron," he asserted. "I would stake my life on it. You all know him. Would he sneak into Urbis in the middle of the night? Would he kill our soldiers to seize power? He doesn't even want power. He just wants to be left alone."

"Who then?" Samos demanded.

"I don't know. The Gallians? They have reason enough to hate us."

"It doesn't matter," Borafin replied. Like Lamathe, Borafin was a viator—one of the priests allowed to use Via to travel to other worlds. "We have to leave. If we stay, we'll be captured or killed."

"But if it's Affron—"

"It isn't Affron," Borafin insisted. "Lamathe's right. Affron wouldn't do this."

"I'm willing to die for Via," Clovis announced. Another young priest.

"What is the point of dying?" Lamathe responded mildly.

"It's better than running away."

"Some of us must survive," Honoria said. She, too, was a viator. "The time will come when we will be needed."

"We are needed now," Samos retorted. He wouldn't have dared to speak to Honoria that way in normal times.

Lamathe tried to make sense of it all. Whoever the invaders were, however they had managed to enter Urbis, they were here. And with the gants, they could not be defeated. And so…

"We must stop them from using Via," he said.

"How can we do that?" Theodosius, another viator, asked. "They possess it. It's theirs." He was close to tears.

"Without Affron or another viator to teach them, they will try to use it, and it will defeat them," Lamathe replied. "It took us all years of training to master it."

"But they have Tirelius, if they haven't killed him," Clovis pointed out. "They may have captured other viators as well."

"No viator will give up the secrets of Via to an enemy," Honoria replied.

"But there is the schola," Borafin murmured. The schola—where young men and women studied for the priesthood and learned those secrets.

"Yes, the schola," Lamathe said. "The books there will tell them all they need to know."

"We must destroy the books!" Samos cried.

"What if the invaders have captured the schola?" Karellia asked. She was not a viator, but someday she would have been, if not for what had happened during the night.

"Perhaps they haven't," Lamathe replied. "In any case, that is where we must make our stand."

"And if we succeed?" Theodosius asked. "The invaders will still control Urbis, and the empire."

"Then, as Honoria says, we must survive—and prepare for the moment when we are needed."

"When will that be?" Clovis asked.

"I do not know," Lamathe replied. "Tirelius has many flaws. Each of us has flaws. But whoever these invaders are, they will not rule as wisely and justly as we have ruled. The time will come when people will understand this and long for our return. We must be ready. Now come, there's no time to waste."

The priests returned to their own houses and changed out of their colored robes to make themselves less conspicuous. They then filled jugs with lamp oil and lugged them back to Lamathe's house. Samos had obtained a horse and cart somehow; they loaded the jugs into the cart and finally set off for the schola.

Lamathe still could not believe this was happening. They were about to set fire to books that had been studied for generations—the accumulated wisdom of Hieron and all who had come after him. And if they couldn't succeed in burning them, they would die trying.

Yet it was the right thing to do.

He looked at Honoria; she had tears in her eyes. "This is awful," he said.

"It is."

"Do you think the Gallians are responsible?"

She shook her head. "I don't know. It makes sense, though."

The Gallians had rebelled decades ago, and the priests had used gants to defeat them. But they had been loyal enough since then. "King Carolus wouldn't try something like this," Borafin said.

"Perhaps he'd do it if he knew it would work."

"It doesn't matter, I suppose," Lamathe murmured.

"No, I suppose it doesn't."

They fell silent as their journey continued. Along the way a few other priests joined them. It felt like a procession. They skirted the main road and approached the schola from behind. Students were milling about on the playing field, looking dazed. When they spotted the priests they surrounded them, begging for news and guidance.

The enemy had not attacked the schola, it turned out. Everyone was safe. So that was good news. Lamathe had to give the students the bad news. He pointed to the cart laden with the jugs full of oil. "We cannot let the schola fall into the hands of the enemy," he told them. "We are here to burn it down."

The students were stunned. They wept. They protested. They begged for a different solution. Like Samos, they wanted a call to arms. Their lives here were just starting, and now Lamathe was telling them those lives were over. They might never become priests or viators. They might never see Urbis again.

But Lamathe would not relent, and the students did as they were told.

Everyone brought jugs into the schola and up to the library where they had spent so many happy hours. Shelf upon shelf of wisdom, reaching up three stories. Lamathe had grown up in Alexandria and had spent many happy hours in its great library, but he knew that many of the books there were filled with nonsense. Here was the truth, of this world and many others. And above all the truth of Via, which provided the entranceway to all those other worlds.

How could this wisdom ever be replaced?

He and the other viators went into the special locked room containing the records of every journey they had taken to other worlds, back to the days of Hieron. They doused the records with oil and departed.

When everyone was back outside, the sun was setting; this felt appropriate. And it was left to Lamathe to take a torch, go inside the schola one final time, and set it ablaze.

He came out afterward and joined them all as they watched the smoke start billowing out of the schola's windows. No one spoke until finally Samos said, "Whoever they are, I will kill them all."

Lamathe put his arm around the young priest's shoulder, and Samos turned and sobbed uncontrollably into the viator's chest.

"It cannot end here," Honoria said.

"It won't," Lamathe replied. "This is what we will do."

And in the gathering darkness he explained his plan.

ONE

Liber

"Io Saturnalia!"

The masked, drunken revelers shouted the ancient exclamation as they pushed past Liber on the crowded street. It was the beginning of Saturnalia, the week-long festival when servant mocked master, the ruled mocked the ruler, and all celebrated the end of the old year and the beginning of the new.

What was there to celebrate? Liber wondered glumly. The old year had been bad enough, but the new year could only be worse.

It was past sunset, although the leaden December sky had offered no glimpse of the sun. Liber hurried down the Palatine, elbowing his way through the crowds, wrapping his cloak tightly around his body to protect it from the biting wind. The sky had been leaden for days now. Perhaps Roma would never see the sun again, he thought. His satchel, filled with books, was heavy, and he felt the urge to throw it into a rubbish barrel. Much good the books would do him now! He had lost his last pupil—a dim-witted youth named Nicomedes who could scarcely remember his own name, much less how to do multiplication and division. His father, a stout, oily merchant, had given Liber the news as he was leaving.

"You are not a bad tutor," the merchant had told him—how

7

gracious of him! "But of course the political situation is so unsettled. Who knows what will happen? We all must be prudent about expenses until we see how events turn out. I'm sure you understand."

Prudent about expenses! And how was Liber supposed to be prudent when he had no money whatsoever?

That wasn't quite true, of course. The merchant, who was a nice enough fellow, had given him a few extra sesterces as a parting gift, and the coins were jingling in Liber's pocket. But what could he do with a few sesterces?

He knew what he wanted to do.

He walked along the winding street that led down past the Forum into the poorer sections of the city. Soon the fancy houses were gone, and he was walking through a castellum where tired people huddled around smoky fires or in doorways protected from the wind. He thought of his drafty room on the fourth floor of a dreary insula nearby. He had plenty of blankets to pile on top of himself, but in weather like this they weren't enough to keep him warm.

He passed a tavern. Inside, he could hear people laughing and singing a bawdy song. There was a tavern on every block hereabouts. Taverns were where you spent your life on cold winter nights, instead of lying on a thin bed covered with blankets.

He kept walking, but he paused in front of the next tavern. More laughter, more singing, a shouted curse. He could smell cabbage, and boiled mutton, and stale red wine. He had failed to eat lunch, he realized. His stomach started to growl, but he didn't enter the place.

Now he was in the castellum where he lived, and he was approaching the tavern where he spent most of the sesterces he managed to earn by tutoring young blockheads like Nicomedes. The Hungry Lion, it was called. On the outside it was no different from all the others, merely a wooden door with a sign above it, and next to the door shuttered windows that were open in the summer so passersby could buy wine without having to bother going inside. He opened the door.

But inside, oh! The warmth, the noise, the smells! This was his place; these were his people! He went in. A few men greeted him, raising their cups and calling out "Io Saturnalia!". He waved to them and found his usual spot in the corner.

These were his people, but he liked to drink alone.

He set his satchel down and warmed his hands over a charcoal brazier next to his table. Janina came over with jugs of wine and water and a cup. She was heavyset and good-natured, and as always she wore an apron stained with food and wine. "Cold out there, eh, my lord?" she said over the din. *My lord.* A joke.

"Bitter cold," he replied.

"Tough on the revelers," she noted.

"They're too drunk to feel the cold."

"True enough. And little enough to celebrate. Will you be eating tonight?"

Sometimes when he was low on money he only drank. But tonight he was hungry, and he had those coins from the merchant. "I will," he replied. "What do you have?"

"What do we always have? Stew, and don't ask me what Iovus put into it."

"I'm sure it will be delightful."

Janina laughed at his joke and went off to fetch the stew.

Liber poured himself a cup of wine, adding a little water, and took his first sip of the night. And then his second, and then his third. Before he knew it, the cup was empty, and now he felt better than he had felt all day.

He looked around. A few men were playing dice, shouting and cursing and laughing. An argument was raging at the next table; he tried not to listen. A stocky man he didn't recognize was drinking by himself in another corner and reading a small book. Reading? That was out of place in The Hungry Lion. Likely he was the only man here besides Liber who had that particular skill.

If only he could afford to buy books other than the ones he carried around in his satchel for his students—books of mathematics and grammar and history and rhetoric, most of which he had all but memorized. He too would spend his evenings reading at a table, alone.

Janina returned and set down a wooden spoon and a bowl of stew. Liber ate the stew greedily. It was better than he had expected. The chicken was probably not rotten, and the onions were probably almost fresh. He poured himself another cup of wine, diluted it again with a few drops of water, and leaned back in his chair, content at last.

But not for long. The argument at the next table was growing louder and more heated. Liber knew the men—sturdy laborers who drank too much and understood too little. They were arguing, of course, about the Gallians who had come out of nowhere not three months ago and conquered Urbis and, with it, the greatest empire Terra had ever known.

"Can't you follow me?" one of the men was saying in irritation. He had long black hair and a scar on his left cheek. His name, Liber thought, was Varius. "It's simple. The Gallians could not have taken over Urbis if the gods did not favor them. How could that happen otherwise?"

"It is payback for what the priests did to King Harald and his army fifty years ago," another man agreed. He was scrawny and had a high-pitched, querulous voice. Marcus? Marcellus? Marcus, Liber decided. "The priests should not have destroyed the army like they did. The Gallians had legitimate complaints."

"Bah," a third man said. His name was Nicator, and he had occasionally bought Liber a cup of wine, so Liber was disposed to like him. "These Gallians sneaked into the city in the dead of night and stole the priests' weapons," Nicator pointed out. "Everyone knows that. It has nothing to do with the gods."

"But how could they sneak into Urbis?" Varius protested. "It makes no sense. There were scarcely more than two dozen of them, I'm told."

"They had help, obviously," Nicator replied. "From Affron and those other priests who were fighting against the pontifex."

"But where is Affron? And where are all those priests?"

"Well, they've joined together somewheres—the priests and Affron."

"But they say that Affron was there," Varius pointed out. "That's how the Gallians found their way into the city."

"No, Affron is gone. Disappeared, long before the Gallians came. Do you understand nothing?"

"I understand that our governor is in league with a bunch of foreigners," a fourth man put in, slamming his cup down on the table. Callias—always eager to pick a fight. Many a time Liber had watched him being thrown out of The Hungry Lion. "We should be attacking the Gallians, not making deals with them."

"Governor Decius is doing what he needs to do," Nicator said. "Winter is here. We need bread. We need work. He can't let his people starve, can he?"

"He has troops!" Callias said. "He should use them."

"Do you think the troops will go into battle against the Gallians with those magical weapons of theirs? It's said they turn a man into ashes in the blink of an eye. Not a chance the army would agree to fight them."

"They can besiege Urbis," Callias countered. "Starve the bastards out."

Nicator spat on the floor and didn't bother to reply.

"If the gods gave the Gallians those magical weapons," Marcus pointed out, "they could surely give them food."

"You are such a fool," Callias responded. "Thinking that the gods would give the Gallians anything."

Marcus stood up, as if getting ready to fight Callias. Nicator shoved him back into his seat. "Let's ask our teacher here," Nicator said. He turned to Liber. "What say you, magister? What is going on in Urbis? Should Decius have made peace with the Gallians?"

Liber sighed. "You realize, of course, that questioning Decius in public may not be the wisest course of action," he pointed out. "They say the governor has spies everywhere."

Nicator waved his hand dismissively. "Decius has more important things to worry about than people like us arguing in taverns. Come, you're smarter than the lot of us—tell us what you think."

Liber wanted no part of this conversation, but he knew that Nicator was not going to give up. "I lost my last remaining pupil today," he replied, "because his father fears that no one will want to build ships with the lumber he has imported from Germania. The times are uncertain at best. Tax revenues have dried up as a result. Decius's soldiers are not likely to attack Urbis; they're more likely to attack *him*, if he can't pay them."

Nicator laughed delightedly and turned back to the other men at his table. "You see? The magister understands the situation." He signaled to Janina. "More wine for my friend!"

"But what of the gods?" Varius demanded. "Why are they doing this to us?"

The gods. Liber smiled. Once upon a time he had believed in the gods, but he was far wiser now, though no happier. "I do not know what to say about the gods," he replied to Varius. "Their ways are too inscrutable for me to understand."

"They must know what they're doing," Varius insisted. "If we are faithful to them, everything will turn out for the best."

Liber tried not to laugh at the poor man's optimism. Nothing ever turned out for the best; Liber himself was a living example of this.

Janina brought over another jug of wine, and he raised his cup to Nicator. "To the gods," he murmured.

The men at the other table automatically repeated his toast, and then continued their argument. They were frightened, of course, and they had every right to be. He, too, was frightened. But now he was drunk, so the fear didn't bother him quite so much.

Eventually, though, the patrons started heading out of the tavern. Time to return to their wretched insulae, their sullen wives and squalling children. Even during Saturnalia they would all need to be up before dawn, ready to put in another day's labor in the cold gray winter, with fear lurking in their hearts. Ah, the tavern was no good when people started to leave. Liber threw his sesterces down on the table and struggled to his feet.

"Good night, my lord," Janina called to him.

He waved to her and headed for the door.

Suddenly the stocky man with the book was by his side. "Your bag," the man said, pointing to the satchel Liber had left on the floor by his table.

"Stupid of me," Liber muttered, going back for it. "Thank you, friend."

"Allow me to help you," the man said. He took Liber's arm and guided him through the tables to the door.

"Very kind," Liber said. He actually did feel a bit dizzy.

"Not at all." The man opened the door, and they walked out into the cold and the biting wind.

Liber looked around in the darkness. His mind swirled. He needed to get home, out of this wind. But where was home? Oh, why had he drunk so much!

"If I might suggest," the stocky man said, "I have a carriage here. Perhaps I can give you a ride?"

A carriage? No one had a carriage in this castellum. How absurd! But there it was. And its driver, all bundled up in a heavy cloak, was approaching him.

"Come then," the stocky man said to Liber. "It will be warmer inside the carriage."

The driver and the stocky man helped him step up into the carriage. The stocky man got in after him and sat on the facing seat. The driver shut the door behind them. Liber realized that the man had bolted the door from the outside; he couldn't get out. He stared at the man across from him. It was as if he were looking at him for the first time. His features were bland; his eyes were half-shut, as if he were preparing to take a nap.

"You aren't taking me home, are you?" Liber said.

"No," the man replied. "Of course not."

"Where are we going?"

"All will be made clear. Now rest, and try to sober up."

"You can't do this to me," Liber argued.

"Of course I can. Now be quiet."

The carriage started moving. Liber closed his eyes. Outside he could hear people singing a lewd song. Why were they still celebrating? Was their life any better now that the Gallians were in power? How could they be so stupid?

And he thought: How could *he* be so stupid? Not just tonight, but his whole life. He felt a surge of pity for himself. He didn't deserve to be here.

But this was exactly where he was. And he knew that no one—and especially not the gods—was going to save him.

TWO

Decius

Marcus Decius, governor of the empire's Roman province, was reading in his study when Corscius arrived. Decius was a bald man, with a fringe of gray hair and piercing gray eyes. He should have been in bed long ago, but this was far too important.

"Well?" he asked his aide.

Corscius nodded. "I found him, my lord. He's in the carriage. Passed out from too much wine."

"And you're sure it's him?"

"Yes, of course. He had a good bit to say at the tavern."

"If you rouse him, will he be sober enough to talk?"

"Probably," Corscius replied. "Shall I bring him to you?"

"Yes. And thank you."

Corscius departed. Decius put down the papers he had been reading and sighed. He had no wish to deal with a drunkard. But the times were dangerous, and he was becoming desperate; he had to take what was available. Perhaps the man could help; if not, Decius would have to look for someone else.

He threw more coal into the brazier and waited. Finally Corscius escorted the man into his study. Decius studied him from the other side of the table. The man was wobbly on his feet; Corscius had him by the

14

arm to keep him steady. His eyes were bloodshot; his robe was thread-bare; his dark hair needed washing and combing. His face was wet—Corscius had presumably thrown water on it to rouse him. He looked like a beggar one would cross the street to avoid.

And yet, bloodshot as they were, there was something about those eyes...

"Gaius Liberus," Decius said quietly.

"My lord," he replied, bowing.

"You know who I am?"

"Of course."

"And do you know why you're here?"

The man gave a small nod. "Quite possibly."

Decius motioned for Liber to sit opposite him and for Corscius to go.

"Would you be so good as to get me a cup of water?" Liber said to Corscius. "And a towel."

Corscius looked at Decius. The governor nodded.

"And kindly don't lose my satchel," he added. "The books in it are my livelihood."

Corscius didn't bother to respond. He left the room, and a few moments later a servant entered with a jug of water, a cup, and a small towel. Liber filled his cup and drank greedily. Decius waited for him to finish. Liber wanted to demonstrate that he wasn't afraid, of course. But Decius knew he was afraid.

When Liber had finished drinking, he wiped his face with the towel and tossed it on the floor. Then he inclined his head to the governor, as if to say: *You may begin.*

"So," Decius said, "why do you think you are here?"

"You perhaps think I have information," Liber replied.

Decius nodded.

"But you must know that if I have the information of the kind you are looking for," Liber continued, "then I have also taken a solemn oath not to reveal it."

"Surely such an oath is meaningless in the current state of affairs," Decius pointed out.

Liber shrugged. "An oath is an oath. And some might say that this is precisely the state of affairs when the oath should matter most."

"Is that what *you* say?"

"I don't know. Perhaps I need to be convinced."

15

"Well then, consider," Decius said. "You are penniless. You are friendless, except for your drinking companions. You live in a wretched insula that is boiling hot in the summer and freezing in the winter. Today you lost your last pupil, and you have no hope of getting another."

Liber looked at him sharply. "The merchant—you told him to get rid of me."

Decius spread his hands. "Does that matter? In any case, I think you see the choice you face. I know what I would do, if I were you. But of course, I am not as brilliant as you. I was not one of the chosen."

"*Chosen*," Liber repeated, as if the word were unfamiliar to him. "You're mistaken, of course. Look at me. I was *not* chosen. But enough. I am tired and drunk. Tell me what you want."

"Let us begin with the obvious," Decius said. "The Gallians have taken over Urbis. They killed most of the soldiers in the city. They possess Via. They possess the magical weapons the priests used to destroy the army of King Harald, the ancestor of their leader. No army will attack them while they possess these weapons. And yet their situation is precarious. The priests fled Urbis, but not before they burned its schola. No one remains in the city who knows how to run an empire, who knows how to deal with the gods. And no books remain to teach the Gallians what the priests knew. They have weapons but no wisdom. They have power but no legitimacy. They have conquered the Roman empire, but they do not know how to rule it."

"They have the pontifex, do they not?" Liber asked.

"Tirelius will tell them nothing. Why should he? He longs for them to fail."

"Find some of the priests who left, then. That shouldn't be difficult. Plenty of them despise Tirelius. They will help."

"They may despise Tirelius," Decius said, "but that doesn't mean they want the Gallians to succeed. They had something else in mind. They looked to someone else to lead them."

"Ah," Liber murmured. "Affron."

"Yes, Affron."

"He wasn't behind it, then? He wasn't there?"

Decius shook his head. "No one knows where he is, or if he's still alive. Apparently a servant boy and girl from Barbarica gave the Gallians one of the magical weapons and helped them sneak into Urbis by night. But then they disappeared. No one knows where they are either."

Liber seemed interested by this. "Are they the children the priests were searching for back in the summer, along with Affron and Valleia and some other man?"

"Presumably. But does it matter?"

"I don't know." Liber poured another cup of water, drank it in a single gulp, and shook his head as if to clear the fumes of the wine from it. "The Gallians, of course, are terrified," he said. "And the thing that terrifies them the most is Via. Perhaps one of them has stuck his hand inside it, and the hand disappeared. Where did the hand go? At least the hand reappeared when he pulled it back out. Perhaps someone was brave enough to walk inside it, but then never returned. What happened to the man? Did the gods capture him? Are the gods angry with the Gallians? If so, what can they do to appease the gods? Perhaps some of them are now arguing that this was all a terrible mistake, but they do not know how to undo what they have done. They need to find someone who *understands*."

Decius inclined his head. "Something like that."

"And then there is you, my lord," Liber went on. "You have thrown your lot in with the Gallians. There are very good reasons for this, but you, too, are terrified. If the Gallians fail, what will happen to you?"

"How can the Gallians fail, with the weapons they possess?" Decius responded. "They can turn a man to bits of dust from fifty paces away."

"But neither you nor the Gallians understand the weapons, any more than you understand Via. If the gods gave them to us, the gods can take them away."

"There are those who say there are no gods."

"Then where did the weapons come from?" Liber asked. "Then what is Via? These things are not from Terra. Surely that much is clear."

"I do not know," Decius admitted. "That is why we need to find someone who understands."

"And you think I am that person."

"I think perhaps you are," Decius replied. "You were once a student in the schola that stood right next to the temple of Via. And you were no ordinary student. You were chosen to become a viator— the highest rank among all priests. You must have read those books that the priests burned when they left the city. You must have learned the deepest mysteries of Via. You must have learned about those magical weapons. But then it ended. You left Urbis and the priesthood. By choice? Or perhaps the priests asked you to leave. Did your fondness for wine cause the priests to give up on you, or was it a result of being banished? Anyway, here you are—tutoring the spawn of rich merchants for a few pitiful sesterces, which you promptly spend on the wine you drink every night. To help you forget how you've wasted your life, I imagine."

"Your network of spies is remarkably efficient," Liber said. "You know much."

Decius shrugged. "It is how I survive."

"And you want me to tell you the mysteries of Via?"

"Why not? Are you afraid of the gods?"

Liber shrugged. "What does it matter? You don't need me, after all. Go read a book about the mysteries—they exist, even if the priests tried to suppress them. I am not the only one to have ever left the priesthood."

"I don't trust the books."

"And you would trust a drunk like me?"

Decius nodded. "I think I would. Because I can look into your eyes and decide if you are lying."

Liber laughed. "A viator knows how to lie and get away with it. But here is the problem, my lord. You want me to work for you. But why should I do that? You would then use the information I give you to ingratiate yourself with the Gallians. Why should I not work for the Gallians themselves?"

"And how would you do that?" Decius asked. "Walk up to the gates of Urbis and introduce yourself? You can only get to the Gallians through me. This ought to be clear to someone as smart as you. But we have sparred long enough. You can help me, in which case we will give you a soft bed in a warm cubiculum, followed by the chance to earn money and possibly even do some good in this wretched world. Or you can refuse, in which case Corscius will be happy to toss you out onto the street and let you find your way back to your insula, where you'll surely be dead by the end of winter. Now choose."

Liber inclined his head. "You are very persuasive, my lord," he said with a smile. "I accept your kind offer."

Decius inclined his head in return. "Then let us begin. With Affron."

Liber stared at him. "What about Affron?"

"Did you know him at the schola?"

"Of course I knew him."

Decius tried to ask the question—the one question to which he needed an answer. But the question was hard to put into words. "Why…what can you tell me about him?"

"What do you want to know?"

"Why is he different? Why did so many priests want him to be the next pontifex?"

Liber shrugged. "Why does this matter? Affron is not the Gallians' problem, unless he's still alive."

It was time to explain, Decius decided. "I met Affron this summer," he said. "And he did something to me. I do not understand what happened. It made me think that he was the most powerful man on Terra. It made me think it would be easy for him to defeat Tirelius. After this meeting we reached an agreement in which I was to help him become pontifex. But instead he disappeared. I would like to know why. I would like to know where he is. I would like to understand his power."

Liber poured himself more water, and then put the cup down without drinking it. "Affron did something, you say. Did what?"

Decius gazed at him and made a judgment. "I think you know," he said.

"I do not," Liber replied. "How would I?" And then he closed his eyes. "I know that I am very tired and still not very sober. Can we continue this conversation in the morning?"

Decius considered, and then shrugged. "Corscius!" he called out. His aide appeared in the doorway a moment later. "Tell Barascus to make our guest comfortable for the night. In the morning, bathe him, feed him, and find him a new robe. Then bring him back to me."

Corscius bowed to Decius and shook Liber by the shoulder. Liber got to his feet, bowed, and followed Corscius out of the room.

Decius leaned back in his chair. His mind returned to that brutally hot day in a cramped room in the bowels of the Circus Maximus. A couple of his soldiers had captured Affron and Valleia and their servant boy, and he was there to decide what to do with them. Turn them over to the priests? He had taken their magical weapon from them; he assumed he had them in his power. But then Affron had looked at him, and…

Decius shuddered. What had happened? He had experienced a moment of pure terror. No, not terror…the word wasn't sufficient. He had been floating, alone, in an immensity of nothingness. And he knew he had always been alone, and nothing mattered, nothing could possibly matter. There was no beauty, no love, no meaning, only a swirling emptiness, but it was the swirling emptiness of all that was and could ever be. But that made no sense. Nothing made sense. And all he wanted to do was die. But he couldn't die, he would never die…

And then he had opened his eyes. He was lying on the floor, and the boy was looking down at him. His face was wet; the boy had poured a bucket of water onto him.

It was over; ordinary life had begun again.

But life would never be quite ordinary after that experience. It lingered at the edges of his mind. He worried that it would return—while he slept, in a meeting, sitting alone at night. Right now.

How had Affron done that? *What* had he done? Decius had looked into Liber's eyes, and thought the man could tell him.

Was he wrong? He didn't think so.

Would this knowledge help the Gallians? Not likely.

But Decius thought this knowledge might keep him from going mad.

He rose from his chair. The room was getting cold. In the morning he would find out what the man knew. And then he would decide what to do with him—throw him away, or bring him to Urbis.

It was unlikely Decius could save the Gallians, but he had to try.

THREE

Flendys

The three strangers rode into town on the King's Road, which led up along the coast from the south and then disappeared inland into the highlands of northern Scotia. The road is mainly used by soldiers and tax collectors; these three were neither. All wore thick cloaks to protect them from the howling wind and blowing snow, but even with the cloaks it was easy to tell they were different. For one thing, one of them was a girl.

And, of course, eventually they spoke. And what they spoke was Latin.

They rode into our town, Flendys as we call it, and we watched them from behind our curtains and shutters, hoping they would ride on. There was nothing for them here, unless they wanted passage on a ship headed to somewhere else. But this they did not want.

They dismounted in front of Grillich's tavern and went in. Grillich speaks no Latin, of course; he barely speaks Erse. It turned out that the girl could speak a little Erse. This did not astonish Grillich—nothing astonishes him—but it astonished the rest of us. It shouldn't have. After all, the woman who had preceded them here had picked up the language quickly, even though most Romans find it unintelligible.

The three travelers asked for food, a place to stable their horses, somewhere to spend the night. And some information. Grillich could provide food; as for the rest, he pointed them to Arva Senth; which was the right thing to do. It's not Grillich's place to tell outsiders our business. But he fed them well—roasted chicken and fresh-baked bread—and they paid him more than it was worth.

The man was dark-haired and handsome. The girl was blonde and pretty, with pleasing gray eyes; young, but of an age to wed. The boy was about the girl's age, perhaps a little younger. He was taller than the girl, with long brown hair and green eyes; he looked tired and worried. He said nothing.

They were all cold. They sat close to the fire and kept their cloaks wrapped about them. They ate the chicken and bread greedily. They refused beer, and Grillich had no wine to offer them.

Eventually they left the tavern and walked their horses to Arva Senth's store. Grillich had had sense enough to send the kitchen boy ahead to tell him they were coming, so Arva was ready.

Arva spent years on merchant ships trading with the Gallians and the Spaniards and the Romans. He has been to Galicia and Anatolia and Dalmatia and any number of places that the rest of us have never even heard of. They say he speaks Latin better than a native. But, more important, he understands these people. Not just the merchants who come on the ships, or the sailors who man the ships—we all understand merchants and sailors. But the people who live in these far-off places, with their different religions and different clothes and different foods. They mean nothing to us.

But Arva's knowledge didn't help him with these three, as it hadn't helped him with the other three—the ones these three were clearly here to find. There was something different about them, something strange and a little frightening; not that they looked so very different from the people he had met in his travels in the empire. To begin with, the strange and frightening thing was simply that they were here. They had no business being in Flendys, like the other three. And the girl had no business understanding Erse.

They were polite enough. They all bowed to Arva, and Arva bowed back. The man did most of the talking, now that they were speaking to someone who knew Latin. The man spoke Latin with a cultured Roman accent and asked again for a place to spend the night and stable their horses. They had been on the road since daybreak. The weather was bad, and likely to get worse. They could pay well.

Arva could think of no reason to refuse their request. We are not known as a sociable people, but we extend great courtesy to anyone who needs our help. So he gave them directions to the Widow Lochen's house. And then he waited for what the man would ask next. He knew what it would be, but still, it was up to the man to ask.

"We are looking for some people," the man said.

Arva continued to wait.

"Three people," the man went on. "Two men and a woman. We are told that they sailed here from Britannia in late summer. But we do not know if they are still here."

"They are not," Arva replied. "They left two months ago. After the harvest, before the winter storms."

"Do you know where they went?" the man asked.

Arva shook his head. "They took the King's Road north. That is all I know." And then he added, "The woman was with child. Perhaps they needed to reach their destination before her time to deliver."

Arva was not sure why he offered that information—hospitality surely did not require that he do so. It seemed to surprise his three guests. "With child," the man repeated.

"Yes. I can't imagine that she spoke of it to anyone, but the women at the market knew. They always know such things. She was showing a little, perhaps, by the time she left with the others."

"Would anyone know where they were headed—besides 'north'?" the man asked. "The women at the market, perhaps?"

"It is possible," Arva admitted. "But this is a small town. If anyone knew such a thing, I would know. Everyone would know."

The man seemed to accept this. But then the boy spoke up. "Where did they stay while they were here?" he asked.

Arva contemplated the boy. His accent was not Roman. It did not sound like any accent Arva had encountered in his travels. The boy was not the man's son, Arva decided. So who was he? A servant? But he had not asked that question as if he were a servant. And the man was not looking at him as if he were a servant. The man, it seemed, was interested in what the boy had to say.

"They lived in a house not far from town," Arva responded.

"We would like to see that house. Would this be possible?"

Why did they want to see the house? Arva shrugged. "They left nothing behind, if that is what you're hoping. I am the owner, it happens. They left the place as they found it—except cleaner and in better repair. For which I am grateful."

"Is anyone living in it now?"

Arva shook his head. "Not often that I can rent it," he said. "Especially at this time of year."

"Can we see it, then?" the boy persisted.

"As you wish," Arva replied. "Tomorrow, though. It is already late."

"Tomorrow," the boy repeated, as if to ensure that Arva would remember.

Then they spoke of the harsh weather, and the food at Grillich's tavern, and Arva asked them about the tumult taking place in the empire—a tumult that we had reason to worry about, even here in one of the lands that the Romans refer to as Barbarica. But they had little to say about it. The Gallians are in charge now, they said. Who knows how long this will last?

"Are you perhaps fleeing from the Gallians?" Arva asked. It was not a question you should ask strangers, but he went on: "We do not see many people from the empire except those who want to trade with us. Especially nowadays. You are welcome here, but we worry. Our town is small. We have little."

"You do not have to worry about us, certainly," the man replied. "We will be gone tomorrow." But that was all he said. And soon they departed for the widow's house.

Arva pondered what this could all mean, but he could make no sense of it. All would be well, he decided...so long as the strangers left, and no more came.

At the Widow Lochen's house, they were quiet and pleasant. The girl dealt with Corin the stable boy about the horses; Corin promptly fell in love with her and offered to teach her as much Erse as she desired. She politely declined. As at the tavern, they paid more than they needed to.

It was Corin who noticed the weapon. He did not know it was a weapon, of course. The girl had loosened her cloak in the warm stable, and Corin stared at her more closely than he should have. He spotted the outline of something in a pocket of her loose black pants. He imagined it to be a tool of some sort, but he could not think what kind of tool it was, or why the girl would possess such a thing. He mentioned this to the kitchen boy from Grillich's tavern, and Grillich sent the boy back to Arva with the information.

And the information troubled Arva greatly. This was no tool in her pocket; he was sure of that. The story of what the Gallians had done in Urbis had reached us, and it was their magical weapons that worried Arva. It was known that the priests had such things, but they had only used them when threatened by King Harald and his Gallian army. Now the Gallians had the weapons. And what did that mean for an out-of-the-way place like Flendys, a small town in an out-of-the-way kingdom like Scotia? Nothing good, Arva surmised.

But the girl wasn't a Gallian; Arva was sure of that. So, did she really have one of those weapons? If so, how had she gotten it? He had no idea. He had no idea about anything. These three made him feel stupid and provincial. He loved our town and wanted to live out his days in it. But great things were happening in the outside world, and they frightened him.

In the morning, the three strangers returned to his shop, and he had to take them to the old house off the King's Road where the other three had lived. The wind off the sea was cold and biting once again, and Arva had little desire to be outdoors. But still, he led them there, as he had promised.

They walked—it wasn't far enough to bother saddling up the horses. The house had once belonged to old Drophus, who kept to himself and came to town only when he needed to get drunk. Two winters past, he stopped coming to town. His daughter found him by the tool shed, stone dead in the snow. It was a blessing the wolves had not found him first. The daughter had no use for the place so she sold it to Arva, who was occasionally able to rent it to a merchant desiring more space and privacy than he could find in a room in the Widow Lochen's house. It had been empty for months before the other three had arrived; it had been empty since they left.

And now Arva was standing inside it with the man, the boy, and the girl, trying to suppress his shivering, watching them look around at the simple furniture, the fireplace, the worn rug. What did they expect to see, to find, to understand, in the place?

He saw that the man and the girl were glancing at the boy, who shook his head finally. "Is there somewhere else?" he asked Arva.

And what did that mean? "I do not understand," Arva replied impatiently. "As I said: this is where they lived while they were here."

The boy didn't reply. He went out of the house and motioned to the shed. "What's in there?" he asked.

25

"I don't know. Tools, perhaps. An axe for chopping wood. A hoe for raking in the garden, come spring. Logs for the fireplace."

The boy went over to the shed. Arva followed. The boy stopped in front and then walked around it. But there was nothing to see from the outside—just a small, windowless wooden building, barely more than a man's height. He raised the latch on the door and went inside. Arva followed once again, although there was barely room inside for the two of them.

The place was dark and musty. It contained a few tools, as Arva had guessed. No logs, but some boards, and a couple of old chairs stacked in the corner. And one chair set down in the middle of the wooden floor. The boy sat in the chair. Why? He stayed there for a while, and then he got out of the chair and knelt on the floor and put his hands out in front of him. For some reason Arva started to become very nervous. What was the boy doing?

And then, just for a moment, Arva felt something else. He felt as if he were falling, falling, in emptiness that went on forever, that multiplied endlessly around him. And he too seemed to multiply, and every self was falling, and he knew he would fall forever.

It was the most awful thing he had ever felt.

And in an instant it passed. The boy was looking at him. "Me paenitet," he murmured. *I'm sorry.* But then he turned away and seemed to stare off into nothingness. And then Arva seemed to *see* the nothingness —just there, above the wooden floor. And how could that be true?

Arva backed out of the shed. He wanted no part of this boy, or whatever he was staring at in the shed. He wanted to run away. But he forced himself to stay. He was not a child; he was not a girl. He had travelled across the world. He would not be afraid of emptiness, of nothingness. Of falling.

He noticed that the man and the girl were standing behind him, their cloaks wrapped tightly around their bodies. They, too, were waiting for the boy.

Eventually he came out of the shed.

"Well?" the man asked.

"Affron was here," the boy replied.

"We knew this," the girl said.

The boy shook his head. "It's different."

"How?"

The boy didn't answer her question. "We should go," he said. "He's waiting for me."

"Where?"

"North, I suppose." He gestured at Arva, as if to say: *We can trust what this man told us.*

They walked back to town. Arva left them at the stable. They politely thanked him for the trouble he had taken. He said it was no trouble; he was delighted to help.

He watched them head off north on the King's Road. When they were out of sight he went directly to Grillich's tavern and ordered a cup of whiskey, even though it was still morning. He drank it down and sat shivering by the fire.

He was not shivering from the cold.

And as he stared at the fire he found himself praying to the gods, for the first time in many years. Even though he had no idea what he was praying for.

The last person to see the three strangers was Corin the stable boy. He followed behind them as they rode, hoping for one last glimpse of the girl with the blonde hair and gray eyes. And yes, finally she turned and smiled and gave him a little half-wave before turning back to the road and her journey.

And that was enough to keep him warm for the rest of the long, lonely winter in our small town.

FOUR

Liber

Liber woke up sober and clear-headed, as he always did.

What was unusual was *where* he woke up—in a comfortable bed, in a warm room. He could not complain. Life was suddenly dangerous, but it was also suddenly interesting; life had not been interesting for a long time.

He rose and went looking for someone. A bored guard was standing by his door; the guard summoned a fat flunky named Barascus. And so the day began.

They gave him a new robe and cloak and brought him a tray of food. And then they put him in the same carriage they had used to kidnap him the night before and drove him to the ornate palatium in the Forum from which the Roman province was ruled.

He was placed in a chilly anteroom, where he sat alone and waited. Finally he was summoned, and once again he sat opposite Decius, this time in a large, high-ceiling room lined with frescoes. The floor was covered with thick rugs. In the corner was a statue of Hieron, the beloved discoverer of Via. Odd that the statue had not been removed, but he supposed that would happen eventually. Two braziers gave off welcome heat.

In daylight, sober, Liber still thought the governor was impressive, with his penetrating gray eyes and aquiline nose. He was short but fit-looking. Even seated he seemed alert, ready to spring into action.

And yet, Liber knew that he was a match for Decius. At least when he was sober. The man was smart, but he was not a viator. Liber bowed, and Decius gestured for him to sit.

"The thing that happened to you in the Circus Maximus," Liber began, without waiting for Decius to start the conversation. "Affron did it to me, as well."

There, that piqued his interest. Decius sat forward, waiting for more.

"It was when we were at the schola in Urbis together," Liber went on. "I do not think he even intended it. I do not think he understood his power back then. We were arguing, and he became angry, and suddenly I found myself on the ground. I did not know how I got there. I still don't know, not exactly. I felt as if my brain had been shattered. I thought at first perhaps he had hit me. But no, that wasn't it. It wasn't his fist; it was his mind."

"Yes, his mind! But how? How did he do it?" Decius demanded.

Liber shrugged. "As I said, I have no idea. And he had no idea either."

"Surely you must have considered this. Surely you must have a theory."

"I have considered it, as you have. But I have no more insight than you do."

"Does it have something to do with Via?"

Liber thought: *Of course it has something to do with Via.* But how could he explain such things to this man, who knew nothing of Via? "Perhaps" was all he could bring himself to say. "But I do not know."

"What happened afterwards?"

"I recovered, as you did," Liber replied. "But not as well, not as fully. To speak the truth, I was a broken man. Before this happened, I was destined to be a viator—the highest honor in the priesthood. Afterwards…as you know, not all priests become viators. There is no shame in it. There are many worthy positions for such priests, in Urbis and throughout the empire.

"But after what happened I was no longer fit for any of these positions. I would not even try to fill one. I left the schola; I left the priesthood; I left Urbis. And I never returned. I became an impecunious tutor to young imbeciles; I became a drunkard. I waited for death."

Both of them fell silent. "So then I was right last night," Decius said finally. "You have experienced this. I could tell that you understood."

"You are perceptive, my lord," Liber replied. "But now I want to ask you about something I do not understand. For months the priests were looking for Affron in Roma. There were crowds in the city demanding that Affron be made pontifex in place of Tirelius. After the Pan-Roman games these demands ceased, but the priests kept looking for him. And then the Gallians took over Urbis. Many people naturally assumed that Affron was working with the Gallians. But you told me last night that Affron was not involved. I believe this; the Gallians would not be ruling so badly with Affron in charge. So, where is Affron?"

"I do not know," Decius said. "As I told you last night, I don't even know if he's alive. After I had that encounter with him in the Circus Maximus, we reached an agreement, as I said. He promised to use his power against Tirelius after the chariot race; he would drive the pontifex mad and take over in his place. In return he would help the people of my province. So I protected him from the priests; I whipped up the people to support him. But he failed, or perhaps he didn't even try—I don't know why. I was angry afterwards; I had risked much on his behalf. I sent soldiers to arrest him, but he and his friends had disappeared. I searched for him, but I did not find him."

Liber pondered this. "It seems unlikely that Affron is dead," he said.

"Yes, I suppose. But for now, I don't care about him," Decius replied. "Tell me what you know about Via. About the weapons. About everything."

Liber shook his head. "I will tell you nothing, unless I tell it to the Gallians at the same time."

"There is no need of that."

"Of course there is. Do I want you to take all the credit?"

"Prince Feslund has sent soldiers into Via," Decius said, "but the men simply disappeared."

"Of course they did."

"And you can do better?"

"I cannot obtain more of those weapons for them, which is presumably what they want. I hadn't progressed far enough in my training to learn how to travel to the world where they are obtained. But I can get the Gallians something else that will benefit them."

"What?"

Liber shook his head. "Bring me to Urbis," he said. "Bring me to the Gallians."

He expected an argument, but Decius gazed at him for a moment and finally nodded. "Very well," he said.

And it was done.

He was sent back to the anteroom as Decius took care of other business that couldn't be delayed. And then he was summoned again and brought to the governor's carriage; finally they headed to Urbis— through city streets still clogged with revelers, and at last onto the long, straight road that led from the old capital of the empire to the new. "Have you been to Urbis since you left the priesthood?" Decius asked.

Liber shook his head. "They would not have me back," he said, "and I could not stand to return."

Could not stand to think about what he had lost. Could not stand the memories. Like the first time he had ridden along this road. On a warm day in the fall, bouncing along in a wagon with a couple of class-mates-to-be, fresh from a sea voyage up the coast, eager to prove himself, eager to conquer this challenge, as he had conquered all the others in his young life.

Ah, and yes, he *had* conquered. In his memory, Urbis was warm, sunlit, filled with joy and triumph. Somehow he had forgotten days like this, with their leaden skies and cold winds. But he had not forgotten Affron.

"There are two people we will need to meet," Decius said. "Prince Feslund, of course. And his mother, Queen Gretyx."

"The king isn't here?"

"King Carolus remains in his castle in Lugdunum. It is said that he disapproved of the raid on Urbis. Also, he is mourning his daughter, Princess Siglind, who died in the raid."

Liber considered. "Feslund is a headstrong fool, I take it," he said. "And Gretyx is the one we must be wary of."

"The queen is a clever woman," Decius replied.

"If she is clever, she understands the Gallians' predicament."

"I suppose she does. But she, too, is in mourning for her daughter. She is not paying attention to the predicament as yet." Decius paused, presumably wondering if Liber would tell him the solution to the predicament. Smart enough by now to know that he wouldn't.

In fact Liber had no solution—not an easy one, at any rate. King

Carolus was correct: even though successful, the raid had been a bad idea. Had the Gallians suffered so much under the yoke of the priests that they had been forced to do this?

He knew why they had done it. The weapons. *Gants*, they were called. The Gallians had been given a gant—why or how, he could not imagine—and they thought: We can destroy the priests with such a weapon. We can rule Terra with it. We can avenge the deaths of our ancestors.

It was not so easy, they were discovering.

No greater issue had faced the priests than what to do with the gants. For decades—since the destruction of King Harald and his army —it had been debated. The priests back then believed they'd had no choice but to use them; Urbis itself was at stake. And so the weapons had been obtained and put to use, and the enemy had literally disappeared. But afterward, many priests had recoiled in horror from the deaths and wanted nothing more to do with the gants. Others had seen a different path. In the long years since a peasant named Hieron had discovered Via, they thought that he and his followers had been too conservative in taking advantage of the wonders that it laid before them. Hieron had worried about the dangers and temptations associated with these wonders, but hadn't the priests proved they could avoid their temptations? And weren't they doing Terra a disservice by withholding the wonders from its people? Not just those who lived in the priests' empire, but those beyond it, in the wilds of far-off Barbarica? The gants were just a means to that end—they would make the complete conquest of Terra simple and inevitable. And then the wonders would start to flow for everyone.

Finally a pontifex was elected who wanted to follow this path: Tirelius. But he lacked the support he needed to begin. Too many priests resisted his vision. Too many didn't want to change what had worked for so long. So he focused on the next generation of priests—the ones being trained in the schola. Surely they could be convinced.

Liber had been convinced. He hadn't actually been much interested in the arguments for and against; what mattered to him was his ambition. The pro-Tirelius faction in the schola needed a leader, and he wanted to be that leader. The anti-Tirelius faction already had its leader: Affron.

Everyone loved Affron. He was charming, funny, and brilliant. A perfect candidate to be pontifex one day. And he wanted no part of a future that included gants. So other students at the schola came to see things as he saw them. And this enraged Liber, as it enraged Tirelius. Because Affron was far from perfect. Liber sensed a weakness in him, an inability to take these issues seriously. Or—no—a feeling that he had more important things to think about than the future of Terra. And what could be more important than that?

Liber recalled the night when it happened. It was like all Urbis nights in his memory—warm, moonlit, sweet-smelling. He had drunk a little too much wine and had gone off wandering by himself. He hadn't seen Affron at first, but then he spotted him—a figure in a white robe sitting alone on a bench in the garden behind the schola.

The figure was doing something strange with his hands—moving them in the air as if trying to grasp something that wasn't there.

Was Affron drunk too? No, Affron had no vices. And—perhaps it was the wine—but seeing his foe calmly sitting there by himself and waving his hands annoyed Liber. "What are you doing?" he demanded.

Affron lowered his hands and turned to look at Liber. He didn't respond. It seemed as though at that moment he barely knew who Liber was.

And that annoyed Liber even more. Ah, wine had never been his friend! "You sit there so calm, so satisfied, snatching at invisible bugs or whatever you are doing," he snarled. "Do you realize how many women die in childbirth on Terra every day? They are dying this very minute. And we know how to save them. But people like you don't care. Let them suffer! Let the deformed babies die horrible deaths! Treat the young girl's cancer with herbs and unguents! Let us all die decades before we should! You don't care."

Affron said nothing. Did he even understand what Liber was saying? Did he even care?

"This world means nothing to you," Liber went on. "Why should you become pontifex? You care about none of us. You care only about what's going on inside your own mind."

Affron said nothing.

And Liber could stand it no more. He rushed over to his enemy, put his hands around his neck, and started to squeeze. He expected Affron to resist, to fight back—why wouldn't he fight back? Where were his hands, which should have been struggling to break Liber's grip? What was the matter with him?

And then it happened. The indescribable terror. The spinning, dizzying whirlwind of nameless immensity and dread. Now Liber was the one who couldn't breathe, couldn't speak, couldn't think.

He opened his eyes, finally, and he was on the ground, looking up at the moon.

"Are you all right?" Affron asked. He was on the ground, kneeling next to Liber. He looked dazed.

Liber tried to say something. But he couldn't—what was there to say? What had happened? Had Affron hit him? No, he couldn't have. What, then? Finally he managed three words: "You did this."

"I didn't mean to," Affron replied. "I'm sorry. It just…happened."

"Happened," Liber repeated.

"I'm sorry," Affron repeated.

The terror subsided. But it didn't go away; Liber somehow knew that it would never go away. Affron's gaze was full of concern. Liber couldn't stand that gaze. He turned his head away. He tried to think of something to do. But what?

And abruptly Liber knew that he had lost—this fight and, likely, every other one. His anger turned to ashes. He had been defeated—by accident, apparently. He looked back at Affron. Why wouldn't he say anything? He was the victor; why didn't he gloat? "You did it with your mind," Liber said. "What is it that you did?"

"You saw…you glimpsed…all that is," Affron responded. "All that could be."

That meant nothing to Liber. "Do you see this too?" he asked.

"All the time."

"Does it have to do with Via?"

"Of course."

"What does it have to do with Via?"

"I don't know."

Liber stopped talking. He would learn nothing from Affron. And what did it matter, after all? His head ached; his body trembled. He got to his feet finally, though standing was an effort. He needed more wine. Much more wine.

Affron rose too. "We can be friends, I hope," he offered.

Liber simply shook his head. "We can never be friends," he muttered. And he wandered away, back to the schola.

And not long after that he wandered away from the schola, from Urbis, from the priesthood. Not many tried to stop him. He had started drinking far too much. He had uttered dark warnings about Affron.

But everyone loved Affron! He ignored his studies. Instead he sat in his room and relived the terror. *All that is. All that could be.*

And finally he left. Even Tirelius was glad to see him go.

He vowed never to return. Today he would break that vow.

And now the city came into view, and beyond its walls Liber could make out the temple of Via, high on a hill in the very center of the city. He felt his eyes start to water, in spite of himself. He closed his eyes. *Via.* The Gallians did not understand it; Decius did not understand it.

But Liber understood the truth of Via. He would have to explain it to them, even though he was unworthy to know the truth, and they were unworthy to learn it.

He would explain it because he needed to survive.

"Are you all right?" Decius asked.

"Of course," Liber replied. "I have never been better."

But the tears pressing against his eyelids told a different story.

FIVE

Q ueen Gretyx sat on an intricately carved wooden armchair in the temple and stared up at the large blue object hovering just above the marble altar.

Perhaps it wasn't really blue. No matter how much she stared at it, she couldn't make up her mind. The color seemed to fade and shift, like ocean waves.

And perhaps it wasn't really an object. She had ventured once up onto the altar and tried to touch it. But there was nothing to touch.

It was what it was. It was Via.

But it was not why she was sitting here, in Via's temple.

She sat here because this was where her daughter had died: Princess Siglind, killed in the glorious raid that had captured Urbis for Gallia. Killed here, somewhere in the temple—Gretyx didn't know the exact location. Everyone who had been here when she died had died themselves—everyone except the boy, who disappeared the night after. And there was no corpse left for Gretyx to mourn, because the awful weapon had turned her child into nothingness, as if she had never existed.

Siglind had ridden off on her own to join the soldiers on their journey to Urbis; Gretyx would never have allowed it. But Feslund—

36

Siglind's own brother!—was in charge of the raid, and he *had* allowed it. Had seen nothing wrong with such a thing, even though he should have known the risks. The fool. Siglind was very persistent, very persuasive; but he should not have let her go with him to Urbis.

The queen closed her eyes. She was tired of Via; she was tired of Urbis. She longed to go back to Lugdunum and run Gallia while Carolus was off on one of his endless hunts. She wanted to calm Siglind down when she complained about something; she was always complaining.

Gretyx missed her daughter's complaining.

She felt a cold breeze behind her; the temple doors had opened. No matter. She was well guarded.

"My lady?" a voice behind her said after a moment.

She ignored the voice.

"Mother?" another voice said. Feslund.

She sighed and opened her eyes. "Yes?"

Three people ranged themselves in front of her.

Feslund was on the left, looking dashing as usual in an elegant blue cape trimmed with gold, white tunic, and flowing black trousers. Was she the only one who could sense the confusion and fear lurking beneath his bold, boastful exterior?

In the center was Decius. Smart, calm, reserved. Ultimately untrustworthy, of course, because he looked only to his own advantage. But that was always the case with such men. And right now it was clear that his needs were the same as theirs. He needed a stable, peaceful empire, and at least for the moment only the Gallians could give it to him. So, that was acceptable.

And to her right stood a third man whom she didn't recognize. Short, badly shaven, with bloodshot eyes and messy black hair. Wearing an ill-fitting robe. And not looking at her, not bowing to her as was her due.

He was staring up at Via.

She thought she saw tears glistening in those bloodshot eyes.

"My lady, this man is named Liber," Decius said, pulling on the man's sleeve to get his attention. He turned to her and, finally, bowed. "Liber was a viator—or as close to one as we have found."

"He's a drunkard," the queen replied. She had seen enough drunkards in Gallia. It seemed likely that her son would turn into one.

Liber bowed again. "I am sober at the moment, my lady," he said.

37

Yes, he was sober. And she could tell from his gaze that he was not afraid of her. That was good. She had no use for people who told her only what she wanted to hear.

"The man says he knows about Via," Feslund said. "He told us that—"

"Do not tell me what he knows," Gretyx interrupted. "I feel certain that he will tell me himself."

She turned her attention back to Liber. "Well, then?"

He shrugged. "I attended the schola here in Urbis until I left, of my own choice. But I learned much while I was here. I learned the secrets of the priesthood. I know what the priests do not speak of."

"And what is that?"

"They do not mention that it is all a lie," he said.

She didn't understand. "What is a lie?"

He gestured around him. "The temple. The religion. The gods. None of it is real. Only Via is real."

She still didn't understand. "The gods are not real?"

"None of it is real," he repeated. "They are lies the priests have told us—or allowed us to believe."

And now she found herself becoming angry. Was the man mad? Why was he wasting her time? "And what is the truth?" she demanded.

Now he sighed, as if speaking the truth were a burden for him. "The truth, my lady, is this: there are numberless worlds—whole universes, really. More than you can possibly imagine. Some that are like ours, some that are very different. And Via is nothing more than a device that lets us travel to these other worlds. In fact, it likely came from one of these worlds. The gants that the Gallians used to conquer Urbis came from a world called Gaia. They are not a gift from the gods. Viators went into Via to obtain them from Gaia and bring them back to Terra."

The one time Gretyx had met that boy—what was his name?—he had said something like this about the gants. But what this fellow said was absurd. "How can there be numberless worlds?" she asked. "There is only Terra."

"No, my lady, there is not. That is the secret the priests have hidden from the ordinary people. And that is the secret you must understand if you are to rule Terra."

"But why would the priests lie?"

"Because most people cannot understand the truth. It makes no sense to them, as it makes no sense to you."

"We have sent soldiers inside Via," Gretyx pointed out. "They have not come back out."

"Via is dangerous unless you know what you are doing," Liber replied. "Visiting other worlds carries with it many risks. Viators know what they are doing, and even so, many of them do not return. I am not surprised that your soldiers did not return either."

"The soldiers died because they disrespected the gods," Feslund said. "Because *we* disrespected the gods. We know better now. We give Via the honor it deserves."

"Then you will fail," Liber responded. "You cannot succeed in ruling Terra without using Via the way the priests used it. You have your weapons, but that is all you have. Eventually the gants will run out of power, and then you will have nothing. People will say that the gods turned against you. But that won't be true. You will fail because you are afraid, and because you will not use the knowledge I am offering you."

"This is absurd," Feslund said. "Decius, why have you brought us this fool?"

"Because he knows abou Via, my lord, and we don't," Decius replied.

"Come with me into Via, my lady," Liber interrupted softly.

Everyone turned to look at him. "What?" Feslund demanded.

"I can talk forever about Via," Liber said, still addressing her. "But you cannot know the truth about it until you experience it for yourself. So come with me. You will be safe—I promise you."

"You are not taking the queen with you into Via," Feslund said. "I will not allow it."

Liber ignored Feslund. "My lady?" he said, gazing at her.

Gretyx stared back at him. She didn't care about her son's opinion, or Decius's. She realized that she had a question. "What do you mean, 'numberless worlds'?" she asked.

"No one knows how many. People on some of these worlds even think that every time you make a decision or take an action, a new world splits off. Every choice of every person in all of history creates another world—one where you turned left, one where you turned right. One where Prince Feslund said yes, one where he said no. So many worlds that it is impossible to count them; it is impossible even to imagine them. These other worlds interpenetrate ours, in ways that I cannot describe and do not understand. They are not far away; they are right here, only not here. You will say that this sounds like drunken nonsense, and I cannot disagree. Other people have other ideas about the number of worlds; they say there has to be a limit to them, that some worlds are more likely to exist than others. But no matter who is correct, Via allows us to visit other worlds and return from them. That is what you must see for yourself."

Gretyx pondered this. "Every world is a choice not taken," she said finally.

"Yes, my lady. Your choices—everyone's choices—branching without end, throughout all of time. Again, I do not pretend to understand this idea, and it may very well be wrong."

"He is a madman," Feslund insisted. "A drunken madman."

The idea was absurd. Yes, of course it was. But it was also absurd that here she sat, with all of Terra at her command, barely able to move, barely able to breathe.

Gretyx stood up. The temple was silent. "I will go with you," she said to Liber.

"Yes, my lady."

She stared up at Via. It seemed as if she had been sitting in the silent temple staring at it forever. Time had stopped; her life had stopped.

"Take me to a world where my daughter is still alive," she ordered the viator.

SIX

Liber

"My lady," Liber replied. "I cannot do that."

"So then you were lying to me?"

"No. I do not have the knowledge; I do not have the ability. Hieron did not approve of traveling to worlds very similar to our own, so viators were never taught how. In any case, it is not something I would recommend. If your daughter is alive in another world, it is likely that you yourself are also alive. That will inevitably complicate things."

"I do not care about complications," the queen replied. "I just want to see Siglind once more—living, breathing, laughing."

"I am sorry, my lady. I simply cannot do it. I can bring you to another world, though—a fascinating world, far different from ours."

Gretyx sat back down and waved her hand in dismissal. "I am not interested," she said. She closed her eyes.

"I am not interested either," Feslund said. "Decius, get rid of this madman."

But Decius slowly shook his head. "I will go with him into Via," he replied. "If you approve, my lord," he added.

Feslund looked as if he wanted to object, but then he merely shrugged. "As you wish," he said.

Decius turned to Liber. "What do we do?"

Liber wasn't happy. It was the Gallians he needed to convince, not Decius. But it appeared that he had no choice. "We cannot go in these robes," he said. "We must find the right clothes downstairs, and then we will enter Via."

He bowed to Feslund and the queen. The queen still had her eyes closed; Feslund ignored him. So he turned away and walked towards the door behind the altar that led to the stairs. Decius followed him.

Liber could feel his heart starting to race. Back into Via! He gazed at it once more as he walked past. He hadn't been allowed to use it often—and then only with a senior viator—but oh, when he did, the excitement, the power! Stepping out into an alien world—ah, there was nothing like it.

"So, you believe me?" he asked Decius as they walked down the wooden staircase.

"It seems absurd, as Feslund says, but I think perhaps I do," Decius replied. "What kind of world are we visiting?"

"You will see."

He found the clothes where they had always been, in the bowels of the temple, in a long room off the main corridor. They were carefully washed after every trip and arranged on wooden hangers with labels above them. The labels were just numbers; the viators had visited far too many worlds to name them all. And of course, most worlds had multiple languages and therefore multiple names: Earth. Terra. Tierra. Terre. Aarde. Zemlya. So many languages. He had learned only a few in his time at the schola.

He found the number he was looking for. "These will fit you well enough," he said, handing Decius a hooded yellow jacket, a brown shirt, thick pants, and boots.

Decius eyed them quizzically. "It is cold there?" he asked.

"You have never experienced such cold," Liber replied. "You will encounter much that you have never experienced."

Decius shrugged and donned the clothes. "The jacket is too light to protect us from the cold," he pointed out.

"You will be surprised."

"I don't know how to close it up."

"Just press the two sides together."

Decius pressed them, and the sides connected. No buttons; nothing. He looked baffled, as Liber had the first time he had donned such a jacket.

Liber put on his outfit. In the old days, devoted temple assistants would have assisted with such mundane tasks and explained clothing items like the jacket. No more.

Behind the racks of clothes were drawers built into the walls.. He opened one and took out some paper currency. "What are those?" Decius asked.

"It's money. Like coins on Terra. We will need it."

"I do not understand."

"No need to understand."

Liber put the money in the pocket of his pants. Then he looked at Decius and nodded. "Good enough," he said. "Let's go back upstairs."

They returned to the temple's nave. Feslund had pulled up a chair next to his mother and was lounging in it, looking bored and irritated. "You look ridiculous," he said when he saw them.

"Yes, my lord," Liber replied. "And your outfit would look ridiculous in the world we will be visiting. We are now entering Via. I do not know when we will return."

"Do you expect us to wait for you?"

"It doesn't matter."

"When you come back, what will you have accomplished?"

"Then, my lord, we will possess the key to your triumph on Terra."

"But I have already triumphed. Here I am—ruling the priests' empire."

"As you say, my lord. But now you must ensure that the triumph continues."

Feslund shrugged and did not bother to reply.

Liber gave the briefest of bows and walked up the steps to the altar, followed by Decius. He stared at Via. How beautiful it was! Oh, how he had missed it! It beckoned to him, like a lover who wanted him to possess her. Oh, yes!

"Pull up the hood of your jacket," he instructed Decius.

Decius did as he was told.

If you looked hard enough, you could see a rectangle of darkness among the shifting blues of Via's surface. That was the right way to enter it. He took a step, and then another, and then he was inside, pulling Decius after him. They stood there together and looked around. They couldn't see out; the temple had disappeared. All they could make out were the shimmering blue waves of light that enveloped them.

There is nothing easier. And nothing more difficult.

That's what his mentor, Tiberius Rufus, had said. Of course, that was not helpful at all; most of what Rufus had to say to him had not been especially helpful. Nothing was helpful, really, except *doing* it. Moving your hands over a set of controls that one could barely feel, that barely seemed real; making the motions that somehow corresponded to the world you wanted to visit. Why did these motions matter? What did these controls do? Rufus didn't know; no one knew. Perhaps they didn't matter. Affron didn't seem to think they did. Only your mind mattered, he insisted. But how did he know? He'd had little more experience with Via than Liber when he made such statements.

In any case Liber had done what Rufus told him to do. He had copied the motions that Rufus had taught him, and together they had stepped out of Via into Tierra, Terre, Aarde...into 14702.

And that is what he did now, hoping that his hands would remember what his brain could not. Because if they got it wrong, who knows what wretched world he and Decius would step into? And even if it wasn't wretched, would it contain the prize he sought?

"What happens now?" Decius asked.

"Now we are silent," Liber muttered. And he set his hands to work. When he was done, he closed his eyes and took a deep breath. Was it right? He had no idea. But he could do no better. "Come," he said.

He walked forward, out of Via, out of the shimmering blue light, into bitter cold and howling wind.

He looked around.

He smiled.

Yes, he thought.

14702.

SEVEN

Decius

Liber grabbed his arm, or else the wind would have knocked Decius into the deep snow. "Come," Liber shouted, pointing to a building of some kind about a hundred paces distant.

Decius staggered forward through the snow, holding on to Liber. If this was what other worlds looked and felt like, he wanted no part of them. Besides the building, he could make out trees and distant mountains. And something…ah, he could scarcely describe it. Something in the distance, in front of the mountains, shimmering and round and impossibly large.

They made their way to the building. Decius realized that he was not as cold as he expected to be. The pockets of his jacket kept his hands warm. The jacket's hood even seemed to warm the exposed skin of his face. How did it do that?

And then he made the mistake of looking up. He saw something gliding in the gray sky far above them. It was far too large to be a hawk or any other bird, and it moved far too fast. He pointed to it. "That," was all he could manage to say.

Liber looked up but said nothing.

Next to the building were rows of black machines resting on the snow. How did they not sink into the snow? What were they for? Liber ignored them and approached the building. It seemed to be made entirely of dark glass. As they reached the building, an opening appeared, as if the building had sensed their presence. They walked inside, and the building closed up behind them.

"Where are we?" Decius asked. "What is happening?"

Liber didn't respond. "Over here," he said. He led Decius to a room that glowed with a strange blue light. In front of the room was a gray table. "Take off your jacket," he said. "Put it on the table."

Decius did as he was told. The table disappeared into the glowing room and then returned, without his jacket. Liber did the same thing.

"How do we get the jackets back?" Decius asked.

"Don't worry," Liber replied. "The room will remember us."

What did that mean? Decius was trembling. The building was warm, though he saw no fireplaces, no braziers. There was light, although he saw no lamps or torches. The air had a strange smell, something like a flower—roses? But he saw no roses.

"Come," Liber said.

"Where are we going?"

"To the city. There are more wonders to see, but we are not here for the wonders."

Now he led Decius to a staircase. It looked familiar enough, except that the stairs *moved*, appearing from beneath the floor and heading down below the building. Next to it was another staircase where the stairs moved up into the floor.

"Hold my arm," Liber said. "It's been a long time since I did this." Then Liber stepped onto a stair and Decius stumbled after him, grasping Liber with one hand and a moving railing with the other.

They headed down, far underground, as if by magic. The staircase finally ended, and they hopped off onto a solid floor. Now they were in a long high-ceilinged hall, with a sunken area in the middle. And here he saw his first people, standing in front of the sunken area. Many of them wore a strange device in front of their eyes. How could they see? Their hair was shades of blue and green and purple. Some had rings in their noses. He had never seen people like them.

"Do not stare at anyone," Liber warned. "Act as if you have seen these sites for your entire life."

Decius looked at the words written on the walls; some of the letters seemed familiar, but the words didn't make sense. This wasn't Latin.

But in any case the letters of the words *glowed*. And every few seconds they would rearrange themselves into different words. "Can you understand this language?" he asked Liber.

"A little. It's easier to learn than many, because it's based on Latin, although much changed."

Decius heard another person speaking. From where? He could see no one. And then he felt a vibration that turned into a rumble. He saw a dark metal machine, at least two hundred paces long, gliding into the sunken area of the hall. It came to a stop and along its length doors slid open—again, apparently by themselves. "Come," Liber said, and he walked through the open door nearest them.

Inside, people were sitting on long benches facing each other. Liber found two empty spaces. "Sit," he said.

They sat.

"Do not stare," Liber reminded him.

Decius couldn't help staring. All the people wore strange, multicolored clothes. Most wore devices that covered their eyes. Many also had devices covering their ears. Only a few were like Liber and himself, their heads unadorned, looking silently out the windows.

And still he smelled roses.

The doors slid closed. The machine started to move, slowly at first, and then impossibly fast. How did it do this? No horses were pulling it; no sails were atop it, catching the wind. Decius was not just baffled; he was terrified. Nothing, no one, should move this fast.

And then they entered darkness.

"We are perfectly safe," Liber murmured. "We are in a tunnel. This is all normal here."

This was not normal. It could not be normal. How did people stand the speed? Why did they not go mad?

"What are we doing in this place?" Decius asked when he felt able to speak.

"We simply need to buy something in the city," Liber replied, "and then we will return to Terra. There is little danger. This is a world like countless others. People live their lives here. They have jobs and families. They worship gods, perhaps; they fight wars on occasion, I'm sure."

"But they don't have those weapons the Gallians used—the gants," Decius said.

"No. Weapons like that destroy a world. You do not want to visit a world with gants, and I was never taught how to travel to any of them."

Decius tried to make sense of what he was seeing and feeling. Countless worlds. How could this be? But here he was, sitting in a machine speeding faster than thought through a tunnel. Above him machines flew through the air. Across from him a woman with green hair, her eyes and ears covered, silently talked to herself.

He felt dizzy. He felt a twinge of what he had felt as Affron stared at him in the bowels of the Circus Maximus.

Eventually the machine glided to a stop, in another long hall. The doors slid open, and everyone got off. Liber led Decius to a long passageway. And the floor of the passageway moved, like the staircase outside the station. No need to walk, no need to do anything except hold on to a railing. It seemed to move slowly upwards after a while. The passageway let them off at a huge, open plaza—far larger than the Forum.

Thousands of people milled, wandered, sat. Decius was used to crowds, used to the mix of smells and sights and sounds of people jostling on the streets and plazas of Roma. But everything was different here. Far above the crowds huge devices hung in mid-air; on them colossal heads were speaking, visions of outdoor scenes moved past, strange devices and strange images appeared and disappeared. Around them shops were selling goods he did not recognize. He heard music playing—at least, he thought it was music, but it sounded harsh and dissonant and without melody. What was everyone doing? Where were they going?

And then Decius noticed something—the plaza was not open. Far above them was some kind of transparent substance that kept out the cold and the snow. They were in an immense bubble.

This was what he had seen in the distance as they stood in the snow.

"The entire city is enclosed in some kind of thick glass," Liber said. "I cannot explain it—I cannot explain any of it. I do not think people go outside often—the weather here is too foul."

This seemed impossible to Decius, but he supposed it was true. "What is the thing you need to buy?" he asked.

"It is merely a cream that you rub on your skin. It is common here —at least, it was."

"What does it do? Why are you buying it?"

"Ah, let me have my surprise. We may have to search for it a bit. It has been many years since I was last here. I don't remember where the shop is."

Decius didn't respond. He just wanted to get out of here; he wanted to go home. How did viators travel to such places without going mad?

After wandering for a while Liber got onto another moving staircase and went up to another level, where there were more people, more shops. Decius followed him reluctantly. The staircase was transparent somehow; they seemed to be moving through thin air.

On the upper level Liber finally stopped in front of a large shop; a yellow sign above the open door flashed blue letters that were meaningless to Decius. In the shop windows were images of smiling, green-haired men and women. "Here, I think," Liber said.

They walked inside. Decius saw aisle after aisle lined with shelves filled with jars and boxes and oddly shaped containers. The same strange, unpleasant music was playing here, but he could see no musicians. Decius thought he smelled cinnamon. Liber walked up and down the aisles until he stopped in front of a row of jars, each with a red paper affixed to the front. Each paper had the usual indecipherable letters on it.

Liber picked up one of the jars. "This is what I came here to find," he said. He brought the jar to a counter at the front of the shop. No shopkeeper stood there to accept his money; instead, he simply set the jar down in front of a device and inserted a piece of the paper money into a slot on the device. A light went on, and Liber picked up the jar. "Let's go," he said.

They walked out of the shop. Liber seemed excited and relieved.

"Did you visit this world often?" Decius asked.

"Several times. My mentor liked to bring me here for practice. It is safer than many worlds, and it has some interesting features."

"Are all the other worlds so different from Terra?"

"Many are. Ours is just one pathway through time. This is another."

Decius felt dizzy again. "Do we return home now?" he asked.

"Yes."

"Can we rest for a moment first?"

"Of course."

They found an unoccupied bench and sat down. Decius looked out at the immense, throbbing scene in front of him. Through the glass-like material he could see huge snow-clad mountains towering above him. Were there other cities in this world? Was each city replicated in world after world?

"What Affron did to you and me," Decius said finally, "is *this*, multiplied thousands upon thousands of times." He gestured out at the crowds in their odd clothes and the strange-looking spectacles, the immense faces floating in the air, the awful music, the pictures that moved, the lights and voices that came out of nowhere—the inconceivable *otherness* of what he was experiencing.

Liber shrugged. "What he did was far worse, I'm afraid. This is real, but it is outside us. We can leave it behind, forget about it. What Affron did was to make it part of us—the whole thing, every world, all at once. Our minds are not built for that. It changes a person, and not for the better."

Decius contemplated that, and decided that Liber was right. And he decided that he couldn't think about it anymore. "This thing," he said, pointing at the jar. "Will it save the Gallians?"

"It will certainly help, if they used it wisely. As I told Feslund, their gants will not be enough, because the gants will run out of power and stop working eventually, and the Gallians won't be able to obtain more. They will look for viators who will help them get these weapons, and they will fail. If the Gallians are smart, they will find ways other than fear to ensure the loyalty of the people."

"Feslund is not smart," Decius noted.

"His mother is."

"Yes," Decius agreed. "But as you have seen, she is not interested in ruling; she is not interested in the empire."

"She will not be able to sit in the temple mourning her daughter forever. Eventually she will decide to live. And then she will take charge."

"And use this jar?"

"Perhaps. There are other ways to rule; none of them very effective in the long term. But perhaps she will not care about the long term."

"I do not understand any of this," Decius admitted.

"No matter. We will see what happens. Let's return to Terra—unless you'd like to stay here longer."

Decius shook his head and stood. The dizziness had passed; he could not wait to leave this world. "The sooner we get back to Terra, the better," he said.

"Come, then," Liber replied. "Via awaits."

EIGHT

Feslund

"The matter is simple, my lord," the man was saying, as if he were talking to a child. "One of the Germanic tribes has crossed the Rhine. For generations they have not been allowed to cross the Rhine. But now they have done so. They are raiding our villages. They are carrying off our women. This must not be allowed. This must be stopped."

The man had a black beard and a swarthy complexion. He wore flowing trousers and a gray tunic. Feslund hadn't caught his name. He was annoyed with the man and the others in his delegation. And with Redegar, Feslund's chief minister, who had insisted that he listen to them. Feslund understood the problem. Did Redegar think that he didn't? The soldiers on the borders of the empire hadn't been paid, so they weren't doing their jobs. And this was the result. "We are doing all that we can," he responded.

"My lord," Black-beard replied, "our people wonder why you will not use those wonderful weapons that the gods have bestowed upon you."

Ah, the gants. The gants were supposed to solve everything. "We can't just send the weapons everywhere people ask us to," Redegar pointed out. He was old, with a high-pitched, querulous voice.

Feslund's father Carolus had sent him to provide counsel to his son. But he was useless.

"But why not, my lord?" Black-beard asked. He sounded desperate. "Surely the gods—"

"Our women are being raped," a younger man from the delegation interrupted, stepping forward. He had absurdly long red hair; his voice quivered with outrage. "Our stores of grain are being stolen. Many of us will not survive to see the spring. Every day that Urbis does not defend us the enemy grows bolder. They sense weakness, my lord. They think perhaps the weapons do not exist, or that they are powerless so far from Urbis."

"Of course the weapons exist," Feslund snapped. "I have one right here in my robe. Would you like to see me use it?"

Black-beard's eyes widened and he pulled the younger man back. "My lord," he said, "We are just reporting what people are saying."

"We of course are very concerned for your safety," Redegar replied, gesturing for calm, "and we will do all in our power to assist you. But there are many complexities in the situation that you do not understand."

Many complexities, Feslund thought. They had no money. How complex was that? Redegar was supposed to figure out who collected the taxes, how the money ended up in the treasury, how the money was paid out, and a thousand other things. As far as Feslund could tell, Redegar had done none of them.

"We are very grateful for your assistance, of course," Black-beard said. "But we wish to point out that it is not just our people. The entire northern border of the empire is at risk. My lords, we need a plan to save it."

Feslund spotted Decius standing in the doorway at the far end of the room, with Liber just behind him. They had returned successfully from Via, it seemed. And they had changed out of those ridiculous clothes they had put on. He had little wish to speak to them, but he had even less wish to listen to Black-beard and the red-haired youth and Redegar. He stood up. "My minister will discuss this matter further with you," he said to the delegation. "I am sure we can devise a plan to help you."

Everyone bowed deeply, even the red-head. Feslund inclined his head and strode out of the room.

He walked up to Decius and Liber. "Well, then?" he said. "You are still alive, I see."

"We are, my lord," Decius responded. "May we have a few moments of your time?"

"Anything to get away from these fools. Come."

He led them out into the hallway. They were in the pontifex's palace, which was even more ornate than the royal castle in Lugdunum. The pontifex, of course, no longer resided here. Feslund assumed that Tirelius was enjoying the jail cell that he currently occupied.

Liber was holding a jar with strange writing on it. "What is this thing?" Feslund asked. "You entered Via and returned with this? I was expecting something interesting."

"I think you will find this interesting enough, my lord," Liber replied. "Will you come to the hospital with us?"

"The hospital? Why?"

"I would like to demonstrate why this jar is interesting, my lord."

"Where is my mother?" Feslund asked.

"Your mother declined to accompany us," Decius said. "She leaves this matter in your hands."

This annoyed Feslund. His mother needed to get over Siglind's death. It was sad—of course it was—but they had an empire to rule. And you couldn't rule it by sitting in the temple day after day, mourning the past. Siglind wasn't coming back to life, and meanwhile the German tribes were pouring over the Rhine. "Very well," he said. "Lead the way."

He had only a vague idea where the hospital was, but Liber knew. He led them out of the palace and across the forum. Darkness was falling, and a cold wind blew into their faces. Feslund longed for excitement. Day after day, sitting in a cold room and listening to complaints…what he really wanted was to mount his horse and gallop across the countryside with his companions from Gallia. With Arminius especially. But Arminius was dead, like Siglind—drowned in the great sea on the way to Urbis. He missed Arminius almost as much as he missed Siglind. But he had no time to mourn. He had to listen to the likes of Black-beard and the red-head.

Did they not see the problem with using these weapons to solve their border problems? Of course they didn't. You couldn't arm soldiers with gants. First of all, there weren't enough gants, and they ran out of power if used too frequently—Feslund himself had experienced this in the raid on Urbis. Second, anyone with a gant was a potential threat to the throne. Did they expect Feslund to hand them out to every legionary? That was impossible. No, the few gants they possessed weren't going to be shipped to the northern border. They would be kept locked up—more securely than they had been locked up under the priests.

Perhaps he himself should go to the border, Feslund thought. Get out of Urbis, get out of the endless meetings with advisors and audiences with petitioners. Of course Decius would object, and Redegar too, although more timidly. But Feslund didn't care. It was all up to him, ultimately. Not them, not his mother, certainly not his father, enjoying himself back in Gallia. The empire was his to rule, his to save.

Yes, he would get out of this place. The idea excited him. This was what he needed to do.

"Here is the hospital, my lord," Liber murmured.

It was a small stone building tucked behind the palatium, with no statue in front, no grand motto chiseled over its doors. It reminded Feslund of the armamentarium where the gants were stored, except that lights shone from its windows, and its door, when they reached it, was unlocked.

Liber led them inside. The building was warmer than most—to keep the patients comfortable, Feslund supposed. A pretty young woman sat at a desk, writing on a parchment. She looked up, and when she recognized Feslund she hurriedly rose and bowed. "Y-yes, my lord?" she stammered.

Feslund simply gestured to Liber, who inclined his head to the woman. "We wish to speak to the doctor in charge," he said. "Will you bring us to him, please?"

"Yes, of course. Come this way, my lords."

She led them down a long, plain corridor. In the distance Feslund could hear a man groaning. He could smell the strong cleanser used in such places. He didn't like being here. He didn't like being reminded of death.

Tomorrow. Perhaps he would leave tomorrow. Why not? He would take Mellor, Escondo, Cymbian—they deserved a new adventure.

The woman stopped in front of a closed door and knocked. An irritable voice muttered something from inside. "I am sorry to bother you, sir," the woman said, "but Prince Feslund wishes to speak to you."

They heard movement inside, and a moment later the door opened. A gray-haired man with a full beard and splotchy skin peered out, saw Feslund, and then opened the door wide and bowed deeply. "I am sorry, my lord," he said. "I did not expect...I am honored..."

Behind him, Feslund spotted a desk, with a jug and a cup on it. He could smell wine on the doctor's breath; his eyes were wide with fear.

"Never mind," Feslund said. "This man is named Liber, and next to him is Marcus Decius, governor of the Roman province. Do what they say. And be quick about it."

The doctor bowed. "Of course, of course. But..."

"I am seeking a patient," Liber interrupted. "Any patient, as long as he is gravely ill, ideally with an infected wound. One who is beyond your powers to cure, with only days to live."

The doctor looked confused. "I do not understand."

"Why do you not understand?" Feslund demanded, although he didn't understand himself. "Do what the man says. Have you such a patient?"

The doctor scratched at his beard. "Well, I suppose. There is a boy upstairs. Will a boy do?"

"What's wrong with him?" Liber asked.

"Cut himself badly with a rusty sword he found somewhere or other. The parents delayed far too long in bringing him here. They are simple folks from outer Urbis, the kind who don't want to be a bother. The poor lad is unconscious, delirious. I do not expect him to last the night."

"Bring us to him," Liber said.

"There is nothing to be done, you know," the doctor insisted. "We used all the means at our disposal, but the wound—"

"Yes, yes. That is perfect. Come, then. No time to waste."

The doctor left the room and led them to a staircase, adjusting his robe as they went. He was unsteady on his feet, Feslund noticed. The drunken fool. He would have the man replaced in the morning.

Upstairs they found themselves in a long open area filled with cots and lit by flickering lamps. Patients lay on the cots, sleeping or moaning. Family or friends sat on stools next to some of them. Nurses walked here and there. The room quieted as people noticed Feslund. A couple of them rose. Feslund waved at them to sit.

The doctor brought them to a cot in the corner near a row of large windows. On the cot lay a boy of six or seven, sandy-haired, pale, eyes closed, breathing irregularly. A young man and woman stood next to him, their faces streaked with tears. "The parents," the doctor muttered.

"My lord," the man said to Feslund, bowing, his voice trembling, "we are so honored."

"Yes, of course," Feslund replied, acknowledging the bow. He turned to Liber. "What now?" he demanded.

"Let us see the wound," Liber said to the doctor.

The doctor turned to the parents. "Perhaps you would prefer to—" he began.

"We will look also," the man said.

The doctor shrugged and drew back the blanket covering the boy. Then he carefully unwound a bandage covering the boy's middle. The wound was long and ugly, filled with green pus. The area around the wound was an angry red. It smelled foul. The woman gasped and started sobbing. "I am sorry," the doctor said.

Liber gestured to Feslund, and they walked a couple of paces away from the bed. Liber had opened the jar with the strange writing on it. It was filled with a white cream. "Put a small amount of this on your hand," Liber instructed. "Rub the cream into the wound."

"I don't want to touch that thing," Feslund protested, looking back at the boy.

"Rub the cream into the wound," Liber repeated. "And the people of the empire will love you. There is no danger."

Feslund stared at Liber, and suddenly he understood. It was all so simple. "Give it to me," he said.

Liber gave him the jar. Feslund smeared some of the cream onto his fingers, and then returned the jar to Liber. The substance, whatever it was, felt cool on his skin. He turned back to the boy and the others.

"May I touch the child?" he asked the parents.

The woman looked at her husband. The man bowed his head to Feslund. "Of course, my lord."

"Thank you."

He went to the boy and bent over him. The boy's breath was ragged. Too young to die, but he would not see the next sunrise. Feslund reached out and forced himself to put his hand on the ugly, suppurating wound. The skin was hot beneath his fingers. He moved his hand back and forth over the wound, rubbing the cream deeply into it. The white color quickly disappeared, leaving behind a glistening, oily residue. "Enough," Liber murmured to him after a few moments.

Feslund removed his hand and straightened up. He stood back. The parents stared at him in confusion. Feslund looked at Liber, who was standing there with his arms folded. Now what? If this fellow was wrong...

"Look," Decius whispered suddenly, pointing to the wound.

Feslund looked. At first he could see nothing in the lamplight that flickered next to the boy's cot.

But then he thought he saw what Decius was seeing. The redness that surrounded the wound—was it fading? Yes, it was. And then the wound itself seemed to fade, crusting over and thinning, as if weeks of recovery were happening in minutes. And the boy's breath sounded more regular now. The doctor reached down and placed a hand on the boy's forehead. "The fever is gone," he announced. "I do not understand this. I do not understand it at all."

And then the boy opened his eyes. He looked up at his mother. "Mamma?" he whispered. "What happened, Mamma?"

The mother buried her face on the boy's neck and embraced him, sobbing uncontrollably. "Publius, my Publius!" she whispered to him.

The boy looked puzzled but happy.

And meanwhile the father had fallen to his knees in front of Feslund. "My lord," he said, "my prince. Blessed be your name. Thank you. Truly you have been chosen by the gods. You are greater than any priest."

Feslund looked over at Liber, who had retreated into the shadows next to the windows. *Chosen by the gods,* Feslund thought. *Greater than any priest.*

Now, finally, it could begin.

NINE

Gratius

The three of them rode along the King's Road, heading north.

Gratius watched the boy up ahead. After all these days and all these miles, Larry was still awkward on horseback. It was understandable; he hadn't grown up with horses on his world. But the girl—Palta—hadn't ridden before she came to Terra, yet she was fluid and graceful on her horse. And she picked up languages easily and was endlessly resourceful. She would have made an excellent viator; Larry would have been helpless without her.

They had spent months making their way here from Urbis. Back in Roma, as the soldiers closed in on them after the chariot race, Gratius had put Affron and two of the others—Carmody and Valleia—onto a ship heading to Britannia. But Palta and Larry had not been with them. And before Affron set sail he had told Gratius: "Bring me Larry."

Why? Affron didn't bother to say. Nevertheless Gratius had striven to obey, finding Larry and Palta in the temple after the Gallians had conquered Urbis, and then convincing them to leave the burning city with him in search of Affron.

But Affron was not at the port in Britannia. Where, then? He and the others had sailed up the coast to Scotia, it seemed. So, the journey had continued. They had stayed at a little Scotian port village called Flendys. But they were there no longer.

Where had they gone?

Larry seemed to know. He said little. Occasionally he looked a little frightened—or perhaps just puzzled, as if he himself didn't understand what was happening, how he knew what he knew. But he did not falter. They headed north along the King's Road, as the townspeople suggested, even though it was the dead of winter and few other travelers were headed for the remote highlands of this wretched little kingdom. But as the days went by and they gleaned no information from travelers and inn-keepers, Gratius and Palta became increasingly worried. Was this all a waste of time? Larry didn't seem to think so.

Now Gratius was tired and cold, and he had no answers to the questions that raced through his mind. "We must stop at the next inn," he called out to Larry and Palta. "The sun is low in the sky, and it will be bitter cold tonight."

Palta looked back at him and nodded. Larry said nothing. He seemed not to hear.

They rode an hour longer, and the sun had set before they finally encountered an inn. It was a dreary place, but this was not a surprise; Scotia was filled with dreary places. This one seemed sturdily built of thick logs, at least. Smoke rose from its chimney, and that meant warmth and cooked food, if nothing else. It was all one could expect of Scotia in winter.

They dismounted, gave their horses over to the sullen, dirty-faced stable boy, and went inside.

The inside was as dreary as the outside. They were the only guests, but the unshaven, barrel-chested proprietor seemed annoyed that they had arrived to spoil his solitude. They sat by the smoky fire and tried to eat the boiled meat he set in front of them. "Is this all you have?" Gratius demanded in Erse, the local language.

The proprietor shrugged. "It's good enough for me," he replied. "Should be good enough for you."

"Have you seen two men and a woman pass by here?" Palta asked him. "They'd have a Latin accent, like us."

The man shrugged. "I've not seen anyone like that. Not lately, anyway."

"In the last few months?"

Another shrug. "We have many guests. I recall none like that."

Gratius didn't believe that the place had many guests, but Palta did not press the landlord further.

There was no wine, of course, only weak, tasteless beer. "We cannot go on like this," he said suddenly.

The other two didn't respond; they just looked at him and waited for him to continue.

"What makes you think we're going to find them?" he went on. "We have asked about them all along the King's Road, and no one has seen them. They could have turned off the road anywhere. For all we know, they could have gone to a port, hired a ship, and sailed back to Roma."

"They haven't," Larry said.

"How do you know this?"

The boy shrugged. "I cannot explain it."

Gratius turned to Palta. "What do you think?"

But he knew what Palta would think. She believed in Larry. There was a bond of sorts between them—not quite sexual, he thought, but not the innocent friendship of childhood either. He had saved her life back in Roma, and they had traveled to Gallia together. And from there, of course, they had led the Gallians to Urbis. They had, in fact, helped the Gallians destroy everything that Gratius had lived for. And still he stayed with them.

"We must find Affron," Palta replied simply.

"But what we are doing now is hopeless," Gratius protested.

She looked at Larry. "It is not hopeless," he said. "You can leave us if you want. We are grateful for your help. But Palta and I have been on our own before. We will continue the journey by ourselves."

Yes, he should simply leave them.

But what then? He thought of the viator Lamathe. In the aftermath of the Gallians' victory Lamathe had come up with a plan, of sorts. But it wasn't a plan to defeat the Gallians; it was simply a way of keeping the viators' dreams alive until Gallian rule collapsed.

Affron was the only one who could save them, who could renew Terra. But perhaps that was a dream too. Gratius had risked his career and probably his life to procure a gant to help Affron escape from jail in Urbis. He had protected Affron in Roma, found him a ship to sail to Britannia as Decius prepared to arrest him, obeyed his instructions as best he could to bring Larry to him....

And here he was, drinking weak beer by a smoky fire in a wretched corner of a wretched country. "Soon the King's Road will end," he pointed out. "And then what? Do we find a boat to take us to the Northern Islands? And what if Affron is not there?"

"He is not far away, I think," Larry responded.

Gratius fumed. He did not understand Larry; he did not understand Affron. He did not understand anything.

He swallowed the beer and finished his wretched meal, and then he went upstairs to the room and bed the three of them would share. They had slept together often on their journey—on the bare ground as they rode north away from the burning wreckage of Urbis, on shipboard as they journeyed to Britannica, and then in inns like this or rooming houses in little villages. Some were better than others, but he'd had no desire to stay in any of them a second night.

The fire burned low in the small fireplace, and the room was cold. The guttering candle revealed a single large bed covered by a few woolen blankets, a white wash basin on a pine table, the usual chamber pot in the corner, and a marble statue of some local cult god on a shelf.

Gratius hung his cloak on a wooden hook by the door, used the chamber pot, put another log on the fire, and then slid beneath the covers. The mattress managed to be both thin and lumpy. The woolen blankets were warm, though. He fell asleep quickly, but awoke when the other two came into the room. They didn't speak as they got into the bed next to him—Larry in the middle, and Palta on Larry's other side. Gratius had awakened often to see Palta snuggled up to Larry, her arm around his waist. This usually caused a faint stirring of desire in him. But he wasn't interested in Palta, who was barely a woman. He *was* interested in Valleia—raven-haired, quick-witted Valleia, his schoolmate, his fellow viator, his friend. She had rescued Affron with him and now she was probably with him somewhere in this godforsaken land. It was the hope of seeing her again, as much as finding Affron, that kept him going.

Valleia wasn't interested in him, however. Instead she had been attracted to William Carmody, who like Larry and Palta had come to Terra from another world. The man was good-looking enough, but what did he have in common with Valleia? How could she think that he would be the right companion for her through life?

Gratius lay awake for a long time pondering such things before drifting off to sleep again. When he finally awoke, the sun was up, and Larry and Palta were gone.

He quickly got out of bed, put his cloak and shoes on, and went downstairs. The proprietor said nothing to him, merely gestured outside, towards the stable. Gratius went out. It was cold and bright, although flakes of snow blew through the air. In the stable, Larry and Palta had saddled their horses and were preparing to mount them. They paused when they saw him.

"You're going on without me?" Gratius asked.

"You're welcome to come," Larry said. "But you seemed to think this was a bad idea."

"Larry knows where they are," Palta said, excitement in her voice. "There is a westerly road somewhere to the north, off the King's Road. That will lead us to them."

"I see." He did not bother asking Larry how he knew.

"Will you come?" Palta asked Gratius. "We are so close. It would be a shame for you to turn back now."

Palta had stabbed him in the hand once, back in Urbis—to capture his gant, so she could use it to destroy the fat fool Hypatius, a viator who had probably been doing awful things to her while her protector Affron was in prison. Well, he could not blame her, he supposed. It was good to see her happy.

Was his long journey really about to end? He found himself trusting Larry. Who else did he have to trust?

"I will come," Gratius said.

And he hurried to join them.

TEN

Palta

Once more they set out—Palta riding in the middle between Larry and Gratius. The day was cold, but every day was cold now. Palta's belly was full, and her horse, her beloved Renni, was content. And perhaps today was the day they would find Affron, and this long journey would at last come to an end.

And what would happen then?

She had been baffled and anxious for this whole journey. It was good that Larry was still here with her on Terra—that he hadn't disappeared into Via to return home and left her friendless in this world. But Larry had changed.

He had tried to explain the change. It had begun back in the temple of Via. He had been confronted by an old woman with a gant as he and the Gallian soldiers had tried to take over the temple. And somehow he had used his mind to destroy her. It was a power that Affron possessed as well. Larry was terrified of it.

But why was this leading him to obsessively search for Affron in the far reaches of Terra? This he could not explain. At least, not very well. "There is a...kinship," he said. "We are the same, somehow. He has sent for me. I have to go to him."

She didn't understand this any more than Larry seemed to. And she knew what she wanted to happen when they found Affron: nothing. She just wanted to live in peace with Affron and Larry. She didn't care about the others. Gratius and Valleia and Carmody could go or stay; it didn't matter to her. What happened on Terra didn't matter to her; let Feslund and the rest of the Gallians rule the priests' empire. She had struggled too much; she longed for the day when the struggle would be over.

But she did not believe that the day would come anytime soon.

The hours passed. The snow fell more heavily; Palta was not used to snow—it seemed unnatural, terrifying. Renni didn't seem to mind it. They did not come across a westerly road. They stopped at mid-day to rest the horses and eat stale biscuits they had bought at the inn. Larry said nothing. Gratius was becoming agitated. Palta knew that it would not be long before he'd point out the folly of what they were doing. But eventually Larry mounted his horse again and set out, and Gratius followed in silence.

The snow grew worse; the road began to disappear beneath it. They kept going. What else could they do? The sky grew darker. A couple of hours later they came upon an inn. "We must stop here!" Gratius called out. "It is madness to continue."

Larry paused. Gratius came up beside them. Larry looked at the inn, looked at the road, and slowly shook his head. "We are not far," he said.

Palta's heart sank.

"We will die if we spend the night in this storm!" Gratius said.

Larry looked at Palta. "We are not far," he repeated.

The snow whipped into her face. She was shivering inside her cape. She recalled the sight of Larry, looking down at her as she lay on the floor of the warehouse in Roma, about to be sold into slavery. He had saved her, as Affron had saved her on Gaia. She owed her life to both of them. Larry would not let her down.

Palta nodded. "Let's go, then," she said.

Larry nodded in return and looked over at Gratius. "Will you come?"

"It is madness," he repeated.

"As you wish."

Larry flicked his reins and his horse moved slowly forward. Palta followed. She looked behind to say good-bye to Gratius, but after a moment he too joined them. It was madness, but he was still part of it.

The darkness deepened. The snow did not let up. And finally Larry stopped again. Was he going to turn back?

"Here," he said, pointing to his left.

Palta looked. She saw nothing—perhaps just a wider gap between the tall pines. "Are you sure?" she asked.

He merely shrugged.

They turned. The snow was deeper, along with the darkness. Palta spotted a deer staring out at them from a clearing. Did he too think they were mad? There were no houses, no farms, no signs that humans lived nearby. But they did seem to be on a kind of path that wound through the trees.

They followed it for half an hour or more. If they had to go back to the inn now, they would have to do it in utter darkness.

And then Larry stopped once again. He pointed to the left—to a faint light glimmering in the distance. "There," he said.

They rode towards the light. The path widened and straightened. The light was in the window of a stone cottage. Palta thought she could see smoke rising from its chimney. Oh, yes! Larry had been right!

They stopped at the cottage and dismounted. Larry went up to the door and knocked, with Palta and Gratius behind him.

The door opened, and they saw Valleia. When Valleia recognized them, she put a hand to her mouth and began to weep. "Oh my friends!" she cried. "You have found us! Come inside!"

They went in. Carmody stood behind her, staring at them in astonishment. Gratius closed the door, and they all embraced in front of a blazing fire.

"Where is Affron?" Larry asked finally.

Palta saw Carmody and Valleia exchange a glance, and her heart sank once again.

"Affron is not here," Carmody said. "He is gone, and we don't know where."

ELEVEN

Valleia

Valleia heated up the remains of the rabbit stew while William helped Larry and the others take care of their horses. When they returned she served the stew and poured them cups of mead. They looked weary and cold as they settled themselves around the hearth. Why were they coming here in the middle of the night? And how had they found this remote place?

It had to do with Larry and Affron, of course. But beyond that she understood nothing.

"Please tell me about Affron," Larry said, after he had taken a few bites of the stew.

"He has been gone a week or more," Valleia said. "He left without a word. We looked—William, especially. But we found no trace of him."

"When we arrived here, Affron would walk away from the cottage every morning and return as the sun set," William explained. "He never told us where he was going; he never seemed especially cold or tired when he returned. And then one day he did not return."

"Could he have walked to a port town and booked passage on a ship?" Palta asked. "Or bought a horse from someone and ridden off?"

Palta looked upset. She had matured since last summer, Valleia noticed; now she was clearly in the early stages of womanhood.

"He had no money that I'm aware of," William replied. "There is a village not far off, but no one there claimed to have seen him."

"Do you think he's dead, then?" Palta asked, with tears in her eyes.

"I do not know, but I can't see how he survived."

"Affron is alive," Larry said, with a certainty that seemed absurd under the circumstances, but nevertheless gave Valleia hope.

"How do you know?" she asked him.

Larry shrugged. "Did he speak of me?" he asked.

"He did not say much in all the time since we left Roma," she replied. "You remember how he was. He would shut himself away from us for hours—days—at a time. But he seemed confident that you would find us, wherever we were. How, I don't know. Why, I don't know."

Larry seemed to ponder this. He too looked older than Valleia remembered. When she first met him on Earth—was it less than a year ago?—he had looked like a normal schoolboy. Now he was taller, and there was a hint of maturity in his eyes. Or perhaps something more than maturity—something that Affron had spotted before any of them. "I saw the shed in Flendys," Larry replied finally. "That's where he spent his time."

And how did Larry know *that*? William nodded. "He would sit in that shed, making those strange gestures with his hands, as if he were searching for something in the air in front of him. As he did in Roma. He never explained what he was doing."

"Yes," Larry said, as if this information did not surprise him.

"How did you find us here?" Valleia asked. She realized that she did not expect a satisfactory answer, any more than she had expected an explanation from Affron about his behavior.

She did not receive one. "I do not understand it," Larry said. "I'm sorry—I would tell you if I could. Why did you leave Flendys?"

"Affron was worried that someone would track us there. He thought we were still in danger."

"Do you know about what happened in Urbis?" Gratius asked.

"About the Gallians?" Valleia said. "Yes, that news reached us. But we know so little about it. You must tell us."

And so they did—Gratius and Palta, anyway. Larry had little to say. It was difficult to believe—Larry and Palta had brought down the priests with a single gant and installed the Gallians in their place. All so that Larry could get back to Via and use it to return home. And yet, in the end, he decided to remain on Terra and find Affron. How did this make sense? What had forged the bond between the two of them?

Larry didn't try to explain it.

And now Tirelius was gone—captured or dead; and all Valleia's friends—viators and priests—were scattered. And the Gallians ruled the empire. "This does not bode well for Terra," she said.

"It does not," Gratius agreed. "But meanwhile, you should be safe here. Larry could find you, but no one else, I think. And I see that you are with child."

Valleia was wondering when someone would point this out. It made sense that it would be Gratius; he had always been fond of her. Perhaps more than fond. She smiled and reached out to grasp Carmody's hand. "We are very happy," she replied.

"I wish both of you health and joy," Gratius said, raising his cup in a toast. Larry and Palta murmured their agreement. "We are sorry to impose on you," he went on.

"It is no imposition," Valleia said. "We are happy for the company. We have lived a quiet life since we arrived here."

"Stay as long as you like," William added.

"You are very kind," Gratius said.

Valleia couldn't imagine that they would stay long. But where else would they go, what would they do, with Affron gone?

"Tomorrow would you help me search for him?" Larry asked William.

"You won't find him around here," William pointed out. "Not alive, at any rate."

"I understand. Still."

William nodded. "As you wish."

With that, it seemed time to go to sleep. The others had traveled far, and Valleia was not used to being up so long after dark. She laid out what blankets they had on the floor by the hearth, and they settled down for the night. It was strange, but not unpleasant, to have guests in this small cottage. Her life here was utterly different from anything she had experienced, and it would change even more when her child was born. The same was true for William, who had been an army officer in the world where he had once lived. Sometimes she worried that she— or both of them—would end up bored, dissatisfied, resentful in their new lives. But that was unlikely, as long as they had each other.

69

She noticed Palta snuggling up to Larry, as she had most nights in Roma. Ah, it was nice to see that this had not changed, even though they had both changed so much. She hoped that Palta's heart would not be broken. Valleia had not been close to her in Roma, but she had no reason to dislike the girl.

Tomorrow Larry would be convinced that Affron was truly gone, and then what? Would he keep searching? Would Palta have to follow him?

Valleia moved closer to William, who put his arm around her. She listened to the regular breathing of her sleeping guests, the patter of snow on the window panes. Oh, it was good to be alive. She wished that Palta and all of them could feel the way she felt right now.

———

Carmody

Searching for Affron was a waste of time, but Carmody was happy to ride out on a crisp winter morning with Palta and Larry. The chores could wait—and, after all, now there were more people to help. Gratius, in fact, was already helping; he had stayed behind at the cottage to reminisce with Valleia and chop firewood. And later he would make the daily trip to the village for food and supplies. He, apparently, had no interest in searching for his old friend.

Palta was confident on her horse; Larry, far less so. And he didn't seem to be searching very hard. He didn't study the ground for tracks; his gaze didn't sweep the distance to see if Affron was rowing a boat on the lake or climbing a rocky crag.

It didn't matter. They would not find Affron in any case.

The day when Affron failed to return Valleia had become increasingly agitated as the sun set and darkness deepened. "He cannot survive the night out there," she said.

"Shall I look for him?" he asked her.

"No, no—what if you get lost? I cannot risk it."

"Put a lamp in the window," he suggested. "I won't go out of sight of the light."

"Yes, all right. But be careful."

The villagers had warned of wolves, although Carmody hadn't seen any. He didn't often wish he were back in his home world, but he would have preferred to have a musket now for protection, or a handgun from Larry's world. At any rate, he took another lamp and went out into the night. He circled the cottage. He went down the path that led to the lake. He tramped through the meadow and the stand of trees that lay beyond it. He stopped and listened for moans or cries of distress.

And he saw nothing; he heard nothing. Affron was gone.

This did not surprise him, and it didn't particularly upset him. He had always assumed that something like this would happen. Affron had already left them in spirit; it was only a matter of time before he left them altogether; and it was just like him to do so without an explanation, without a good-bye. Carmody returned to the cottage. "He will return if he wants to return," he said. "He will be safe if he wants to be safe."

Valleia nodded. "Still, we must try to find him."

"Of course. I'll go out again at daybreak."

Daybreak came, and he left the cottage once again, and once again found no trace of Affron. No tracks in the snow, no scrap of clothing caught on a bramble. No frozen corpse lying on the ground, staring sightlessly at the sky.

Day after day he wasted time searching; day after day he found nothing. Affron was gone.

He was the only reason they were here, in this beautiful, desolate spot. He was the reason for everything they had done on Terra, really —and now he was gone.

Now there was just the two of them, with their unborn child. And that was fine with Carmody. What did Affron matter to him? He had no interest in these disagreements among the priests; he did not care whether they or the Gallians ruled the empire. The only reason he was here on Terra was Valleia. Without Affron, they could concentrate on building their life together.

And now Larry and the others had arrived. How had Larry discovered them? Carmody had met Larry before any of them, back on Carmody's own world, a scared boy trying to talk his way out of a refugee camp in Boston. It seemed so long ago now, when he had been a soldier trying to use Larry and his friend Kevin to win a war. Much had happened; they had both changed. But it seemed that Larry had changed far more than he had.

And that was strange, because Carmody felt that he himself had changed completely. Until he met Valleia, he had been focused on finding out the secrets of Larry's world—guns and motors and flying machines—and bringing them back to his own, so that his nation could defeat its enemies. But when he met Valleia, such concerns slipped away. What did they matter, next to her smile, her touch? He had no desire to be anywhere but where Valleia was.

"Stop!"

Larry had raised his hand and pulled up for no reason that Carmody could see. They were at the base of a hill, a few hundred feet high. Carmody tried to remember if he had searched it. Probably not; he hadn't bothered climbing all the numberless hills that dotted this landscape. Why would Affron climb to the top of a hill? Larry got off his horse and tied it to a scrub pine.

"What is it, Larry?" Palta asked.

"Just wait here," he replied. "I'll be back."

And with that he started to scramble up the hill.

"Is anything up there?" Palta asked Carmody.

Carmody shook his head. "Trees and rocks. Grouse, rabbits, squirrels."

Palta looked worried. "Should we follow him?"

"Why? He's not in any danger. He will come back down eventually. And then we will keep looking."

"You think this is a waste of time."

"Of course it is."

They watched Larry make his way up the hill. He was awkward; he stumbled over a rock, fell, and slid back down a few feet, then got up with difficulty. He wasn't used to climbing. Finally he made it to the top and disappeared from view.

Palta and Carmody waited. "I do not understand Larry," she said finally.

"Nor do I," Carmody replied.

"What do you think he's doing up there?"

"I have no idea." He paused, and then asked: "Did he tell you how he found us?"

"Not very clearly. He had a sense, a feeling…He can't explain it—or won't." After another pause, Palta asked, "Do you like it here?"

"It is very beautiful—far nicer than Roma. But if we stay, Valleia and I will have to figure out how to make a living in this place. I'm not a farmer, though I suppose I can learn. It is difficult living in a world that is not your own. As you know."

Palta did not respond. She seemed to be a smart, accomplished girl. But she, too, was an outsider here. What did she want to do with her life?

"You're welcome to stay, you know," he went on. "All of you, actually. Away from the struggle and the strife."

He stole a glance at her. She sat motionless on her horse, but it was not hard to spot the concern on her face. Was she even listening to him?

"There he is!" she exclaimed.

He looked up and saw Larry at the top of the hill. He seemed to be gazing off into the distance. At what? There was little to be seen—the lake, the village, small cottages like theirs, flocks of sheep, hills and meadows and snow. Finally he started back down the hill.

"Did you discover anything?" Carmody asked when he reached the bottom.

"Nothing," Larry replied, untying his horse. But he didn't seem disappointed.

"Shall we continue?"

"I don't think so. We can return to the cottage, if you like."

"As you wish," Carmody said. He waited for Larry to mount his horse, and then they started off in silence.

Back at the cottage, Gratius and Valleia were preparing dinner. In addition to the food, Gratius had bought extra blankets in the village. He apparently had plenty of money, which was helpful, because Valleia and Carmody had to be careful with what little they had left. Carmody told them about their lack of success.

"So, you have searched; what will you do now?" Valleia asked Larry.

Everyone looked at him. Larry was silent for a long time. And then he said, "Can we stay here for a while?"

And Carmody thought he saw a hint of the scared boy he had met outside that refugee camp in Boston. Larry had expected to find Affron here. But Affron had disappeared. And now he was baffled, lost.

But the fundamental question remained: why this obsession with Affron? Why hadn't he taken the opportunity to return home when he'd had it, back in Urbis? He knew how much Larry had wanted to go home, on Carmody's world and again here on Terra. Carmody had felt the same regret and longing when he'd been trapped in Larry's world. So many friends and relatives, so many customs and habits and ways of thinking, lost forever. Carmody had found something—someone—better, someone who made up for all he had lost. But Larry—what did he have? Palta, of course. She clearly cared for Larry. What did Affron offer him?

"You can stay," Valleia said to Larry, repeating what Carmody had said to Palta. "You can all stay. For a while, or for longer. The searching, the yearning…It can all stop. Now. Here."

No one said anything. And finally Larry nodded. "You are most kind," he murmured.

Palta put her hand on Larry's. Gratius smiled. Carmody himself felt a sense of relief.

The mood was cheerful as they ate the meal. Gratius had purchased jugs of ale that all but Valleia consumed gratefully. There was little talk of the future, but that was all right. It was good to have friends and shared memories and the warmth of a fire.

Later, Carmody went to the outhouse, and when he returned Valleia was standing outside the cottage door, her cape wrapped around her shoulders. She smiled at him, and he smiled back. "I was getting used to our privacy," she said.

"I know." He put his arm around her, and they stood in silence. The night was clear, and the sky glistened with stars.

"Larry will not stay," Valleia said at last.

"How do you know?"

"It's just a feeling. Whatever he is searching for, he won't find it here. So he will leave."

"Perhaps Palta will stay," he replied. "She could help with the childbirth."

"That would be good. But she loves Larry, and she will not want to leave him."

This seemed likely. But he couldn't worry about them. He touched Valleia's belly lightly. Everything was quiet inside it at the moment. But it was good to know that the baby was there, growing every day, getting ready to join them. "Let them stay or leave," he said. "It doesn't matter, does it?"

Valleia didn't bother to reply; the answer was obvious. Instead she laid her head against his chest, and together they looked up at the stars in silence.

TWELVE

Larry

Larry had read something about memories once—in science class, maybe, or somewhere on the web. Memories are stored in the synapses of your brain; scientists aren't exactly sure how. But your body is always changing, developing, aging. Your synapses today are not the same as your synapses last year. And you think you remember things, but really you don't, at least not very well, certainly not perfectly— maybe your memories today just remember old memories, and so they get less and less accurate over time, like in that game where a conversation is repeated from person to person, and eventually the last person ends up hearing something that is nothing at all like the original.

Nowadays he felt his memories of his life in Glanbury slipping away, as his synapses changed here on Terra. He had an image in his mind of what his father looked like, but was it real? What about the sound of his brother Matthew's voice, the excitement of Christmas morning, how it felt to ride in a car…?

It hadn't been that long.

It had been forever.

He lay on the floor of this isolated cottage under a woolen blanket. The fire in front of him burned low. Palta lay asleep next to him. He was in northern Scotia, which was a part of what people in the empire called Barbarica, which was in a world called Terra, although the Scotians themselves probably had a different name for it.

A few months ago he had set in motion events that had killed hundreds or even thousands and brought down that empire.

What was next?

There was much he didn't know. But he was learning; every day, he was learning.

It was impossible to explain, though, just exactly what he was learning. This was not math; this was not history; this was not riding a horse or speaking a foreign language. This was…unlocking things inside himself that he didn't know existed. And if you don't know they exist, how can you figure out how to unlock them?

Affron could help, he knew. But Affron was gone.

And once he had learned what he needed to know, what then?

Not even Affron could tell him that. Larry had caused much suffering and death here. It wasn't his fault, he could tell himself. He hadn't asked to come to Terra; he hadn't asked to be held in Urbis against his will, then hunted down once he and the others had escaped.

But he knew better. It was his fault. He had done what he had done.

He closed his eyes and tried to sleep, but as usual sleep was slow in coming. And when it did come, it was not restful. It was never restful. He did not dream of Christmas mornings at home, or of family expeditions to the beach, or of long, silly conversations with Kevin, but of the temple of Via, and the carnage he had unleashed there. The bodies of Siglind and the Gallian soldiers disappearing before his eyes. The hatred on the face of the ancient woman who guarded the temple, who had killed them with her gant, who was now prepared to kill him…

Until he reached into her mind and caused her pain and terror beyond imagining. Caused her body to fall from the balcony to the temple floor, where it lay broken but still alive, until his own gant had disposed of it.

He had much to atone for, although he did not know how.

He knew what his next step should be, though. If he could bring himself to take it.

Because he knew where Affron had gone.

Sort of.

The knowledge now haunted him. It was not what he had wanted;

it was not what he had expected. He was tired. Tired of strange worlds and hard decisions. Tired of leaving people behind.

How could he bear to leave anyone else behind?

Everyone rose early, although there wasn't much to do. No books, no entertainment, just conversation and chores. He recalled how Palta and he had explored Roma every day when they went to buy food, and she had taught him Latin along the way. He missed those days.

After breakfast, he volunteered to go to the village to do the errands. Palta offered to go with him, but he shook his head. "It's better if I go by myself," he said.

He wasn't sure why he said that. Palta looked upset. "You'll get lost," she pointed out, with good reason. She had a much better sense of direction than he did.

"No, I won't," he insisted.

No one argued with him. Valleia told him what they needed and how to find the store. Outside, Palta helped him saddle his horse. "Come back," she whispered before he left.

"Of course I will."

And he left with a wave. He found the village without difficulty, a couple of miles along a rutted path, next to a river that apparently fed the lake. It was no more than a few dozen houses and shops. The villagers looked at him with curiosity and perhaps suspicion, but he wasn't worried; Gratius had had no difficulty yesterday. Larry had learned enough Erse to explain what he needed to the short, bald proprietor of the tiny store. The man wanted to chat. Did Larry know the other stranger—the one who had been there yesterday? Would they be here long? Were they related to the nice couple in the cottage by the lake? They were from the empire, right? What was the news from the empire? People here were always interested in news. So many strange goings-on in the empire.

Larry had the same news that Gratius had given the proprietor yesterday, but he tried to be pleasant. The man was happy that they were buying food and supplies for five now, and Larry didn't haggle over the price. When the purchases were made, he got back on his horse and left the village.

He didn't return directly to the cottage. Instead he went back to the hill where they had stopped yesterday. He looked up at it. His horse snickered as they stood there, wondering what his rider was up to. Larry dismounted. He stroked the horse's mane. He continued to stare at the hill. Finally he walked a few steps towards it, stopped, and then abruptly turned around and came back.

"Not today," he murmured.

He remounted his horse and continued on to the cottage.

It wasn't that day, and it wasn't the next. Everyone did chores, and reminisced, and speculated about the Gallians and the priests and what would happen to the empire. And they started making tentative plans for the spring. How should they make a living? Should they farm? Fish? Hunt? Should they add on to the cottage? Build a new one? Gratius and Palta had skills to offer; Larry had none.

Occasionally one of the others would look at him questioningly, but he said nothing. And at night he stared at the fire and felt the pressure of Palta's body against his.

And then one morning he woke up, and he realized that it was time. He roused Palta. "Come with me," he whispered to her. It was early, barely dawn, and the others were still asleep.

"Where?" she asked drowsily.

"Just come."

They got up, put on their sandals and cloaks, and left the cottage. Outside, snowflakes blew past them in the frigid air. "Are we riding?" Palta asked.

Larry considered, and shook his head. "Let's walk."

It was a long walk. Mid-way, he sensed that Palta knew where they were headed. She said nothing. He too was silent, but he took her hand.

Finally they reached the hill. They paused and looked up. Their breath came in clouds; the snowflakes stung his eyes. "We're climbing it?" Palta asked.

Larry nodded.

They started up the hill. Occasionally Palta would help him when he stumbled. This is stupid, he thought. He shouldn't be making her do this. But he couldn't just...

They reached the top. The wind was stronger here. Fog was blowing in from the lake, obscuring the view. They seemed to be isolated in their own cold, barren world.

Palta looked at him. *Now what?* her gaze seemed to be asking. Why are we here?

"I have to leave," he told her. "There are things I need to learn, things I need to accomplish. But I can't—I can't take you with me. I'm sorry."

She looked around. "Where? How?"

He didn't reply. She didn't seem to expect a reply.

He felt tears welling in his eyes. Palta's eyes, too, were filled with tears. He held his arms out to her, and she moved into his embrace. They kissed. He stroked her golden hair, wet from the snow.

"You are coming back," she said.

Her voice rose at the end of the sentence, so it became half-statement, half-question. "If I—" he began to reply, and then he stopped himself. "Yes," he said. "Yes, I'm coming back. But I don't know when."

She hugged him tight then. And finally he had to gently move out of her embrace.

And he had to turn away from her and walk into the fog, alone.

———

Palta

Palta watched him walk away.

And then she saw him disappear. Not into the fog, but into nothingness.

She knew what that meant.

She stood there for a moment, not moving, not breathing. And then she couldn't stand it anymore and she ran forward to where he had disappeared and moved her hands in front of her body, searching desperately for the nothingness, for the spot where her hands would no longer be visible as they encountered the magic of Via, of the portal.

But she found...nothing. No way out of this world, no way to follow Larry to wherever he had gone.

And finally she gave up and sank to the frozen ground, howling with despair as she realized that she was finally and utterly alone, in this world and every other.

———

Afford

It was not, Affron thought, a particularly well-run world. But people seemed happy enough. The streets were always crowded with vehicles —small, odd-looking, three-wheeled machines of a kind he had never encountered before. But there were no traffic lights, no one directing traffic, and not much evidence of rules that people were following. But the drivers didn't seem upset; no one shouted or cursed or gesticulated out the window. Instead the drivers just patiently wended their way through the mess towards their destinations.

Some major festival or religious holiday seemed to be approaching —or perhaps this was always the way the streets and shops were decorated—with green and yellow streamers everywhere, along with statues and paintings of the same bearded, smiling man, with one hand raised in a pleasant greeting.

People were generally smaller and darker than Affron, with thick, muscular bodies, but no one stared at him, and everyone happily put up with his efforts to speak their language, which seemed to be a strange variant of Latin with a strong admixture of something else— Chinese, perhaps. They used a Latin-like alphabet, though, which helped him decipher the names of shops and streets.

He was walking along a busy sidewalk, carrying a satchel of food he had just bought. He wore flowing pants and a loose shirt, like all the other men. The day was hot but dry; so far he had experienced nothing like the enervating heat of a Roman summer. He paused at an intersection. On a platform high above it a couple of young women wearing nothing but shorts were enacting some kind of dance to the accompaniment of drums pounding out an intricate rhythm. Was it art? A religious ritual? A sporting event? Sometimes they ran towards each other and appeared to be struggling to throw each other onto the floor of the platform. The struggle would last for a few seconds, and then abruptly they would back away and continue their dance. Affron watched, fascinated, until the dance ended. When the girls were done there was no applause, no cheering. They simply slipped on shirts to cover their bare chests and made their way down from the platform. People who had stopped to watch them now walked on.

As did Affron. Sometimes worlds fit into familiar patterns; sometimes they seemed inexpressibly alien. There were learned treatises about this in the schola at Urbis. Although perhaps those treatises no longer existed.

Affron turned a corner. Ahead of him was the warren of interconnecting rooms and apartments and houses where he lived. Communal baths, communal kitchens, communal everything, really, except you had your own room to sleep in and another little room that was identified by a word that seemed to mean something like *shrine*. You stayed away from other people's shrines.

As usual he got lost as he made his way through the warren to his own room. As in Roma, there were no street signs or house numbers; you simply needed to know where you were going. He entered the wrong room at one point, and its inhabitant shooed him away with a grin and a burst of words Affron didn't understand.

Finally he found his room. He put the satchel on the floor and lay down on the bed with a sigh. A pleasant breeze blew in through the open window. Outside, he could hear the sounds of distant music and children playing—high-pitched shouts and laughter. Affron smiled.

And then he thought he heard something else.

He lay still and listened. Yes. Of course.

He stood up and walked across the room. He slid back the curtain that separated his bedroom from the shrine.

There, sitting cross-legged on the floor, his eyes closed, was Larry Barnes.

Eventually Larry opened his eyes and looked up at him.

"It took you long enough," Affron said.

THIRTEEN

Lamathe

Lamathe had been born near Alexandria and now, finally, he returned to it. He and the other priests settled in a ramshackle building in an anonymous neighborhood not far from the harbor. And, more important, not far from the library. The director of the library, Olef-Nan, was an old friend, and she was able to assist, secretly, with money and supplies. But his plan worried her.

"You have a long task ahead of you, I fear," she said to the viator one evening as they dined at her villa, soon after they had arrived.

"Yes, I know. But what else can we do?"

"Fight, perhaps?"

"We do not know how to fight, any more than you do. And they have the gants. No one can defeat them if they choose to use those weapons."

"So, what hope is there?"

"The gants will eventually lose their power. We must be prepared for when that happens."

"They can't replace them?"

"To replace them—to find any weapons like them—they'll have to learn how to use Via. And they are likely to fail at that without a viator to teach them. And we will not help. We would kill ourselves first."

"How long will it take?"

"A few years at most. Even if the weapons aren't used, their power leaks away over time."

"And then what?"

"I do not know," Lamathe admitted. "The Gallians may succeed for a while, or they may fail utterly. But when their rule finally collapses, we must be ready. And we must not forget all that the priests have learned over the years. Regaining power may take longer than our lifetimes to achieve. But our wisdom must not be allowed to die out. And so we will write it down. Create our own library."

The director nodded. "You know better than I, of course. But if you live here you must remain quiet and inconspicuous. This is still part of the empire, after all."

"Yes, of course," Lamathe replied. "I would love to visit your library again, but we want nothing more than to be inconspicuous."

"And the others—the ones who aren't with you?"

"They are living outside the empire. They will be safe, I pray."

"Well, I wish all of you every blessing," Olef-Nan said. "I fear that the world is about to become a very turbulent place, and I hope you will be the ones to save it."

Lamathe nodded his thanks. He could use all the blessings she could send his way. It was an awful time. He felt as though all his wisdom, all his knowledge, now counted for nothing. He no longer wore the purple robe of the viator; he no longer had the certainties that came with his role and status. He was just trying to do his best to solve the awful problem with which he had been presented.

He walked back from Olaf-Nen's lovely villa to the building where he and the other priests now lived and worked. He didn't feel especially safe walking through the streets of Alexandria at night, but he had no choice. The others were asleep except for Samos, who had waited up for him, looking weary and upset. Samos always looked upset, it seemed to Lamathe.

"I have written for twelve hours today," Samos informed him.

"I admire you, Samos," he replied, "but there is no need—"

"I have nothing else to do. If I don't write, I think about the Gallians, and I don't want to do that."

"I understand."

"I do not like it here," Samos continued. "The food, the smells, the language. It is ugly. It is alien."

83

"If you had become a viator," Lamathe pointed out, "you would have encountered places far more alien than Egypt."

"*If*," Samos repeated. "And now that will never happen."

"You must have faith, Samos."

"Why? Why must I have faith?"

Lamathe stifled a sigh. Samos was a good man, but dealing with him was always difficult. "If you don't have faith, you will go mad," he replied.

This answer didn't satisfy the young priest, of course. But what answer would? "Some worlds end badly," Samos replied. "That is in the nature of things. Progress ends; people give up. Empires collapse into savagery and never return to their former glory. That is what I have been taught. That is what *you* taught me."

"Not all worlds," Lamathe pointed out. "I taught you that, as well."

"Which kind do we inhabit?"

"That is up to us—our choices, our actions."

"We are pebbles on the shore," Samos said. "The tides of history overwhelm us."

"That is foolish," Lamathe responded. "A year ago the Gallians probably felt as you do. But they changed history."

Samos waved a hand wearily, as if dismissing the Gallians—or Lamathe. "As you say. I will do what I can. But still I feel like a pebble."

Lamathe smiled. "You are far more than a pebble, Samos. Get some rest."

Samos went off to bed, and Lamathe was left alone, sitting in the empty room and pondering history in the warm Egyptian night.

FOURTEEN

Tirelius

W hy was he still alive?
For months Tirelius had expected some Gallian thug to enter his jail cell in the dead of night and slit his throat. Or they would hang him in the forum in front of cheering crowds. What were they waiting for?

He had no reason to live, and yet still he lived.

Once he had been the pontifex maximus, the high priest, the leader of the greatest empire that Terra had ever known. An empire that treated its citizens with dignity and justice, that used the wisdom and knowledge of Via to make people happier, healthier, and stronger.

And in one night it had all been destroyed.

How? How had he let Affron and the others slip away from Urbis? How had he not found them as they hid in Roma? How had he failed to secure the armamentarium and properly guard Urbis? Day and night he thought about these things and a thousand others like them. He had nothing else to occupy his mind, just the monotony of eating and sleeping and waiting for death.

He was an old man, and he had nothing to show for his life except failure.

The cell where he now lived was in the bowels of the palatium. It was cold and damp and smelled of mildew and piss. For all he knew, it was the same one in which Affron had been held before he escaped. His guards had little to say to him. The food was tolerable, but he could scarcely bring himself to eat it. He had lost weight here, despite doing nothing all day but thinking.

Beyond all the bad decisions and missed opportunities, his mind kept returning to his final moments in the temple of Via. Feslund and the others had rousted him from his bed before dawn. The surprise had been complete; Urbis had fallen before he even knew it was under attack. The Gallians aimed gants at him and shoved him out of his room. Occasionally they killed a frightened servant, as if for sport. Tirelius had never seen a gant being used before; the destruction was instantaneous, total, and terrifying.

But he'd had no chance to ponder this. They half-pushed, half-dragged him across the forum and up the stairs to the temple. Inside, he stood before Via while the Gallians conversed. What did they want from him? It didn't matter. He stared at Via, for so long the center of his life. Now it belonged to others.

And then the boy spoke. He wanted Tirelius to send him home in Via. He *demanded* it. Tirelius was confused and annoyed. What did this have to do with him? He refused. *Ask Affron,* he had said. *Or Valleia.*

The boy told him they were dead. Tirelius hadn't believed him then; he assumed that they were behind the Gallians' raid. Later he would find out that both he and the boy were wrong. The boy waved his gant at him. But Tirelius could not be threatened. He was old and defeated; he welcomed death. He turned away.

And then the boy did…something.

Not with the gant; with his mind. His mind was inside Tirelius, overpowering him with fear and dread. Terra was nothing, he suddenly saw; even Via was nothing. And he himself, of course, was nothing—a bug about to be squashed by a sandal. He staggered and would have fallen if a guard hadn't grabbed him. He shrugged off the guard and looked at the boy.

The boy returned his gaze and then turned away.

And that was all.

The dread subsided but did not entirely disappear. It would be like a wound that never properly healed; the memory of the moment would be with him as long as he lived.

"Get up!" the guard called to him from outside his cell. "You have a visitor."

Tirelius raised his head. The guard was unlocking the door of his cell. This was different; this was new. He had come to think that he had been forgotten. The pontifex struggled to stand but found that he couldn't. Behind the guard was a man in a bright blue robe. Tirelius thought he recognized him but was unsure. Who was he?

"This place is dreadful," the man said to him in cultured Latin. "Let's take you someplace more comfortable." He gestured to the guard. "Help him up," he ordered.

The guard got Tirelius to his feet. "I am...slow," the pontifex muttered. His voice sounded odd. How long had it been since he had spoken?

"No matter," the man in the blue robe replied. "We have all day."

They started walking. Out of the cell, down the dark, foul-smelling corridor.

"You don't remember me," the man said.

"You are familiar," Tirelius said. "But my mind is not what it was."

"Yes, of course. My name is Liber. I attended the schola once."

Tirelius stared at him, and finally the memories came. Liber. A drunkard. Still a drunkard, he surmised. But what was he doing here? Helping the Gallians, apparently. *Traitor.* "You disappointed us," Tirelius said.

"I disappointed myself."

Tirelius did not reply. They walked past the guards' desk, then out into a hallway. The hallway was dreary, but at least it smelled better than the corridor outside his cell. It was good just to see something, to be somewhere, different.

Liber opened a door and went inside. "Come," he said. Tirelius knew what was inside; he could smell it. The smell made his knees weaken. He followed Liber into a small room. In the middle of the room was a table covered with platters of food.

"You do not look well, my pontifex," Liber said. "Sit. Eat. It will be good for you."

Tirelius sat at the table. Was the food poisoned? Not likely. Why would they bother? There were easier ways to kill him. Liber sat down on the other side of the table and was helping himself to a chicken leg.

"Wine?" Liber asked, gesturing to a jug. "It is very good."

Tirelius shook his head.

"As you wish," Liber said and poured himself a cup, diluting it with water from a second jug.

Tirelius took a chicken leg and bit into it. It was so delicious he thought he might pass out.

Liber was watching him. Enjoying himself, Tirelius thought. Enjoying his power over the man who had ruled his life at the schola. What did he want?

"Well, then," Liber said, tossing the remains of his chicken leg into a bucket, "I am very sorry for your imprisonment. I am here to discuss how we can bring it to an end."

"Bring it to an end?" Tirelius asked. "What power do you have here?"

"Ah, I should have explained. I am chief minister. Prince Feslund has given me wide latitude to make decisions for the good of the empire."

"You? That's absurd. How did this happen?"

Liber smiled at Tirelius. "Governor Decius had me kidnapped from a tavern in Roma. I was a tutor to rich men's children, and not a very good one. But I attended the schola, and I am not a fool. I am smarter than Prince Feslund, at any rate, and smarter than his former chief minister, and Feslund is smart enough to recognize this. So here I am."

Tirelius ripped a chunk of bread from a loaf, soaked up some of the chicken drippings with it, and took a bite. He considered. "You are not a fool, but you are talking to me because you need my help," he replied after he had swallowed the glorious food. "The Gallians are incompetent, and you know nothing."

"Think of me as you will," Liber said. He poured himself some more wine. Yes, Tirelius remembered him now. Smart enough, like everyone who attended the schola, but he drank too much and lacked self-control. He'd had some kind of run-in with Affron. Ah, Affron. At first he had thought Affron was behind the Gallians. But that had been absurd, a consequence of his confusion and fear. He and Affron had disagreed on much, but Affron would not bring down the empire. He would not hand it to the Gallians.

The boy, on the other hand…

"The old world is gone," Liber went on, "and it is not coming back. But we can control what the new world looks like."

"*We?*"

"Why not? I know what you wanted when you were pontifex: to use the wonders we found on other worlds to help us here on Terra. All we seek is wisdom, Hieron taught us. But he was wrong—you and I both know that. There is so much good we can do, if only we can break free of the shackles that Hieron's words placed upon us. You never said it quite like that, but it is what you meant. Well, the shackles have come off, my lord. We can do whatever we want."

"*You* can do whatever you want," Tirelius replied. "This has nothing to do with me."

"You can make my work so much easier, though. The Gallians are in possession of Via. But they don't know how to use it, and neither do I—at least, not very well. To learn will take them many years of trial and error, as it did for Hieron and his followers. But why must we wait? You can teach us."

"Ask other viators," Tirelius replied. "I am old and tired."

"Viators seem to be hard to find. But here you are, sitting a few hundred paces from Via. So consider: you can wither away in your cell, contemplating the injustices that have been done you. Or you can help me change the world. The riches of the multiverse—medicines, inventions—are at our disposal. Help me make Terra a better place."

Tirelius ate a handful of grapes. He longed now for a cup of wine, but he knew even a single sip would render him unable to think clearly. "Help you make the Gallians succeed," he replied.

"Does it matter who gets the glory, if we help Terra?" Liber asked.

"The Gallians won't help Terra; they will help themselves."

"Everyone will benefit. The sick will be healed. Life will become easier for all."

Tirelius was tiring of this. "What happens if I refuse?" he asked.

"Why would you refuse?" Liber responded. "Come, I am offering you the chance to achieve what you have always wanted to achieve."

"You did not answer my question."

Liber sipped his wine and stared at him across the table. "Ah, well. If you do not help me, what need do I have of you? The only reason to keep you alive is the possibility that you will change your mind."

Tirelius shook his head. "I cannot, will not teach the Gallians how to use Via." He thought a moment and added, "And even if the Gallians knew how to use Via, Affron would destroy them, if he is still alive."

"Where is he?" Liber demanded. "Do you know?"

"I do not. But do you think he will approve of Prince Feslund and the rest of them? Do you think any of you will be safe from him?"

Tirelius was pleased to see the effect this had on Liber. The man was frightened of Affron. Affron had a powerful effect on people. "Very well," Liber said. "We will see about Affron."

Tirelius inclined his head. "If there is nothing more…"

Liber waved his hand in dismissal. Tirelius got to his feet with difficulty and returned to his cell. Liber didn't bother accompanying him.

The guard seemed surprised to see him return. "Back so soon?" he asked.

Tirelius did not reply. The guard led him down the corridor and locked him into his cell, where he collapsed onto his cot. Even this trivial exertion had exhausted him. His body was giving up. He lay back and closed his eyes.

Perhaps he had done wrong by reminding Liber about Affron. It didn't matter, he supposed. Affron could take care of himself. And if Liber was concentrating on Affron he wouldn't give a thought to the boy.

The boy.

It had been the boy all along. The boy had led the Gallians to victory. And the boy had not gone home; Tirelius was sure of it, though he didn't know why. And he knew that the boy would return to Urbis. The Gallians had far more to fear from him than from Affron.

He hoped the boy would destroy them all.

FIFTEEN

Larry

"What am I doing here?" Larry asked.

"How should I know?" Affron replied with a hint of a smile.

"You wanted me to come," he pointed out.

"True, but you were the one who came."

"How did that work, exactly? All the way from Urbis I tracked you, without knowing what I was doing or where I was headed."

"How should I know?" Affron repeated. "There seems to be an… affinity," he added.

"You're not going to make this easy, are you?"

Affron shrugged. "It hasn't been easy for me, either," he pointed out.

"That thing on the hilltop in Scotia—was it the portal?"

"*A* portal." They were speaking in English, where the difference between *a* and *the* was clear.

"And you created it," Larry said. "With your mind."

"With my mind. With my hands. With…something."

"How? Okay, don't bother answering that. *How should I know?* —right?"

Affron smiled.

Larry considered. "An affinity," he repeated. And then: "I have the same ability you have—the one you used on that pawnbroker and on Decius. I killed a woman with it in the temple of Via. Then later, I didn't use Via to return home when I had the chance. Gratius offered me the choice: he would take me home, or we could go in search of you. I chose you. I don't know how I found your portal on that hill in Scotia, but I did. And when I found your portal, I used it. Just now. I left Terra behind. Walked away, into nothingness. And somehow I managed to make the portal disappear behind me, so Palta couldn't follow. How did I do that? Why did I do that?"

"Yes, those do seem to be the questions."

"And what other abilities do I have?"

"Perhaps we'll find out. By the way, welcome to Kravok-Li."

———

Larry found Affron's attitude irritating but also somehow inevitable. Something was working itself out, and whatever it was, it was inside him. It wasn't up to Affron to explain it, even if he could. Affron had expected his arrival, and now he had arrived, and a new life began.

It was a terrible life, at first. The food on Kravok-Li was so spicy that he couldn't even eat it. And when he did eat it, he had the worst diarrhea of his life. He recalled that awful disease—*drikana*—that had almost killed Kevin when they had been trapped in Carmody's world. Larry had been lucky so far in his travels; his health had been good. But maybe his luck had run out. Maybe he would die here of some nameless disease.

And there was the language. It was incomprehensible—an endless succession of meaningless syllables, spoken in rapid-fire staccato. He was sure he would never understand it. And the music. It was played everywhere, at all hours, and it sounded even weirder than the music on Terra, filled with percussion and dissonance. And the crowds, and the smells…Every time he went outside, he felt as if his senses were being assaulted.

But most of all, the loneliness. What was he doing here in this strange world? What was happening on Terra? Was Palta happy? Did she miss him as much as he missed her? What were Feslund and the Gallians up to?

And what was happening on Earth? His family must have given up on him by now. Would Kevin have told them about the portal? If he had, would that have given them any hope? It didn't seem likely. He would be just another missing teenager, like the ones you saw shows about on TV—kidnapped or murdered by a pervert. Just what his mother had always worried about.

He had made her life hell. And he was sitting here in this weird world with a portal in the next room. Could Affron take him back to Terra, back to Earth?

Larry didn't ask. He sat in their room and waited.

Affron was gone most days, working as a laborer to earn money. He didn't say much about it. Larry thought sometimes that he should help, but he didn't see how he could without knowing the language.

When Affron arrived back at the room one night, Larry finally said, "I don't understand what's happening. I still don't know why I'm here."

Affron didn't respond.

"I want to go home. To Earth. My Earth. Can you take me home in your portal?"

"I don't have much practice yet, but I suppose so."

"Will you do it?"

Affron shrugged. "As you wish." But then he added: "Let's go in the morning, shall we? Just to be sure you want to leave."

"All right. But I do want to. Being here is a waste of time. Nothing is happening. I don't know why I'm here."

"It's your choice. Let's do it in the morning, though."

Affron cooked dinner in the communal kitchen. Larry helped, even though the food, whatever it was, was barely edible. Back in their room, they ate the food and drank some kind of mildly alcoholic wine that always made him drowsy. Which was good, because otherwise he didn't know how he'd ever get to sleep.

They snuffed out the candles and settled down on the floor. Distant music thumped and clanged, as always. People shouted good-naturedly outside their window. But finally Larry drifted off, to confusing dreams of Palta and Scotia and Glanbury and his old nemesis Stinky Glover. Professor Gardner, from Carmody's world, was explaining it all to him. But he couldn't quite hear him, couldn't quite understand his words. If only he could understand...

He awoke to find himself sitting in what Affron called the "shrine," next to the bedroom. He was just a few feet away from the portal. A cool breeze moved through the open windows. It was still nighttime.

What was he doing in the shrine? Was he awake? Dreams faded, returned, rearranged themselves.

He felt his arms start to move. Was this too a dream? No, it seemed real. Had he willed the movement to happen, or were his arms moving on their own?

And then he saw his hands making strange motions in the air in front of his face. As if he were conducting an invisible orchestra. As if he were searching for something in the dark.

As if he were Affron, seated by the window of their insula back in Roma, doing exactly the same thing.

"Well then," Affron said from behind him. "I think we're ready to begin."

SIXTEEN

Liber

"Decius is waiting for you, my lord," Cingulus informed him when he arrived at his office in the palatium.

Liber sighed. "Very well." It irked him that Decius felt he could simply walk into the office of the chief minister, and that Liber's secretary would allow this, but he let it pass. He strode into the room. "What's the news?" Decius asked him. "Has King Carolus finally arrived?"

"He has."

"Was the queen happy to see him?"

"The greeting was warm enough, I suppose," Liber replied. "What I saw of it, anyway."

"Do you think he'll bring her out of her stupor?"

Liber considered. "Yes, I suppose he will. It couldn't last forever, in any case. She has required my presence tomorrow morning."

"That could be bad. Feslund has mostly let us do what we like."

"True. But his lack of interest has not always been helpful. Perhaps Gretyx will see things our way."

"This seems unlikely, my lord."

Liber wondered if the "my lord" was meant to be ironic. But this, too, seemed unlikely. He and Decius were allies, weren't they? They knew what they had to do: to try to ensure that Gallian rule was fair and just and benefited the people. And to keep the empire from falling apart. Decius knew far more about such matters than Liber, but Liber, as chief minister, now outranked him. Feslund had appointed him to the position out of gratitude for making him a hero with the miraculous medicine, and also because his predecessor had been useless. But that didn't mean Liber knew how to run an empire.

Decius had arrived with yet another list of policy changes he wanted to make. Liber glanced through them. They all seemed worthy. Except, of course, there was no way to pay for them. He put the list aside. "Not enough revenue," he murmured.

"The key to revenue collection is to prove to citizens that their taxes will be spent wisely," Decius pointed out. He always pointed this out.

"Yes, yes," Liber agreed. "But we can't build new aqueducts when we can't even pay our troops. In any case I have another issue to discuss: Affron."

"What about Affron?"

"I want to hunt him down and kill him."

"Ah." Decius considered this. "Is your hatred of him that deep?"

"It is deep enough. But he is also a danger to the empire. He is the only one who can unite the priests against the Gallians. And he has a power that could be stronger than gants."

"True. But I doubt that Affron would be interested in leading a rebellion. I don't think he cares enough."

"We can't take that chance. Do you have any information about him—where he went after he disappeared from Roma?"

"We searched for him afterward," Decius replied. "My spies on the waterfront found out that he'd boarded a ship headed to Britannia, along with Valleia and Carmody. I sent a letter to the governor of Britannia inquiring about them. His information was that they sailed from Britannia to Scotia, although he couldn't be certain of this. In any case, by the time I received his reply, the Gallians had taken over, and no one cared about Affron anymore—including me."

"Scotia," Liber repeated.

"A little kingdom north of Britannia. Full of wild men and wilder weather, I'm told. The empire never bothered to conquer it—not worth the trouble. If you wanted to hide out from us, it would be as good a place as any."

"Perhaps it's worth sending someone there to track him down."

"Why?" Decius asked. "Affron could be anywhere by now. Finding one person in all of Barbarica is an impossible task."

"Affron is worth it," Liber replied.

Decius appeared uninterested. "As you wish." He returned to his list of policy changes. But Liber wasn't paying attention.

He was thinking about Scotia.

———

Gretyx

Gretyx no longer went to the temple every day, but she was left with a hard ball of anger inside her.

Her daughter was dead.

Her son was a drunken braggart.

Her husband was an ineffectual fool.

And the empire they possessed was falling apart.

At long last, it was time to do something.

She was meeting with Feslund's new chief minister, the ex-priest whose only qualification for the job was that he had managed to turn Feslund into some kind of god. This was not an insignificant accomplishment, but hardly sufficient for running an empire.

The man bowed low as he entered the room. Feslund sat sullenly at the table next to her. Carolus cowered in the corner. Her husband didn't want to possess the empire; he was sure this would all end badly. As always, he underestimated his wife.

She gestured for Liber to sit. He seated himself opposite her and folded his hands on the table. He returned her gaze; he did not look nervous. He had once been in training to be a viator; presumably viators did not get nervous. "We are in trouble," she said to him. "This does not surprise me. You are chief minister. Tell me what needs to be done."

He nodded. "Thank you for asking my advice, my lady," he began. "Our greatest problem is money," he said. "People aren't paying their taxes."

"Can't we punish them if they don't pay? Throw them in prison?"

"We have no way to punish them. Our administration in many provinces has effectively collapsed."

"Can we not simply mint more coins?"

"Not easily, not quickly. We could use less silver in the coins, but that would reduce their value."

"Then we can demand higher tribute from foreign lands."

"They will only pay tribute if we can enforce payment. But we can't pay our soldiers, so the army is shrinking."

Gretyx was annoyed. "What, then?" she demanded.

"We need to collect taxes differently," Liber said.

"How?"

"Put tax collection in private hands, my lady. They did this in the old days, before the priests. Enter into contracts with rich merchants and landowners in each district. They hire their own people to collect the revenue; how they do the collection is their business. They pay us for the right to collect the taxes, and then they pay us a percentage of what they collect. The more they collect, the richer they become."

Gretyx considered. "But we lose that percentage of the revenue."

"Yes, we will collect less than is fair, but more than we are capable of collecting on our own."

This seemed like a reasonable idea. "We will do it, then," she said. "What else?"

"The magic cream, my lady," he replied. "We should obtain a larger supply of it and—"

She waved aside this suggestion. "The cream has done its job," she replied. "We need some for our own use, that is all."

This got Feslund's attention. "The people want me to cure them," he protested. "Why should I stop?" He enjoyed being a hero, of course.

"You have created the legend; that is enough," Gretyx said. "Using the cream was a good idea, but now it is a waste of time. In the future, we can simply make up stories and circulate them around the empire. Why do they need to be true? The people will tire of this trick eventually and demand ever greater miracles. We will then simply invent the miracles."

Feslund pouted; Liber merely shrugged. "Yes, my lady."

"What else?" she asked.

"The legions, my lady," he replied. "Even if we find the money to pay them, they must be put under Gallian generals to ensure their loyalty."

"Surely you can help with this, Feslund?" Gretyx asked her son.

"I thought I had."

"My lord," Liber said, "you promised to provide me with a list, but—"

"Yes, yes," Feslund muttered.

"How about Ploterus?" Carolus asked, speaking for the first time. "I have always liked Ploterus."

"We need many more than just that one general, my lord," Liber pointed out.

"Work with him, my dear," Gretyx said to her husband. "I do not know these military men."

"Delighted," Carolus said. He was happy to have a task.

"Good. And what about viators?" Gretyx asked Liber. "I have been told we need viators if we are to obtain more of these gants. Have you found any?"

"No, my lady. We started our search too late, it seems. The viators disappeared after the fall of Urbis, and we've been unable to find them. But we believe we know where one of the most influential of viators is. His name is Affron, and he is thought to be in Scotia."

"Scotia?"

"A kingdom to the north of Britannica. It is possible that he has other viators with him—he has always had followers. I would like to send some men to capture them."

"Of course. Do whatever you need to do. If the viators will not cooperate, kill them."

Liber inclined his head. "Very good, my lady."

The meeting continued. Liber was better than she had expected, but she still did not trust him. She trusted no one but herself. And there was much more to be done.

———

Liber

The meeting could not have gone better, Liber thought. But now he needed the right man to find Affron. He didn't trust soldiers; they wouldn't understand Affron, so they could not hope to capture him. Who, then?

The answer was clear, if unpleasant.

His name was Harmalo. Liber dispatched Cingulus to find the man, and after a search his secretary found him on the waterfront, where he had an unsavory job handling smuggled goods for one of the gangs there. Cingulus brought him directly to Liber's chambers in the pontifex's palace, where Liber was reading by firelight.

Harmalo stood just inside the door, saying nothing, waiting. If he bowed, it was just the slightest inclination of his head. Liber waved Cingulus away and gestured to the jug on the table next to him. "A cup of wine after your journey?" he asked Harmalo.

Harmalo shook his head. "No thank you, my lord."

He rarely drank wine; Liber should have remembered that. It was one of many irritating things about Harmalo. He was taller than Liber, and more distinguished looking—beardless, his hair now streaked with silver. He had the dark, piercing eyes of a viator. But, like Liber, he was not a viator. Unlike Liber, he had not quit; he had been dismissed. Not because he wasn't smart enough, but because of a streak of cruelty so powerful that it overcame even his ambition. Liber had never liked him; no one had liked him, really. But Harmalo didn't seem to mind.

And if he was impressed at Liber's sudden rise under the Gallians, he wasn't going to show it. If he was desperate for respect, or success, or money, he wasn't going to show that, either. But he had come. He could have refused. He could have laughed at the very idea of helping the Gallians or Liber. But he hadn't.

"Sit down, then," Liber said.

Harmalo came over and sat opposite him in front of the fire. Liber fought the urge to pour himself another cup of wine. He was in control here. He could have Harmalo killed if he chose. He had no need to be frightened of the man.

"Do you remember the viator Affron?" he asked.

"Ah, Affron. Somehow I knew this would be about Affron."

"I need to have him killed."

"That is to say, you want me to kill him," Harmalo replied.

Liber nodded.

"So, the first time you have any power, you decide to kill your own enemy."

The key to dealing with Harmalo was to not let him anger you. "He is a danger to the Gallians," Liber pointed out. "He can rally other viators to oppose them, if he chooses."

"Where is he?"

"A land called Scotia, we believe."

"Scotia?" Harmalo shook his head. "Scotia is...nowhere," he

murmured. "A strange place from which to start a rebellion. Why is he there?"

"It's a long story."

"I have time."

Liber could see no harm in telling him the story, and so he did.

Harmalo listened, eyes half-closed.

"So, he may or may not be in Scotia," he said when Liber finished. "He could be anywhere."

"True. He could already be dead."

"And he may or may not have two other people with him—Valleia and some man who was with them in Roma. Probably a man from another world."

"True."

"Does Affron have a gant?"

"I don't think so," Liber replied. "He *had* a gant—Decius saw it. But he apparently gave it to the boy and girl who were with them. The boy and girl ended up in Gallia, and they used the gant to help the Gallians conquer Urbis."

"Very odd. And where are they now?"

Liber shrugged. "No one knows. Dead, probably."

Harmalo steepled his fingers under his chin. "And why me? You are chief minister of the empire. Others can do your bidding."

"Others do not know Affron's true power. I think you do." Liber had made the mistake of talking to Harmalo about Affron once, years after both had left the priesthood. It was clear that Harmalo hated Affron too; but then, Harmalo hated everyone associated with the priesthood.

"You have told me of his power," Harmalo agreed. "And that means I know the risk I'll be taking."

"I'll pay you a thousand denarii. And I will give you a diplomatic retinue and make you an official representative of the empire."

Harmalo shook his head. "Five thousand denarii."

Liber was shocked; this was an absurd amount of money. Then again, he had the queen's support. "Very well. Half now, half when you return with his head."

"That is acceptable. But there is one more condition."

"What is that?"

"I will need a gant."

Liber shook his head. "I can't give you a gant."

"Why not? You are chief minister. Surely you have access to them. Without a gant, how do you expect me to defeat Affron? Either you want this done or you don't."

Liber hadn't considered this. The idea terrified him; gants terrified him. But he understood Harmalo's argument. To defeat Affron, he would need a power comparable to Affron's own; a gant was the closest thing on Terra to such a power. "You will use it only on Affron," Liber said. "If you encounter Valleia or other viators, you will bring them back to Urbis. We need them here. Do you understand me?"

"Of course. When do I leave?"

"We will need to make preparations. Cingulus will summon you when we are ready."

Harmalo nodded and arose. "This should be quite interesting," he said.

Liber watched him leave; he was already wondering if this was a mistake.

Nevertheless, he proceeded.

Obtaining the gant was surprisingly easy. He had been prepared to invoke the queen and Feslund, but the officer in charge at the armamentarium deemed Liber's authority sufficient. Perhaps he should institute greater restrictions, along with all the other security changes that he had already made. A matter for another day.

The officer was named Armindor, a gruff red-headed Gallian. He unlocked a room on the second floor of the armamentarium and led Liber inside. They gazed upon several shelves lined with the small weapons, all glowing a pale blue.

"Take any that you like, my lord," Armindor said.

Liber walked over and picked one of them up. It was heavy and slightly warm. He understood nothing about the object.

"You'll be returning it, my lord?" Armindor inquired.

"Eventually," Liber replied.

Liber put the gant in a pocket of his robe. Armindor leaned over and made a notation in a book sitting on a table in the corner. Then they left the room, and Armindor locked it behind them. And that was all that needed to be done.

Harmalo was summoned again a few days later, and this time they met in Liber's office in the palatium.

"Cingulus has given you what you need?" Liber asked, gesturing at the satchel Harmalo was carrying. "The documents? The funds?"

Harmalo nodded. "Your secretary is most efficient," he replied. "The ship and men await me. But of course there is one item remaining."

Liber took the gant out of his pocket and handed it to him.

Harmalo stared at it. "How does it work?" he asked.

Liber shrugged. "I don't know. It's not hard to figure out, I'm told. Do not use it unnecessarily—if used too often, its power fades. When you are done with it, you will return it to me. If you do not, we will hunt you down and kill you. Do you understand?"

"Of course. For Affron alone. And how do I bring you proof of his death, if the gant is as powerful as you say?"

"That is your problem to solve."

———

They both fell silent and stared at the blue glow of the gant. Finally Harmalo placed the weapon in his pocket and stood up.

"Do not fail me," Liber said.

"Affron is as good as dead, my lord," Harmalo replied. And then he left the room.

A mistake, Liber thought once again. But it had to be done. And Harmalo was the man to do it.

He returned to the business of the empire. But he couldn't wait for the day to end and he could go back to his chambers, and the jug of wine awaiting him there.

SEVENTEEN

Larry

Affron would watch him from the other side of the room. Occasionally he murmured a suggestion; the suggestions never made sense.

"You can't will a portal into existence," he said once. "You need to dream it into existence."

"What does that mean?" Larry demanded.

"It means that trying too hard won't work. I tried for years, and nothing happened. I knew it was there—somewhere—but I couldn't find it."

"So how did you find it?" Larry asked.

"I didn't. It found me."

"That doesn't help."

"It's the best I can do."

It wasn't good enough.

———

How did the brain work exactly? Larry didn't really know. Did anyone know, in all the worlds of the multiverse? Trillions of neurons, all connected in endlessly branching and looping networks, firing and pausing, sending and receiving their tiny electrical signals. And out of it all came thought and desire and intention and wisdom. Works of genius and acts of inexplicable heroism. And sometimes, it seemed, something more. Sometimes the neurons thought about themselves thinking about themselves, an infinite regress, a hall of mirrors. And sometimes, in the thinking, things happened.

What things?

"Can anyone create a portal?" Larry asked.

"Anyone?" Affron replied. "That seems unlikely, don't you think?"

"How should I know?"

"There is a reason you and I are sitting here," he replied. "It says nothing about our virtue or our temperament or our hard work. It is a gift, but a gift that no one has given us. A trick of history, a mistake of the multiverse."

"Why not just ignore it then?"

Affron shrugged. "Go ahead and try. You don't need to be here. You can go home. You can go back to Terra. You can do anything you want. I think perhaps that my telling you I would take you home was what caused something to break free in you, what got you started. But I don't know. My offer still stands."

But Larry couldn't leave. He knew that the gift was there if he could find it—if it could find him.

———

Time passed. A month? A year? Larry ate. He slept. He felt himself growing, changing. He moved his hands through the air.

And nothing happened.

It didn't take this long with Yoda and Luke Skywalker, he thought. But that was just a movie. And Affron, apparently, wasn't Yoda. He didn't have any ancient wisdom to impart; he just had his own experience, which had been long and tortuous. Larry was going to have to do it by himself.

But he couldn't sit there all day, every day; he'd go mad. Affron had a job, which he explained as best he could: unloading strange-looking pots from an endless series of wagons and storing them in a warehouse, then sometimes taking them from the warehouse and loading them into a different set of wagons. Sometimes statues arrived instead of pots. Were they for sale? Were there shops that sold pots and statues somewhere on Kravok-Li? Affron assumed there were, but he didn't really care; he simply did what he was told. Larry joined him one day and helped with the unloading and loading. No one questioned why he was there. No one seemed to mind; no one told him to go away. At the end of the day a man clapped him on the back and put a few coins in his hand, and Larry felt absurdly grateful. He had a job, too!

So they worked during the day and went back to the room at night. Sometimes they stayed in the city, ate food at a café, and listened to the incessant music, which Larry somehow grew to like. He began to learn the language, which was far more complicated and alien to him than Latin. Palta would have mastered it in a week, but he did his best.

And when he felt the urge, he sat in the shrine in the middle of the night and moved his hands. He tried to dream a portal, and sometimes he thought he had succeeded. But when he reached out to grasp it, it wasn't there. He was discouraged; he was frustrated. He began to believe finally that he wasn't going to succeed. He had wasted a year, two years, more, trying to do something that he could not do. He had some kind of power, but not *this* power. And why did he want this power anyway? What good would it do him? What good had it done Affron? He had used his portal once, to come to this strange world. For what? So that he could load and unload pots and statues and give Larry useless advice? How had this helped either of them?

He cried one night. It was all so awful. "I hate this," he said. "I hate all of this."

"The food's not bad," Affron replied.

"Yes, it is."

"Fair enough. Is this the point where you talk about going home and so on?"

"Yes, it is."

"So, it's also the point where I say that we'll leave tomorrow?"

"Why not right now?"

"Fine."

They didn't move.

"Well, then," Affron said after a while.

"Shut up," Larry replied.

Affron shut up.

It wasn't that night, or the next night. But soon enough the dream of a portal became more vivid, the neurons shifted and branched, the movement of his hands became more assured, more purposeful, and finally, effortlessly—as if it had been destined to happen at this moment, in this place, since the beginning of the multiverse—he reached out his hand, and it disappeared into nothingness.

And it was as if everything made sense at last.

EIGHTEEN

Harmalo

Scotia was a vile place.

His carriage rattled over the rough road as they headed to the king's castle. More than once he'd had to get out as the carriage got stuck in the spring mud, and his soldiers had to lift the thing out of the mud and set it right. The whole voyage had been like that. Bad winds, bad storms, bad food. Harmalo had spent half his days on shipboard leaning over the railing in the wind and rain as he puked up the wretched slop he'd eaten. Then, finally, landfall, only to be confronted by obtuse customs agents and officious diplomats demanding to know his business in their godforsaken land.

Oh, how he'd longed to take out the precious gant and show them that he was a man to be feared and obeyed, not interrogated.

He was a man who carried death in the pocket of his robe.

But he was also a man in control of his passions. The gant stayed in his pocket. It was not needed for underlings.

He folded his arms and gazed out the carriage window. Leaden sky; bare trees, with leaves just starting to bud and rain dripping from their branches. In a month or two he supposed the place would be lovely. He had come from such a place, on the northern border of the empire. Beautiful in late spring, but wretched most of the year. He had not real-

108

ized it was wretched until he left and learned that the world was a far bigger place than he'd imagined, with different weather, different people. Better weather, smarter people. He'd left because the priests had recognized that he, too, was one of the smart people. They needed people like him in Urbis.

Eventually they changed their minds. Claimed it was a question of temperament. He had beaten up a younger student—a wretched, sniveling creature who had spilled wine on Harmalo's robe. Did they expect him to do nothing? They claimed there was a history of similar behavior. There was not. He had a temper, but he could control it. Didn't they see how well he could control it?

The carriage stopped. After a moment one of his soldiers loomed at the window. "Emissaries from the king, my lord," he said. "They ask to speak with you."

"How far are we from the castle?"

"Two miles, my lord. Perhaps three. You can see it up ahead."

Harmalo sighed; couldn't this wait until they were all sitting in front of a warm fire? But he got out of the carriage. Twenty paces away two burly, bearded men stood next to their horses. In the distance he could make out the castle, a darker gray against the gray sky. It did not look inviting.

The men fell to their knees in the mud as Harmalo approached them. "Get up, get up," he said impatiently. "What do you want?"

The men arose. The one on the right spoke, in wretched Latin. "Sire, King Glamys sends his greetings and asks the purpose of your visit to Scotia."

"Tell King Glamys that I will explain my mission to him alone. I believe I have already made that clear."

The man looked uncomfortable. "As you say, sire. His majesty insists, however, that—"

"You may tell the king that I am an official representative of the Roman empire," Harmalo interrupted. "Upon my arrival the king's officials were shown documents attesting to this. All further communication will take place with the king himself. Do not displease a representative of the empire."

The two men glanced at each other. They were not happy. Harmalo did not care. "Very well, sire," the man on the right said without enthusiasm. "If you would please follow us, we will lead you to the castle."

Harmalo turned and went back to his carriage without replying.

It seemed clear what was happening. Like most lands in Barbarica, Scotia had been left alone by the priests, except for occasional demands for tribute. Now the empire had new masters. What did these new masters want? Perhaps King Glamys feared the demand for tribute would increase, or they would offer less money for Scotia's timber or whatever it was that it sold to the empire. Perhaps the king wanted to display his strength to them. Harmalo was uninterested in such matters. He had only one job to do. And he didn't like being bullied.

Soon enough the road turned from mud to cobblestones, and the carriage headed uphill. It passed through open gates at which more burly men stood staring at them, and came to a halt in the castle's inner courtyard. Harmalo got out once again.

A row of soldiers stood at attention. Harmalo waited. After a few moments a large wooden door opened and a wizened man with a long white beard hurried out. He wore brown trousers and a thick green coat. He shot a glance at the two burly men, and then turned to Harmalo and bowed deeply. "Good day, my lord," he said in a surprisingly strong voice. "My name is Orthan, counselor to King Glamys, and on his behalf I—"

"Where is the king?" Harmalo demanded. "My business is with him, not with you or these men."

"In due time, in due time," Orthan replied, apparently unperturbed. "Please, let us show you to your rooms so that you have a chance to recover from your journey. Tonight we have arranged a feast in your honor."

His Latin was good, although spoken with a thick accent. Harmalo considered demanding to see the king instantly, then decided not to bother. A rest would be welcome. "Very well," he said. "But my mission here is urgent. I will not tolerate delay."

Orthan nodded. "So I am told. But before we go to your rooms, if you would kindly let me peruse those documents I have been told you possess...?"

Harmalo waved to his secretary, who fetched the documents from a case and presented them to Orthan. The king's counselor glanced at them quickly and then handed them back to the secretary. "We have so few visitors from Urbis," he said to Harmalo. "You must understand our surprise when we heard of your arrival."

This man's surprise did not concern Harmalo, but still he managed to remain polite. "Much has changed in the empire," he said. "And if the empire changes, so will all of Terra."

"Yes," Orthan agreed. "Let us hope the change is for the better."

Any change in this place would be for the better. Orthan led him into the smoky castle, putting him under the care of an unctuous servant with scarcely any Latin at all, who brought him to a large bedroom heated to excess by a blazing fire. It would do. The servant left finally, and Harmalo lay down on the canopied bed to rest for a couple of hours before the feast.

Everything about Scotia was dreary and pitiful. It occurred to Harmalo that with his gant he could seize power here. But the place wasn't worth ruling. Better to return to Roma; five thousand denarii could buy a lot of pleasures in Roma.

He took the gant from his pocket and held it, running his fingers over its warm, hard surface. He had used it only once, for practice. It was at night, on the eve of his departure from Roma. He had walked the streets of the city until he found what he was looking for: a sickly black dog, with matted coat and watery eyes. It limped towards him, half afraid, half hoping for a scrap of food. Harmalo took out the gant, aimed it, and destroyed the wretched thing, which disappeared without a sound, leaving behind only a faint, bitter smell in the air.

It was disappointing, actually. He had known the weapon was not like a sword, but he had not expected it to do away entirely with the reality of death—the terror and blood and pain—but that was what it did.

He liked the terror and blood and pain.

Finally he arose and prepared for the feast. Hot water was not to be found, of course. Scotians probably bathed once a year, if that. He put on a new robe and cleaned himself as much as he could, and then waited for Orthan to escort him to the banquet hall.

"Who will be at this feast?" Harmalo asked Orthan when he finally arrived.

"Ah. Many nobles will be in attendance. We are honored by your presence."

"Do they live in the castle?"

Orthan seemed puzzled by the idea. "No, of course not. They live in their own castles, among their own people. But the king often summons them to hear their counsel on important matters."

Harmalo understood this kind of kingdom. It was no more than a loose collection of clans, ruled by a king who was the strongest among the clan leaders. Some societies endured such a model endlessly; the strong king died, his weak sons failed to hold onto power, and war started up all over again until someone else emerged. So dreary and predictable.

He followed Orthan down a dark staircase and through a set of large wooden doors to the banquet hall. It was high-ceilinged and drafty. The fire in the huge fireplace was not sufficient to heat the room; the tapestries on the walls were faded and threadbare. In the middle of the hall seven or eight long wooden tables were arranged in a rough rectangle. The benches were half-filled with large, bearded men who stared at him suspiciously—the noblemen, Orthan explained; the king himself had not yet arrived. A couple of large dogs lounged on the stone floor nearby. Orthan introduced Harmalo to the nobles, who seemed to speak no Latin. Harmalo inclined his head to each of them and promptly forgot their names. He had no interest in these men, unless they could lead him to Affron.

Orthan led him to one of the tables, and a server placed a tankard of ale in front of him. He didn't touch it. The nobles ignored him, babbling away in their own language. It was called Erse, he'd been told. Strange name for a language. People who mattered on Terra spoke Latin. He wondered if the king spoke it.

"These men know what goes on in their domains, yes?" he asked Orthan.

Orthan nodded. "Of course. Our nobles are very close to their people."

"Good. Are all of them here?"

"No, not at all. If we'd had more warning of your arrival, my lord—"

"No matter," he muttered.

He waited for King Glamys. Ten minutes or more passed. This was outrageous, he decided. Was the man deliberately insulting the empire?

Finally the wooden doors opened, and the king made his entrance. He was tall and thin, unlike most of the men Harmalo had seen in Scotia. His hair and beard were red; he wore a fur cape over his robe. Orthan and the nobles got to their feet as he approached; Harmalo stayed seated. The king bowed to him; Harmalo nodded back. "My lord Harmalo, you are welcome to Scotia," the king said in Latin. His voice was deep; his Latin was tolerable.

"I bear greetings from the new rulers of the empire," Harmalo replied. "And I have a request."

King Glamys waved away the request. "First we feast, my lord. Then we shall talk." He sat down opposite Harmalo, next to Orthan.

Harmalo tried not to look annoyed. A servant filled the king's tankard, and he emptied it with one long swallow. The nobles cheered and did the same. Other servants carried in trays of food—a roast pig, baked apples, and vegetables Harmalo did not recognize. "Let us eat and drink and thank the gods for their blessings," the king called out in Latin. Then he spoke again in his native tongue, and the nobles cheered again. The dogs thumped their tails on the floor. The servants heaped food on plates and passed them out—first to the king, then to Harmalo, then to the others.

Harmalo tried the food. It was overcooked and tasteless; the Scotians stuffed it into their mouths with delight. They shouted at each other and at the king; the king shouted back at them, laughing. No one paid attention to him until the king noticed that he wasn't drinking. "Give us a toast, my lord," the king demanded.

Harmalo sighed and stood up, raising his tankard. "Long life to all in this hall," he said simply. The king shouted out a translation, and the nobles cheered yet again and drank. Harmalo forced himself to swallow a mouthful of the ale; it was as bad as the food. He sat down and hoped that he was done with drinking. But now the king rose and toasted the empire, and next each of the nobles stood and toasted something or other, and Harmalo had to force himself to take a sip of the ale after each toast.

It occurred to him that the king wanted him drunk. But that would not happen.

The drinking and feasting continued. Harmalo ate little and drank less. He was tired of these boorish people; his patience was running out. Finally the servants cleared the plates and Orthan arose. "Now that we have eaten and drunk together," the counselor said, "King Glamys will hear the reason for Lord Harmalo's visit to his kingdom."

Orthan sat. Was Harmalo supposed to stand? He supposed he was. He got to his feet. "My lord," he addressed the king, "The empire requests a simple favor of you. Last summer a man sailed from Roma to your kingdom. He was accompanied by a couple of others—a man and a woman. The man we seek is named Affron. Black-haired, in his thirties. He is a former priest accused of serious crimes against the empire. We want information about his whereabouts, and we request the right to seize him when he is found."

King Glamys scowled. "This is a troubling request," he said, without standing. "Scotia has a right of sanctuary that all in the land recognize and support."

Harmalo sat down. "We would not make such a request if it were not important," he replied.

The hall had fallen silent. The nobles could evidently sense that something serious was taking place.

"The priests always left us alone," the king pointed out. "They have let us follow our ways. We allow their merchants to trade here, and we pay a tribute as well. We have caused Urbis no trouble."

Harmalo shrugged. "The priests are not in charge anymore," he replied. "The world has changed."

"The gods have not changed," the king countered. "The gods will not allow me to do what you are asking."

Harmalo was becoming angry. "Do you know where this man Affron is?" he demanded.

"I have never heard of him. I have no knowledge of him."

"Do you?" he asked Orthan.

"No, my lord. Of course not," Orthan replied.

"Do they?" Harmalo gestured at the silent nobles.

"I will not ask them," the king said, folding his arms. "If the man has come to us for protection, we will protect him. That is the way our people have always lived."

"This is very foolish," Harmalo noted. "Prince Feslund will not be pleased."

"Nevertheless, we cannot agree to your request. We can discuss many things of interest between us. But not this."

The king was sweating, Harmalo noticed. From the heat of the fire-place, the ale, the tension? This was absurd. They lived in drunken squalor, but they would not hand over a criminal to their betters. He sighed and felt in the pocket of his robe. "You do not understand the importance of this request to our new rulers," he said.

"It does not matter," the king replied. "We must follow our ways."

Harmalo's patience was at an end. He took out the gant and held it up in front of him.

The king stared at the weapon. "What is this?" he demanded.

Harmalo didn't respond. What did words matter? He aimed the

gant at one of the dogs, sleeping contentedly on the floor, sated from scraps of meat thrown it during the feast. Then at the last moment he changed his mind and swung the gant up till it was pointed at Orthan. The old man's mouth opened, and his eyes went wide with fear. Then Harmalo squeezed the gant's handle, as he had learned to do, and the counselor disappeared in a flash of white light.

Harmalo assumed that there was a commotion among the nobles, but all he heard was the howling of the dogs. They had smelled the bitterness in the air, and somehow they knew what it meant. Meanwhile he stared at the blankness where Orthan had been, and he felt the satisfaction of death.

"What have you done?" he finally heard the king shout. "Where is Orthan?"

The nobles too were shouting and gesticulating. Harmalo ignored them and turned his gaze to the red-faced, terrified king. "What have I done?" he replied calmly. "I have shown what happens to those who defy the power of the empire. Orthan is gone; you are next. Tell me where Affron is."

"But I do not know!"

"Then ask your nobles, who I think may understand more Latin than they let on."

Glamys turned and spoke to the nobles, who began babbling in response. They shook their heads; they raised their hands and gestured at ceiling, as if calling on the gods to witness the truth of what they were saying.

And then one of them said something to the king, who nodded in response. They conversed for a moment, and then the king turned back to Harmalo.

"Lord Macver knows something," he said. "Three people from Roma landed in Flendys this past summer. Two men and a woman. One of them must be the man you seek."

"Flendys," Harmalo repeated.

"It is a port town south of here. They stayed there a while, then left in the winter, heading north along the King's Road. That is all Lord Macver knows about them."

Lord Macver was a stout man with beady black eyes. He said something more. He seemed eager to please, now that he had seen the gant. Harmalo realized that he was still holding it in his hand.

"You are not the first to come looking for them," the king went on.

"There were three others—again, two men and a woman. A girl, actually. They came to Flendys, then followed the first three north."

Three others? Was he not the first one Liber had sent in pursuit of Affron? "These others," Harmalo said. "Were they sent from the empire?"

The king conferred with Lord Macver, and then responded. "It does not seem so. They arrived overland. They spoke Latin but had no papers from Urbis like yours."

This was puzzling, but it scarcely mattered. One man, or six men and women—they would be no match for Harmalo. "And no one knows where they ended up after they left Flendys?" he asked.

"None of us have any knowledge of this," the king replied quickly. "The lords of the highlands do not come here often. The journey is long, and they like their freedom."

Harmalo stared at the sweating, frightened king, and decided that he believed him. "Very well," he said. "You are to send out word that no one is to impede me in my search for this man."

The frightened king nodded.

"There will be no sanctuary for him, or for any of his friends."

The king nodded again.

Harmalo stood. He looked at the dogs, who like the nobles cowered before his gaze. They knew, he thought. How odd. "I leave at first light," he said. "I thank you for your hospitality."

And then he strode out of the hall, still clutching the warm gant in his hand.

NINETEEN

Feslund

F eslund did not like being summoned to his mother's chambers. He was no longer a child—he was the ruler of an empire! But the queen saw things differently, of course.

And she knew what was best.

She was sitting in a high-backed chair by the window; his father was seated next to her. As usual, the king looked nervous, uncertain, out of place. He clearly hated Urbis and what was now demanded of him. He had spent his life doing the priests' bidding, and he was comfortable in that role. He wanted to be back in Gallia, feasting in the great hall, hunting with his friends. Feslund didn't blame him. He wanted to hunt, too! But here they were. And they had to succeed.

"I wish to speak of two matters," the queen said.

"Yes, mother." Feslund sat opposite her. Her dark eyes never failed to frighten him. What had he done wrong? What problem had he failed to foresee? There were so many problems.

"First, the weapons. I have received letters from friends in the provinces. Some people are saying the Gallians defeated the priests by trickery, not with the magical weapons. If there were weapons, the priests would surely have used them against the Gallians. If there were weapons, surely *we* would be using them now against the treasonous legions and invading tribes."

"But we do not have enough gants to defeat all our enemies," Feslund pointed out. "And every time we use the ones they have, they lose some of their power. They cannot be sharpened like a sword."

"I understand this," Gretyx snapped. "But the people do not. And we don't want them to know how limited our ability to use the weapons truly is. This is the problem we need to solve."

She wouldn't have raised the problem if she didn't have a solution. "What do you suggest, mother?" Feslund asked.

"You must demonstrate to the world that we possess the gants and can use them. You must show the world what happens to our enemies."

"How?"

"First, you must choose a time and a place when the eyes of Terra will be upon you."

"The Pan-Roman games," Feslund responded, getting the idea.

"Indeed. After the chariot race. In the past the pontifex has crowned the winner of the race."

"I know. I was already going to do that myself."

"Yes, but this year you are going to do more. I have learned that the old pontifex is still being kept prisoner in the palatium. Why, I do not know."

"His name is Tirelius," Feslund replied. "Liber hopes he can convince the fellow to help us."

"That is surely a vain hope," Gretyx said with a dismissive wave. "But it is good that he is still alive. Because after the chariot race, in the full view of uncounted thousands in the Circus Maximus, you are going to execute him with a gant. If anyone doubts that these weapons are real or that you won't use them against those who oppose you, they will learn the truth when the old pontifex turns to ashes, as my dear Siglind did."

Feslund was delighted with the idea. "Execute Tirelius—yes, of course! He deserves it, certainly."

"Do you not risk making him a martyr?" his father suggested. "I'm sure that many people still feel some fondness for Tirelius, especially if their lives have gotten worse lately. It is only natural."

"They will not have any fondness for him when they learn of his crimes."

"But what are his crimes?" Carolus persisted. "Surely it is not right to—"

"We will make up crimes!" Feslund shouted. "What does the truth matter? The people will not know the difference."

Gretyx nodded. "He did unspeakable things as pontifex. We just need to decide what they were."

His father's face reddened with anger, but he did not lose his temper. Instead, he raised another point. "Will this not end forever the chance of finding viators who will cooperate with us?"

"Perhaps they will cooperate if they know they face death otherwise," his mother replied.

"The priests do not strike me as the kind of people who will respond to fear," Feslund observed.

His mother turned her terrible gaze upon him. "That is because they have not dealt with me," she snapped.

At this both Feslund and his father fell silent. It was decided: Tirelius would die.

"Have you explained this to Liber?" Feslund asked finally.

"You can do that," his mother replied. "Liber has some good ideas, but not enough of them. He and his friend Decius are soft. They wish to placate the people whenever they can. We do not have the time or the inclination to placate people. Anyone who stands in our way—anyone who resists us—must pay the price."

Feslund liked Liber; Liber had made him a hero. But he wasn't going to argue with his mother. "Fear," he murmured.

"Yes. Fear is how we will survive. Starting now. On to the second matter. We must find you a wife. You have enjoyed yourself without thought of the future these past months. That must come to an end. You must give me grandchildren. You must carry on our royal line. That is your obligation and your highest duty."

Feslund had been expecting this. A wife was acceptable to him, as long as his mother didn't require him to give up his other pleasures. "Do you have anyone in mind, mother?"

"The king of Aquitania has offered us his daughter, along with a rich dowry. It is a reasonable alliance for us—and we need the dowry."

"Do you know anything about the girl?"

"You mean, is she pretty? Her father says that she is, of course. He sent along a portrait I can show you. And she can ride a horse and play the lyre and dance. Perhaps she can even read. But none of that matters. What matters is that she is healthy enough to bear your sons."

"Yes, of course," he replied meekly. "I will do whatever you think is best."

His mother nodded her approval. "That is well said, my son. We will speak more of these things. There is much to be done."

Feslund realized that he had been dismissed. He bowed to his parents and left the room.

He noticed that his hands were shaking. He thought he had done well enough, although he could not be sure.

It was simple, really. All he had to do was to submit to his mother's will. She was in charge now, and that meant everything would be all right.

TWENTY

Palta

The baby was born just before dawn, after a long night that left Valleia exhausted but determined, while Palta gripped her hand and urged her on and Carmody stood by, fearful and helpless.

It was a boy—small, red-faced, and angry. But he quickly settled down when Palta wrapped him in a blanket and placed him in his mother's arms. Valleia wept tears of joy and relief, leaning back in Carmody's arms as Palta cleaned up.

She had never assisted at a birth before. She had urged Valleia to send Gratius to fetch the village midwife, but Valleia refused. She wanted Palta. Palta had been terrified that something would go wrong and she would be responsible for the deaths of Valleia and her baby, but after a night of fear and pain and uncertainty, all appeared well.

Gratius came in later to pay his respects, and then he and Palta went outside to give the new family some privacy. The late-spring morning was cool but cloudless, and the day promised to be beautiful. "I thought he'd never arrive," Gratius remarked. "You must be exhausted."

"I'm not," Palta replied. "I'm just happy that it's over. Did you take care of the horses?"

"Of course. I'll be riding to the village in a while. Do you want to join me?"

She shook her head. "I'll stay here, I think."

"As you wish. But rest. Valleia will need you."

"Yes, I'll rest."

She sat down under an oak tree, leaned back against the trunk, and closed her eyes. *I should wash the dirty clothes in the lake*, she thought. *I should bring back water. I should tend to the garden.*

Instead, she fell asleep. When she opened her eyes, the sun was high in the sky. She got up and went inside. Valleia, Carmody, and the baby were all asleep—Valleia in the crook of Carmody's arm, the baby nestled against her breasts. Gratius was gone. Palta tore off a hunk of yesterday's bread and ate it by herself at the small table. The cottage was silent except for the family's regular breathing.

She thought again about her chores and decided to ignore them; there was nothing that couldn't wait. Instead she went outside and got on Renni. Palta had ridden many horses since Arminius taught Larry and her to ride in Gallia, but this was her favorite. The purest joy she felt was in riding Renni, just the two of them, wandering through this harsh but beautiful land.

First they took the short path to the lake. She stripped off her clothes, dived in, and paddled gently for a while in the cool water, hoping that Gratius didn't happen by and see her naked. Not that he would do anything to her; it would just embarrass them both. Her body had grown and filled out in the past year; young men in the village stared at her as she walked by. Attention from men had been part of her life on Gaia, her home world; it would surely be part of her life here on Terra. She assumed it would be part of her life on any world.

Finally she got out of the water, donned her robe and sandals again, and rode away.

Renni knew where to go. They traveled through thin woods, across wide meadows, and stopped at the foot of the hill. Palta dismounted and stroked Renni's mane. "I won't be long," she whispered to him.

Then she scrambled up the side of the hill, as she had so often. It was easier now that the snows had melted and the rainy season was past. It was easier also because she had worn a path amid the rocks and bushes.

At the top, she paused to catch her breath and look out at Scotia. The lake sparkled in the distance. Streams made their way from it through meadows, heading perhaps to the ocean. She saw flocks of sheep. She saw their cottage and the distant village. She saw hawks circling in the cloudless sky.

Palta turned away from it all. She walked over and stared into nothingness. She extended her hands and groped the nothingness. It was here that Larry had disappeared, presumably to follow Affron to another world. *I'm coming back*, he had promised her. But he had not come back. She had visited this spot almost every day since he left. But why? What he said hadn't really been a promise. Perhaps he had said it only to soften the blow of his departure. And if he came back, he didn't need her to be here on this hilltop, waiting for him. He knew where the cottage was. He knew how to find her, if that was what he wanted.

Still, she came. It was beautiful here, especially in spring. Why not climb this hill, stare into the distance, and feel a little closer to him? Was there something more important that she should be doing instead?

She stood on the hilltop for a while, and then she scrambled back down.

Gratius was waiting for her at the bottom. She said nothing to him as she untied Renni.

"Affron and Larry are not coming back, Palta," Gratius said. "You know that."

"I like it up there," she replied. She got onto Renni and started off. Gratius went with her.

She'd had to tell the others about Larry's disappearance, back when he left her that morning in the winter. They were as baffled as she had been. A portal, on a hilltop in the highlands of Scotia? Where had it come from? Had Affron created it?

And if it was a portal, where was it now?

In any case, there was nothing to be done. The portal—if it had been a portal—was gone, along with Larry. He had come here to find Affron. He had apparently done so, and then followed Affron to another world. Or perhaps he went somewhere else—to his home on Earth. And the rest of them were left behind here on Terra. And that was that.

"I'm leaving, Palta," Gratius said as they rode side by side back to the cottage.

She looked at him. "What do you mean?"

"Leaving the cottage, leaving Scotia. Travel will be better now that it's spring. I know nothing of farming or fishing or tending sheep. I have been here for months and learned little. The baby has been born; Valleia and Carmody will be all right. It is time to go."

Palta had always suspected that Gratius was a little in love with Valleia. It made sense for him to leave, she supposed. It must have been hard seeing her with someone else.

"Where will you go?"

"To a place called Hibernia," Gratius replied.

"Where is that?"

"It is a small kingdom off the coast of Britannia."

"Why Hibernia? Is that where you come from?"

Gratius shook his head. "Some priests went there after the Gallians took over Urbis. We burned down the schola so they wouldn't be able to learn how to use Via from its books. But we didn't want to lose that knowledge forever—someday the Gallians will be gone, and we will need to start again. So the priests are recreating that knowledge."

"They are just writing down whatever they know?" Palta asked.

"That was the plan. There and in Alexandria—so if one place is discovered, the other can carry on. It could all have fallen apart by now, I suppose. But if they are still there, I will join them."

This information saddened Palta. "This is my fault—mine and Larry's," she said. "We should have stopped when we met Feslund. We knew he would be a bad ruler."

"You could come with me," he pointed out. "You could help us with our task."

"How?"

He shrugged. "You could be a scribe, perhaps. Write down our knowledge."

"What makes you think I know how to write?" she murmured.

He looked embarrassed. "Ah, I'm sorry," he said. "But you are a smart girl. Surely you can learn. And what would you do here? Marry a village boy and bear his children? Stay unmarried and be a servant for Valleia and Carmody? You don't belong here any more than I do."

"I am safe here," she pointed out. "My entire life, I have never felt safe."

"You have a gant in your pocket, don't you? That surely gives you a measure of safety. It will give you a future more interesting than this." He waved at the meadow, the lake, the birds chirping in the trees.

Palta didn't respond. She realized that she was crying. She hadn't expected that. She hadn't cried since Larry left her.

"You don't have to decide right now," Gratius said gently. "They will need us for a while yet."

"Yes, of course."

They made their way back to the cottage. And they *were* needed. Carmody and Valleia were both intelligent, self-sufficient people, but even they found caring for a newborn to be a struggle, and they were grateful for any help. So Palta cooked meals, and procured supplies from the village, and washed their clothes, and fished in the lake. And occasionally she just held the sleeping baby in her arms, and she felt a kind of peace she had never felt before. She did not return to the hill.

A week went by, and then another. And finally Gratius spoke to her again. "It is time," he said. "I leave tomorrow."

"Have you told them?"

He shook his head. "I will speak to them tonight."

She didn't respond, and finally he walked away. Palta closed her eyes and tried to imagine a thousand different futures, on a thousand different worlds. Would she be happy in any of them?

Gratius told Valleia and Carmody of his decision after dinner. They didn't seem surprised, and they didn't try to talk him out of it. "We wish you every success and happiness," Valleia said. "We owe our lives to you."

They also approved of Gratius's destination. "There was so much knowledge in the schola," Valleia said. "I'm sorry to hear that it's gone. But I suppose you had no choice."

"We didn't think so, at any rate," he replied. "The priests used that knowledge wisely—as wisely as they could, at any rate. We feared that the Gallians would not do the same."

They didn't say anything more. Gratius wanted to get an early start in the morning, so they went to bed early. They rarely stayed up long after dark in any case.

Palta still slept near the others, on the floor in front of the hearth. It felt familiar to her, comfortable, although not as comfortable as lying next to Larry, as she had so often. She had no wish to be by herself at night.

But tonight she couldn't sleep. Affron was gone, and Larry, and soon Gratius would be gone as well. And she needed to make her own happiness. But she didn't know how.

125

She heard movement in the room, and she opened her eyes. Valleia had risen from her bed. Was the baby fussing? Palta hadn't heard him.

No, Valleia wasn't going to the baby. She squatted down on the floor next to Palta. Palta sat up. Valleia said nothing at first. The fire was burning low. Carmody was snoring peacefully. Palta waited.

"We were never close in Roma, you and I," Valleia began finally, speaking softly in the darkness. "I didn't see why we needed you or Larry. You just seemed to complicate things, when all I wanted to do was save Affron. I was wrong, of course. We wouldn't have survived without you. I still need you, but in a different way. But you and I both know that you don't belong here. You must go with Gratius, even if I don't want you to leave."

"What if I don't belong anywhere?" Palta responded. "Least of all Hibernia."

"Go wherever you like," Valleia said. "I don't know what you will do, but I know that you will accomplish something important."

"I wish I could believe you."

Valleia put her arm around Palta's shoulders and pulled her close. "Ah, but you must," she said. "I have visited many worlds, and I have done and seen many things. So trust me. Believe me. Obey me."

Palta leaned into Valleia and closed her eyes. She didn't know if Valleia was right. But she was a mother now, and that seemed to make a difference to Palta. Palta had never known her mother. "I will go," she whispered.

"That's good," Valleia murmured. "It will be fine," she added. "It will be fine."

In the morning Palta announced her decision to the others. Gratius was surprised, of course; Carmody was not. Presumably Valleia had told him about their conversation. "It is hard to make a life in a world that isn't your own," he said to her. "I know this. But perhaps you will be fortunate, as I have been."

"I hope so," she replied.

So everyone agreed that this was the right thing to do. Why, then, did it feel so wrong?

She packed up her few possessions and went out to put on Renni's blanket and saddle. She realized with a pang that she would not be able to take Renni to Hibernia with her; she would have to sell him in Flendys or whatever port town they chose as the start of their long sea voyage. "I'm so sorry," she whispered to him. "It seems that I must leave everything behind."

Gratius approached her. "They have packed food for us," he said. "They could not be kinder."

"Well, then," she replied. "Whenever you are ready."

They said their final good-byes, and Palta held the baby in her arms one last time. And then they mounted their horses and took the path that would lead them back to the King's Road. Away from the cottage, away from Valleia and Carmody, away from the hill that had taken Affron and Larry to some unknown world.

Palta knew that, like them, she would never return.

TWENTY-ONE

Larry

"It's not what I thought," Larry said.

"How could it be?" Affron replied.

"I mean—it's *there*. It's everywhere. You just have to see it. Except not with your eyes."

"More or less."

"But it goes in and out of focus. It…flickers."

"The flickering will go away."

"And I can't make it stay."

"Yes, you can."

"Is this how it happened for you?"

"More or less."

"How long did it take you?"

"I'm not sure. Forever?"

"But you succeeded."

"Yes. And here we are."

———

Time passed. Months? Years? Larry noticed that his voice had changed, and hair was growing in places where it didn't before. He was a man.

It didn't seem to matter. What mattered was what he was creating in the air in front of him. It grew and dissolved, grew and dissolved. Sandcastles destroyed by the incoming tide. No: memories he was trying to recover, words at the tip of his tongue. Almost there, and then gone.

But so much more. A network of neurons transferred outside his brain, rebuilt synapse by synapse in the air.

No, not in the air. *Through* the air. Tunnels. What was the word? Wormholes.

But wormholes went to single points, if he understood them, if they even existed. These wormholes were networks, infinitely branching, infinitely looping.

Or something. Metaphors were useless. Words withered when they confronted this. It was why Affron was so maddeningly vague. Understanding came only gradually, from the inside out.

But it came.

His hand disappeared into nothingness and came back out. And then his hand couldn't do this again for a week, a month.

Where did his hand go? He should have been terrified, but he wasn't. It would be all right; wherever his hand had gone, he could make it come back.

———

One night Affron forced Larry to take a break. They went outside and wandered through the crowded, sultry streets. They bought spicy food at a café and ate it in some kind of park. There seemed to be a festival taking place; but then, there always seemed to be a festival taking place. Men wearing nothing but loin cloths beat drums or played some kind of pan flute, their bodies gleaming with oil and sweat. Women, naked except for long bright scarves, twirled and shook and strutted. Fireworks exploded in the sky, to shouts and cheers from the crowds. One of the women grabbed Larry and pulled him into the dance, laughing at his awkwardness. He laughed too.

And her lovely, bouncing breasts suddenly reminded him of Siglind and Palta, bathing naked with him at the Gallian consulate in Roma. Siglind, who gave up her life to save him at the temple of Via. Palta, his companion in all his journeys on Terra, abandoned so that he could come to this place, to sit in a room and wave his hands in the air.

His laughter faded.

Eventually the woman let go of his hands and twirled away.

Affron handed him an icy green drink he had bought in the park. Larry took a sip. It was sweet, and very alcoholic.

"People are happy here," Larry said to him over the din of the music.

"They certainly seem to be."

"Do you think they know the secret to living?"

"Perhaps the secret is to die young. Medicine is not very advanced in this world."

"Ah." Larry took another sip. He could feel his brain starting to spin like his body during the dance. Siglind, Palta, Gratius. Valleia, Carmody, Kevin, Professor Gardner. Mom, Dad, Cassie, Matthew, Stinky Glover, Nora Lally—the girl he'd had a crush on back in Glanbury. They all spun with him. "We can't stay here forever, right?" he said to Affron.

"No, this is not our final destination," Affron replied.

"What is our final destination?"

"I don't know. We'll figure it out."

Larry swallowed the rest of the drink and closed his eyes. His brain was filled with fog now. But even as the fogs beclouded the looping, branching networks of neurons, he knew one thing: tomorrow he would return to the shrine and continue his work.

———

A hand, then two hands, and then eventually the gap, the tunnel, the wormhole was big enough for an entire body. But it did not persist; the gap closed, the wormhole faded into mere air. How did you make it persist? How did you create something that you could leave behind for someone else to find on a Scotian hill, or in conservation land in Glanbury, Massachusetts?

"Right now it is just you," Affron murmured. "It is outside you, but it isn't really real. You need to make it real."

"How?"

"You have to give it up. You have to leave it behind."

"*How?*"

Affron shrugged. "I didn't say this would be easy."

But why was it so hard? Why wasn't it as easy to find as the power he had found within himself in the temple of Via—the power to inflict a vision of the multiverse on someone else, to overwhelm them, torture them, with its immensity? He had needed that power to save his life, and there it was, waiting for him. The old woman aiming the gant at him staggered back in agony, tumbled thirty feet to the floor below, and he had triumphed.

It was far easier to destroy than to create, apparently.

But he did not give up. If he gave up now, what was left of his life?

And eventually he saw what he needed to see, felt what he needed to feel. Create it, and leave it behind. Like a mother giving birth. It's part of you, you give it life, but finally you know that it is not yours. And somehow it knows this too. The parting has to come from it, not from you.

And it is agony—like childbirth. Your mind is shattered, your brain is turned inside out. You cannot do this. But you cannot *not* do this. It is too late to turn back, to return to playing video games and surfing the internet and practicing the piano. To thinking about college and jobs and girlfriends. *This must happen.*

And so, finally, it does.

———

He was on his feet. Trembling, sweat-soaked, facing the emptiness.

"Go ahead," Affron said, from somewhere far away.

Larry took a step, and then another. Into the emptiness, surrounded by fog. Another step, and then one more. And he was out the other side.

He stood on a featureless plain. The sky was gray; the air was cold. Birds circled high overhead. He looked down. He was standing on hard-packed earth. A few tiny weeds poked up through it.

No trees, no houses, no roads.

He was alone. He shivered, but he did not move.

He was *somewhere*. And he had come here on his own.

After a long time, he turned and walked slowly back through the fog and into the shrine room, where Affron stood waiting for him.

"Well, then," Affron said.

———

It was a long time before Larry could speak. And when he finally did, he surprised himself. "There are others," he said. "Not just us."

Affron nodded. "Yes, I believe there are others."

"Have you seen them? Have you met them?"

Affron shook his head. "How would I do that? I've been here with you, carrying pots and statues."

"How do I know that there are others?"

"I don't know. How do *I* know that?"

"Where are they?"

"I have no idea."

Larry considered, and finally he said, "We have to find them."

"Yes," Affron replied. "Yes, we do."

TWENTY-TWO

Gratius

G ratius and Palta traveled south all day on the King's Road. It was a far more pleasant journey than the one they had taken along this same road in winter. His heart was light; he knew he had made the right decision.

There were concerns, of course.

What if he couldn't find the priests in Hibernia? What if their effort had fallen apart?

He could go home, of course. To Comum, in northern Italia. It was not an important place, just a small town next to a beautiful lake, with beautiful mountains in the distance. But you could swim with your friends in the lake, or lie back at night in the hills and stare at the stars. You could chase each other in the narrow streets and amid the stalls in the marketplace, laughing with each other over jokes that no one else could understand.

Ah, but it would not be the same.

Someone, sooner or later, would turn him in to the Gallians. He would not help them, of course, but what would they do to try to convince him? Perhaps they would leave him alone if he refused to help. But he did not think that's what would happen.

He would be lucky if his death was painless.

No, he could not go home. If he couldn't find the other priests, he would have to change his identity, become a teacher in some foreign city. Perhaps marry, have children—lead a normal life at last. Perhaps he would end up as happy as Valleia.

He glanced at Palta, riding next to him. He had not expected her to come with him; he had expected her to wait at that cottage forever, hoping for Larry's return. But here she was. "Are you all right?" he asked her, not for the first time on the journey.

Palta shrugged. "It is a lovely day for a ride," she replied.

"We have days of riding ahead of us," he pointed out.

"There's nothing I enjoy more."

"That's good. It's growing dark. We must find an inn before long."

"We can sleep in the open if you wish. We have food and blankets. We just need pasture for the horses."

"It will not be comfortable lying on the ground."

"Neither will lying on a hard bed in a Scotian inn. We have done both, Gratius."

"True," he agreed. "We will find a spot, then."

"Not just yet, though. The further we go, the less chance I have of changing my mind."

Gratius nodded. "As you wish."

He wondered if Palta would fit in with the priests. Would they even want her to join them, once they found out her role with the Gallians? He thought they would; Borafin and the others understood such things. They would welcome her help. And if they didn't, if Palta was unhappy there or anywhere, she could always return to Scotia. She would be all right.

In the distance a solitary man on horseback approached. They had met far more people on the King's Road today than when they had ridden along it back in the winter—merchants and farmers mostly, this far north. No noblemen, no soldiers. He assumed they would encounter them further south, near the larger towns. All who passed had been friendly, and Gratius now knew enough Erse to carry on a conversation with them.

The man wore a long brown cloak. He was beardless, and his hair was streaked with silver. He didn't look like a farmer. But if he was a merchant, where were his wares? Gratius nodded to the man as he drew near. "Good day to you, sir," Gratius said, in the polite way of the locals.

The man simply nodded and said nothing.

Ah, but his eyes! It felt as if Gratius had seen those eyes before.

But he could not recall where. He had seen too many eyes, encountered too many strangers. It would be good to be with other priests once again, even in a place like Hibernia.

He began searching for a spot where they could spend the night.

———

Harmalo

The man wore Scotian clothes, but he was not Scotian. That much Harmalo was sure of. He had spoken only a few words in Erse, but his accent had been Roman. And the self-assurance with which he carried himself, the power of his gaze, in the instant their eyes had met...

Was he a viator? Not Affron, of course. He did not look like Affron. But perhaps one of the others in the complicated story of Affron's disappearance from Roma. And the girl? There had been a girl in the story as well. Three people landed in Flendys looking for Affron. One of them had been a girl, according to the story the Scotian lord had told. Perhaps these were two of those three.

But where were they headed? Why were they traveling south? Had they found Affron? More likely: Had they failed to find him?

Harmalo's journey up the King's Road had proved frustrating. He had dismissed his retinue, hoping to travel fast and carry out his mission without fuss. But these Scotians were a tight-lipped people, though friendly enough. If they had any knowledge of Affron, they weren't going to share it with a stranger. He could threaten them with the gant, of course. He could kill one or two of them, if they were unclear about the gant's power. About *his* power. Oh, how he longed to do this! But what was the point, if they didn't know anything?

But these two...

Harmalo slowed his horse and pondered the situation. Finally he turned around and headed south.

His horse was tired and disinclined to speed up. This annoyed Harmalo; he had no wish to be riding in the dark. "Come on then, you filthy beast," he muttered.

The horse did not go any faster.

Harmalo wrapped his cloak more tightly around him and pressed on as darkness fell and the air grew colder. His anger increased—at the horse, at the stubborn, ignorant Scotians, at the man and girl who were making him chase them through the night.

The stars came out. He should just stop. Go into the woods, tie up the horse, and try to sleep on the hard, cold ground. If he didn't find the man and the girl tomorrow, he would simply turn around and head north again.

But then Harmalo spotted something up ahead, in the woods on the right. A flame. Firelight. It was they who had stopped for the night. He halted and quietly dismounted. He tied the horse to a sapling by the side of the road and then walked slowly through the woods towards the firelight.

When he saw movement, he stopped and took out his gant.

The two of them sat by a small fire in a clearing. The man and the girl. The girl had long, flowing hair, and her face was pretty in the firelight. She was holding a stick with meat on it over the fire. It smelled delicious. Harmalo hadn't eaten since morning.

Would they understand the gant's power? The man would, if he was a viator.

Harmalo moved forward. They looked up.

"Good evening," he said in Latin. "I am sorry to bother you, but I seek information."

They stared at the gant. Yes, they understood.

"Who are you?" the man asked.

"My name is Harmalo, and I'm seeking a man named Affron. Perhaps you've heard of him?"

"What is that thing in your hand?"

"I think you know," Harmalo responded.

"We don't know anyone named Affron," the man said.

"I think you do."

"You seem to be threatening us. Why?"

"I simply want information. I mean no harm to anyone."

"Well, we have no information for you. I'm sorry."

Harmalo moved a step closer. "Perhaps I'm mistaken," he said, "and you don't really understand what this device can do to you. So I will tell you. With the slightest movement of my finger, it will destroy you and leave not a particle behind. I do not know if it causes any pain, but I expect it does—one instant of agony as you are obliterated. This need not happen. I do not ask much. I think you, too, came from Roma in search of Affron. Did you find him? If so, I want you to tell me where he is."

The man did not seem nervous. "We did seek Affron," he replied. "But we did not find him. He has disappeared."

Harmalo considered. "I don't believe you."

The man shrugged. "I cannot help what you believe," he said.

He *was* a viator, Harmalo suddenly decided. With a viator's supercilious attitude—even when faced with a gant. "I mean no harm," Harmalo repeated, "but I need to find Affron."

"We do not know where he is. I am telling the truth."

Harmalo felt himself becoming angry. The man showed no fear, no respect. "But you have already lied to me," he pointed out. "First you said you didn't know him, now you admit you were seeking him. Which is it?"

The man seemed unfazed. "We came here to find him," he said. "We did not find him. We wanted him to help us fight against the priests. This was months ago—before we found out that the Gallians had done our job for us. Kill us if you choose, but that is the truth."

Harmalo raised the gant. "I need to find Affron."

The man shook his head. "Then you are wasting your time talking to us. Actually, you are wasting your time in any case. Threats won't help you."

"I think perhaps you are mistaken," Harmalo said quietly.

"I know where Affron is," the girl said.

He looked at her. This was the first time she had spoken. She had dropped the stick, and the meat sizzled in the fire. She seemed calm, like the man. Too young to be a viator, though.

"And where is that?" he asked

"There is a tiny village off the King's Road, in the highlands about a day's ride north of here. The villagers call it Glendolland, when they call it anything. He lives in a hut on the outskirts of Glendolland. I found him by chance. The people in the village told us nothing—that's their way—but I spotted him outside his hut as I rode by in search of him, and we spoke. He told me he wants to be left alone. He is tired of struggling with the priests. He doesn't care about the Gallians. He is happy living by himself, far away from everything."

The man sitting next to her looked startled. "You should have told me," he said.

"I'm sorry, Gratius," she replied. "It didn't seem to matter. The

Gallians have already taken over. So what was the point? Just leave him alone." She turned away. Was she crying? Who was she? Her Latin accent was slightly off; was she from another world?

Harmalo looked at the man. Gratius. Did he know hom from the schola? He was staring intently at the girl, but he said nothing. Something wasn't right here.

"Why did you keep looking for him," he asked Gratius, "once you found out the priests had been destroyed?"

"The time may come," Gratius replied, "when the Gallians will need to be defeated as well."

"You are a viator," Harmalo noted.

Gratius shrugged. "There is no such thing as a viator anymore. There are only rulers and the ruled. Right now, I am one of the ruled."

This made Harmalo smile.

"What is your name?" Harmalo asked the girl.

"Palta," she said softly.

"Palta, you will come with me."

She looked surprised. "But why? I have told you where you'll find him."

"But it's easy to lie. You are obviously smart enough to know this."

She considered this, and then nodded. "I understand. Do we leave now, in the dark? Or wait till morning?"

"Now, I think. The sooner the better."

"And Gratius—he doesn't have to come?"

"He doesn't know where Affron is. You do. I will take you."

"Very well." Palta got to her feet, brushing the twigs from her robe. "I will miss you, Gratius," she said to the man.

He smiled at her. "Come visit me someday," he replied.

"I will."

She turned away. And then Harmalo aimed his gant and killed Gratius.

———

Palta

Palta didn't have to turn to know what had happened; she could smell the bitter odor. Oh, she had smelled that odor before.

But still she turned. Gratius was gone, as though he had never existed. The man was aiming the gant at her.

She began to tremble. Tears coursed down her cheeks.

"This is a very powerful weapon," the man noted.

"Why?" she whispered. "Why did you have to do it?"

"I didn't trust him. He knows where we're headed. He could try to get there first and warn Affron."

Palta fell to her knees, looking at the empty space where her friend had just been sitting. This had happened to her so often. Too much.

"Come along, then," the man said.

"You know where to find him," she replied. "You don't need me."

"I don't trust you, either. If you are lying to me—and I think you may be—I will kill you, too. I am actually quite fond of killing people."

"Then kill me now. I don't care."

Her idea had been that her lie would free Gratius, and then she could take care of this man when she had a chance. He didn't know she had her own gant. That was all the advantage she needed. A moment would come when he wasn't paying attention, and that moment would be enough.

Now, what did it matter?

"No," the man said, "you're coming with me."

"Why? I *was* lying to you. Affron isn't in that village. He isn't anywhere. He built his own Via and disappeared from Terra. He's never coming back. He wants nothing to do with us. So you don't have to kill him. That's why you were sent here, isn't it? Someone is still worried that he'll show up in Urbis and take over the empire. So they need to make sure he doesn't. Tell them they don't have to worry. And kill me."

The man was silent. Palta tensed, awaiting the moment of her disintegration. But it didn't come. "No," he finally repeated. "I will not kill you simply because you want me to. I will kill you because *I* want to. Once I'm sure what the truth is."

"You are a fool," she whispered.

"You are mistaken," he replied. "Now roast me some of your meat. I'm hungry. Then we ride north."

Palta did as she was told. It didn't matter. The man sat by the fire and stared at her. Was he clever enough to search her? Would he spot the bulge in her pocket? His face was hard, and his eyes were intelligent. Intelligent enough? He ate most of the mutton she and Gratius had brought. Should she offer him wine, to make him sleepy? Or would that make him suspicious instead?

She decided to offer him nothing. She would simply obey.

"Let's go," the man said finally, rising.

Palta stood up as well. "My horse is over there," she said, gesturing into the woods.

"All right. I will be behind you. Don't try to run. I am faster than you, and stronger. And as you saw, I know how to use this weapon."

"Of course," she said. "What will happen to Gratius's horse?"

"I don't care."

"Can I at least untie him? He'll starve if I don't."

"As you wish."

She untied Gratius's poor horse, who simply stayed where he was, staring at her. Then she went up to Renni and put on his saddle, always aware of the man watching her, gant in hand. Did he really think this was a good idea? He would fall asleep before they reached the village— or at least nod off. Or his attention would wander. He would be vulnerable in countless ways. Why not just kill her and remove the risk?

Because killing her would make her happy.

Very well, then.

Renni seemed puzzled by what she was doing, but as always he obeyed her. She walked him back to where the man's horse was patiently waiting for him. They mounted their horses and started riding slowly north in the darkness. Palta led the way, with the man following close behind her. It was a clear night, and a half-moon had risen. They were silent.

It was only a matter of time, she thought. Minutes, hours. It didn't matter. It would happen.

She remembered riding away from Urbis with Larry and Gratius in a cart the night after the raid that had handed the empire to the Gallians. Riding away as the city burned behind them. Riding through the night—they weren't sure where—and into the dawn. Larry had decided not to use Via to go home, even though he could have, and she had been so relieved and grateful. She wouldn't be alone; she would have a friend. And they would somehow find Affron, hiding in Barbarica, and all would be well.

But here she was; Affron and Larry had disappeared, and Gratius was dead.

Alone, she thought. Always alone.

And then the moment came. "Halt!" the man said.

Palta stopped.

He dismounted. "I need to piss," he muttered.

She dismounted too.

"Stay where you are," he ordered. He walked over to the side of the road. He half-turned and fumbled with his robe; he still held the gant.

The fool.

She waited. The pee started to flow. She reached into her robe for her own gant.

He turned to face her, still peeing. "Stay where you are!" he repeated.

She didn't bother to respond. She took out the gant.

"What are you doing?" he cried.

He raised his own gant, but he was too late. She aimed and shot.

The man disappeared.

The arc of his piss disappeared as well. That was strange. No matter.

The man was dead.

Palta stood there, by the man's horse. She took off the horse's saddle and threw it to the side of the road. "You can go too," she murmured. But the horse didn't move.

She put the gant back into her pocket and took a deep breath. Renni stared at her.

"What should I do now?" she asked the horse.

But Renni didn't respond. Palta was alone, and it was all up to her.

TWENTY-THREE

Gretyx

"My lady, he is here," Liber told her.

"What is his mood?" Gretyx asked.

"He is angry, of course."

"He is a fool. Send him in."

Gretyx waited while Liber fetched Decius from the anteroom. Decius was perhaps not a fool, but she had little time to waste on those who disagreed with her.

The governor strode in with Liber following behind. Decius could scarcely bring himself to bow. He thrust a piece of paper towards her. She knew what was printed on it. She took it from him.

"My lady, have you seen this decree?" he demanded. "It forbids all political meetings in Roma, on penalty of death. This is absurd!"

"Why is it absurd?" Gretyx inquired.

"It says three people or more constitute a meeting. So, three people complaining about the price of bread is a meeting. Will those people be put to death? And why was I not consulted? Roma is my province. I must approve all decrees."

"The empire is in crisis," Liber observed. "We needed to take immediate action."

Decius turned to Liber. "Were you involved in this decision? Was everyone involved but me?"

"We cannot allow the situation to get out of hand."

"These are my people!" Decius shouted. "I know them better than anyone. They will not stand for this!"

"If enough of them are put to death, the remainder will stand for it," Gretyx said.

"You will start killing my people? I demand that you rescind this decree!"

"Sit down," she ordered.

Decius looked as if he wanted to argue, but he obeyed her.

"We are making changes," she said.

She gestured to Liber to continue.

"You have been replaced, along with your generals," Liber told Decius.

"Replaced? You can't do that! The Roman people elected me. There are laws! Sacred laws!"

"The laws have been changed. Nothing is sacred."

Decius stared at him, and then turned to Gretyx. "My lady, you can't do this. The people are hungry. They are worried. You must get them on your side."

"Fear will get them on our side. I think we are done here." She gestured to Liber once again.

He stood up. "Come then, Decius," he said.

Decius ignored him. He stared at Gretyx with hatred in his eyes. But he said nothing more. He merely stood and quickly left the room. He did not bow to her.

It didn't matter to Gretyx. Decius had lost his job. If he made any trouble, it wouldn't be long before Decius lost his life.

————

Decius

"I take it that you have not been replaced?" Decius asked Liber as they left Gretyx's residence.

"As a matter of fact, I have," Liber replied. He looked uncomfortable.

"Well? You are no longer chief minister?"

"I am to be your replacement," he said. "The queen herself will act as chief minister. In effect, she has already been doing that. I am very sorry, Decius."

Decius was too angry to respond. He tried to calm himself and finally said, "I cannot believe you are going to be part of this, Liber. It will end badly for everyone—for you, for the empire, for Terra."

"I wish you well, Decius, but you are mistaken. The Gallians are doing what they must do. We can work with them, or we can die."

Decius shook his head. "Do you think you will be spared, Liber? You are doomed whether you work with them or not. Your only choice is whether or not you go to your death believing you fought for what is right."

"When I first met you, you thought that helping the Gallians was the right thing to do."

"Clearly I was mistaken."

Liber did not respond. But in any case his response didn't matter. Liber had his choices to make; Decius had his own. He assumed that he was in danger. It was only a matter of time before Gretyx decided he was too dangerous to live.

She had set him free, in a way. And now it was time to take advantage of his freedom.

———

Liber

They parted at Decius's carriage, and Liber returned to his office in the palatium.

First, chief minister, now governor of Roma…. soldiers saluted him; minor officials bowed deeply to him. It was absurd. But here he was.

It couldn't last. But he had survived till now. If Gretyx didn't like him, at least she didn't find him as objectionable as she had found Decius.

"Any word?" he asked Cingulus.

"None, my lord," his secretary replied.

Harmalo had disappeared. They had heard from his deputy: Harmalo had gone off on his own in search of Affron, and the deputy now wanted instructions. Should he and the others await Harmalo's return or sail back to Roma without him?

Liber didn't know what to tell him.

He wondered when Gretyx would remember to ask him about Affron. They still had not found any viators. This is the sort of thing that would anger her. Well, at least it wasn't his responsibility anymore.

He had a far more difficult responsibility now. He had to ensure the obedience of the people of Roma.

And if they didn't obey, he would have to put them to death.

It was early afternoon, but Liber wanted a drink very badly. Being a poorly paid tutor to the doltish children of wealthy merchants hadn't been so bad, he supposed. But that life was gone now, and he had to be successful in his new life. Or he, too, would be put to death.

TWENTY-FOUR

Larry

At last they left Kravok-Li, the world that had been their home for months, for years. The laughing people, the clanging music, the endless stream of pots and statues—all gone now. Larry supposed that he would never return.

They stepped through Larry's portal into a barren, rugged world, not unlike Scotia. The sun was low in the sky. A strong wind blew out of the east.

"Are they here?" Larry asked.

"I don't think so," Affron replied.

"But…this is the place we need to be."

"I think so."

"And now we just have to…"

"Take the next step."

"Whatever that is."

"Yes."

The next step was to stay alive here. Find food, warmer clothes, a place to sleep. They saw a village in the distance and started walking towards it. How would they get what they needed without money, without being able to speak the natives' language?

The village was a small collection of wooden buildings lining both sides of a narrow street—it looked a little like a movie set for a Western. A few people were walking along the street. They men were dressed in dark jackets and flowing pants; the women wore wide-brimmed hats and long skirts. They all stopped and stared when they spotted Larry and Affron.

"Smile, and don't appear threatening," Affron murmured.

Larry did as he was told.

They walked up to a man and woman. Affron began to speak, but the couple shook their heads and hurried away from him, disappearing inside one of the buildings. Everyone else was leaving the street as well, as if they were expecting a gunfight.

Everyone except a stoop-shouldered white-haired man with bloodshot eyes and a scraggly gray beard who was sitting on a bench on the wooden sidewalk. So they approached him. Again Affron started to speak. The old man raised a hand to stop him. He rose with difficulty from the bench and gestured for them to follow him.

He walked slowly along the sidewalk and paused in front of a door. Next to the door was what Larry supposed was a sign, in some indecipherable script. The old man looked back at the two of them, and then he opened the door. Inside was a large room. People were seated at long tables, eating. Was it a restaurant? The food smelled familiar. What was it? Finally Larry realized: potatoes. There had been no potatoes on Terra or Kravok-Li. How long had it been since he'd eaten them? His eyes swam with tears as he remembered the mashed potatoes his mother made back home in Glanbury.

The people in the room were staring at them. The white-haired man pointed to a couple of empty spots at one of the tables.

"Come on," Affron said.

They sat down. The people at their table said nothing to them. A child pulled on his mother's sleeve and whispered something to her; she shushed him. Finally a man brought them plates of food. Some kind of meat, and boiled carrots and, yes, a potato. And a knife and fork. There had been only spoons on Kravok-Li.

The food was bland and tasteless compared to the food on that world. His potato needed salt; it needed something.

People started talking again after a while. "Any idea what they're saying?" he asked Affron.

Affron shook his head.

After they finished eating, the white-haired man reappeared and motioned to them again. They rose from the table and followed him, this time through a set of swinging doors that led down a short corridor to a small room, empty except for a table with a candle on it and a chamber pot. Another man arrived with a couple of blankets. The man dropped them on the floor and left without looking at them; the white-haired man nodded to them and then shut the door, leaving them by themselves.

"Now what?" Larry asked. "Do we just go to sleep?"

Affron shrugged. "I suppose so. Then we see what tomorrow brings."

They lay down on the floor. Larry tried to sleep, but the silence bothered him. The incessant music on Kravok-Li had worked its way deep inside him, and he found that he missed it, along with the food.

Was he homesick for that world along with all the others? Would every world he visited make him homesick?

Eventually he fell into a fitful sleep. He awoke finally to a gentle knocking on the door. Affron opened the door, and the white-haired man stood outside, holding a pair of dark jackets that Larry had seen on most of the men. He handed one to each of them. They put them on. Then the man led them back to the long room where they had eaten the night before. No one was there except the man who had served them. He motioned for them to sit down and brought them plates of food, which was much like what they'd had the night before. He and the white-haired man stood in a corner watching them. When they had finished, the two men stepped forward. The server removed their plates; the white-haired man motioned to them to follow him.

He led them out of the building. Outside, things had changed. Hundreds of people were lined up on both sides of the narrow street, holding torches. A pair of horses were tied up to posts by the building. The white-haired man gestured to them.

"Tulf," he said in a raspy voice, and he pointed to the left, to where the sun was just rising over a distant mountain. It was the first word anyone had spoken to them.

"Tulf?" Affron repeated.

The man nodded energetically, as if delighted at Affron's clever-ness. "Tulf!"

And then the crowd began to chant the word: "Tulf! Tulf! Tulf!"

"I think these people have gone through this before," Affron murmured to Larry.

"What do we do?"

"I suppose we go and find Tulf," he replied.

Affron mounted one of the horses, and Larry mounted the other. The white-haired man smiled a toothless smile up at them. And they headed off down the street through the chanting crowd, riding slowly towards the rising sun.

TWENTY-FIVE

Palta

With Gratius dead, Palta had no reason to go to Hibernia—to search for people she didn't know, who might not even be there, and who might not want her help. But she couldn't bring herself to return to Valleia and Carmody. Gratius had been right: she needed to find a life for herself.

So she decided to return to Roma. She was familiar with Roma; it was huge and exciting, and it would offer her opportunities. And she had been happy there, after a fashion, walking through its streets with Larry and teaching him Latin. Perhaps she could be happy again.

She made her way back to Flendys, sold Renni to the stable there though it broke her heart, and booked passage to Britannia. In Britannia she found a ship that would take her back to Roma.

The voyage to Roma almost destroyed her. At the best of times her fear of water was barely under control. Twice in her life she had almost drowned, and now she had to sail through constant rough weather on an overloaded ship with a surly crew and leering fellow passengers. Every moment had been a nightmare, and every moment reminded her that she didn't have to be doing this. It was a choice. But the choice had been made, and there was no turning back. She was headed to Roma, and a new life.

Always a new life.

After the long, difficult voyage the ship finally pulled into a busy wharf, and Palta set foot on land once more, tired and filthy but grateful to leave the water behind and still be alive. Now what? She stood on the wharf as the passengers pushed past her, and she considered. The first thing to do was to get away from the waterfront—the smell of the salt air was almost unbearable, and the port had its own bad memories for her—of being kidnapped and held in a warehouse here, waiting to be sold into slavery, until Larry saved her.

Palta made her way into the city. She needed a place to stay and a good meal, but she had little money left. She would have to find work soon. But not today.

She stopped at a tavern and bought a small meal of bread and olive oil; it cost far more than she had expected, and this worried her. While she ate at a table outside, she looked around. Roma seemed much as it had been. It was a hot summer day, and children played in a fountain. Women carried jugs of water on their heads. She saw banners flying by the fountain; she heard a band in the distance. The Pan-Roman Games were coming, she realized. Or perhaps they had already begun. More memories overwhelmed her: of attending the chariot race at the Circus Maximus with Larry, expecting that Affron was going to use his powers to destroy Tirelius after the race and begin the revolt against the priests. And, most important, give Larry the chance to go home. It didn't happen, and at that moment they hadn't known why; they only knew that Larry was trapped here on Terra. The two of them had left the Circus in despair, finally running in the rain through the streets of Roma because there was nothing else to do, and she had felt so sorry for him. He had a wonderful home to return to, unlike hers, and now he had no way to get back to it. They stopped, in a colonnade finally, breathless and wet, and kissed as the rain poured down. That moment had been so sweet. Nothing was going right, but at least they had each other.

And then the kidnappers had shown up, she was ripped from Larry's arms, and nothing was the same again.

Palta shook her head to rid herself of the memory. She was off the accursed ship. She was here in Roma. She was safe, for now. The bread was expensive but freshly baked; the olive oil was full of flavor; the summer heat was bearable. She had money enough for a few nights' lodging, although inns would certainly be charging more for a room during the Games. She was young and healthy; she could find work.

First, though, she would need to find a bed for the night. She rose from her chair and started walking through the city again. She heard a roar in the distance. It didn't seem to be coming from the direction of the Circus. Perhaps it was some kind of performance—dancers, acrobats, musicians…They filled the city during the Games. She walked on, towards the roar.

She realized that she was heading towards the Forum. What was happening there? A stream of people were heading in that direction as well—families; young women her age with flowers in their hair; fat, drunken men.

They all seemed to be in a hurry. She started hurrying with them.

The Roman Forum was a large, open square lined with massive buildings and a majestic temple dedicated to Via. Before the priests had built Urbis the Forum had been the center of power in the empire, and it was still the heart of the Roman province. And now the Forum was filled with people. Palta pushed her way through the crowds and up a long set of stairs leading to one of the buildings. Finally she turned and looked back.

And that was when she saw the human heads, spitted on poles and displayed at the entrance to the temple.

She gasped, unable to look away from them. Men, women. A dozen or more. Their eyes were closed but still they seemed surprised. *Why am I here?* they seemed to be saying. *What did I do wrong? Why have I become a grotesque object detached from my body?*

What was going on?

Someone was tugging at her sleeve. "Another one," a woman next to her was saying, pointing out towards the middle of the square.

Palta turned her gaze there. She saw a large platform surrounded by blue-caped soldiers. On the platform was a large stone block, stained red with glistening blood. Next to it stood a burly, bearded man holding a large ax. Two soldiers were dragging a young man howling with fear across the platform towards the block.

The crowd howled back at him, shaking their fists, screaming for his death. "Occidere! Occidere!" *Kill! Kill!*

His hands and feet were tied, and he could do nothing but writhe in despair as he approached the block. He was no more than a boy, really. What had he done? The soldiers positioned him on the block and held him in place. The bearded man raised his ax. Palta closed her eyes and put her hands over her ears, but still she heard the crowd's roar when it happened. When she finally opened her eyes, she made sure to look away from the platform; she did not want to see what took place after the beheading. She was trembling; she felt as though she was going to vomit. She turned to the woman next to her. "Why are they doing this?" she asked.

The woman was short, gray-haired, red-cheeked, stout. Her hands were gnarled; her robe was a dingy gray. She looked surprised at Palta's question. "What do you mean, love?" she replied. "He was stealing our food, plotting against us. They all are. Prince Feslund has to stop them before it's too late."

"What do you mean, 'stealing our food'?"

"You know what's going on, love. We all do. The grain shipments from Egypt—they never come anymore. It's all the fault of the priests and their followers. They pay off the Egyptians so they sell most of the grain to Barbarica, and the priests keep the rest for themselves and their favorites. That's why prices are so high. That's why honest folk like us are going hungry. The priests are trying to make the Gallians fail. The priests have always been against us."

"But—"

"Tirelius is behind it all, of course. I never liked that one. But don't worry, Prince Feslund has plans for him. They haven't said anything, but everyone knows—tomorrow. At the Circus Maximus, after the chariot race, after the prince crowns the victor. Then he will do what they should have done long ago."

"What's that?"

"Execute him, love. With that weapon the gods gave the prince. In front of all of Roma. Oh, I'll be there, that's for sure. Look—they're going to do another one."

Do another one. Palta did not look. Instead she turned away and walked up to the top of the stairs. She sat down behind a pillar, closed her eyes, and wept as the crowd howled in ecstasy at the next beheading.

Kill! Kill!

This cannot be happening, she thought. This was another nightmare, like all her other nightmares. She had returned to Roma to endure beheadings in the Forum?

Kill! Kill!

She should get out of the city. Right away. Find another ship. Return to Scotia, to Valleia and Carmody; it had been a mistake to leave them. Go anywhere but here.

But she didn't want to go to Scotia, or Hibernia, or anywhere.

She didn't know what she wanted, except not to be alone in this awful world.

TWENTY-SIX

Gretyx

They brought the bride-to-be to Gretyx for approval of the dress she would wear to the Circus Maximus. Her absurd name was Bathanala, which Gretyx still had a hard time remembering. Everything about the girl was forgettable, actually. If she had a spark of personality, Gretyx had yet to detect it. The portrait her father had sent during the negotiations had been utterly misleading. It had shown a lovely young woman with rosy cheeks and lively eyes. In person, the girl's skin was pale and splotchy, and her eyes were dull and fearful. Feslund was, of course, disappointed. But he would do his duty and put a son in her.

"My dear, you look lovely," Gretyx lied to her.

Bathanala blushed and curtseyed. "Thank you, my lady."

Gretyx hated her curtsey. "Don't do that," she admonished her. "Simply bow. If someone is more important than you—like me—bow deeply. If the person is an inferior, simply incline your head. Do you see?"

"Yes, my lady."

"Good." Gretyx inspected the dress. "This shade of blue flatters you," she said. "But the dress bares too much flesh. You are going to a chariot race, not a dinner party." She gestured to Bathanala's maid.

"Find something to cover her shoulders," she ordered. "A shawl, perhaps. She will be hot, but this is the kind of sacrifice one must make."

"Yes, my lady," the maid replied.

"Go then," Gretyx replied irritably when the girl did not move.

The maid bowed and left the room.

Gretyx turned her attention back to Bathanala. "You know what is going to happen tomorrow," she said to her.

The young woman's eyes widened in fear. "I…think so," she replied.

Gretyx stifled an urge to throttle her. She thought of her own daughter, and how smart and brave Siglind had been. Gretyx would not have needed to tell Siglind what was happening and what she had to do. "Tomorrow they will hold the chariot race in the Circus Maximus. We have talked about this, yes?"

"Yes, my lady. It sounds very exciting."

"This will be the first time the people of Roma see you. It is vital that you make a good impression on them. Once you marry my son, you will be their queen. They are not used to having a queen. But they will love you if they see that you are beautiful and gracious and strong. Do you understand?"

"Yes, my lady. Of course."

"You will walk by Feslund's side across the field and sit in the royal box," Gretyx went on. "You will gaze at him lovingly from time to time. You will smile at his jokes, if he manages to make any. But you will not laugh. Have you ever seen a chariot race?"

"Yes, my lady. They are very popular in Aquitania."

"Then you know that there are collisions. The charioteers and their horses may be injured; some may die. The crowd will find this delightful. They will cheer every collision, every death. But you must not become too excited. Nor must you seem too squeamish. You must appear to be entertained, but you must keep your composure. Is that clear?"

"I think so, my lady."

She *thinks* so. "Very well. Now afterwards. You know what is happening after the chariot race?"

"Feslund puts the laurel wreath upon the head of the victor," Bathanala said.

"Yes, yes. After that."

"After that the pontifex is to be executed, my lady."

"Yes, very good. And do you know how it is to happen?"

"My lord Feslund will kill him with the magical weapon."

"Correct. This will be different from the chariot race. Do you understand that? It will not be bloody. Tirelius will be there, and then Feslund will aim the weapon at him, and he will disappear. We do not know how the crowd will react when this happens. Perhaps they will be terrified. Perhaps they will roar their approval. In any case, you yourself must not react. You must stand next to Feslund like a queen and look solemn. He is dispensing justice, and you are there to support him. You believe in him, you love him; you love what he has done. It is for the good of the empire and its people. Do you see?"

"Yes, my lady." Bathanala's eyes were watering, and her chin was starting to quiver. She looked as though she were about to faint from the stress of trying to remember all these rules. It was too much for her.

It couldn't be helped. She had to play her part, and she would do her best. Gretyx was more worried about Feslund, who might have his own ideas about the part he was supposed to play. She hoped he was smart enough not to trust his instincts and to obey his mother instead.

"You may go, my child," Gretyx said to Bathanala, as gently as she could. "Get a good night's sleep. Tomorrow will be tiring for all of us."

"Yes, my lady." Bathanala started to curtsey, then corrected herself and instead bowed deeply. "Thank you, my lady."

Gretyx waved her out of the room. She sat back in her chair and closed her eyes. It was so hot, even with a breeze wafting in through the open window. Summer here was vile. How did the Romans stand it? Most of them had no choice, of course.

Twenty-two executed in the Forum today, she had been told. It was a start. The crowds had loved it, apparently. Of course, there would be those who wouldn't love these executions—those who would be terrified by them, and those who would be outraged, smart enough to understand that these people were innocent, the cases against them fabricated. But terror was acceptable to Gretyx, as long as it produced obedience. And as for those who were outraged—she would find them, and they would become the next victims.

Like Decius. She should not have waited to kill Decius. Now he had disappeared, and who knew what mischief he would foment?

The danger—always the danger—was losing one's nerve. Carolus was one of those who was terrified, and Feslund—he simply wanted to be loved. He thought that he *should* be loved. He needed to understand that he could not be loved by everyone; with love came hatred. You had to accept the hatred if you wanted the love. Both her husband and her son would likely crumble without her. They would let themselves be overwhelmed by details, by scruples, by the truth. Real leaders made their own truth.

She slapped a mosquito that had landed on her neck. Such an awful place. She was tired. She was worried. But she couldn't wait for tomorrow, in the Circus Maximus.

———

Feslund

Feslund sat on the grass outside the armamentarium, drinking wine with some of his mates—Mellor, Cymbian, Escondo. They had been with him on the journey from Gallia to Urbis. They had fought the guards in this armamentarium. They had freed the gants and used them to kill the soldiers in Urbis, to capture Tirelius, to claim the temple of Via, to defeat the priests and avenge King Harald. They were still with him. And tonight they were getting drunk and reminiscing.

"Do you remember the shock on the faces of those guards in there?" Escondo asked, laughing and waving at the armamentarium. "The last thing they expected was a bunch of soggy Gallians rushing in on them in the middle of the night."

"True," Mellor replied. "But they fought well enough, once they woke up."

"It was a good fight," Cymbian said. "A real fight. Once we got those gants, though…"

Feslund sighed and poured himself more wine. His soldiers had never liked the gants. Soldiers liked to win, but they liked to win because they were smarter and stronger than their opponent, better trained and better led, better with their horses and better with their swords—not because they possessed magical weapons and the other side didn't. "We took the risk and it paid off," he said, somewhat defensively. The others muttered their agreement. There were times when they could have turned back, when perhaps they *should* have turned back. After the storm on the great sea, especially, when one of their ships had been lost and half their soldiers had drowned. Including Arminius, his closest friend, his wisest comrade. "I miss Arminius," he said.

Muttered agreement again. "There was no one like Arminius," Mellor said. "Best soldier I ever met."

"He would have helped afterward," Escondo pointed out.

If he were alive, we wouldn't be in this mess was what Escondo meant. Feslund felt a surge of anger. The men had always thought better of Arminius than they had of him. Feslund was the prince, but Arminius was the one they looked up to.

Still, he did miss Arminius. Arminius never gave him bad advice, and was never afraid to say what he thought. Could he have stood up to Gretyx? Probably not; no one could stand up to his mother, once she felt strongly about something. But perhaps he'd have had ideas about how to work with her, soften her....

Avenging King Harald had been the easy part, it turned out. What came after was the hard part.

Oh, it didn't matter. Arminius was at the bottom of the great sea. And today the executions had started.

"You know who I miss?" Cymbian asked. "The boy and the girl."

"The boy couldn't ride a horse," Mellor pointed out. "The girl was a natural, though."

Yes, the boy and the girl. Larry and Palta. Feslund hadn't thought of them in a while. "Palta knew how to get us in to Urbis," he said. "She found that postern. And she could speak Gallic, a little."

"And she knew the route to the armamentarium," Escondo added. "Plus, she figured out where the key was to the room with the gants. She was a smart one. The boy wasn't much."

"Where did they go?" Cymbian asked. "They were supposed to be guarding the temple for us."

"Must've walked into Via, is what I think," Escondo said. "Pass me the wine, will you?"

Feslund handed him the jug. "You walk into Via, you don't come back out," he said. "Unless you know what you're doing."

"Via scares me," Cymbian said. "Nothing else in this world scares me, but Via does. Why would anyone just walk into it?"

"They were different from us, Larry and Palta," Mellor said. "I liked them. Without them, we wouldn't be here."

At that, the soldiers fell silent. They didn't want to be here. They wanted to be home in Gallia. Feslund knew that. Some of them had asked him already if they could leave—maybe all of them had asked. He couldn't remember. They wanted to be with their families, be with their own kind. They would be heroes in Gallia.

But he couldn't stand to let them go. He couldn't stand to be here alone. Or worse, with his bride.

"We're introducing Bathanala at the Circus Maximus tomorrow," he said. "The wedding will be sometime in the fall."

The soldiers stayed silent.

And that made Feslund angry again. "What's the matter?" he demanded. "Don't you approve of her? She's a princess! She's better than the lot of you!"

"Don't really know her, my lord," Escondo replied mildly.

"Seems very pleasant," Cymbian added.

Feslund grabbed the jug back and took another long swallow. "She's stupid," he said abruptly.

At that, the soldiers burst into laughter. Feslund laughed too.

"But at least she's beautiful," Mellor replied.

The soldiers laughed some more.

"Well, at least her name is beautiful," Cymbian said. "Babanana."

"No, no," Escondo said. "Balabala."

Feslund smiled. "I just call her 'Bath' for short," he said. "But I think she'll answer to anything."

"She'll answer to anything your mother calls her, anyway," Cymbian said.

Feslund lunged at Cymbian then, grabbing his throat and pushing him back onto the ground. Went too far. The fool. The idiot. "Do not insult my mother!" he shouted. He could feel hands on him, trying to pull him away. Finally he loosened his grip on Cymbian and let the others drag him back.

"Sorry, my lord," Cymbian croaked. "Wasn't meant to be an insult. Just fooling about." But Feslund looked into his eyes and saw something different: rage, perhaps. Or, worse, contempt.

He struggled to stand up. By the time he was on his feet he couldn't remember why he'd been angry. His head spun from all the wine. He suddenly felt sick. He needed to go to bed. But which way was he supposed to go?

"We can take you home if you like, my lord," one of the soldiers said. Feslund couldn't tell which.

"You should get some rest, my lord," another one said.

"Tomorrow is an important day, my lord," a third said. "You must be ready for it."

He felt their hands supporting him, leading him. He let himself be led. They were good lads, even if they went too far sometimes, overstepped boundaries. They were his mates. A man needs his mates.

And tomorrow he had to walk into the Circus Maximus and, before a hundred thousand people, take out a gant and execute Tirelius.

––––––

Cymbian

Cymbian stayed outside as his mates staggered into the barracks. He too should get some rest; they would all need to be sober in the morning. But he didn't feel like sleeping.

He was not especially upset that Feslund had attacked him. They all knew how Feslund got when he was drunk. It was the other things that upset him—the executions in the Forum, for example. It was obvious that none of those people were guilty, that the story about the priests stealing the grain was a lie. Was he the only one bothered by this? He had tried talking about it with Escondo and Mellor, and they had just shrugged it off. It wasn't their job to bother themselves with such matters, they said. Princes rule; soldiers obey.

Fair enough; but it didn't seem right somehow.

He looked up at the temple of Via. Ah, things had been easier when there was just a battle to be fought. Now the world had changed, and he didn't know what to do about it.

Arminius would have known.

Cymbian sighed. Perhaps someday he would be as wise as Arminius.

––––––

Liber

Liber waited till late at night to go to the palatium. The night was warm and muggy. Urbis was quiet except for the trilling of insects; the forum was deserted, the palatium was dark. He carried a torch and nodded to the guards as he went inside the building. He was the governor of Roma now, not the chief minister, but still they seemed to accept his right to be here. With some difficulty he found the staircase that brought him down to the prison.

It was a tiny place, of course, just a narrow hallway of cells guarded by a couple of sleepy soldiers. The only excitement here had been when Affron and Valleia had managed to escape from their cells on the night before they were to be executed.

Liber had not been in Urbis then, but he had thought about that escape a lot.

The guards stood at attention when he entered. They looked a bit confused. "I wish to speak to the prisoner Tirelius," he said.

"Yes, my lord. Do you want him brought to you?"

"Yes. I'll be in the room where we met before."

"Do you wish food and drink, my lord? We can perhaps—"

"That won't be necessary."

Liber found the room and put his torch in a bracket on the wall. Then he sat and waited until one of the guards produced the pontifex.

Tirelius looked worse than he had at their previous meeting—a shriveled, gaunt figure with a single wisp of white hair on his head. He was wearing a thin, dingy white robe. His eyes were bloodshot; his hands trembled.

The guard lowered him into a chair opposite Liber. "Shall I stay, my lord?" he asked.

Liber waved him away.

He stared at Tirelius in the flickering torchlight. Tirelius met his gaze for a moment, and then his eyes slid away, uninterested. "Do you know what is going to happen tomorrow?" Liber asked him.

Tirelius did not respond.

"You will be brought to the Circus Maximus. After the chariot race, you will be led out to the platform where Prince Feslund just crowned the victor. You will then be found guilty of committing numerous crimes against the people of the empire. You will have committed few if any of these crimes, but that doesn't matter. Prince Feslund will then pronounce sentence upon you, and the sentence of course will be death. He will then raise a gant, aim it at you, and, in front of the screaming mob whose thirst for blood has not been sated by the race, he will obliterate you.

"None of them will have seen such a thing before. When it

happens, they will go mad with excitement. But of course you will not experience any of this excitement, because your life will be over."

Liber fell silent. Tirelius said nothing.

"But there is an alternative," Liber said finally. "Come with me. Now. We go upstairs, out of the palatium, then across the forum to the temple. I tell the temple guards that I am granting your last wish, which is to visit Via one final time. They let us inside. But we do not simply stare at Via; we enter it. You take us both to another world. A world where the Gallians cannot follow us, cannot find us. A world where you can live out your life in peace and comfort."

This time Tirelius responded. His voice was a hollow croak. "The last time we spoke you had other ideas," he pointed out.

"Ideas that you rejected," Liber replied. "You wouldn't help the Gallians, so I could do nothing for you. And here we are."

"I wouldn't help, so now you are putting me to death?"

"It isn't me," Liber said. "Our rulers have decided that you are of most use to them if you are executed."

"And you don't agree?"

"I don't care. At this point I simply want to survive. I fear that survival is going to be increasingly difficult in the empire."

"Why don't you leave the empire yourself? Why take me?"

"Because I am not a viator. I only know how to get to one other world. It is cold and alien, and I don't know how to survive in it. Also, I have had to show the Gallians how to get there, so they might be able to track me down if they wanted to. You and I could go to another Roma—a place we both understand—only without the Gallians. Surely you know how to reach such a world."

"Of course I do," Tirelius replied.

"So, you can go to that world and live, or you can stay here and die. Which is it?"

Liber watched Tirelius ponder the choice. He didn't ponder very long. "I will die in any case," the pontifex said. "And I prefer to die here."

"To die tomorrow," Liber said.

Tirelius shrugged. "Dying will be a blessing. You might consider it yourself," he added.

"I am trying to help you," Liber insisted.

"I do not wish to be helped," Tirelius replied. "I wish to die. The

Gallians have granted that wish. I am grateful to them for their kindness. Please take me back to my cell, so I can prepare for my death."

I should have known better, Liber thought. The man would give him nothing. He summoned the guards and watched them escort Tirelius back to his cell. Then he left the palatium and looked across the forum at the temple in which Via hovered, its magic forever unattainable to him.

Like Tirelius, he was doomed to die on Terra.

TWENTY-SEVEN

Carolus

This will not end well, King Carolus thought. What had they achieved, after all? Revenge? Fine, fine, his grandfather had been avenged. At the cost of Carolus's daughter. But now what? After revenge has been satisfied, life must go on. And did they really want this life, in Roma, struggling to hold on to an empire they had no clue how to rule?

His wife did.

Gretyx thought she knew how to rule it: with terror. And perhaps she was right. Perhaps she would succeed. But ah, wouldn't it be better to be back in their palace in Gallia? Under the thumb of the priests, yes, but that was not so bad…life went on pleasantly enough. There were no executions, no heads spitted on poles.

Now they were headed to the Circus Maximus, and more horrors. He sat in the open carriage next to his wife and opposite Feslund, Bathanala, and Bathanala's father. The women held parasols to block out the blazing afternoon sun. Feslund's eyes were bloodshot; he'd been out drinking last night, of course. Bathanala looked frightened, as usual. She was pale but pretty, and she had seemed pleasant enough, the couple of times he had spoken to her. He had tried to reassure her that everything would be all right. But she didn't believe him, he was sure; he didn't believe himself.

Gretyx herself had once been such a bride, given to Carolus when she was seventeen by a nobleman eager to please Carolus's father. She'd had no choice in the matter; neither had he. But she had been dazzling: beautiful and intelligent and totally sure of herself.

He thought sometimes that he had been afraid of her since the day they met.

Now they were traveling through Roma, and crowds lined the streets. Many of the people were cheering; not all. "They love us," Gretyx remarked with satisfaction, waving to the crowd.

Did she really believe that? She had spent countless denarii to buy their love—money she had gotten from Bathanala's father for the privilege of having her marry Feslund. But perhaps she was right. The executions had gone well, he'd heard. Some of the people, at least, were convinced that the Gallians were protecting them from the evil priests. But in truth the only priest the Gallians were protecting them from was a shriveled little man who had been locked away for months and probably wanted only to die.

"It's too hot," Feslund muttered. "I can't believe how hot this city is."

"Don't complain," Gretyx ordered. "Never complain."

Feslund fell silent.

The carriage came to a stop in a plaza outside the Circus Maximus, and they all got out. The heat seemed even fiercer here. Flags hung limply from poles. Soldiers held back the crowds, who shouted and waved. Liber rushed up to meet the carriage, bowing deeply and explaining what was going to happen. Liber was not the worst of the Romans who worked for them. He looked haggard and beset today. He led them past the crowd and into a dark passageway inside the Circus; it was blessedly cool there. "That's better," Feslund muttered.

Bathanala looked as if she were about to faint.

It was only going to get worse for her, Carolus knew. First the chariot race, and then the execution. Perhaps Bathanala liked chariot races; many people did, even young women. Carolus found them dreary and artificial. He, and most other Gallians, preferred the excitement of the hunt. When you were hunting, it was your own body that was at risk, not a stranger's; it was your achievement, your glory when you killed the beast.

Perhaps Bathanala liked public executions as well as chariot races; he didn't think so.

No one asked him if he'd wanted to come to the Circus Maximus, of course. No one asked if he liked chariot races and public executions. It had been assumed; it was his duty. It was Bathanala's duty, as well.

Perhaps they could become friends.

At the end of the passageway, they waited. Feslund went to find a toilet. Gretyx looked annoyed. A fat little man bustled up and conferred with Liber, who apologized to them for the delay. Feslund returned, looking no better. Finally everything was ready. A band began to play. The fat man gave a signal. They walked out of the passageway onto the field—Feslund first, with Bathanala on his arm, then her father, then Carolus and Gretyx.

Carolus had never seen such a crowd. Everyone in Roma must have been here. But it wouldn't do to show surprise, or even interest. They walked slowly, solemnly across the field, as befitted the rulers of Roma and its empire. There were cheers, but perhaps not very loud ones. The charioteers were lined up to salute them; they looked a bit foolish to Carolus in their colored uniforms. A couple of them would soon likely be dead or gravely injured, and one of them would be crowned with glory.

Past the charioteers, the procession finally reached the far side of the field, where they walked up a short set of stairs to their seats, protected from the sun by a purple canopy. "You may wave," Gretyx murmured to the family. They waved.

And then they sat and waited for the chariot race to begin.

Carolus liked to think he was beloved in Gallia. Common folk lined up for the touch of his hand on their shoulder or cheek. Families named their sons after him. His rule was constrained by the priests, who insisted on certain policies, certain laws, but all Gallians agreed that he was just and merciful. And they were astounded and delighted when the news came of Feslund's triumph. Surely life would be even better now!

And for some, surely it was. But he wondered for how long. And he wondered when the love would turn to mistrust, and then to fear, and then to hatred. Because there was no way to rule this empire other than with fear and hatred. And surely it would reach Gallia as well as everywhere else.

The chariots were lined up. The crowd was on its feet. Carolus stood along with everyone else.

Gretyx leaned over to him. "I know you're not interested, but try to look excited," she murmured.

"Yes, my love."

"But not too excited."

"That won't be hard."

Gretyx squeezed his arm. "It will be over soon."

But Carolus was sure that it would not be over soon.

————

Bathanala

Bathanala hated chariot races. She had told the truth to the queen: they were popular in Aquitania. But she had never attended a race; she couldn't bear to see the horses abused. She hated bloodshed; she hated suffering.

There was much that she hated.

She hated Roma: the heat, the people, the wretched smells, the noise.

She hated Gretyx and her son.

She hated her father for selling her to them.

And most of all she hated herself, because she could not bring herself to act on her hatred. She would lie awake at night, imagining her future in this place, with these people, and she would be consumed with anger and dread. She would rehearse things she could do, could say, that would show them who she really was, what she really felt.

And in the morning she would rise, and smile, and pretend that she was content, that nothing pleased her more than the life she had been given.

She assumed that the queen could see through her, could feel the hatred raging beneath her simpering acquiescence. But what did it matter? Let Gretyx send her back to Aquitania in disgrace; let her father rage at her. She would be content.

She was standing, as she was supposed to, as the beginning of the race approached. She clutched the shawl she had been told to wear, despite the oppressive heat. She smiled; she looked mildly excited, as instructed. Occasionally she turned and gazed lovingly at Feslund, who ignored her.

And then the race began.

It was a blur of color and sound: the pounding of the hooves, the roar of the crowd, the charioteers' tunics: blue, green, red, brown… The waving flags, the glistening bodies of the horses, the fierce expressions of the charioteers. Feslund was gripping her arm: too hard. He would leave a bruise. On the track, chariots veered close to one another, then moved away when a collision seemed inevitable. Orange was ahead, then blue, then green. A wheel came off red's chariot, and he had to slow up and pull off the course. One circuit of the track, then another, and another. How long did it last?

Despite her distaste for the race, Bathanala was drawn into it. She found herself rooting for orange. Why? His long black hair? The way he gritted his teeth? She had no idea. *Faster, orange, faster!*

The horses thundered; the crowd roared. Surely orange was going to win—oh no!—blue was coming closer and closer…

And then it was over.

Blue had won; orange was second.

The chariots slowed to a stop. The charioteers climbed down. Men rushed out to take care of the horses. Gretyx applauded, so Bathanala did too, even though she was disappointed that orange hadn't won. Finally they sat down.

"No collisions," Feslund pointed out. "No one was injured. No one died. The crowd won't like that."

Why not? But of course, she knew. Because they were bloodthirsty savages who cared nothing for beauty or grace or goodness. They just wanted their fill of blood and death. They wanted broken limbs and screams of agony.

"This is good," the queen said. "It means that they will enjoy the execution more."

Bathanala smiled pleasantly. She clutched her shawl in the heat and waited for what was next. She wanted to kill Gretyx. She wanted to go home. But she was not going anywhere.

———

Tirelius

They held him in a dark passageway under the Circus Maximus. He was heavily guarded; his hands were bound. No one said a word to him. The soldiers were embarrassed, perhaps. Ashamed. It didn't matter.

How many times had Tirelius been here in better times, waiting as they formed the procession of priests and dignitaries who would then cross the field and take their seats of honor to watch the chariot race?

The crowd would cheer or not, depending on the price of bread and wine or the quality of the acrobats and dancers and musicians who had just performed. But even if they booed, underneath the boos there would be respect, because the priests had brought peace and prosperity to the empire for generations, and no one could imagine a world without them.

Now they had such a world, and he had no use for it. Now they would put him to death, and he welcomed it.

He heard trumpets blaring, the roar of the crowd. The race was over, and Feslund would be crowning the victor, probably some burly fellow from a distant province for whom this was the ultimate achievement of his life. Strangers would buy him meals, women would offer their bodies to him. He would have a happy life. Or not. Perhaps he would sink into degradation and despair and slit his throat some cold gray morning, regretting everything he had ever done.

This too didn't matter. Nothing mattered anymore. Tirelius had lived his life, and now it was over. He had visited many worlds, made many friends and many enemies. He had done what he could.

He found himself praying. Not to the gods—there were no gods; there was no life to come. He prayed to Hieron, who had created all this. *Do not let it die,* he prayed. We have done much good. There are no slaves; the water is clean; wars are infrequent and distant; women can live as equals of men. Don't let the Gallians destroy it all. Don't let the empire return to what it had been before Hieron. We made mistakes, of course. We were human, but we were not evil.

I must die, but Via must not.

"It's time," a gruff voice said.

Someone gave him a shove, and Tirelius started to walk. Slowly— he could go no faster, no matter how much they pushed him. From the darkness and into the light. He blinked his eyes against the light. The crowd roared when they saw him. Roared with hatred and bloodlust.

Tirelius looked down at the dirt, the grass. He did not want to stumble. He saw the platform in front of him. It wasn't far. He looked up at the people waiting there. He recognized none of them except Feslund, wearing a purple robe and holding something in his hand. Ah, he knew what that was.

Could he make it up the steps? He didn't think so. Two soldiers grasped him by the elbows and helped him. Absurdly, he felt grateful to them. When they reached the platform the soldiers stepped aside, leaving Tirelius alone there, facing the man who was going to kill him. The man's eyes were bloodshot. His hands seemed to tremble a bit. *He is frightened*, Tirelius thought. He doesn't know what he's doing. He will never know what he is doing.

Feslund spoke, but it was impossible to hear what he was saying over the roar of the crowd. It didn't matter; Tirelius wasn't interested in what he had to say. He stared at Feslund. *Now,* he thought. *Now. Make it end.*

Finally Feslund stopped talking and raised the gant.

Yes. Now.

Hieron save us all.

TWENTY-EIGHT

Palta

P alta watched him walk slowly across the field, hands tied, to the platform where he would die. Such an old man, pitifully small, so insignificant now. The crowd jeered, but their jeers were half-hearted, uncertain. This wasn't quite what they had hoped for.

Palta hadn't expected to have any sympathy for Tirelius. He had, after all, condemned *her* to die, along with Affron and Larry and the rest. But she couldn't help but feel a twinge of pity for him. Why did so many people have to die?

She shouldn't have come. But still, here she was.

She had been flooded with memories of her previous visit to the Circus Maximus. It had all ended badly, but at first she had been filled with excitement and optimism; she remembered buying a little circlet of flowers for her hair on the way to the Circus—she hoped Larry would think it made her look pretty. There were so few times in her life when she had felt pretty.

She hadn't felt pretty today. She felt tired and lonely and worried. She had walked for hours the night before, searching for somewhere to sleep, finally finding a place on the floor of a large communal room in a wretched inn. She scarcely slept at all, with the heat and the noise and the terror of being attacked.

She knew she should leave Roma however she could, as soon as she could. But first she had to witness the execution of Tirelius.

She didn't know why. After what she had seen yesterday in the Forum she had no love for Feslund and the Gallians, whom she had helped to defeat Tirelius. So what did it matter whether one of them killed the other? It had nothing to do with her anymore.

But still...

She had joined the crowds heading to the Circus. She felt their excitement, their anticipation. Everyone knew what was going to happen. Everyone had an opinion.

"That's what he gets, stealing our bread."

"I never liked him. Or any of those priests."

"There was a good priest, though...what was his name? What happened to him?"

"I don't believe in those magical weapons. That's so much nonsense. If they do kill him, they'll chop his head off, like the ones yesterday."

"That was something, wasn't it? Never seen anything like that."

"Speaking of foreigners, I don't like those Gallians. Especially the queen—she's a hard one. The priests had their faults, but—"

"The priests are stealing our bread!"

Palta made her way into the Circus and, as before, couldn't help but feel awed by it. So many people jammed in one place! The colors! The music! The chanting! The waving flags! The naked athletes running and jumping!

She wished Larry were with her.

Finally preparations began for the chariot race, followed by the slow procession across the field. Last year it had been priests; this year it was the Gallians. She had met most of them—Feslund and Gretyx and Carolus; she thought she recognized a few of the soldiers as well. So strange to see them here.

They took their seats. The chariots were arranged for the race. The crowd's excitement increased. Everyone stood up. Trumpets sounded. Palta felt her heart pounding.

And the race began.

It was absurd. She didn't care about this race! But along with the crowd she, too, was excited. And then she looked at Feslund's bride-to-be, smiling as she gazed out at the chariots thundering by.

She hates this, Palta realized. The race and Roma and Feslund. She was doing her best, but she couldn't hide what she felt. She was terrified.

Suddenly Palta felt so old. She had seen too much, suffered too much. And this young woman—who, surely, was older than Palta—was about to learn what it was to suffer.

Finally the race ended, and the crowd cheered endlessly for blue and whatever province blue represented. Palta remembered last year, with Larry—now, as the pontifex crowned the victor of the race, was the moment when Affron was supposed to use his power to destroy Tirelius. And that would allow Affron to become the new pontifex, which would allow Larry to use Via to return home.

She had wanted so much for Larry to be happy. But she hadn't wanted him to leave. And so when the victor had been crowned and nothing happened, she had felt such relief....

Ah, and at last Larry had left anyway. And Affron was gone too, and Gratius was dead...And she alone of all of them was here in Roma.

Now Feslund had crowned the winning charioteer, and now Tirelius was making his way slowly towards the same platform.

He ascended the steps, with the help of two soldiers, and the crowd started to roar. The crowd wanted death, she realized. They had been denied it in the chariot race, and now they were demanding it.

Now Feslund stepped forward, and he had something in his hand. Something the crowd had never seen before. Something small and hard; bluish-gray metal, impossibly smooth. Oh, they knew what it was, even if they had never seen it. It would bring death to Tirelius, triumph to Feslund.

Feslund seemed to be saying something—reciting the pontifex's crimes, perhaps? He looked annoyed as he spoke. No one could hear him, no one was paying attention to what he was saying, not even Tirelius. What did the crimes matter at this point?

Finally he stopped talking and raised the gant. Was his hand trembling? The roar of the crowd increased. Palta could feel the sound; it was almost painful. She found herself shivering in the heat.

"Occidere! Occidere!"

And then Tirelius was gone.

The roar abruptly ceased. People looked at each other. Was it over? What had happened? They knew what had happened. They had heard of King Harald and his army. But to see it…to see the power of this weapon…

Feslund lowered the gant and simply stood there on the platform, as if he didn't know what to do next.

And then the sound began again—a hundred thousand voices, a hundred thousand men and women screaming out their bloodlust. Where was the blood? They wanted blood!

Feslund turned finally and walked down the platform steps, followed by the rest of the Gallians. They were leaving; the show was over.

But the roaring didn't stop.

And then the fighting began. People were hot and drunk, and they wanted something they had been denied. So they were giving it to themselves. All around her Palta saw men and women screaming at each other, wrestling, exchanging blows. About what? It didn't seem to matter. The fights spilled out of the stands and onto the field. The Gallians, protected by their soldiers, disappeared into a passageway. The chaos had nothing to do with them.

Palta pushed her way through the crowd. People pushed back, snarled at her, reached out to grab her. But she was small and quick and avoided them all. She reached a passageway reeking of piss and stale wine, and she raced through it, out into the plaza that surrounded the Circus. It, too, was crowded, but at least she felt as if she could breathe. It was late afternoon now, but the heat was still intense. She longed for the cleansing thunderstorms that had drenched Larry and her last year as they ran away from the Circus.

She slowed down and looked around. People were walking aimlessly or sitting on the ground, dazed, bewildered, upset. A man stood by a fountain, washing away the blood that flowed down his face. A woman tried to comfort a crying child. The front of a girl's robe had been ripped and, weeping, she had to hold it in place to cover her breasts.

Too many people. Palta was tired of people. She walked away from the plaza. The crowds thinned until there was just one man, weaving drunkenly along a narrow street. She tried to get by him, and he bumped into her as she passed.

"Watch yourself," he muttered. And then he looked at her. "Ah, you're a pretty one," he said. "Why don't you come with me?"

He grabbed her arm. His hand was thick and sweaty. She shook him off.

"Come on, then," he said. "You've hurt my feelings, little one. I can pay you handsomely for your time."

He reached out for her again, and Palta tripped him. He fell heavily onto the cobblestones. "Damn you," he said.

Enough, she thought.

She took out her gant. "Do you know what this is?" she hissed. "This is the end of your worthless life."

The man raised a hand. He knew what it was. He had seen its power in the Circus. "Please," he whimpered. "No." A wet stain appeared in the middle of his robe.

She gestured with the gant. "Go," she said. "Your life is not worth the time it would take to move my finger and destroy it."

The man scrambled to his feet and staggered away.

Palta waited until he had turned the corner, and then she put away the gant. She leaned back against the doorway of a building and closed her eyes. Her heart was pounding. She thought the rage inside her would split her in two. She had to do something.

And she supposed she knew what it was.

TWENTY-NINE

Affron

The land became increasingly barren and rugged as they traveled through it, looking for Tulf. They spoke the word in every town and village they entered, and always the townspeople and the villagers pointed to the east. They provided food for the journey, and shelter if night was falling, but they never spoke to either of them. They didn't seem afraid, exactly, just eager to send them on their way.

Today Affron and Larry had ridden since dawn without seeing anyone or anything. Now the sun was low on the horizon behind them, and the wind was picking up. "We'll have to camp soon," he said to Larry. "The horses are tired."

"I suppose," Larry muttered. Larry always wanted to keep going.

They stopped at sunset next to a brook. Larry took care of the horses. Affron gathered kindling and started a fire. Finally they sat by the fire, ate bread and cheese, sipped bitter ale, and looked up at the stars and the quarter moon low in the sky. It was lovely here, wherever they were.

"Tulf isn't far," Larry said finally.

"I think you're probably right."

"It may not be a place," Larry went on. "It could be a people, a tribe."

"Will they be any more talkative than anyone else on this world?"

Larry smiled. "They will tell us what we need to know."

Affron smiled back at him. Larry was no longer a boy. He was tall and strong and capable. He had done the impossible—as Affron himself had done. "We have come a long way, you and I," Affron said.

Larry nodded. "From a park in Glanbury. In a world with gigantic cell phones. You were giving a sermon. Aimed at me, I thought."

"I used to love giving such sermons," Affron replied. "A waste of time, of course. We were supposed to be gathering ideas for ruling Terra. Always looking for ways to improve the lives of our subjects. But really, no one did that anymore. We knew what worked and what didn't. So I used to go to worlds and say what I was thinking, to whoever would listen."

"I listened."

"Yes. An audience of one."

Larry lay back and looked up at the sky. "Is that the same moon?" he asked. "Or does it change as the Earth changes?"

"Everything changes," Affron replied. "Or can change. The moon, the sun, rocks, birds, history. There appear to be certain pathways... universes that are more probable than others. That is what I'm told, anyway. I never tried to understand such things."

"I tried, after I went home. I studied; I read books. But the multiverse never seemed to make much sense. At least to people in my world."

"Your world is just beginning to understand such things. Other worlds are much farther along. But none have reached final understanding, complete knowledge. That we know of. Truth is always just out of reach. Sometimes much is learned, and then it is forgotten, or misunderstood, or simply disbelieved. Progress is never certain."

Larry was silent. Clouds scudded across the moon. Leaves rustled in the wind. The two of them were utterly alone.

"What do you think is happening on Terra?" Larry asked finally.

"I don't know. Does it matter?"

"You have family there. Friends. Don't you miss them?"

Affron pondered the question. "I should. But this is something that happens to viators. We are taken from our families at a young age. And then we wander too far. We experience too much. We touch the inexpressible immensity of existence. It changes you."

"But your home is your home," Larry said. "Your family is your family."

"Of course. But you found another family on Carmody's world, did you not? The same but different."

"Not entirely the same."

"True. But everything, everyone is always changing. The moon, the stars. You are not the same person that you were when you first stepped into Via. And neither am I."

Larry fell silent. "And now it is time for a new adventure," he murmured finally.

Affron nodded. "And now we change again."

They fell asleep then, and arose at first light. They splashed water from the brook onto their faces, ate more of the bread and cheese, and set out.

They rode through the day. And late in the afternoon they reached a village—little more than a collection of huts, really. A sentry must already have spotted them and brought word, because all the villagers were standing outside their huts, as if waiting to be inspected. They were different from the others Affron and Larry had met on this world: small but thickset, with long black hair and dark eyes. They wore woolen tunics and leather leggings.

Affron and Larry dismounted. A young man ran forward to take care of their horses. An older man walked up to them. His eyes were fixed on the ground, as if he were afraid to look at these powerful strangers. He wore an odd headdress made out of colored feathers. Affron assumed he was the chieftain.

"Tulf?" Larry asked.

The chieftain raised his eyes, smiled, and gestured to the people, the village. "Tulf."

The chieftain then turned and gestured to Affron and Larry to follow him. He led them to the largest building in the village, which turned out to be a single room in the middle of which was a huge fireplace. The smoke from the fire escaped through a wide circular hole in the ceiling; over the fire a pig was roasting.

"They seem to have been expecting us," Larry said.

Affron nodded.

The chieftain gestured for them to sit on thick woolen rugs near the fire. He sat next to them, and it looked like the entire village crowded in behind and around them.

179

Women approached with their eyes lowered, offering bowls fill with a dark liquid. Affron took his bowl, raised it to the women in thanks and took a sip. It was some kind of fermented grain—hot, earthy, and very powerful. He set the bowl down. He noticed that Larry had done the same thing. "Drinking the whole thing would probably kill us," Affron murmured to him.

Then the feast began in earnest. Everyone drank from the bowls. Serving women carved up the pig and heaped up plates of meat and vegetables on polished wooden platters, which they placed around the fire. People reached out and took what they wanted from the platters. At first everyone was silent, but as the feast progressed people began talking and laughing, and finally singing. Their language was harsh and guttural, but Affron found their singing surprisingly tuneful.

After the singing stopped half a dozen young girls came forward and performed an intricate dance to the accompaniment of drums and an odd-sounding three-stringed instrument. They were charmingly serious as they worked their way through the steps. At the end everyone cheered. Affron and Larry cheered too, which seemed to delight the children, who broke into smiles and hurried off.

And that seemed to be the end of the entertainment. The drinking continued. The fire died down. Men and women settled back on the woolen rugs; some were already starting to snore. Finally Affron left the building to pee. Night had fallen; he couldn't make out a latrine or an outhouse, so he simply relieved himself against a nearby tree. When he had finished, he heard a girl's voice, speaking softly in the darkness nearby. He turned. He could make her out by the starlight. She was standing by herself, facing him. Was she speaking to him?

She repeated what she had said.

"I don't understand," Affron replied. "I don't speak your language."

She said something else.

"I'm sorry, I don't—"

"Est non procul," she said this time.

And that he did understand. Latin. *It's not far.*

"What?" he asked in Latin. "What is not far?"

She paused for a moment, as if considering. "Hoc quaeretis," she said finally. *The thing you seek.*

"Can you take us there?"

"Possum." *I can.*

And then she ran away into the night.

Affron thought about following her, but instead went back inside the building. Inside, Larry was already asleep; he had drunk more of the liquor than he should have. Affron spotted the chieftain, who was sitting against a wall in the shadows of the hut. He couldn't tell if the man was staring at him. Did he know about the girl? Had he sent the girl?

Affron lay down next to Larry and closed his eyes. It was always difficult understanding other worlds, other societies. You think they are doing you a favor, and it turns out they are trying to kill you. Or vice versa. But he thought—he hoped—that he understood what was happening here. A ritual of sorts. A ritual that had taken place before. Many times? He didn't think so. But often enough, perhaps, for that girl to learn Latin. And to learn how to take them where they wanted to go.

Affron gave up pondering the situation finally and drifted off to sleep.

When he awoke, Larry was gone from the hut, as was the chieftain. Affron made his way outside through the sleeping bodies. It was just after dawn. Larry was standing in the narrow path that led through the center of the village. He was staring off into the distance, to where the sun was just peeking over craggy highlands.

"There," he murmured, gesturing at the highlands.

"I spoke to a girl last night," Affron replied. "In Latin. She knows the way."

Larry nodded, as if this didn't surprise him. "Then let's find her."

They walked through the village. Smoke was rising through the holes in the roofs of the huts. A baby cried. A dog barked. People who saw them looked down as they passed.

The girl was waiting in the corral where the horses were kept; the chieftain was with her. Affron hadn't seen her clearly in the night, but he knew it was her. She was slighter than other women in the village, but with the same black hair, and her dark eyes radiated intelligence. She had reached womanhood, but just barely, with small breasts visible under her tunic.

"Can she come with us?" Affron asked the chieftain in Latin.

The girl spoke to the chieftain, who made a brief gesture towards the highlands in reply.

"Possum," the girl said to Affron.

"Eamus," Larry said. *Let's go.* He went over to his horse.

The girl raised a hand. "Relinque equos," she said. *Leave the horses behind.*

"What about our food? Our supplies?" Larry asked in Latin.

The girl shook her head. "Et relinque." *Leave them also.*

Larry looked at Affron, who nodded. Then the chieftain dropped to his knees in front of the two of them, murmuring something that the girl didn't bother to translate.

"Gratias tibi," Affron said. *Thank you.*

The chieftain seemed to understand.

The girl ignored him and strode out of the corral. Affron and Larry hurriedly followed.

She headed east along the rutted path, towards the rising sun. Affron tried asking her questions: What is your name? Where are we going? How do you know Latin? But she didn't respond. Larry was silent.

What awaited them up ahead? Affron didn't know, but he remembered when he was back on Terra, and Scotia pulled him ever northward until finally he spotted a barren hill, indistinguishable from a hundred others, and thought: *here.* Why?

The girl was moving quickly. They could have travelled much faster on horseback. But of course horses could not clamber up the kind of hill he had been drawn to in Scotia.

The morning was chilly, but the exertion quickly warmed him. He wanted to go faster, he realized; he wanted to run. All his life, he thought, had been pointed towards this. "It is finally happening," he said to Larry.

Larry didn't respond, but Affron knew that he, too, was excited.

They travelled several hours without a break. Affron was tired and hungry. It was beginning to seem like a mistake to have left their food behind. The path had disappeared, and now they trudged through high grass and crossed a narrow stream.

"Mox," the girl muttered. *Soon.*

They made their way through boulder-strewn ground until they reached a long rocky slope heading up to a plateau. A hawk soared overhead. The sun was high in the sky now. The girl gestured up to the top of the slope. "Ibi." *There.*

They stood in silence for a moment, and then the girl abruptly said, "Eo." *I go.* And she turned as if to leave them.

"Wait!" Affron commanded.

She turned back obediently.

"What can we do for you? What can we give you?"

The girl paused, and then she knelt in front of them as the chieftain had done. "Benedictio tua," she whispered. *Your blessing.*

Affron looked at Larry, who shrugged his agreement. Affron reached down and put his hand on her head; then Larry did the same. The girl seemed to shiver beneath their touch. Finally they removed their hands, and she stood up. "Gratias tibi," she murmured, and then she walked quickly away.

They watched her go, and then they turned and started up the slope.

It was hard work. Affron was exhausted now. Larry was younger, but even he looked weary as they scrambled upwards, grasping on to stunted trees and seeking footholds among the loose rocks.

Occasionally Affron spotted a footprint in the ground. Others had scrambled up this slope before them.

Finally they made it to the top. Affron stood up; his knees were scraped and sore. He looked around. They were on a wide, barren, windy plain.

Empty. Nothing. His body ached. The wind whipped against his face.

He felt a stab of disappointment, but then he recalled the hill in Scotia. Empty. Nothing. And he had built Via there. He had left Terra from there, leaving his Via behind for Larry.

"It's here," Larry said.

They stood up and walked forward. Nothing.

Until suddenly there was something—a force pushing back against them. Not the emptiness of Via, into which you could step and then travel to another world. Just a transparent nothingness, with no way in or through.

They followed it for fifty paces perhaps, probing it, pushing against it. Whatever it was, it was far larger than Via.

Finally they stopped and stared into the nothingness. "What do we do?" Affron asked.

Larry didn't reply for a long time, and then he said, "I know how to get in."

THIRTY

Decius

Decius walked out of the meeting in the afternoon, worried and discouraged. The rebel general, whose name was Hippolytus, and the admiral, Eukippus, seemed unable to agree on anything, starting with who had ultimate command of the rebellion. And meanwhile the days passed and the soldiers grew restless. They could not stay in this port town forever. They needed to attack before winter. They needed to defeat the Gallians before the Gallians figured out how to defeat them. The strategy was obvious to Decius, but they were dismissive of his ideas. What battles had he ever won?

He strode across the plaza, heading to his cramped room in an inn on the waterfront.

It was then that he heard the woman calling out to him from the other side of the plaza.

He stopped and looked at her as she approached. She was young, with blond hair and gray, intelligent eyes. "Yes?"

"My lord, are you Governor Decius?"

She spoke Latin with a slight accent that he couldn't quite place. "I am," he replied, "although I am a governor no more. Who are you?"

"A friend of the viator Affron, whom I think you know."

He stared at her, puzzled. She met his gaze. "How do you know Affron?" he demanded.

"May we speak in private?" she asked, gesturing at the people passing by.

He shrugged. "Come, then," he replied. He led her to the inn. His room was on the third floor; in it, Corscius was writing at a table. "Please leave us for a while," Decius said to him.

Corscius glanced at her with curiosity and then stood, bowed, and left without a word.

Decius took his place at the table and pushed the papers aside. She sat opposite him. The room was hot, but at least a cool breeze blew in through the open window. They were in Misenum, a port town on the great sea. It was the right place for the rebels to be, if they could decide what to do next.

"Your name?" he asked.

"Palta, my lord."

"And how do you know Affron?"

"I was one of the people Tirelius was seeking last year, along with Affron and the others. The ones who escaped from Urbis."

"You and Valleia and the boy," he said.

"Larry Barnes, yes. You met Larry in the Circus Maximus, when Affron did whatever it as that he did to you. Larry and I were separated from the others and ended up in Gallia. We were with Feslund when he and his men took Urbis. Then we left to find Affron. We finally tracked him to Scotia. But Affron had already left Scotia and gone someplace else—I don't know where. Larry went after him. I do not think either of them is coming back. But I returned to Roma, and from there I came here to Misenum."

The tale was told so simply, so quickly. Here, sitting opposite him, was the girl who had helped the Gallians and then disappeared. Had he heard her name before? He didn't think so. "Why did you come to Misenum?" he asked.

"I helped to destroy the priests," she explained. "And that was a mistake. Now I want to destroy the Gallians. So I need to join your rebellion."

Decius recalled Liber's obsession with Affron. Had he tried to track him down and kill him? "We knew that Affron went to Scotia," he said. "The Gallians may have sent someone to find him. So he could be in danger."

"He is not in danger," Palta replied. "Not from the Gallians, at any rate. And they did send someone. I killed him. With this."

She reached into the pocket of her robe and took out a small metal object that gleamed with a strange blue light.

He stared at it.

"You know what it is, I think," she said.

"I do," he said. And it terrified him. She was young, but her gaze told him that she was capable of using the thing. He thought of her accent. "You are not from Terra," he said finally. "You and the boy."

"That's right—I see that you understand such matters. In fact, I'm from the world where the priests obtained these awful weapons. But that doesn't matter. I live here now. I want to help Terra. I want to help the rebellion."

"But you helped the Gallians," he pointed out. "Why have you changed your mind about them?"

"I never cared about the Gallians. Larry and I just wanted to get back to Via so he could return to his own world. Now I have seen what Feslund and his mother are doing to the empire. They need to be stopped."

Decius nodded. "They do need to be stopped. Would you kindly put that weapon away, please?"

Palta put the gant back in the pocket of her robe.

"Thank you. You say you come from the world where the priests obtained these weapons. How much do you know about them?"

Palta shrugged. "I don't know how to make them, if that's what you're asking."

"No, no. Of course not. I'm told that the weapons lose their power eventually. Do you know how long this takes?"

"It depends on how often you use them."

"What if you don't use them?" Decius asked. "What if they are sitting in the armamentarium in Urbis?"

Palta recalled talking about this with Gratius. "The world where I lived is called Gaia," she said. "Viators would have to return to Gaia every couple of years to restore the power of the gants in Urbis. And those gants weren't being used at all."

"Yes, I see."

"The Gallians can't find any viators, can they?" Palta said. "They've all disappeared."

"That was the situation when I left Roma. I doubt that it has changed."

"Without any viators to bring the gants back to Gaia, the weapons will lose their power, and the Gallians will no longer be able to use them. So that's good news for the rebels. The Gallians can't rule by lies and fear forever," she said. "Eventually they can be beaten."

"I hope you are right." Decius sighed. He stood up abruptly. "It is too hot in here," he said. "Let's go outside."

They went down into the streets of Misenum. People hurried by. Women carried woven baskets on their heads. Couples held hands. Children skipped and laughed. A cloud passed over the sun. They walked along the waterfront. Finally they stopped and looked out at the dozen or more ships moored in the harbor.

"You have a lot of ships," Palta remarked.

"We do," Decius agreed.

"I hear that you may attack Roma before long."

"Where did you hear that?"

"I'm a serving girl at a tavern. The soldiers talk."

"The soldiers know nothing."

"So you're not going to attack Roma?"

"Would you?" Decius asked.

Palta considered, and then shook her head. "Not while the gants still have their power. It would be like King Harald all over again."

She was a smart girl, Decius thought, although the answer should have been obvious to anyone with a brain.

"But you probably can't maintain an army for a couple of years while you wait for the gants to run out of power," she went on. "And there is always the chance the Gallians will find a viator who will help them."

Yes, she was certainly a smart girl. "Soldiers need purpose," he said. "And they need to be paid. Otherwise they'll just drift away."

"So what will you do?"

Decius shrugged. He wasn't going to tell her their plans—such as they were.

They fell silent. The girl looked worried. "Can my gant help you?" she asked.

Decius found himself liking her. And believing that she wanted to help. "Perhaps," he said. "But do not tell anyone you have this weapon.

Or that you are from another world. Or that you helped the Gallians defeat the priests. But I expect that you understand these things."

"Of course I do. But how can I help? I won't just hand my gant over to you. And I don't expect that I'll be made a legionary."

He considered. "Join my staff," he proposed. "It may be boring, but it will surely be better than working in a tavern. We will find a way for you to help us."

"What is your role, my lord?"

"That is to be determined, along with much else. Our military leaders understand that they will need civilian administrators at some point if they are successful. I am the best they have."

"Larry spoke highly of you."

Decius tried to remember him. He recalled being doused with water in that room beneath the Circus Maximus, but little about the boy who had doused him. "I am grateful for his praise," he said. "So, will you join me?"

"Yes, of course," she replied. "What will I do? I know nothing of civilian administration."

Decius nodded. "Now would be a good time to learn. Come, let's find Corscius and get started."

THIRTY-ONE

Larry

Larry probed the invisible field with his hands, with his mind. It pushed back against him, but not completely. It felt as though he and the field were two magnets with the wrong ends aimed at each other. If only he could get the ends lined up right, he and the field would snap together.

Or something.

So he needed to turn his mind backwards, or inside out. Make it positive instead of negative, or vice versa. Maybe the metaphor didn't make any sense. He didn't know how to turn his mind inside out.

Here was another metaphor. This was a portal, except it was locked. To open it, you needed a key, a combination, a password.

Yes, that was better. A password.

After a while it came to him. Well, something came to him.

He placed his hands on the field, and he filled his mind with thoughts of home. Earth-home. Arguing with Cassie. Playing video games with Matthew in their room. Riding his bike with Kevin. Making Christmas cookies in the kitchen with his Mom, listening to carols on the radio. Tossing a football to his Dad in the backyard. Oh, and wait: there he was playing the piano for Professor Gardner in Carmody's version of Earth; there he was with that world's version of his father and mother, a simple farmer and his wife who had buried their son once and then saw him magically returned to them. Oh, how could he have left them?

And there was Palta, gazing at him in the colonnade after the chariot race in Roma, as the rain poured down and his dream of returning to Earth had been destroyed.

Home.

He felt the field give way.

"Let's go," he said to Affron. He held out his hand. "Take it," he said.

Affron grasped his hand, and they walked inside.

———

They were in a garden. A rose garden—roses of every type and color, lining a narrow dirt path. His mother had a couple of rose bushes in their back yard, but they barely managed to bloom every summer, despite all her efforts.

"Looks like we're in another world," Affron murmured.

"It's a beautiful one," Larry replied.

They set out along the path. It wound through the garden, and eventually the roses gave way to other flowers, most of which Larry didn't recognize. Not that he had ever spent much time studying flowers.

Eventually he saw someone up ahead—an old black man wearing a wide-brimmed straw hat, baggy green pants, and a loose gray tunic. He was on his knees, weeding. They approached him. He looked up, squinting against the sun. "Salve!" he said in oddly accented Latin. *Welcome!*

"Salve!" Larry and Affron replied.

"Who are you?" the man asked.

"Um, we just arrived," Larry said.

"But there are two of you," the man pointed out, looking perplexed.

"That's right."

The man appeared to ponder this, and then he stood up. "Well, it makes no difference, of course. You are still welcome. My name is M'Nasi."

Larry and Affron introduced themselves.

"Where did you come from?" M'Nasi asked.

Affron explained.

"Very good," M'Nasi said. "Very good. You have no idea how you got here, but here you are. That's as it should be. Let's take a walk."

He led them further along the path. They passed a vegetable garden: Larry didn't recognize most of the vegetables. Then they went through a patch of woods. In among the trees they saw a brown-haired woman sitting on the grass, her legs crossed, her eyes closed.

Her hands were making motions in the air.

"Well, that looks familiar," Affron murmured.

"I expect that it does," M'Nasi replied.

"Does this world have a name?" Larry asked.

"It has many names," M'Nasi said. "So many that I can't remember them all. Some of us call it *Elysium*."

The word was familiar to Larry, but he couldn't quite place it.

"Have we died?" Affron asked.

M'Nasi smiled. "You are very much alive, my friends. And you are young. That is good."

Once they came out of the woods, Larry saw two- and three-story stone buildings in the distance. "Almost there," M'Nasi said. "Many people to meet."

They walked into what seemed to be a small town. The streets were made of cobblestone, but there was no traffic. The first person they saw was an old man sitting on a bench, staring straight ahead and trembling slightly. "This is Jubal," M'Nasi said. "He doesn't speak, alas."

"Why not?" Affron asked.

"Ah, there is much to learn, much to explain," M'Nasi replied.

Which explained nothing. On the bench next to Jubal sat a bearded man wearing a ragged olive-colored Grateful Dead t-shirt. Larry found this very strange. The bearded man was reading a book; Larry didn't understand the title on its cover. The man lowered the book as they approached and smiled at them..

"You're new here," he said. He, too, spoke Latin with an odd accent, though different from M'Nasi's.

Larry and Affron nodded.

"And two of you!" he pointed out, just like M'Nasi. "That is excellent."

"This is Rigol," M'Nasi said, and he introduced them.

"Nice t-shirt," Larry said, in English.

Rigol laughed. "You are the first person who has ever said such a thing," he replied, also in English.

"Are you from Earth?"

The man shook his head. "I am not. But some art transcends the world on which it was created, don't you think?"

Larry considered. "You're joking, right?"

Rigol laughed again. "I think we'll get along well. Come, let's visit Amelia. She is probably indulging in some sort of healthful exercise. Amelia is very irritating that way. In her favor, she likes to make people feel at home here in Elysium."

"I will sit with Jubal," M'Nasi said. "Best not to leave him alone."

Rigol rose and led them across the street to a stone building with a black door.

They went inside and found themselves in a large, high-ceilinged room, with a fireplace to their left and open windows ahead of them looking out into yet another garden. A woman was doing pushups in front of the windows.

"Salve, Amelia," Rigol called out. "We have new arrivals. Two of them."

She smiled and leapt to her feet. "Wonderful!" she said. She grabbed a small towel from a chair. She was tall and, Larry thought, beautiful, with dark eyes and long brown hair tied back in a ponytail. Although she spoke Latin, she was wearing Earth-like exercise clothes —black workout pants, a blue tank top, and running shoes. She wiped her face and arms with the towel as she walked over to them. She held out her hand.

Larry shook her hand and introduced himself. She had the gaze of a viator. The combination of her beauty with that gaze was a bit overwhelming. He glanced at Affron as she turned his gaze on him and shook his hand; yes, he felt it too.

"I expect they're tired and hungry if they came to us through the world of the Tulf," Rigol said. "Also curious and perhaps frightened, although how they could be afraid of you or me or M'Nasi is beyond me. Why don't you bring them to Lucia's café, feed them, and start the explanations? I will find them lodgings. There are empty rooms in the building next to mine. They should do while we sort things out."

"And Jubal?"

"M'Nasi is sitting with Jubal. His roses can wait."

Amelia smiled. "Come then, Larry and Affron. Let's get started."

She led them back outside, and the three of them walked through the streets of the town. They met more people. All spoke some form of Latin; all were surprised that there were two of them; all of them made Larry feel at home. "Has everyone here—you know—built a portal?" he asked Amelia.

"Via. Portal. Gateway. Mystical connection to all that is," she replied. "Yes, we are all quite different, but this is what we have in common."

"And you used your portal to come here?"

"Through the world of the Tulf, yes. We don't make it easy to get here, I grant you. But we have our reasons for that."

"It seems very peaceful," Affron noted.

"If you don't like peace, you don't stay in Elysium."

Eventually they reached an open-air café, with small tables scattered around a brick patio. Two women sat at one of the tables. One of them stood up as they approached. "New arrivals, Lucia!" Amelia called out.

Lucia was a stout middle-aged woman with frizzy black hair turning gray. She wore a flowing blue suit covered by an apron. "How delightful!" Lucia exclaimed. And she gave them each a hug.

The woman next to her didn't rise, didn't look at them. She was younger than Jubal, but like him she stared straight ahead; her hands didn't tremble, but her eyes were watery, as if she were on the verge of crying. "This is Veronique," Lucia said, gesturing to her. "She doesn't speak, but she is glad you're here as well. I'm sure."

"I expect our guests need to be fed," Amelia said to Lucia.

"Of course! That's why I'm here. Where are you from? Perhaps I have foods you will enjoy."

"I grew up in a world called Terra," Affron said.

Lucia's eyes widened. "Terra! Ah, that is interesting. So, you know Roma? Urbis?"

"Yes, very well. Are you from—?"

"No, no. I know *of* it, you see. We know of many worlds here. Anyway, I have bread I baked this morning, cheese, olives, wine, lovely tomatoes…I'll be right back."

Lucia bustled off into the café. Veronique's gaze didn't follow her, but she looked distraught after a moment, as if she sensed Lucia's absence. Amelia took hold of her hand, and she calmed down. Larry wanted to ask about her, but he decided it wasn't right to do that in front of her. There was plenty of other stuff to learn. So he asked Amelia the first question that came to mind. "How many people live here?"

"It's hard to say," she replied. "A couple of hundred, perhaps. Once you have found Elysium, you can come and go as you please, without having to travel through the world of the Tulf. Some people find Elysium rather boring after a while; other feel that it is the haven they have been seeking all their lives. There are no rules or rulers here. We do what we want to do. And we support each other." Amelia glanced at Veronique as she said this. "It is a lovely place."

"Is Elysium separate from the world of the Tulf?" Affron asked.

"It is in that world, but we control Elysium—its climate, its resources. People far smarter than I am created it long ago. It is quite small, but suited to our purposes. If we wanted to make it larger, I suppose we could figure out how."

"We knew that we needed to go to the world of the Tulf, even though we'd never been there before," Larry said. "And then we figured out how to enter Elysium. How did we know these things?"

Amelia shook her head. "Some of us spend our lives pondering such questions, but I don't think we have satisfactory answers, any more than we have an answer for why we can build portals."

"What is your story?" Affron asked. "How did you come to be here?"

"Ah, my story isn't interesting. Like most people here, I had no idea that I was building a portal. It was a compulsion that came over me in my twenties. I wasn't spiritual; I wasn't interested in science. I was supposed to finish my schooling, perhaps get married, have children. I had no time for sitting alone and using my mind in strange ways. But I had to make the time; it was a compulsion. I expect it was the same for you. Before long, nothing else mattered. And then, at last, it happened, the portal was there—I had spun it out of nothingness. And I walked through it, into another world. My own world hadn't any conception of a multiple worlds, so I had no idea what had happened to me. I thought at first I had gone to heaven—are you familiar with the idea of heaven?"

Affron and Larry both nodded.

"But the world I ended up in was nothing like either heaven or hell," Amelia went on. "It was just…different. It was a wildly confusing experience at first. I started exploring. And I couldn't stop. I was so excited. I wanted to tell everyone. I wanted to bring my friends with me. I wanted to become rich and famous."

"But you did none of those things," Affron said.

"No, of course not. Those who try to use the portal to become rich and famous do not end up in Elysium. Or, they learn their lessons and change before they are destroyed. Then I thought: I will use the portal to improve my world. Bring back the wisdom and knowledge I discovered in my travels. Many of us have tried this. But it is always harder than we expect. Much, much harder. It was impossible for me. I am not especially clever. I am a woman, and that counted against me in my world. I was ignored; I was laughed at; friends left me; my family sought help for me."

"It made you unhappy," Affron said.

Amelia smiled. "It makes everyone unhappy, Affron. Each in his own way, for his own reasons."

"But you found this place," Larry said.

"I did."

"Do you ever return home?"

She shook her head. "For me, Elysium is home."

Lucia returned then with a platter of food, a jug of wine, and cups. "Now you must eat and tell us about yourselves," she announced, sitting down next to Veronique.

The food was delicious. Affron and Larry then told their stories. They seemed wildly strange to Larry, but Amelia and Lucia simply nodded in sympathy. "Every story is different," Lucia said, "and every story is the same."

"You were lucky you had a friend to help you," Amelia said to Larry.

"I'm beginning to realize that."

Larry couldn't help noticing the way Amelia gazed at Affron while he spoke. Perhaps she thought that Affron was in fact different.

When they had eaten their fill, Lucia shooed them away. "Go and settle yourselves," she said. "But come back whenever you like. Many of us congregate here as darkness falls. It is a good time to eat and drink and talk about the day."

So Amelia, Affron, and Larry left her with Veronique and walked back to the center of the town. "Lucia is lovely," Amelia said.

"Is everyone lovely here?" Affron asked.

Amelia shrugged. "I wouldn't say so. I wouldn't call Rigol lovely, I suppose, although he is quite entertaining. And there are those who have been…damaged."

"Like Veronique and Jubal?" Larry said.

"Yes, and many others."

"What damaged them?"

"It is hard to explain, if you haven't experienced it. Not all of us have. This power of ours—this ability to create portals—has a way of projecting itself out of you and into other people. And in that instant, both of you feel all that is or could be—all of this in a single instant. Some people do not recover from the experience. Their minds are destroyed—at least, they are no longer able to communicate with us or care for themselves."

Affron and Larry glanced at each other.

"Well, I see that you know what I'm talking about," Amelia said.

"I'm afraid so," Affron replied.

"If you have done this, then I beg you, do not do it anymore. The danger is too great. You will see people like Jubal and Veronique throughout Elysium. We care for them, we love them, but we cannot cure them. We cannot bring them back."

They fell silent for a moment. Larry recalled the instant that he had first used this power—on the old woman in the temple of Via—and he shuddered at the memory. "I wonder how many people have done this and didn't end up here," he said.

Amelia nodded. "Yes, they may be dead, or living out their lives in darkness, on a world not their own, cared for by someone who has no idea what is going on in their minds. We have no way of knowing. But here is Rigol. Let's see what he has done for you."

They were on a side street near the center of the town. Rigol sat on the steps of a two-story building. As before, he was reading his book. He looked up as they approached.

"Did your book distract you from your task, Rigol?" Amelia asked with a smile.

"It did not," he replied, with a hint of indignation. "Come see what I've done."

They followed him inside the building and up to the second floor. A small corridor separated two doors. Rigol opened the door on the left. It was empty except for a bed on one wall, a sink and toilet on the other, a table with an oil lamp on it, and a wooden chair. On the bed was a pillow, a blanket, a blue shirt, and a pair of black pants.

"Two rooms, very similar," Rigol said. "This one is Larry's. For the clothing, I guessed at your sizes. If the clothes don't fit or you don't like the style, come visit me next door. I have a large stock of clothing, along with much else. People here make fun of me, but if they need a new pair of boots, they know where to go."

"We couldn't survive without Rigol," Amelia said.

Rigol bowed to her. "Thank you, my lady," he replied.

"Also, if you don't like these rooms," Amelia told them, "if you want more space or more privacy, there are other places where you can live. Or we can help you build a new home. Whatever you like."

"No electricity and that sort of thing, of course," Rigol added. "But we do have public baths on the south side of town. Very refreshing."

"And now we will leave you," Amelia said. "I expect you have much to ponder. Come to the café tonight and meet more of us."

"Thank you both," Affron replied.

And with that Amelia and Rigol left them. Larry sat on the edge of the bed; Affron sat on the wooden chair. "Well, here we are," Affron said. "Home at last."

Larry recalled how he had found his way into Elysium: thinking about home.

But was this really home? Was this where he was supposed to be? "Everyone is very nice," he replied.

"Amelia is the most beautiful woman I've ever seen," Affron said.

"She's stunning."

"I wonder—" Affron began, then stopped. "We have much to learn about Elysium," he said instead.

"There's a lot to learn about everything." Larry suddenly felt very tired. "But first I want to take a nap."

Affron smiled and stood up. "It's been a long day. Let's meet later and walk over to the café."

"Of course."

Affron left the room, and Larry lay back on his bed. It was comfortable enough. He would try the new clothes later. Elysium was utterly silent. How many worlds had he visited? It felt as though he might be losing track. Was this the end of his wandering? Was this home?

And then he recalled the hollow eyes of Jubal and Veronique, and he shuddered. It was good that he had found people who understood him, who would take care of him. But he didn't want to end up like Jubal and Veronique.

He closed his eyes. After a while he must have dozed, because he was awakened by a soft knock on the door. It was growing dark, and he realized it was time to return to the café. "Come on in," he called.

The door opened, but it wasn't Affron. It was a white-haired old man, wearing shapeless pants and a ragged blue top. His eyes looked sad. He seemed vaguely familiar. Had Larry seen him on the street? No, that wasn't it...

"You are the young one, then," the man said in Latin. "Larry."

"That's right."

"And your friend—Affron?"

"Across the hall," Larry replied.

"Ah," the man said. "Come with me if you would, Larry. Let's go visit Affron."

Larry rose from his bed and obediently followed the old man. They crossed the hall, and the man knocked on Affron's door. After a moment they heard Affron's voice from inside. "Enter," he said, in English.

The man opened the door, and Larry followed him into the room.

Affron was sitting in a chair by the window. He stared at the man, who didn't speak. Affron looked puzzled, and then a very different look came over his face. He stood up, and then he dropped to his knees in front of the stranger.

The old man inclined his head and smiled. "Salve, Affronius," he said. "Nomen mihi est Hieron."

Hello, Affron. My name is Hieron.

THIRTY-TWO

Affron

Every town in the Roman empire had a statue of Hieron in front of its temple. In most of these statues he leaned forward, his hand outraised, as if striving to see the future and lead his people safely into it. His likeness was on the empire's coins; it was drawn in the empire's schoolbooks. He was the humble peasant to whom the gods had given Via. He was the man who had used Via to bring back the secrets of the gods, for the betterment of all the people of Terra.

His followers had conquered the empire through the force of their ideas, and Terra had become a better place. And then he had disappeared. The gods had called him to them, it was said. His job on Terra was done.

The priests knew this was not true. Hieron had stepped into Via one day and had not returned. Many viators did not return from their visits to other worlds; there was always danger in those visits. Hieron hadn't been summoned by the gods; he had caught a disease, or been eaten by a tiger, or struck by lightning.

But...but...here he was, standing in this room, two paces away from Affron.

"Come, come—arise," Hieron said.

Affron got slowly to his feet. "It is you," he whispered.

"It is."

"How? How are you here? How are you alive?"

"Ah, you have not been told everything about Elysium, it seems."

"People don't die here?"

"Oh, we all die eventually. But the passage of time slows for us. I cannot explain it, any more than I can explain many things I have seen and experienced. Lucia told me you were from Terra, and that excited me. It has been many years since I was there."

"You left Terra when you found this place."

"I did. It was time. I had done what I could for Terra. I had no more to offer. Best to let others carry on."

Affron made a connection. "You saw the problems coming."

"You mean, arguments about weapons and medicines and such? Yes, I had my opinions about such things, but I could not convince everyone. And tell me: did the problems come?"

It seemed strange and troubling that Hieron did not know. "They did, my lord. It has been years now since Larry and I left Terra. But things were not going well in the empire when we left, and I doubt that they have improved since then."

Hieron sighed. "I tried. It was never easy, but…You must tell me the story, of course, but not now. I don't think I could bear it just yet."

Affron had another insight. It should have been obvious to him, ever since the first time his hands made motions in the air, but here was the truth of it, standing in front of him. "You always said that you discovered Via on that hillside outside Roma," he said, "but that wasn't what happened, was it? You created Via, the way I created my own Via and Larry created his. Out of your mind. Out of yourself."

"Yes, that's right," Hieron replied. "And then I tried to use it to help people. I thought it would be easier for them to accept it if they thought it came from the gods. I visited many worlds, made many decisions about what would work and what would not. All I wanted was to help. I like to think that I did."

He looked upset. And that upset Affron. "My lord, you helped many millions of people," he said. "Your memory is sacred on Terra. You did not fail."

"In the end, Affron, everyone fails," Hieron replied. "Time is a long, long river, and we are just ripples in its current. Eventually all those ripples disappear. But I think perhaps you know that."

Affron thought perhaps he did.

"Come," Hieron said. "Let's go to the café. You have many people to meet, and we have much to say to one another."

So they left his room. The night was lovely; probably every night was lovely here. He couldn't stop staring at Hieron—alive! Walking next to him and talking about Lucia's pasta! Ah, life was beyond strange.

But when they arrived at the café, Affron found himself staring at Amelia instead. Her hair was down, she wore a simple yellow dress, and she was lovelier than the night. She came and sat next to him. "I didn't realize your connection to Hieron," she said. "Lucia just explained it to me."

"He is like a god in my world," Affron replied.

"He doesn't speak of it, at least to me. But it's good when we can do something for others with our powers."

"We struggled on Terra to do the right thing with the power Hieron gave us. How we struggled."

She reached out and covered his hand with hers. "No need to struggle anymore," she murmured.

They talked till late at night. He met many people, heard many stories about many worlds. He finally told Hieron about Terra; he was troubled by what he heard but not surprised. Affron ate too much of Lucia's food and drank too much of her wine, but that didn't matter. It was glorious.

And after it was over, he walked with Larry back to their rooms.

"What an amazing world," Affron said.

Larry didn't respond.

"Are you all right?" he asked.

"I don't know," Larry said. And then he added: "I'm not sure I belong here."

"Why not?"

"I'm so much younger than everyone. The people are wonderful, but do I want to spend *forever* with them?"

"You can leave and come back whenever you like," Affron pointed out. "I was talking about this with M'Nasi. People build their own portals in the woods—we saw someone doing that. You don't have to go through the Tulf now that you're here."

"I suppose." They stopped in the street outside their building. "Maybe I don't belong anywhere," Larry said.

"You're tired, Larry," Affron said. "You've been here less than a day. Your life is changing too fast to make sense of it. Don't try. Not yet."

"Okay. But when? When do I try?"

"I don't know. I'm not the right person to ask. Ask Hieron, or Rigol, or Lucia. Any of them. They will know how to adapt."

"I don't want to end up like Jubal or Veronique."

"We must be careful of that, of course. It never felt right, using my power the way I did."

Larry looked at him in the moonlight. "Amelia likes you," he said.

Affron felt absurdly pleased at this. "Well, I like her," he replied. "We have a lot in common."

"She's a reason to stay here."

"Yes, I suppose that's true."

"I miss Palta," Larry said.

Palta. Affron scarcely thought of Palta anymore. "She must be... older," he said. An obvious thing to say.

"If she's still alive," Larry pointed out.

"Yes. Of course."

But Larry changed the subject. "I miss my family back on Earth," he said. "I miss my mom and dad, I miss my brother and sister. I miss French fries. I miss playing the piano."

"Of course."

"I miss that other world you saved me from—the one with Lieutenant Carmody, and Professor Gardner, and another version of my family."

"Yes, I remember," Affron said. "Leaving that world was a hard choice for you to make."

"I even miss Kravok-Li. The food. The stupid pots and statues. The happy people."

"The food was terrible," Affron said. "But I understand."

"I was thinking about all this this afternoon, when we were trying to get into Elysium. I think that's how I got us in. It was something they expected."

"I wonder who 'they' are," Affron remarked. "Who created this place? How? There's so much we don't know."

"I wouldn't have found it without you," Larry said. "I owe you so much. You've given me years of your life."

"I didn't want you to suffer the way I suffered, trying to figure this out. It was good to have a partner on the journey."

"And I'm so very grateful."

This, too, please Affron. He felt a pang of sympathy for Larry. He had felt many pangs of sympathy for him over the years. And for himself. "You're free now," he pointed out. "You can do what you want. There are many more things to learn, I suppose, but you know how to learn them."

"Haven't I always been free?" Larry asked.

"Have you felt free?"

Larry shook his head. "Not for a long time."

"Let's get some sleep," Affron said. "All will be clear in the morning."

Larry laughed. "Not likely."

They went inside the building and prepared to spend their first night in Elysium.

THIRTY-THREE

Amelia

Amelia and Affron walked together in silence through the woods. Weeks had passed since he had arrived in Elysium, and they did this every day now. When they tired of the silence they talked about their pasts and their struggles. They had so much in common—everyone in Elysium had much in common, it seemed—but so much was different, as well. She had grown up in a world with an advanced technology and collapsing governments. Constant wars loomed over everyone's lives, even as people lived in comfort. And he had lived on Terra, the world that Hieron created! So strange to view that world—and Hieron—through Affron's eyes. Amelia had never heard Hieron say much about what he had done on Terra, although surely he had talked about his past with Lucia or M'Nasi or one of the others. But now everyone knew how much Hieron had struggled to improve his world, and the ways he had ultimately failed. It was sad.

Much about Elysium was sad, she often thought. Not just because of Jubal and Veronique and the others like them, the constant reminders of the danger their powers presented to each of them...no, beyond that, there was a sense of sameness about the place. Increasingly she found herself traveling to other worlds, just to see what they were about. Of course, there was danger in doing this, but so what? You had to live your life.

But she had felt no desire to use her portal since Affron arrived. He, of course, loved Elysium, loved the absence of danger, loved being able to live with others like him. That was common with new arrivals here. She sensed—she knew—that they were kindred spirits. For Amelia, Affron had made Elysium enchanting once again.

They stopped by the brook that gurgled through the woods. They sat on its bank, took off their sandals, and put their feet into the water. They had done this often. Affron placed his hand on hers; as usual, his touch made her shiver. She squeezed his hand and pressed it onto her thigh.

"I was in love once," she said. She hadn't mentioned this before.

"Should I be jealous?" he asked.

She smiled and shook her head. "It was before I understood myself, before I started to build a portal. I was unhappy, and I thought Friedrich was the solution."

"But he wasn't."

Amelia shook her head. "He was wonderful, actually—kind, funny, generous. He tried so hard to please me, to understand me. But that turned out to be impossible."

"So you left him behind?"

"I did. I left many people behind, of course—as you did, as all of us here did. I think of them, once in a while. But Friedrich more than most. He was wonderful, but I needed a different life. I found it here."

"Do you ever think of going back to your world?"

"No, not seriously. What would it accomplish? And everyone I loved might have died in some horrible war. That's likely, in fact. I don't want to find that out."

They fell silent yet again. And then Affron said: "I'll try to be like Friedrich. Except I'll be sure to understand you."

Amelia laughed. "You certainly have a head start." And she leaned over and kissed him then. And nothing had ever felt sweeter.

"We are going to be a wonderful couple," Affron said after the kiss.

"I'm sure of it."

———

Hieron

Nothing had been the same for Hieron since Larry and Affron arrived.

This was good in a way. It was good to feel unsettled, even worried. Good to help the newcomers. It made him feel useful. It made him feel alive. Still…

As always, he discussed matters with Lucia.

"Everything I tried to build on my home world has been destroyed, it seems," he said as he wiped down the tables for her.

"You don't know that," she pointed out. She had heard Affron's story, and she had strong opinions about it. She had strong opinions about everything. "Affron has been gone for a long time, helping Larry build his portal," she pointed out. "Anything could have happened while they've been away. All may be well on Terra now."

"That's not likely, though, is it?"

Lucia shrugged. She was feeding Veronique, who wasn't cooperating. "Then go back and find out," she said. "Nothing is stopping you. Many of us return to our home worlds."

"Most of us don't, though. I can't go back. It's been too long. It would be too painful."

"Then stop complaining about it."

"But I enjoy complaining about it."

Lucia wiped Veronique's chin and fed her another spoonful of oatmeal. "Well, as long as you're enjoying yourself," she muttered.

"It's strange that it all started on Terra because Larry *wanted* to go home," Hieron said. "He needed to get back to Via, and he ended up overthrowing the government I had created. And then he decided *not* to go home."

"That is strange," Lucia agreed. "I like Larry, though. Don't blame him. He is still young. He was even younger when he did this."

"I like him, too. And I don't blame him. But I worry about him."

Lucia looked concerned. People mattered to her, not worlds, Hieron knew; she was more interested in Larry than in the fate of Terra. "Larry is young to be here," she repeated. "It would have taken him far longer to build his portal and find us if Affron hadn't helped him. Look at how old you were when you arrived."

"Yes, I know. But I was busy."

"He doesn't have to stay, of course."

"But he doesn't know where to go," he pointed out.

"Then he's just like all the rest of us, poor dear."

"What should I do? What should I tell him? He likes to talk to me."

"Then you must listen," Lucia said.

"I'm good at that, at least."

Lucia smiled. "I need another towel," she said. "You keep feeding Veronique."

She bustled off into the café.

Hieron picked up the spoon and got Veronique to swallow some oatmeal. "What would you tell Larry?" he asked her.

But Veronique, as always, did not reply. Instead her eyes stared off into the distance, and she kept her thoughts to herself.

————

Larry

Life on Elysium was not going well. He should have been happy, but he wasn't. Everyone was wonderful to him, but it didn't seem to matter. And it shouldn't have mattered that Affron had fallen in love right away and was spending all his time with Amelia, but somehow it did. He had spent years with Affron, and now he was…gone. Not physically gone, of course, but less interested in him. For Affron, this was his final destination, what he'd been searching for all his life. For Larry, it was…what?

He didn't know. But it wasn't his final destination.

Larry found himself spending more time with Hieron than with Affron. Hieron didn't mind talking to him about Terra and Earth and Kravok-Li, didn't mind hearing his memories and regrets and worries. He didn't have much advice to offer, other than to give things time. Which was fair enough, but of course it solved nothing—it was the kind of advice that Affron used to give to him. It meant that he had to find answers inside himself, not have them handed to him by someone else. So every day he would wake up and think: *have I given it enough time?* And it would turn out that he hadn't.

And then one day he had.

He and Hieron were walking through the woods when they saw Mollia—a thin, black-haired woman—seated on the ground and making those familiar gestures in front of her. "Mollia is building a portal," Larry said.

"Yes, she is," Hieron replied. "I'm surprised she hasn't built one before this. Let's leave her alone. One does not interrupt someone building a portal."

They walked on. Finally Larry stopped and looked at Hieron. "It's time, isn't it?" he murmured. "Time to build my own portal."

"Yes, I think it probably is."

"I'm not good at it," Larry pointed out. "I've only built one, and that took forever. I never really learned how to control it—you know, the way you could control Via. Figuring out my destination and so on."

Hieron shrugged. "You've mastered the hard part," he replied. "The rest will come to you. You will get plenty of advice, if you need it."

"Where do I do it?"

Hieron gestured vaguely at the woods. "Choose a spot. The woods are big enough if you want privacy. But go somewhere else if you like. You won't be in the way."

Larry looked around and made up his mind. "I'll do it here."

Hieron nodded. "That's fine. And I will help however I can."

That was settled, then. There was just the one remaining question. When he finished the portal, where would he go?

THIRTY-FOUR

Palta

Palta won the battle of Alexandria.

She didn't mean to; she hadn't expected to. She had spent the voyage from Misenum below decks, seasick and ignored. Decius liked her, but he had given her little to do, and everyone assumed she was his concubine and resented her for taking up space on the fleet's flagship.

Alexandria was the capital of Egypt and its most important port. The rebel leaders had finally agreed with Decius that conquering Egypt should be their first objective. Roma survived on Egyptian grain. If the rebels could take Egypt, Urbis would be brought to its knees. They hadn't expected much opposition; that turned out to be a mistake.

Palta made her way onto the deck to see what was happening as they approached the city. The empire's fleet was arrayed at the entrance to the harbor. "Not good," Corscius muttered, coming up next to her. "There's far too many of them." She spotted Decius and Hippolytus arguing with Eukippus, the admiral of the rebel fleet. "Hippolytus and Decius want to turn the fleet around," Corscius explained, "but the wind's shifted."

"So we'll have to fight?"

Corscius nodded. "I expect so."

Corscius was holding a sword, she noticed.

The enemy vessels began to approach; rebel soldiers shot flaming arrows towards their sails, without much effect.

Palta watched the ships as they approached. The soldiers on the flagship were holding their swords; the sailors were bringing out grappling hooks and ladders. She heard Eukippus shouting orders, the whizzing of arrows, the lap of water against the ships. The sky was cloudless; the day was hot.

Decius came up to her and Corscius. "Eukippus thought we could surprise them," he said. "They do not look surprised."

"Shouldn't the flagship be behind the line?" Corscius asked.

"Eukippus doesn't want to look like a coward, apparently."

"Are we going to lose?" Palta asked.

Decius shrugged. "I do not like our chances."

She felt the gant in the pocket of her robe.

"I can improve our chances," she pointed out.

Corscius looked puzzled; Decius did not.

She did not want to do this. But what choice did she have? "Should I?" she asked Decius.

"I did not expect things to happen so quickly," he replied. "I thought we could save it."

"You need to tell me," Palta insisted. "I cannot do this on my own."

He sighed. "Can it sink a ship?" he asked.

"I think so."

"Then yes, you must use it, I suppose."

Palta took out the gant and waited.

"What is that thing?" Corscius asked, staring at the gant.

"It is Death," she replied.

A ship neared them. Palta could see the faces of the men onboard —dark, bearded, confident. A couple of them spotted her, pointed, and laughed. They shouted lewd comments to her. Was the ship close enough? She thought so. She walked to the railing and steadied herself, Then she squeezed the handle of the gant.

A hole opened up in the side of the ship, and water began pouring in. The laughter stopped. A bitter smell filled the air.

She shot again and again, and the ship began to list. Men jumped over its railing into the water. Men on the flagship stopped what they were doing and watched her. A cheer went up as they realized what was happening.

"What's this?" Eukippus demanded, coming up to them.

Palta ignored him. She sprinted towards the port side of the ship, where another ship was approaching. The men made way for her. "Let 'em have it!" one of them shouted. She could see the sailors and soldiers on the enemy ship, now terrified instead of laughing. They moved back when they saw her, but it didn't matter. She simply shot again and again at the ship itself, and it began to disappear underneath them. In moments what was left of it started to sink, and those men fell into the water, flailing helplessly.

Palta hated the water, and she began to hate the gant and what she was doing with it, hate the sight of men drowning in front of her. She wanted to destroy the empire, but she no longer wanted to kill anyone. And how many more deaths would be required?

The gant was warm in Palta's hand. She noticed that Decius was still beside her. She held the weapon out to him. "You do it," she said. "It's not hard, but I am sick of it." And then she turned and vomited on the deck.

But little more needed to be done. Decius sank one more ship, and then the rest of the enemy fleet turned and fled. The battle had been won.

Palta sat and closed her eyes. People crowded around her, but she ignored them. The rebel ships headed into the harbor of Alexandria. She disembarked as quickly as she could.

The enemy troops had pulled back, leaving the city to the rebels. It was agreed that Hippolytus would pursue the soldiers; Eukippus would pursue the remaining enemy ships; Decius would stay behind to administer the city. Meanwhile Palta was a hero, but she didn't care; she just didn't want to kill anyone else.

But first she had to answer the general's questions about the gant. No, that was the only weapon she possessed. No, she wouldn't tell him who she was or how she came to have it. No, she wouldn't give it to him. Or, rather: Decius possessed it now. What he did with it was up to him.

Decius shrugged. "It will do you little good," he said to Hippolytus. "We've used it too much. It is cold in my hand. Its power is weakening."

Hippolytus seemed not to understand. He was not very clever, Palta thought. "I saw its power on the ship," he pointed out.

"The power does not last," Decius replied. "It is the nature of the weapon."

"Can we not…do something to increase its power?"

"No, my lord," Palta replied. She was tired of this. "Give him the weapon," she said to Decius. "Let him use it as he wishes. He will discover the problem."

Decius shrugged and handed it to him. Hippolytus seemed delighted to hold it in his hand. Palta recalled how Feslund had looked when he had first held a gant back in Gallia. "We can defeat the empire with this," Hippolytus said.

"No, you can't," Decius replied. "The empire has its own weapons, which they are sure to use once they find out what happened in this battle. We are in as much trouble as ever."

"Our troops will be a match for them. But I must hurry. I leave the city in good hands."

Decius bowed to the general. "I thank you, my lord."

Later Palta stood with Decius and Corscius in the main plaza of the city, outside its massive library, guarded by a small squadron of troops. They looked around at the city they would rule.

"It is a great city, a great country," Decius said. "We have started well, but still we face many difficulties."

"Gretyx will use her gants now," Palta said. "She'll have to."

"And Hippolytus and Eukippus are both fools," Corscius added. "You are the only competent leader we have."

Decius did not disagree with him.

Palta found herself looking at the library. She was fascinated by the idea of a building filled with books. "I don't think I've ever seen a such a place," she said.

"It is the largest library on Terra, I believe."

She felt a twinge of longing. There was so much to learn. She could scarcely read. She had never read a book. Did that matter? Perhaps not. "We must protect the library," she said.

"Of course," he replied. "But there is much else to be done."

———

Olef-Nan

Olef-Nan looked out her window at the plaza below. "I see some of the rebels down there," she said to Menander.

"Yes, my lady," the young man standing behind her replied. "What are they doing?"

"Nothing. Talking. Looking up at us."

"Maybe they love books," Menander suggested.

No one loved books more than Menander, so it was a natural guess for him. "Doesn't seem likely, does it?" she replied.

"Well, the priests—"

"Don't speak of the priests," Olef-Nan said sharply.

"Sorry, my lady." Menander wanted nothing more than to keep her happy.

"It's all right," she murmured. She turned away from the window and walked back to her office, a little room on the top floor of the library. Menander followed her, awaiting orders. But she had none for him. There were always tasks to be completed, but the tasks didn't matter if their new rulers didn't care about the library.

What the new rulers should do, of course, was leave the library alone. For centuries it had stood on this spot—before the priests and after them—the center of learning for the empire and beyond. Why would anyone want to change this? Just let the people here do what they knew how to do—collect the books, care for them, teach people about them. What higher calling was there than this? What greater service to humanity?

"My lady..." Menander began.

Olef-Nan waved him away. "It's all right," she said. "Go home. Nothing more will happen today."

"Yes, my lady." Menander bowed and departed, leaving her to her thoughts. She knew nothing of the people who now held the library's fate in their hands. The rumor was that they were disaffected generals seeking to overthrow Gallian rule. Olef-Nan had no love for the Gallians. But did the rebels seek to re-establish the rule of the priests? Or did they just want power for themselves? Was the empire returning to the old days, when generals endlessly battled each other for supreme rule, with no concern for the suffering of the people—or for the knowledge contained in books?

If so, she feared that chaos would result. And chaos was what she feared most. It was when the world was in chaos that the library was at most risk. Who cared about books and manuscripts when there was no food and no law? Better a dictator than anarchy.

And then, of course, there were the priests.

That night she paid a visit to Lamathe.

THIRTY-FIVE

Larry

L arry set to work.

It didn't seem any easier, to begin with. You built it out of your very being, step by step, only to see it collapse like a house of cards if your concentration wandered or your confidence failed. You dreamed it, but then the dream dissolved with the snapping of a twig or a sudden memory. You moved your hands through space, but the movements felt rehearsed, unnatural. You groped for something, but it was just out of your reach, somewhere you couldn't go.

The first day, he failed. And the second. And then he began to lose track of his failures.

People were sympathetic, understanding. Each day Lucia left a plate of food beside him in the woods. He never heard her come. He worked till after dark, as he had on Kravok-Li, then wandered back to his room by starlight, exhausted and perplexed.

"Why can't I use someone else's portal?" he asked Hieron. "Like on Terra."

"No, Larry, you need to do this yourself," Hieron replied. "There are things that only a creator can do with his portal. Don't worry. It will come."

And he knew that Hieron was right. Even if he could use someone else's portal, he wouldn't want to.

And after countless days and nights, it began to take shape, as it had before—an extension of his mind, an endless dream of endless worlds, a gateway to the multiverse, this time in the woods of Elysium.

When he thought it was complete he stood in front of it, alone in the dusk, in the silence.

He stepped into it and through it.

He was standing on a rocky shoreline looking out at a gray, swirling sea. The sky was overcast. Nearby, a few bearded men stood outside a tent, staring at him. They wore thick robes and brown headscarves. Curved swords gleamed in their hands. They pointed at him and shouted in a language he didn't understand. He didn't respond. Then they started walking towards him.

Well, this wasn't Glanbury; this wasn't the Earth he knew. Larry stepped back into his portal, pulled it out of this alien world, and returned to Elysium.

It was time to get some advice.

He made his way to the café, where people had already gathered for dinner. They were delighted to see him.

"It's done, then?" Hieron asked him.

"Yes, but I don't know how to use it. How do I go where I want to go?"

"Ah, it will come to you with practice."

"How do I make sure that I arrive in the world I'm going to at the same time I leave Elysium?"

"You will arrive when you want to arrive."

He should have expected this kind of response. No one seemed to disagree with Hieron, so it seemed that this was the best advice he was going to get.

"Where do you want to go, Larry?" M'Nasi asked.

"Home," he replied. It was the only answer that made sense.

"You mean Earth?" Affron asked. "Your Earth?"

And that was the question that needed to be answered, wasn't it?

"Yes," he said. "My Earth."

"It's been a long time," Affron pointed out.

"I know." He closed his eyes and felt tears pressing against his eyelids as he thought about how much time had passed, how much his family had probably suffered because of his disappearance.

"Going home is hard, Larry," Amelia said. "I could never do it."

"But you must do what your heart tells you to do," Lucia added.

"You'll need clothes," Rigol pointed out. "You can't go home looking like that," he said, gesturing at the white tunic and loose red pants Larry was currently wearing. "I have the right kind of clothing, if you think you need it."

"Yes, okay, that would be helpful."

And so it began to become real.

The next day he went to Rigol's rooms, which looked like they belonged to one of those hoarders Larry had once seen on a TV show. The place was jammed full of books, clothes, and assorted junk. Even the narrow bed was covered with stuff. Where did he sleep? "You could move into a bigger place, couldn't you?" Larry asked.

"Yes, I suppose I could," Rigol replied, as if this were the first time the idea had occurred to him. "Really, though, I should just clean this place up. But I never seem to get around to it."

You have absolutely nothing to do all day, Larry wanted to point out. But he didn't. Rigol was wearing his Grateful Dead t-shirt. Larry realized that he'd never seen him wear anything else. He was a refugee from a world where people thought he was a sorcerer and had wanted to burn him at the stake. That could affect a fellow, he supposed. Rigol's hands shook a little as he searched for clothes. He seemed amused by the difficulty he was having in deciding what he could spare.

"What about these?" Larry asked, grabbing a pair of faded, paint-stained khakis. "Can I borrow these?"

"Of course. But be sure to bring them back—I've been meaning to wear them."

Rigol would never wear them, Larry suspected. He tried them on. The waist was too large, and the legs were too short. But they would do. He found a t-shirt that look like it was for the American tour of another rock band. But he didn't recognize the band's name, and he only recognized a couple of the cities on the tour. Perhaps it was from another Earth? The shoes were too big; the socks had holes in them. But again, they would do.

"If you happen to come across a Milli Vanilli t-shirt on Earth, kindly bring it back for me," Rigol said.

"Sure thing." Larry had never heard of Milli Vanilli. "Why do you have all this junk, by the way?"

Rigol shrugged. "Because I have a psychological disturbance, perhaps? I'm definitely not normal, I will grant you that. But then, none of us here are especially normal."

"I can't disagree with you."

Later that day, Hieron helped him practice with his portal.

"Earth is there, in your mind," Hieron said. "We have all spent a lot of time understanding such things. But it is impossible to describe them with words."

"It was misty inside Via," Larry pointed out. "I thought there was a control panel you could use to set your course."

"It was an illusion I created for Via," Hieron replied. "The viators needed to be trained. The controls were an aid in their training."

"OK, but when I found the portal on Earth, I just walked into it and came out on some random world. I don't want that to happen now."

"We will make sure it doesn't, Larry. You need a different kind of training than viators had. Because you are now much more than a viator."

And so Hieron led him through his portal into and out of world after world, until Larry began to sense what he needed to sense. It took him a long time to understand what he was doing, but nowhere near as long as it had taken him to build a portal in the first place.

"Shall I go with you to Earth, to make sure you arrive safely?" Hieron asked.

Larry shook his head. "I want to go by myself," he replied.

"I understand. I'm sure you won't have a problem."

He decided to do it the next day. He slept badly, and in the morning he went to the baths and then put on Rigol's clothes. Several of his friends walked with him into the woods—Affron, Amelia, Hieron, Lucia, Rigol. It felt like a procession, he thought.

He was nervous. What would he say? How would he act? How would he explain where he had been all this time?

Would he ever return to Elysium? Would he ever use his portal again?

Larry stopped in front of his portal. He looked around at the others. They looked back at him with sympathy, with understanding, with love. He hugged each of them in turn. "Thank you," he whispered.

And he walked into the portal.

It was misty inside, as usual. There were hints of objects just outside his field of vision. But that was an illusion, his mind trying to make sense of where he was.

He took a step, another step. And Elysium disappeared.

THIRTY-SIX

Ploterus

The first thing Ploterus noticed as he rode up to Roma was the human heads on spikes above the gates to the city. A dozen of them, perhaps, men and women, wizened and pathetic-looking. He glanced at the officers traveling with him, but they seemed unconcerned. They had witnessed enough horrors that something like this wouldn't bother them.

It bothered him, though.

Tomorrow he would be meeting the woman who had ordered those heads displayed there.

He and his men made their way into the city, dusty and tired after their journey from the north. Ploterus had never been to Roma before, and he didn't like what he saw: the streets were dirty and crowded, the people were sullen, the buildings large and pretentious. Ah well, he hadn't expected anything different. And he didn't expect to be here long.

They made their way to a barracks near the center of the city, where he dined with Gregorius, the general in charge of the legions in the Roman province. Gregorius was white-haired and rheumy-eyed; his hands shook, and he leaned on a stick when he walked. He looked as though he wouldn't survive the winter. He was happy to finally meet

Ploterus. "You have done wonders keeping the German tribes under control," the old man said. "We are most grateful for any good news from our armies in the north."

"Conditions are bad in Roma, I take it."

Gregorius shook his head. "Alas, yes. Bread must be rationed, taxes are high, and our legions are undermanned. But we carry on."

"Do you have any idea why I've been summoned to Urbis?"

Gregorius smiled wearily. "You are our savior, don't you see? You are from Gallia, and you were friends with Prince Feslund. You are trusted."

"I wasn't quite friends with him, but I knew him of course," Ploterus replied. "I was in charge of the garrison in Massalia when he and his mates showed up looking for ships and men for his attack on Urbis. I was dubious about the attack, of course, but no one asked my opinion."

"No matter. You have been successful where others have failed. And that is what we need."

"Prince Feslund has failed in Egypt, I've heard."

"Yes," Gregorius said. "Things did not go well for him there, even with his magical weapons. The rebels are still in power, and the grain does not arrive. Queen Gretyx was displeased, as you may imagine."

"Queen Gretyx is the real ruler here, I take it," Ploterus said.

"Ah, we don't say such things out loud. But that is the truth of it."

Ploterus had always liked King Carolus, as every Gallian did. But Queen Gretyx had always seemed cold and distant. She enjoyed power, and she'd had precious little of it in Gallia. She had it here, though, if she could hold onto it. "Will the queen send me to Egypt?" he asked.

"Without a doubt," the general replied.

"Do you think I should go?"

"I don't see that you have much choice, I fear. A competent general with enough men should be able to defeat the rebels, I think. In any case, going to Egypt will keep you away from Roma. You should stay as far away from Roma as you can. It's harder for them to kill you when you're a thousand miles away."

"You're here in Roma. Are they going to kill *you*?"

"Oh, no, I'm old and feeble. I'm no threat to them. But you are. You are popular and successful. The queen is neither at the moment, and she will see you as a threat. Go far away, my friend, and stay there."

Ploterus inclined his head. "I thank you for the good advice."

Gregorius bowed in return. "These are difficult times," he replied. "I pray that you survive them."

The next day Ploterus went to the baths early, put on his best military robe, and rode to Urbis. He was pleasantly surprised by the reception he got—soldiers lined the road in Inner Urbis and saluted him as he passed. Was Gregorius behind this? Or perhaps even Feslund? In the old days a victorious general returning to Roma would have been accorded a triumph—a parade, a feast, a crown of olive leaves. Those days were long gone, but he would take what was offered.

"A moment, general?" a soldier murmured to him after he had dismounted. The soldier wore Gallian blue and looked familiar.

"Cymbian?" Ploterus guessed. A companion of Feslund's if he recalled correctly.

"Yes, my lord. The same."

He shook the man's hand. "You look well," he said. The man didn't, actually. He looked hung over, unshaven, and worried.

"My lord, there is no time to speak, but you must save us," Cymbian said. "I don't know who else will."

"Save you?" Ploterus asked, confused.

"Save all of us. It's gotten very bad, general. You must know that."

This was strange. Was it a trap? He wouldn't put it past Gretyx to test his loyalty. But Cymbian didn't look like the kind of fellow you'd use for that sort of thing.

"Well, Cymbian, we must all do what's best for the empire," he said.

Cymbian seemed to consider this, and then he shrugged and walked away. Ploterus went into the palatium to meet the royal family.

Carolus looked tired and thin—feebler than Gregorius, it seemed. Feslund looked annoyed. And Gretyx—ah, she had the same cold, appraising stare she'd had back in Gallia. He bowed deeply to each of them. Carolus embraced him. "So wonderful to see you," he said. "You have given us good service in the north. We are very proud of you."

"Thank you, my lord."

He too will not last the winter, Ploterus thought. And he thought: everyone and everything here is dying.

They sat down to an elegant luncheon; at least Ploterus was being well fed. Afterwards Carolus retired, needing to rest, and Ploterus was left with Gretyx and Feslund. Feslund had drunk too much wine at lunch and looked very unhappy.

Gretyx got directly to the point. "We need to retake Egypt," she began.

"Yes, my lady," Ploterus replied.

"We cannot survive without it," she went on. "The grain shipments are vital."

He knew all this. "Yes, my lady," he repeated.

"Besides the grain, the rebels are now emboldened. Before long they will invade Italia. As things stand now, we will not be able to resist such an invasion."

This statement puzzled Ploterus. "My lady, forgive me, but do you not still possess those magical weapons—the weapons that defeated King Harald so long ago?"

Gretyx and Feslund exchanged a glance. Ah, that glance was interesting! "I am about to tell you something," Gretyx said to him. "You are forbidden to repeat it to anyone."

"Of course, my lady."

She folded her hands on the table. "We had such weapons, but they no longer work. They have lost their power."

This statement confused Ploterus. Of course, he knew nothing about such things. "Lost their power?" he repeated.

"We knew this would happen eventually, but it has taken place faster than we expected. Prince Feslund took some of them with him to Egypt, but they proved to be ineffectual."

"Can't you, uh, obtain more?"

"To do this we must find a viator who will cooperate with us. So far, we have been unsuccessful."

"This is not what I understood," Ploterus said carefully. "In the north, we always wondered why—"

"Now you understand," Gretyx replied. "We must defeat the rebels the way you defeated the German tribes—with swords and spears and arrows. With superior strategy and overwhelming force. And with fear. And we want you to lead the army who will defeat them."

"I heard a rumor that the rebels had one of those weapons," he pointed out.

The queen shrugged. "They apparently used a single weapon in their initial attack on Alexandria. How they got it, we do not know. They used it to great effect, sinking three of our ships. After that, we

223

have little evidence of its use. It is likely that it has lost its power as well."

Ploterus considered. This was good news, he supposed. He knew how to fight wars with swords and spears and arrows. He did not know how to fight them with magical weapons from Via.

"Very well, my lady," he said. "I will go to Egypt. And we will win the war without the weapons."

The queen's expression relaxed. "Thank you" was all she said in response.

"I know nothing of the strategic situation in Egypt," he went on. "I will have to discuss this with Prince Feslund. But I expect that the rebels will have trouble recruiting more soldiers. We must raise an army large enough to crush them."

"We also find it difficult to recruit soldiers, as you well know," Gretyx pointed out.

"We must pull legions from the north," he said. "The tribes on the borders are less dangerous than the rebels at this point. We must scour the countryside for every able-bodied man. And we must do it quickly, before the rebels gain the courage to attack."

Gretyx nodded. "Yes, very well. Talk to Feslund. Determine the number of men you need. We will see that you get them."

Ploterus inclined his head to her. "Thank you, my lady."

Gretyx left the room then to check on Carolus, leaving Ploterus alone with Feslund. The discussion with Feslund was difficult. He was defensive, argumentative, and not altogether coherent. "We can't defeat the rebels in Egypt," he insisted.

Of course, this was what someone who had lost to the rebels would say. "It seems that we must try, my lord," Ploterus murmured.

"Alexandria is impregnable if properly defended," Feslund insisted.

"Then we will attack them elsewhere."

"Hippolytus is a wily general. His soldiers trust him."

"Any general can be defeated, my lord. You were unlucky, I'm sure. Every general risks defeat in the face of events he cannot control."

"Yes, yes, of course. You too may well fail."

"I will need your help, my lord."

This seemed to make the prince feel better. He finished his wine and pushed the cup aside. But he wasn't ready yet to discuss Egypt any further. "Remember that night in Massalia, Ploterus? All of us staying in your barracks before we sailed to Urbis?"

"It was unforgettable, my lord."

"Ah, I had dreams back then."

"We sit here in Urbis," Ploterus pointed out. "Your dreams have come true."

"I do not wish to sit in Urbis," Feslund retorted. "I hate Urbis. We are going to build a palace in the Forum, did you know that? To be nearer to my people."

"I did not know that, my lord." This seemed to Ploterus like an extraordinarily foolish and wasteful thing to do while the empire was in grave danger, but it was not his place to say so.

"And I'm married now, of course. I will be a father soon."

"Yes, I heard about your marriage. Congratulations, my lord."

Feslund played with his empty cup. Ploterus found himself feeling sorry for him, which was an odd emotion. How did the prince end up being so unhappy? And, of course, how had he managed to lose the war in Egypt? He had been trained—better than Ploterus, perhaps. And Hippolytus was not a wily general, he knew. From all accounts, the man was barely competent.

Ploterus was the youngest son of a poor farmer in Gallia. He had entered the army only because the family farm wasn't big enough to support him along with all his brothers and sisters. The army wasn't a glamorous, or particularly dangerous, occupation under the priests—its role was mainly to protect the borders from occasional raids, and to dissuade foreign powers from considering an invasion. Until Feslund conquered Urbis, Ploterus had never even been in battle. He expected to live out his life in Massalia or someplace like it, a competent administrator, a man who accomplished whatever he was asked to do. But then suddenly the Gallians ruled the empire, and there were threats on all sides, and the royal family needed military men they could trust.

And now Ploterus knew that he had a talent for war—a talent that Feslund apparently lacked.

"My lord," he said, "I must learn everything you know about Egypt and the rebel army. And I need to know how many men I'll need to defeat the rebels. We cannot delay."

"Yes, yes, of course," Feslund replied. And finally they got down to work.

This would not be easy, Ploterus decided after a long afternoon of discussion with the prince. But of course it could be done.

Many men would die, but he was going to retake Egypt for the empire.

And as he began his planning, he thought of Cymbian's plea: *Save all of us.*

Could he do that as well?

THIRTY-SEVEN

Larry

L arry stepped forward, out of the portal, and the mist turned to snow.

What?

He looked around. He was in the woods. It was cold, and snowing lightly. He looked down. His shoes were buried in white.

He hadn't thought about the weather on Earth. He had assumed it would be the same as on Elysium, but why would that be true? Why hadn't anyone pointed this out to him?

He should just turn around, return to Elysium, to his friends, who would still be standing in the woods. Get a jacket and hat from Rigol, perhaps some boots.

But he didn't go back. He couldn't go through this again. He had made his decision, and he would put up with a little discomfort. He started walking.

He didn't recognize where he was. Somewhere in that conservation land behind his house in Glanbury, maybe. Or perhaps he had screwed up, and he was in some random forest in some random world. At least he could follow his footprints in the snow back to the portal—unless the snow got heavier and covered his tracks. He kept going.

This was stupid, he thought after a few minutes. A horrible mistake.

How far should he walk before he gave up? Maybe he was in Glanbury but headed in the wrong direction. Or maybe he was in some other world and wolves were watching him, waiting to attack. Maybe he'd get frostbite.

He trudged on, shivering and worried.

And finally he saw a jungle gym. *Their* jungle gym. *His* jungle gym. Oh, the hours he had spent playing on that thing! And beyond it, a house. His house. He started to run. Into the yard, past the jungle gym, up to the back door.

And he stopped.

What was he going to say? How was he going to act? Years had passed. Would they even recognize him? He had obsessed about this, but he had decided nothing.

All he knew was that he missed them so much.

He turned the knob. The door was locked. His heart thumping, he knocked.

No answer.

He went out to the driveway. There was a car parked in it, covered with snow. He didn't recognize it: an SUV of some kind. They wouldn't have the same car, of course. He went around to the front of the house and up the steps. The front door, too, was locked. He rang the doorbell over and over. No answer. Should he break in? Why not? He couldn't just stand here in the snow.

Then he noticed the mailbox next to the door. He opened it and took out the mail. Bills and magazines and circulars. He read the names on the address labels.

Mr. and Mrs. Charles Rossetti

The Rossetti Family or Current Resident

Ms. Lauren Rossetti

Gail Rossetti

He dropped the mail and went over to the bay window looking into the living room. He pressed his face up to the glass and stared inside. The furniture was different. The piano was gone. He saw photos on the wall: images of smiling faces that he didn't recognize.

His family didn't live here.

Maybe this was another version of Earth, and they had never lived here, and he had never been born. No, he was sure that wasn't true. This was the right world. This was the right house.

His family had moved away. That was the obvious explanation.

Why wouldn't they? He had disappeared without a trace. Why would they want to stay here and be reminded of that?

He had destroyed their lives.

So now what? He sat on the Rossettis' front steps and let the snow fall on him.

Destroyed their lives. They could be living in California now, or Canada. His parents could be divorced; Cassie could be an addict; Matthew could have dropped out of high school. Anything could have happened.

They were gone.

He stood up finally and walked away. Down the street and past the houses he knew so well. The McKenzies and the Gabbards and the Hitchcocks and the Bergsteins. There was the basketball hoop where he and Jimmy Hitchcock had played one-on-one. There was the big maple tree he had climbed with Jimmy, terrifying his mother when she spotted him. Did Jimmy still live there? Did anyone of their friends and neighbors still live where they used to live?

He kept walking. He didn't feel the cold now. He couldn't seem to feel anything, except a kind of numb dizziness. Maybe he would end up like Jubal or Veronique, trapped inside his own mind. Maybe it was impossible to avoid. In world after world after world, people were living out their lives, making choices that were right or wrong, good or evil, or just random—turn left or turn right, step on that crack in the sidewalk or avoid it. The worlds don't care, the multiverse doesn't care. There are no gods. It's just you--*this* you, here and now, walking aimlessly in the snow through a town that no longer belongs to you.

No other.

Larry looked up after a while. He was downtown, standing outside the 7-11. He recalled the last time he had been inside the store, buying Doritos with Vinnie Polkinghorne. That was when he had spotted Valleia. That was the start of the choices that had led him to Terra— the choices that, finally, had led him back here.

He went inside. The sudden warmth took his breath away, made him dizzy. The lights were brighter than any on Elysium. The store seemed empty. He walked down an aisle at random. The packages for the food looked absurd: bold colors, smiling faces, cartoon characters. But he suddenly felt hungry. He grabbed a bag of ranch-flavored Doritos and brought them up to the counter at the front of the store. He put the blue bag down. Nothing happened. What was supposed to happen? It had been so long. The clerk behind the counter was staring at him.

He was supposed to pay for the Doritos. But he had no money, he realized. He should have asked Rigol for some.

Larry stared back at the clerk. Fat, with unwashed hair, scruffy beard, acne. He looked vaguely familiar. He read the clerk's nametag: *Julian.*

It was Stinky Glover. His seventh-grade nemesis.

Oh, Stinky!

Stinky was older now, like Larry. Larry almost greeted him, almost said his name. *How's it going, Stinky?* But he didn't. "I guess I don't have any money," he admitted, stupidly.

"Gotta pay for stuff," Stinky pointed out, also stupidly.

They kept staring at each other. Did Stinky recognize him? Larry didn't think so. It didn't matter, he decided. "Sorry," he murmured. He left the Doritos behind and walked out into the parking lot. And suddenly he bent over and threw up into the snow.

Then he sat down on the curb and put his head in his hands.

After a while he heard a voice behind him. "Hey man, I think you need some help. The cops can bring you to a homeless shelter—there's one over in Quincy, I think. The cops are okay—they won't arrest you or nothin'. And then maybe the people at the homeless shelter can get you into a rehab place somewhere."

Larry looked back. It was Stinky, standing coatless in the snow, trying to help. The bag of Doritos was in his hand, and he was holding it out to Larry.

"There's no shame in it, man," Stinky went on. "I've got a cousin, he got hooked on painkillers after he broke his leg skiing. You got to fight through it. But you can't do it alone. Believe me."

And somehow, Stinky's words seemed to make everything okay.

Larry smiled at Stinky. "I love you," he said to him. "I will always love you."

But he couldn't stay here. Not now, perhaps not ever.

And so he got to his feet and walked away from the 7-11, through the cold and snow back to the portal, and Elysium.

THIRTY-EIGHT

Hieron

The others left eventually, but Hieron stayed by Larry's portal, sitting on the grass, wanting to be there when he returned. If he returned.

Hieron was in no hurry; he had all the time in the world. He closed his eyes. It was a hot, cloudy afternoon. Insects buzzed; birds chirped. A trickle of sweat made its way down his neck.

And he thought of Terra. Larry'd had the courage to return to his home. Why didn't he? Were things as bad there as Affron and Larry thought they might be? Had all his work really been for nothing? He could find out, if he had the courage.

Finally he heard a noise and opened his eyes, and there was Larry, stumbling out of the nothingness of the portal—wet, shivering, snow in his hair. He collapsed onto the ground next to Hieron.

He didn't speak for a while. Then, finally, he said, "It was winter. Cold, snowing."

"Ah," Hieron replied. "We should have thought of that. Did you come back for warmer clothes?"

Larry shook his head. His shivering had subsided in the warm air of Elysium. He sat up and took off his soggy shoes and socks. "My family moved away," he said. "I don't know where."

When Larry didn't say anything further, Hieron said, "You could find out."

Larry shook his head again. "I don't think I could face them. I don't think I'm strong enough."

"You can always change your mind."

"Sure. I don't know."

"No need to decide anything now," Hieron said. "You should change out of those wet clothes, perhaps have a cup of wine."

"Okay."

They arose and made their way through the woods and into the town, where they stopped at Lucia's café to pick up a bottle of wine. "My poor darling!" she exclaimed when she saw Larry. "You must take off those clothes. Let me find you something to wear. And I'll warm up some soup for you."

Lucia bustled off to her room in the back of the café. Larry didn't look happy. "I don't want to stay here at the café," he said to Hieron. "And I don't want to talk to anyone besides you. Not yet."

"Of course," Hieron replied. "I'll tell Lucia. She won't mind." Hieron went back and explained Larry's mood to her.

"Then take a blanket and wrap him in it," she instructed him. "And don't argue. He's a mess. It's never a good idea to go back to your home world. You've never been home, have you?"

Hieron didn't argue with her; he wasn't likely to win the argument. He took a gray woolen blanket and returned with it to Larry, who accepted it gratefully. "Let's go to my room," Hieron said, picking up the bottle of wine.

Larry wrapped himself in the blanket, and they walked to Hieron's small, bare room in a building on the outskirts of the town. Larry took long swallows of the wine as they walked. In the room, he quickly changed into one of Hieron's robes, and then slumped in a chair and took another swig from the bottle.

"We should dilute the wine perhaps," Hieron said mildly.

Larry nodded and sighed.

"Tell me what happened," Hieron suggested. "You're sure it was the right world?"

"Yes, the portal ended up right where it should have been—in the woods behind my house. What used to be my house. But another family lived there."

"Ah, that is too bad," Hieron replied. "But not unexpected, I think?"

"No, not when you think about it. Would've been strange if they still lived there, I suppose. After I found out, I just wandered around Glanbury for a while. Remembering stuff. I ended up going into a store to buy some food, but I didn't have any money. And the clerk was someone I knew from school. Everyone called him Stinky, which was cruel, of course, but that's the way we were. Stinky didn't recognize me. He thought I was a homeless drug addict. He tried to help me. That was so…different."

"And then you came back?"

Larry nodded. "Then I came back." He was silent for a while. Hieron thought he might be falling asleep. But he wasn't. "How do you deal with it?" he asked Hieron. "I lived on Terra for less than a year, I guess, but I think about it all the time. I think about Palta—this girl I met there—all the time. How do I leave her behind? How do I leave anyone, anything behind?"

Hieron felt a great wave of sorrow and regret wash over him. "I don't know the answer to this, Larry," he replied. "The problem is not unique to the people here in Elysium, is it?"

"I suppose not. What do I know? You've lived a lot longer than I have."

"That is certainly true. To be human is to have regrets. And the longer you live, the more regrets you have."

"Well, that's certainly encouraging." Larry took another swig of wine. "Do you mind if I stay here tonight?" he asked. "I'm feeling a little woozy."

"Of course not."

He brought Larry over to his narrow bed and arranged Lucia's blanket over him.

"I told Stinky I loved him," Larry murmured, closing his eyes.

"Was Stinky a friend?"

"No, not a friend. The opposite, really. But still—I think I love him. He's Stinky. There's only one of him, in all the multiverse."

"That's true," Hieron said. "No matter how many worlds there are, there's really only one of each of us."

"Stinky," Larry repeated. And then his breathing became regular, and he was asleep.

Hieron sat in the chair and watched him as the sun set on Elysium.

Larry would be all right, he thought. He was just growing up. It was an odd way to grow up, of course, but we do not control the trajectory of our lives, much as we'd like to.

Ah, but that was not entirely true, he knew. We are always making choices: to live in one world or another, to leave your past behind or to embrace it. Hieron had left his past behind. And now?

Now he should be wandering over to the café to spend the evening with the others. Perhaps afterward he would play chess with Rigol. Perhaps he would help put Jubal to bed. Small pleasures, small kindnesses. A good enough life.

He did not go to the café. Instead, as evening fell, he went to visit Rigol to borrow an item or two, and then he walked back to the woods, alone. With some difficulty he found the spot that belonged to him, in a small copse of trees near the brook.

He had not used his portal in years. He would use it tonight.

THIRTY-NINE

Sulpicius

The harvest had been good, and it was a mild winter, but no one was happy. No one was ever happy anymore, it seemed. His wife didn't like for him to go to the tavern at night. *We haven't the money,* she'd point out. And: *Wine doesn't change anything. It just makes you feel worse the next morning.* Which was true enough, he supposed. But it changed things for the time you were drinking it, and there was something to be said for that.

Anyway, she couldn't stop him, and probably she was happy to have him gone from their cottage, so she could sit in peace by herself and mourn their lost son. So she let him go with only a little fuss.

The usual men were there—he had known them all his life. They were so familiar to him that he could tell what they were going to say before they said it. Which was not so bad. Too much had changed; he didn't want his friends to change as well. They sat in the little tavern and drank their wine and complained, and reminisced, and even laughed a little bit. It was good to laugh. His wife didn't laugh anymore.

And then the stranger entered. Who was he? Why was he here, in their tavern? This was a small village, far inland from the Via Appia. No one came here, except tax collectors and soldiers looking for recruits. But he didn't have the cold gaze of a tax collector or a soldier. He was old, gray-haired and gray-bearded, although he seemed spry enough. He wore a dark-blue cloak, belted in an old-fashioned style. He seemed vaguely familiar, though Sulpicius couldn't say where he might have met him. It was not as if he saw many strangers, year in and year out.

The old man bowed to them all, and then sat at one end of the long table and ordered a jug of wine and a loaf of bread from Flavio, who seemed delighted to have a patron who wouldn't make a single cup of wine last the entire evening. "Please join me," he said to the men, gesturing to the food and drink. "I've been traveling a long distance and could use some company."

His Latin was odd, although Sulpicius couldn't say why. He didn't seem like a foreigner, though. And there was something about his voice…it was soft, like leaves rustling in trees. It made you want to listen. The men filled their cups and mumbled their welcomes and their thanks. They didn't see many strangers, but they knew how to be hospitable. They would be sure to repay his kindness.

"How are you all?" the stranger asked after he'd taken a sip of wine. "The weather is mild, it seems."

They agreed that the weather was mild.

"Very pleasant," the stranger said. "And yet…"

His words hung in the air.

The men stared at their cups and said nothing. Sulpicius stole a glance at Marcellus, sitting by himself in the corner. It was dangerous to complain. They all knew that, especially Marcellus. Marcellus said nothing.

But perhaps the stranger was only talking about the weather. Better to take it that way, in any case. "The weather can change at any moment," Sulpicius said. "It is in the hands of the gods."

The stranger nodded deeply and didn't respond, as if Sulpicius had said something so wise he needed to pause and contemplate it. And then he said, "It is hard to know what the gods are thinking nowadays."

And what did this mean? Surely he wasn't talking about the weather now. Marcellus looked at the man then. "The gods have much to answer for," he muttered.

That was not a wise thing to say. The stranger seemed harmless enough, but one could not be too careful. Spies were everywhere; everyone had a story to tell. Marcellus had a story—a son hauled away to the mines for a mild joke he had told about the Gallians. No trial, no appeal. The son's life ruined. The father's life ruined.

"I was merely talking about the changeable weather," the stranger said mildly, as if to give Marcellus a chance to retract his statement about the gods. *We're all just talking about the weather here.*

"The weather be damned," Marcellus replied, and he picked up his cup and finished off what was left of his wine.

They were all silent for a bit. Strangely, it was old Pompey who spoke next. He rarely had anything to say. "We are all doomed," he announced. "Doomed," he repeated, as if he liked the sound of the word. "We all complained about the priests, but we never knew how good we had it until the damn Gallians threw them out. Now the Gallians build their fancy palaces and fight their awful wars, and we are the ones who suffer."

Well, then. There it was. A statement plain enough to get Pompey executed, if the stranger was a spy. "Now, now, I'm sure you're jesting," Flavio said, glancing nervously at the stranger. No telling what the Gallians would do to Flavio if he let patrons say such things in his tavern.

But Pompey wasn't about to be silenced. "I mean it," he said. "I don't mind the taxes—I have no money to begin with. It's the fear I mind. Why should I be afraid, at my age? And the wars. Everywhere a war."

"The Gallians have to put down the rebellion," Flavio pointed out. "They have to stop the invaders. That's only natural."

"Then let them do it with their own sons, not ours!"

At that, everyone looked at Sulpicius.

Sulpicius said nothing. But the feelings he kept inside him started to well up and threatened to break free.

"War is a terrible thing," the stranger murmured.

Sulpicius should have ignored this. What did it matter? Everyone said such things, and he always ignored them. But there was something about the stranger—his sad eyes, his soft voice—that made Sulpicius feel as if the man had experienced war himself, over and over again, and his simple words summed up all that anyone could ever say about war.

And so Sulpicius started to weep. The other men continued to stare; he didn't care. He was talking to the sad-eyed stranger. He wanted the man to understand what he, too, felt. "My boy didn't want to be a soldier," he said. "He was too young. He wanted to stay here with his family. But the legionaries came to town and they just took him —some of you were there. They just pointed to him and said: *You*. And they grabbed him and threw him into their wagon. And that was the last we saw of him."

He looked around to see the other men nodding sympathetically. That had been a terrible day. And then he turned back to the stranger. "Marcus was a good lad," he said. "Gave us no trouble. His mother doted on him. But the Gallians needed bodies to fight the rebels, and no one was volunteering. Who would want to fight for the Gallians? Pompey's right—it's their war, their problem. No one asked them to throw out the priests.

"Marcus ended up in Egypt. Egypt! He wrote us, you see. He learned how to write in school. His mother insisted he go to school and learn such things. There's talk the Gallians will close the schools. They think that peasants like us don't need to read and write. But schools are good—the priests knew that. Marcus was such a good lad—didn't want us to worry. He said they treated him well enough, but we knew better. He said there were awful, bloody battles in the desert, but he was safe. He said they expected more battles soon enough. And then, nothing. Nothing."

The stranger was nodding like the other men; his eyes were moist with sorrow and sympathy. He understood. Of course he understood.

"Never a word to us from the Gallians, either," Sulpicius went on. "We heard rumors about the war. The Gallians claimed they were pushing the rebels back. Claimed they were fighting the evil priests, who were going to take our land and give it to the barbarians, nonsense like that. I know some folks believe such things, but not me. The priests were never evil. Stupid sometimes, I'll grant you. But not evil.

"Well, finally we got a letter from a mate of his who had deserted. Said Marcus died in one of those battles. Said his arm was sliced off, and he died of the fever later. Said Marcus was a good comrade— cheerful, friendly, helpful. Said none of the soldiers knew why they were fighting. They just had to fight or they'd be beheaded. His mate said he'd be beheaded if they ever caught him. So he was on his way to someplace in Barbarica and never coming back.

"What I want to know is this," Sulpicius said, addressing the stranger, as if the old man possessed some wisdom that the rest of them didn't. "If the Gallians have these magical weapons, why don't they use them against the rebels? That's what the priests did in the old days against that Gallian king. Why make lads like Marcus fight and die for them? And if Prince Feslund has the power to cure the fever like people say, whey won't he use it to save a lad like Marcus who is fighting to save his empire? Where's the justice in this? Where's the justice in anything?"

He fell silent. He looked at his wine cup. It was empty, but he made no move to fill it.

"Times are hard," Flavio murmured.

"We need to stop those bastards," Pompeo growled.

In his seat in the corner, Marcellus too was weeping.

"Your suffering must be immense," the stranger said to Sulpicius. "And I can offer you nothing but hope. Strangers pass by on winter nights, and sometimes they can make a difference—the gods know how. I will not forget you."

With that he rose and placed his hand on Sulpicius's shoulder. Sulpicius shivered at the touch. Then the stranger laid some money on the table—ancient coins that none of them had seen before—and left the tavern.

The men fell silent.

Later Sulpicius went out into the night and looked for him, but he was nowhere to be found, and no one in the village recalled seeing the man arrive or leave.

It was as if the stranger had disappeared into thin air.

He told his wife about the man, and she dismissed his story. "You're having fantasies," she said. "The lot of you drink entirely too much. It's addling your brains. You should all stay home at night."

But Flavio had those coins. And he showed Sulpicius one of them. "Do you see?" Flavio asked.

Sulpicius stared at the face on the coin. It looked not unlike the stranger's face.

"What do you make of that?" Flavio asked him.

Sulpicius had no idea what to make of that. He was a simple man, and the ways of the gods were far beyond his ability to understand.

FORTY

Hieron

The next day Hieron found Larry sitting on a bench next to Jubal. Poor Jubal looked especially bad today. His hands occasionally jerked up, as if trying to guard himself from someone or something. Then he would moan and drop his hands, as if he realized that his hands couldn't help him.

Perhaps someday they would learn how to cure Jubal, Veronique, and the others. For now, people like Larry could do nothing but be with them as they endured their terror.

Larry looked glum. Hieron sat down next to him. "I returned to Terra," Hieron said.

That got Larry's attention. "Why?"

Hieron shrugged. "You and Affron thought things would not be going well there, under the Gallians. I decided to see for myself."

"You've never been back there since you left."

"No, never."

"And what did you find out?"

"Ah, it is worse than I feared, Larry. The priests are gone, justice is gone, hope is gone. In their place are poverty, repression, and despair."

"Gone," Larry repeated.

Hieron nodded. "It seems that life in the empire has returned to what it was before me. For century after century the Roman empire survived. Sometimes there were good emperors; sometimes there were bad. But mostly they didn't matter to ordinary people. The lot in life for such people was disease and privation, with no hope of improvement. And, of course, endless wars, large and small: an invasion here, a rebellion there. I changed that. Now Feslund and his family have overturned everything I tried to do. They care only about their own wealth and power. They kill or imprison those who oppose them or mock them. They levy unbearable taxes. They impress peasants into the army against their will."

Larry seemed to ponder this. "But you came back here to Elysium," he said finally. "Like me."

Hieron nodded. "I came back. Perhaps I shouldn't have gone to Terra in the first place. I am old; I have lived far too long. I don't have the energy I once did. I do not know what to do about this."

"It's all my fault," Larry pointed out. "The empire was working well enough until I came along."

"Don't be absurd, Larry. I understand what happened. You did what you had to do. You were only trying to get home."

"Sure. But when I had the chance to use Via I turned it down. And now, when I actually did go home, I turned around right away and came back."

"Going home is hard," Hieron murmured. He thought of the little village he had visited. The kerchiefed peasant women sweeping their doorways. The distant sound of a girl's voice singing a song. The bitter taste of the wine in the tavern. The men weeping over their lost sons.

They were silent for a long time. And then Larry said: "I'm going back to Terra."

Hieron had half-expected this. "That is you choice," he replied, "but don't expect to defeat the Gallians. And it doesn't matter, perhaps. They will defeat themselves, eventually."

"I won't worry about the Gallians," Larry said. "But I want to find the girl I abandoned there. Palta."

Hieron considered telling Larry that this would likely just cause him more heartache. Palta would have disappeared by now. Or died. Or—perhaps worse—married and borne children. Created a life for herself that didn't include Larry. But he didn't say such things. Because it seemed better to Hieron now to know the truth than to live in ignorance. Hieron himself had lived in ignorance for too long. He had just learned the truth of what had happened on Terra, and perhaps someday that truth would not hurt him the way it did at this moment.

"Yes," he said to Larry. "If Earth is unbearable to you, I think you must return to Terra."

Then they were silent again. A soft breeze blew along the silent street. Jubal raised his hands to protect himself against his invisible enemy. Larry touched him on the arm and murmured something to him, and Jubal lowered his hands, at peace once more.

FORTY-ONE

Valleia

"Mama, someone's coming!"
Henry stood in the doorway, pointing outside.

Valleia was busy nursing Emily. "Who is it, Henry?" she asked from her seat by the hearth. "Is it Papa?"

"No, silly. Papa's at the barn. It's a man. He's walking. I don't know who he is."

That was strange, Valleia thought. Henry knew everyone, and everyone knew Henry. Of course, strangers occasionally showed up in the village, even this far north, even this far from the King's Road. But you had to go out of your way to reach their cottage.

Valleia got up and walked over to the door, standing behind Henry as the man walked up the path. "Salve!" Henry called out. "I'm Henry!"

"Salve, Henry," the man replied.

Then the man looked at her, and she looked at him. He smiled and inclined her head to her in greeting. She was confused for just a moment. And then recognition flooded through her, and her eyes filled with tears.

He was a young man now, with broad shoulders and deep-set eyes.

He was quite handsome, actually. But he was also still the boy she had first seen in that little store on Earth.

"Salve, Valleia," he said.

"What's your name?" Henry asked him.

"My name is Larry. I know your mother. And your father. But I don't know who that new person is that your mother is holding."

"That's Emily. She's my sister."

"Salve, Emily."

"She can't talk yet," Henry pointed out.

"Ah. I see."

"Larry is a funny name," Henry went on. "People in the village say that Henry is a funny name, too. But I like it."

"I think it's a fine name," Larry replied. "I once knew a boy named Henry."

"Come in," Valleia said to him. "I don't know—I didn't expect—"

"Of course."

"Henry, can you run to the barn and get your father?" Valleia said. "Tell him Larry is here."

"Yes, Mama!"

Henry rushed off.

Larry walked into the cottage. "What a wonderful boy," he said.

"Yes, he's very…energetic."

"And you have a daughter, too. So much time has passed. I was wondering if you'd even recognize me."

"It took me a moment, I confess." They sat down by the hearth. Emily fussed and Valleia changed her to the other breast. She wiped the tears from her eyes. "Would you like water?" she asked. "Ale? Are you hungry? William will be so excited."

Larry shook his head. "Perhaps when Carmody—when William returns."

"Oh, Larry," she said, "we thought you'd gone back home to Earth. We were sure you'd never return."

"It's a complicated story," he said, "but here I am." He hesitated. "I was wondering," he said, "if Palta…"

Valleia shook her head. "She's not here, Larry. She left with Gratius, not long after you disappeared."

"Ah."

He was silent for a long moment. His disappointment was obvious.

He had come back for her, she realized. She ought to have realized that. "Do you happen to know where...?" he said finally.

"She's in Egypt."

"Egypt?" he repeated.

"She *was* in Egypt, I should say. But she could be anywhere by now. News travels slowly here, of course. She sent us a letter—we can show it to you. But that was months ago. It was a miracle that it even arrived here. You would like to see it, I assume."

"Yes, yes I would."

But before she could get it she heard Henry chatting on the path, and a moment later he and William showed up in the doorway, Henry pulling his father by the hand to go faster and meet the stranger. "Here is Papa!" Henry announced.

And there was William, grinning as he entered the cottage. "Welcome back!" he said. Larry stood up, and they embraced. "It's good to see you," William went on, in English. "You've grown so much. You're a man now."

"Papa, what are you saying?" Henry demanded.

"We'll speak in Latin," Larry said to him. "Don't worry."

"I'm saying how much he's grown, Henry," William explained. "We haven't seen Larry since before you were born."

Henry had little idea what life was like before he was born, of course. But he was a curious boy, and someday he'd learn that they hadn't always lived in this cottage here in Scotia. What would he make of the story they would eventually tell him?

A question for another day. Emily had gotten all the milk she wanted and fallen asleep. Valleia brought her over to the crib by the big bed that she and William shared. Emily fussed for a moment when Valleia put her in the crib and placed a blanket over her, but then she quickly settled herself.

Meanwhile William had poured cups of ale for himself and Larry. Valleia sat back down, and Henry climbed up onto William's lap.

"The letter," Larry reminded her.

"Ah yes." Valleia rose and retrieved it from the bottom of the chest next to their bed. She handed it to Larry.

"It was brought to us by a merchant, who received it from another merchant," William explained. "Palta paid them, I'm sure, but still, it was long odds that it would arrive safely."

"Who is Palta?" Henry asked.

"Another old friend," Valleia explained.

Larry unfolded the letter and began to read. He looked up almost immediately. "She is with Decius in Alexandria?" he said.

"The news is stale, I'm afraid," William replied. "She apparently joined a rebellion with Decius, and the rebels somehow conquered Egypt. The last rumors we heard were that the rebels were under attack, and their grip on Egypt was loosening. The Gallians have apparently come to their senses and are throwing all their forces against them."

"She says that she is ignoring her work and spending time at the library," Larry said. "That seems odd."

"The library at Alexandria is the greatest on Terra," Valleia pointed out. "I think she wants to learn—she never had much of a chance to learn anything in her life."

"That's true." Larry returned to the letter. Moments later he spoke again. "And Gratius is dead?"

"Yes, alas," Valleia said.

"I don't know *any* of these people," Henry complained.

"You may go outside and play," Valleia said to him. "But stay close."

"Yes, Mama." Henry squirmed down from William's lap and scurried outside.

"It seems that the Gallians were looking for Affron," Larry said. "And possibly you."

"Possibly us. But Affron is who they want, I'm sure."

"Have you had any trouble since Palta and Gratius left?"

"None," Carmody said. "It's been a quiet life."

"Affron is still alive, you know," Larry said. "I saw him yesterday. He sends his love."

And that made Valleia's heart lurch with joy and wonder. She felt almost dizzy hearing it. "Is he...well?"

"He's never been better, actually."

"And is he here—in Scotia?"

Larry shook his head. "That is part of my story. But let me finish reading."

Larry looked down at the letter again, and finally he read aloud the sentences that Valleia knew would interest him the most. "*If Larry ever returns, tell him that I had to leave, but I will never forget him,*" he said softly.

They were all silent for a moment. "She really did have to leave,"

William said finally. "It's lovely here, but she couldn't stay. She had to find a life for herself."

"Of course she did," Larry replied. He handed the letter back to Valleia.

"Perhaps you could tell us your story," Valleia said to him.

"Of course," he said. "You'll find it strange. Beyond strange, I suppose."

And he began. Yes, he was not mistaken about the strangeness. She and William interrupted him constantly, trying to understand. Affron had created his own Via. Then Larry had followed him to another world, and Affron had taught Larry how to do the same thing. Valleia had already half-imagined something like this; it was the only way to make sense of their odd behavior and sudden disappearance. But the next part of his story seemed beyond belief. "You have met Hieron?" she gasped. "How can that be?"

Larry tried to explain. Hieron still existed, in a world built only for those like him, a world where time passed differently than in other worlds. He got up in the morning, read books, drank wine, talked to his friends. *Elysium* was the name given in the old religion to the home of the blessed after their death, Valleia knew. Is that how the world where Hieron now lived had gotten its name?

And then there was this: Affron was in love! It was hardly strange, yet Valleia felt a swift twinge of regret, of lost possibilities, of worlds forever closed off to her. She had been in love with Affron once. Now that seemed like a very long time ago. She was happy for him, in any case. He deserved the happiness he had found.

"Frankly, I don't understand any of this," William said. "But then, there's much I haven't understood since I first encountered the portal."

"I don't understand these things myself," Larry replied. "Why I can do what I can do, why I'm sitting here talking to you in this world…"

They sat in silence for a long while. Valleia found herself listening to make sure Henry was all right. He had a tendency to wander. She thought of the particularities of her life: the way William snored. Henry's delight at seeing a rabbit in their yard. Emily's fine golden eyebrows. Where had she gotten that color hair? The well-trod path to the village. Fishing in the lake. The health of their pig. The food she would cook for supper. It was all so very real to her. She loved her family. She had no wish to go to Elysium. Or Egypt.

She was where she belonged.

But Larry wasn't.

———

Larry

They went to bed soon after dark. Henry was full of energy until suddenly he wasn't, and the whole family seemed to collapse when he did. Valleia and Carmody worked hard and didn't have the leisure to sit at a café and talk by torchlight till early in the morning.

But Larry couldn't sleep. Finally he removed the blanket Valleia had given him, rose from his spot on the floor, and left their cottage. He walked a few steps down the path. The night was cool and clear. Insects chirped. He smelled hay and sweet flowers. He looked up at the stars.

Here he was, back on Terra. These were the same stars he had seen in Roma and in Gallia, and on the great sea. And on Earth. Gratius had taught him the names of the constellations on their journey to Scotia. He picked them out: *Scorpius. Aquila. Canis Major.*

It was good to see Valleia and Carmody again. And their children. He smiled at the thought of little Henry. Henry reminded Larry a bit of his own brother. Younger, of course. But still: the same energy and curiosity. The same endless questions. Matthew was probably in high school now, he realized with a pang.

"It seems as if people are always leaving us," Valleia said from behind him. "Affron, Palta, Gratius, you."

Larry turned. She was standing in the doorway.

"I'm not leaving right now," he replied. "Just enjoying the night."

She came up beside him. "It is beautiful here," she murmured. "But I understand why all of you have had to go."

"I wish Palta had stayed with you," Larry said. "It would have made things easier."

"You will have to travel to Egypt."

"Yes."

"It's a long journey. Can you use your portal to get there?"

He shook his head. "It doesn't work that way."

"No, I thought not."

She reached out and touched his arm. "I'm glad you're here, Larry. In this world. Even if you leave us tomorrow."

"I *am* leaving you tomorrow."

248

"So be it. Perhaps you'll return."

Larry didn't respond. But finally he said, "Watch the stars with me for a while."

"Of course," Valleia replied.

So they stood there together, looking up at all those constellations, until finally Larry decided he was ready to sleep.

In the morning he said good-bye to his friends and left for Egypt. Palta had said she would never forget him; now he only hoped he could find her.

FORTY-TWO

Ploterus

The war had been difficult and lengthy. Uncounted thousands had died in ferocious battles in this cultured but alien land. Now the fighting was all but over, and the empire had won.

And Ploterus had returned to Alexandria to rebuild the city.

It was a daunting task, but he rather enjoyed it. War had its excitement, of course, but peace offered greater satisfaction. He liked to think he was good at both.

Alexandria needed peace. Ordinary life in Alexandria had been ignored during the war, and now that the war was winding down it was important to get things back to normal—to rebuild houses that had been destroyed, to give work to peasants and laborers who would otherwise be restless and therefore dangerous. The rebel administration had been competent enough, Ploterus had decided, but it never had the money or the men to accomplish much.

Ploterus was doing what he could. He spent the warm morning inspecting building sites. Some people actually cheered him. He was usually cheered only by his soldiers.

But he knew he had enemies. He might be popular, but the Gallians surely weren't. And so, alas, he had started investing in spies. It was a sordid business, but he was an outsider here. He did not speak

Coptic; he knew little about Egyptians and their customs. But for now he was their governor, and he needed to understand what was happening if he was to be successful.

In the afternoon he spoke to Babaef, a local man whom he'd placed in charge of the spies. Babaef was short and thin and smiled a great deal, and how was Ploterus to know whether he was telling the truth? You have to trust someone, of course, and Babaef seemed honest enough, even if unctuous and too eager to please.

Babaef bowed almost to the floor when he entered the room. "My lord, I am most grateful to be allowed to make my report," he said in passable Latin.

"Yes, of course. Please sit."

"Thank you, my lord." He sat.

Babaef liked to begin these discussions with fulsome praise of the general and all he had accomplished, but today Ploterus was not interested in being praised. "I want to know about rebel activity in the city," he said. "Have you discovered any?"

Babaef produced a scroll from a pocket in his robe. "My lord, here are the names of people who have been overheard complaining about the imperial government or you personally. As you can see, it's quite long."

Ploterus unwound the scroll and glanced at it. "Everyone complains," he replied. "Are any of these people actively plotting against us, or planning to join the rebels?"

"As you say, my lord, some people seem to enjoy finding fault with even the most enlightened ruler. We have uncovered no active plots, however."

"What about the woman Palta—the aide to Decius—she was seen here even after the rebels evacuated the city. Have you found her?"

"No, my lord. Alexandria is a very large city, as you are of course aware. Palta was known to frequent the library, but to our knowledge she hasn't been seen there lately. I expect that the sighting of the woman must have been an error."

Ploterus had learned about Palta only recently, and he wondered if this was the same young woman he had met with Feslund and the others in Massalia, when they arrived there to sail for Urbis. How many Paltas were there in the empire? Strange if she had joined the rebels; stranger still if she had left the rebels behind. "Have you talked to the director of the library?" he asked Babaef. "What's her name—Olef something?"

"Olef-Nan, my lord," Babaef replied. "No, we do not ask people directly about such things, of course. We merely listen, and report."

"Of course." Ploterus contemplated this. Palta was unlikely to be important, but her presence in the city did seem odd. She could be trying to stir up trouble, but where was the evidence of it? The information about her could have been incorrect, certainly. Rumors, mistakes, suppositions…this place was full of them. "And what about priests?" he asked. "Any more sightings of priests?"

"Ah, no, my lord. Any priests who are here are too smart to make themselves known, I fear."

"But you have heard rumors."

Babaef inclined his head. "There have been many rumors. But I fear that priests will not be found easily."

"Well, keep looking."

"Of course, my lord."

Ploterus dismissed the man and thought some more. Then he made up his mind to visit the library.

He had never entered the library before, even though it was the largest building in the city—a massive stone structure near the harbor —and some called it Egypt's greatest glory. He wasn't especially interested in books. He could read well enough, certainly, but books frightened him; they seemed to possess a kind of magic that he did not understand. Utter foolishness, of course. At any rate, he wasn't interested in the books right now.

The people at the library were predictably taken aback by his unannounced arrival, and then predictably effusive in expressing their joy at his presence. Someone ran off to summon the director. While he waited for her he stood in the bright, high-ceilinged entrance hall that extended up six stories or more, lined on all sides with long shelves filled with books and scrolls. He found it difficult to imagine how so many books could actually exist. What was there to write about?

Before long he spotted the director coming down the main staircase. He recalled meeting her at a dinner for the city leaders after he had retaken the city. She was stout, middle-aged, dark-skinned, and spoke perfect Latin. She wore a crimson robe with a white vertical stripe on the left side. Was it some kind of uniform? She bowed deeply to him. "My lord, this is a great honor," she said. "Have you finally come for the tour I offered you?"

Ploterus vaguely remembered the offer. "Some other time, perhaps," he replied. "Today I only wish to have a brief conversation."

Olef-Nan looked puzzled for a moment, and then smiled and inclined her head in acquiescence. "Of course, my lord. Will you follow me to my office?"

She led him up the stairs to a large, crowded room also lined with bookshelves. A marble statue of a naked woman with the head of a bird stood in a corner next to a door. From the window of the office he could see the lighthouse on Pharos. A table in the center of the room was covered with scrolls and manuscripts. She offered him a seat on one side of the table, and she sat on the other. "Would you like something to drink?" she asked.

People in Egypt drank beer, which was a vile beverage, but there was nothing better to be had. He nodded. Olef-Nan made a signal, and a servant quickly brought in two cups on a tray and placed them on the table.

"Now, how can I help you?" the director asked.

She was less obsequious to him than others in the city, he noticed. He supposed that her position was quite important. He was happy to talk to people as equals. "I am told that one of the rebels—an aide to Decius—stayed on in the city after the rebels left. Her name is Palta. She is a young woman. Fair-skinned, blonde-haired. Not Egyptian, of course. I met her once, years ago, in Gallia."

Olef-Nan shrugged. "I vaguely remember such a woman. If she was an aide to the rebel governor, I'm sure I must have met her. As to whether she stayed on after the rebels left, I cannot say. And the rebels departed quite some time ago."

"So you know nothing about such a woman."

Olef-Nan shook her head. "I can make inquiries. Or you can search the library, if you like. But what is the concern? I hope you do not think that the library is involved in a plot against your rule."

"You worked well enough with the rebels, I'm told."

"Ah, but that is my job! You can see that the library is a very large place. People from all over Terra are constantly arriving and leaving. Roma, Gallia, all of Barbarica…We do not inquire about their political beliefs or allegiances. They seek knowledge here, and we strive to provide it for them. We strove to work with priests when they were in power, and we will strive to work with whoever comes after you. We need to ensure that the knowledge in this building is preserved for generations yet to come, living in a world we cannot imagine."

"I am not interested in future generations," Ploterus pointed out. "I am interested in doing my job, which is to rule Egypt. Now, about the priests."

Olef-Nan raised an eyebrow. "Yes, my lord?"

"They are enemies of the empire, as are the rebels."

"Of course."

"Have you had any dealings with them? Have you seen any of them? Have they come to the library?"

"I am unaware of any priests living in Alexandria," she replied. "But even if they were here, why would I have knowledge of them?"

Ploterus shrugged. "They, too, are interested in knowledge, as I understand it. It would be natural of them to come here."

"It would be more natural of them to hide their identities and entirely disappear from view, don't you think? They are clever and resourceful, I imagine. And they must know the empire is looking for them."

"Perhaps they let down their guard while the rebels were in control. There have been rumors."

"Rumors of what, my lord? Of people who claimed to be priests? Who acted like priests? Who have the same name as a priest? I can only repeat: I know no priests in Alexandria."

Ploterus took a sip of beer from his cup and stared at Olef-Nan. She sounded somewhat exasperated. She herself was obviously clever and resourceful, he thought. Was she also truthful? He could not tell, but he suspected that she wasn't. What should he do about his suspicion, then? Arrest her? Torture her? And then what? She presumably had a lot of powerful friends, and he needed the cooperation of those friends. He probably needed her cooperation as well, although he wasn't sure why. He put down his cup. "You will please tell me if you obtain any information about this woman, or about any priests," he said. "The last thing you want, I think, is further war and destruction here. I am your best hope of avoiding these things. Please keep this in mind."

"I shall certainly do so, my lord," she replied. "And I hope you will keep in mind how important the library is to the city and the world."

They both rose then and bowed low to each other, and the interview was at an end.

Not especially satisfying. Ploterus returned to the government palace. He closed the door of his office and then sat for a long while alone in the afternoon heat. Finally he took two letters out of a locked drawer. The first was from Cymbian. Cymbian had written before, imprudently. Ploterus had read his most recent letter often since it arrived. It was filled with news, some of which he had already heard from other sources: King Carolus had finally died, alas, and Feslund had been crowned as his successor. General Gregorius, leader of the legions in Roma, had died as well. The new palace had been completed on the Roman Forum, and the royal family had left Urbis to take up residence in it. Queen Bathanala had miscarried yet again, so Feslund still did not have an heir. He spent his nights drinking and womanizing, and his days complaining. The people were sullen and angry. So were many of the soldiers.

"You must return," Cymbian concluded. "You must come back to Roma and end this. The people have heard of your successes and respect you. They will follow you. You are our only hope."

Such a letter would surely destroy them both if it were discovered. But still he held onto it.

And now a new letter had arrived, which he opened and re-read. It was from Gretyx. It praised his many successes in Egypt and ordered him to return to Roma, where he would be appropriately honored and given a new assignment worthy of his great abilities.

He remembered old General Gregorius's advice: *Go far away, my friend, and stay there.*

He had much to ponder. He liked his life in Alexandria. The war had been won, but there were people to be tracked down. Where was Governor Decius? Where was Palta? Were the rumors of priests in Alexandria true? He could make excuses to stay in Egypt.

He couldn't stay here forever, though.

Eventually he would have to decide what to do about Gretyx, and the empire.

FORTY-THREE

Larry

Larry's ship reached Alexandria late in the day.

To get here had taken a long ride through Scotia, then two endless sea voyages, with little to do on them but hope and worry. The food had been bad on both ships, and his fellow passengers made no effort to be friendly to him. At least neither ship had sunk, which was what had happened the last time he had sailed on the great sea.

And now at last he was here.

Larry left the ship and wandered into the city. Alexandria reminded him of Roma: the same teeming streets, the same high fountains and wide plazas, the same majestic architecture, the same blistering heat, even as twilight approached. On the other hand, the people's skin here was darker, and they spoke a different language. And they dressed in extremes—some wore robes more colorful than any he had seen in Roma, while many women, despite the heat, wore austere gray robes with hoods that all but covered their faces.

He made his way immediately to the library, an immense stone building situated not far from the harbor. It was dark, except for lamps shining in a couple of windows. Two stone lions sat on either side of the large entrance. He went up to it and tried the doors, which were covered with panels showing scenes of ancient Egyptian gods; they were locked.

Then he sat on a bench in the plaza across from the library.

If Palta walked out of the building and past him, would he recognize her? Would she recognize him?

You are coming back, she had told him on that hill in Scotia, as he stroked her hair.

I'm coming back, he had agreed.

But years had passed, and what did those words matter anymore? He and Palta had been young—old enough to kiss, old enough to fall in love, perhaps, but not old enough to make vows that could never be broken. He had walked away from her into the portal, and then he had made the portal disappear so she could not follow. Slammed the door in her face and locked it behind him.

She had said in her letter that she would never forget him. Was that true? He didn't know. But they had spent so many days and nights together, endured so many hardships. They had kissed in the colonnade during the thunderstorm. He had saved her life, helped her survive a shipwreck. And she had done all she could to help him return home, even though she was putting her life at risk. There was a bond that could never be broken.

Wasn't there?

Larry sat there for a long time, looking at the library, and then he walked away to find a place to eat and sleep. He couldn't afford to spend much money; he had already used up much of what he had brought from Elysium; he hadn't expected the search to take him all the way to Egypt. And what if she wasn't here? Where would his journey take him next? Finally he settled on a run-down inn in a poorer section of the city; the proprietor spoke a little Latin and provided him with a cheap meal and a tiny, airless room.

He slept badly. In the morning he bought a hard roll from a street vendor and returned to the library. The streets were filled with people and camels and donkeys. The air was filled with the odor of spices and excrement. A sea breeze made the heat tolerable.

A couple of legionaries stood next to the stone lions now. He took a deep breath, and then walked up the steps, past the soldiers, and through the heavy doors.

And then there was silence, as if the bustling city outside did not exist. He stood in the entrance hall and looked around. It looked more or less like libraries he was familiar with on Earth, except far larger. He saw long rows of bookshelves, disappearing into the distance, and long tables at which people sat reading or writing. People hurried past carrying books and scrolls in small satchels. No one paid any attention to him.

Where to begin? He walked down a passage to his right and found himself looking in on a classroom—a gray-bearded man lectured twenty or more young men and women seated on benches in a semi-circle around him. He was speaking Latin. Larry listen for a moment; the man was saying something about *being* and *essence*—philosophy, apparently. Larry was quickly bored.

He wandered through more passageways. He came upon an indoor garden filled with statues—he spotted one of Hieron. Why hadn't the Gallians removed it? There were signs over doorways, but he didn't understand the script—it didn't look like hieroglyphics, but it wasn't the Latin alphabet either. He got lost, but finally managed to find his way back to the main hall. Next he climbed the stairs and started wandering through the rest of the library.

So many books. But of course they were the old-fashioned kind: hand-printed on scrolls or parchment; People at the long tables weren't just reading books or taking notes; some of them were laboriously copying them. Larry had asked Hieron about this back on Elysium. He could sort of understand not introducing inventions like cars and tele-phones from other worlds. But why not the printing press? Why not save people all this effort? Books were good, right? "It's a question of what kind of world you want," Hieron had replied. "Books contain knowledge and wisdom and beauty, but they also contain ignorance and hate. Are the worlds filled with books any happier than those like Terra, where books are rare and precious? Not in my experience."

So here were Terra's rare and precious books. But right now Larry didn't care about them. He wanted to spot Palta seated at a table, care-fully turning the pages of a hand-stitched book or copying a scroll, her blond hair falling down over the words, her gray eyes moving over them, understanding, learning.

But she wasn't here. He saw old men reading heavy books, their eyes equally heavy, their hands trembling. He saw fierce-eyed young men reading scrolls as if their lives depended on the words in front of them. He saw young women too, quiet and studious, or shy and giggly, but they were not Palta.

Occasionally someone addressed Larry in the Egyptian language, probably asking if he needed help finding something. But Larry just shook his head. By afternoon he had become discouraged. She wasn't here. Or she was in some corner of the place that he hadn't found. Or she had come and gone while he was elsewhere in the building. Just wandering around wasn't going to work.

But what was the alternative? Palta had fought for the rebels, but they had been driven out of Alexandria. Would people think he was a rebel too and arrest him? Was she wanted by the authorities? Could he be putting her in danger?

Finally he decided he had no alternative, so he started asking people. Have you ever seen a young woman here? Named Palta. Light-skinned, blonde hair, gray eyes. Eager to learn. Probably quiet, probably kept to herself. It turned out that everyone in the library spoke Latin, though some much better than others.

He had little luck, though. Many people had seen light-skinned blonde women in the library, but no one could recall their names. It was a large library, and people came and went here frequently.

And then he felt a hand on his shoulder. He turned and saw a burly Egyptian staring at him. "Sir, I could not help overhearing your query," he said quietly, in perfect Latin. "Perhaps you would be kind enough to bring your request to our director. She may be able to help you."

"Of course," Larry replied. The man led him to a small waiting room and then left him there. Larry didn't know whether to be excited or terrified. Did the director know something about Palta? Would she have good news for him or bad?

Finally the door to her office opened and another Egyptian, this one young and thin, gestured for him to enter.

In the office Larry saw a middle-aged woman wearing a bright green robe. She stood behind a table in the middle of the room with her arms crossed. She seemed puzzled when she saw him. He bowed politely, but she did not incline her head. Was that not the custom here? "You are a Roman, then," she said in Latin. "Or a Gallian. Not an Egyptian."

Larry didn't respond. He didn't know what to say.

"But this seems foolish," she continued. "I told your general just the other day that the woman wasn't here. Does he think I am a liar?"

"My lady, I don't know what you're talking about."

"I won't have the visitors to my library bothered," she went on. "I won't have Ploterus using these subterfuges. Tell him he can search if he likes, but he must do it openly. Bring in his soldiers and be done. We have nothing to hide."

A general was searching for Palta? Ploterus, the head of the garrison in Massalia all those years ago? So she was in danger, if she was here. "My lady, Palta is a friend of mine," he said. "I heard that she was in Alexandria, so I have come from a long distance to find her."

"How do you know she is here?"

"She sent a letter—not to me, but to mutual friends in Scotia, a land far to the north. The letter was sent some time ago, and I understand that much has happened since then. But I mean no harm to anyone. I only wish to find her. We were close many years ago."

Larry felt a lump in his throat as he said these words. He noticed that the director had uncrossed her arms and place her hands on the table. "What is your name?" she asked.

"Larry Barnes," he replied. Her eyes narrowed in response. Was she puzzled? Suspicious? "It is an odd name, I know," he added.

"Larry Barnes," she repeated, and his name certainly did sound odd when she said it. And then she paused before saying, "I will see if I can find out something about this woman for you, Larry Barnes. But you may not ask anyone in the library about her. She is not here. You will not find her on your own. Is that understood?"

He bowed. "Yes, my lady. And thank you. But can you tell me if—"

"Return to me in two days. But do not speak to anyone about this."

"Two days, my lady."

The director inclined her head to him, and then turned away. The meeting was over.

———

Olef-Nan

Olef-Nan watched the man leave her office, closing the door behind him.

She felt a shiver of something, and after a moment she realized what it was.

Joy.

But it was not unmixed with fear.

She considered what to do. There was no time to waste.

She summoned Menander.

Larry

In the plaza outside the library, Larry sat on a bench and watch the sun set over the harbor. Lovers strolled by, holding hands. Laughing children chased each other, Women filled jugs in the fountain and left, balancing the jugs on their heads. Life went on as usual in this alien city, in this alien land.

He had been alone for months, traveling, searching. He had friends in Scotia, but he had left them behind. He had friends in Elysium, on Earth...but here he was. Another day had passed, and he had not found Palta.

Had he made any progress today? He couldn't quite tell.

His brief interview with the director had been perplexing. She had offered to look for Palta, hadn't she? But was she just being polite? Or trying to get rid of him? He didn't know. He couldn't get a sense of what was behind her formal Latin words.

But she had also made it clear that Ploterus was searching for Palta. So she was likely to be in hiding, or, more likely, had left the city altogether. And then what would he do?

For now he would have to obey the director and stay out of the library. But he could sit here and watch the entrance, couldn't he? And in two days he would talk to her again. He had no other choice. But finally darkness started to fall, and he stood up and made his way back to the inn. He would return in the morning.

Menander

The fair-skinned man was easy enough to follow, even in near darkness. He walked slowly, as if in no hurry to reach his destination. And, of course, he had no idea he was being followed, and probably couldn't tell one Egyptian from another—probably wouldn't have remembered the fellow who had opened Olaf-Nen's door for him. Easy enough to follow, even if Menander had never done such a thing before and felt awkward and out of place. Menander loved books, not intrigue.

Finally the man entered an inn in a dismal section of the city, on a street lined with ramshackle shops and empty lots. Was this his destination? Menander waited outside for a while, and then made up his mind and went in.

The inn itself was as dismal as the area in which it was located—a few small tables crammed into a narrow, stiflingly hot space. A staircase at the back led up to the second floor, where there were sure to be a few hot, small, dirty rooms.

The man sat by himself in a corner. Menander walked quickly to the other corner and sat in the shadows. A fat woman brought a cup of beer and a plate of something to the man. He took a sip of the beer and set the cup down. The stuff was undoubtedly wretched. Then the woman approached Menander, eyeing him with suspicion, as if it was inconceivable that a stranger would enter this place.

"Beer," Menander muttered.

The woman walked away without responding. Menander studied the man, paying more attention to him than he had in the director's anteroom. He looked like he could have been a Gallian. Or, if not from Gallia, then elsewhere in the northern reaches of the empire. There were circles of sweat under his arms; he wasn't used to this heat. He could have been a soldier, Menander supposed, though he didn't have the confident stride of a soldier. He didn't appear to be waiting for anyone; his gaze didn't move to the door whenever it opened. So perhaps he wasn't a spy, waiting to tell his master what he had learned at the library. He seemed uninterested in everyone and everything, including the beer.

The fat woman brought over Menander's own beer. He took a sip; it was sour, barely drinkable.

What now?

Menander waited. He had been given one task, and he would have to perform it. He wasn't going to drink any more of that beer, though.

An argument broke out at the table next to his. One man owed the other money, and they disagreed about the amount. Menander hoped they didn't start fighting. Finally the two of them left, overturning their chairs in anger. The fat server came over, placidly picked up the chairs, and wiped the table with a rag.

The man in the corner put a couple of coins down on his table and stood up. Menander tensed, getting ready to follow him again. But the man didn't leave the inn; instead he walked up the rickety wooden staircase at the back.

This was where he was staying, then. Menander waited for a while to be sure. Perhaps he was visiting a friend; but why wouldn't the friend have come down to drink with him? Perhaps he went upstairs in search of a woman. Menander couldn't imagine what kind of women would use a place like this.

The man didn't return.

Menander took out his own coins to pay for the wretched beer. Then he, too, stood up and left the inn where the man was staying.

His task had been accomplished, as well as he could accomplish it.

What next? It was up to Olef-Nan, of course. But he supposed he knew what she would decide, and he didn't look forward to it.

He wanted to be among his books; he didn't want to go on a journey.

But for Palta, he would.

FORTY-FOUR

Palta

P alta was in the vault below the compound when Cetonia found her. Palta liked being down here, where it was always cool, even during the mid-day heat. As usual she was sitting at a table, copying a manuscript. She had gotten better at this over time, and she liked to think her copies had become much easier to read than the originals.

"My lady," Cetonia said, breathless, in Coptic. "A man…here… courtyard…for you."

Cetonia was a lovely child, with a bright gap-toothed smile. She adored Palta, who adored her in return. On the other hand, Cetonia was not always the most reliable of messengers. "Say it again," Palta instructed. "And take a deep breath first."

Cetonia took a deep breath. "A man has arrived from the city, my lady," she said. "He asks for you. He is waiting for you in the courtyard. My lord Lamathe sent me to fetch you."

"Do we know who this man is?"

"My lady, I do not."

"All right. Run back and tell them I will be there shortly. Can you remember that?"

"Yes, my lady. Be there shortly."

Cetonia bobbed her head and raced off.

Palta leaned back against a wall and closed her eyes. There were few breaks in the routine here. What did this one mean? Lamathe would not have said she was here if he thought the man was dangerous.

She opened her eyes finally, picked up the lamp sitting on the table, and made her way to the staircase leading out of the vault.

Upstairs, she hurried across the tiled floor and through the airy but hot rooms, out to the courtyard. Under a palm tree the man was seated at a table next to Lamathe, drinking a cup of beer. Cetonia sat on her haunches in a corner of the courtyard, gazing in fascination at the man. He wore a dusty white robe and a white headdress circled with a red band. He was young and dark-skinned, with a thin mustache and soft brown eyes.

It was Menander. He hadn't had the mustache when she had last seen him, but otherwise he was the same, sweet young man she had known at the library.

He jumped to his feet when he spotted her and bowed deeply. "My dear lady Palta," he said.

She went over and embraced him. "Menander," she replied, "it is so good to see you. The mustache makes you look older."

"Thank you, my lady. I am the director's assistant now."

"Congratulations! And don't call me 'my lady', Menander. We know each other too well for that."

Menander smiled. "Thank you, Palta. May we speak in private?"

Palta glanced at Lamathe, who quickly rose and departed with a bow. Cetonia followed, looking disappointed.

"A man came to the library in search of you," Menander said quietly when they were alone. "The director thought you should know, so she sent me here."

"Who is he?" Palta asked. "Did he give his name?"

"Palta, he told Olef-Nan his name is Larry Barnes."

She could not speak for a long moment after she heard that name. Did she dream it? And then the years melted away, and she was standing on a hill in Scotia…

"Larry Barnes," she repeated finally.

"Yes, Palta. I remember the name. As did Olef-Nan, of course. You spoke of him often."

"What does he look like?" she asked.

265

"He is young, Palta. About your age, perhaps. Brown hair, fair-skinned, of medium height."

"Did you hear him speak?"

"Only a few words. He spoke Latin with an accent I did not recognize. But Palta, my lady the director is worried. General Ploterus has asked her about you and about the priests. As you have told us, the general has met you, and he has met Larry Barnes. Also, the Gallians have captured many rebels. Perhaps you spoke of him to one of them. So the director fears that this may be a trick, and the man who calls himself Larry Barnes could be a spy. But she does not know for sure. She thinks he may have been telling the truth."

Palta felt a thrill as Menander spoke those words. "What does she suggest I do?"

"Olef-Nan says it is your choice, Palta. We can bring him to you. Or you can return to the city with me to see him, but that is of course a risk for you."

Palta wondered if Menander suspected that there were priests here; Olef-Nan knew it, of course—she had found the place for them when they'd been forced to flee the city. If this person—Larry!—was an imposter, bringing him to the compound would risk the priests as well as her. Really, there was no choice. And if she went with Menander, she would find out the truth faster. "I will go to Alexandria with you, Menander."

Menander bowed. "Thank you, Palta. That is the choice Olef-Nan expected you to make. I have brought a hooded cloak for you. I think you will not be recognized in it."

"Thanks you, Menander. I know you've had a long journey, but can we leave early tomorrow?"

"Of course, my—Palta. As early as you like."

"It was good of you to come so far," she said.

Menander smiled. "This is important, is it not?"

"Yes, it is very important."

Palta fetched Cetonia. "Show Menander to one of the empty rooms so he can rest after his journey," she instructed her. "Bring him water and fresh linen. Ask your mother to provide him with refreshment."

"Yes, my lady."

Menander followed Cetonia into the compound.

Palta then found Lamathe, who was sitting in the garden behind the compound. She sat down next to him and told him what had happened.

"Ah, this is wonderful news," he said. "We should let the others know."

"Not just yet. They will find out soon enough."

"Samos will be suspicious," he suggested. "Theodosius will be worried, and Karellia will be overjoyed."

Palta smiled. "We are all rather predictable, aren't we?"

"We know each other well. And you, Palta? How do you feel?"

She considered. "I have thought about this for so long, imagined how it might happen, what he would say, what he would look like. And then I forced myself to stop. It seemed foolish—the dream of a child. I'm a child no longer. And now…"

She felt herself starting to weep. She hadn't wept in a long time. She was not the kind of woman who wept. And this was not an occasion for weeping. "I have been happy here," she said to Lamathe at last.

"Yes, but still you must go."

"But what if—"

"Still you must go," he repeated. "You know this."

Of course she knew this. "Larry Barnes is in Alexandria," she murmured, wiping her eyes with the sleeve of her robe. The words sounded so strange.

Later she said them again to the others: Samos, young and easily outraged; Theodosius, older and easily upset; and his wife Karellia, always ready to calm him down. They were the only ones left of the many who had first come to Alexandria with Lamathe. They did not want her to leave, but they understood what she had to do. How could they not understand? They had heard her story often since she arrived. "You can bring him back here, my love," Karellia pointed out.

"Where else would you go?" Theodosius asked.

"I don't know," Palta admitted. "I haven't thought."

"What is there to do here?" Samos demanded. "For him, or for any of us. We have written what we can write. We are just sitting here, waiting for something to happen. But what will happen?"

"Our work will not be in vain," Lamathe murmured.

Samos grimaced. He complained, but he never did anything about his complaints. Palta had grown very fond of him. "I will come back," she said. "I'm sure of it."

"You must," Karellia said, grasping her arm. "We couldn't stand it otherwise. We have lost too much. We don't want to lose you."

Ah, this was going to be hard.

Palta slept little that night. Tomorrow she would leave, and what would life have in store for her then?

———

Menander

The journey back to Alexandria was both tedious and tense. Palta had little to say. One could barely see her face behind the close-fitting hood, but Menander knew she was excited. He would have liked to talk to her, but about what? He assumed that the people she was living with were priests, but Olef-Nan had forbidden him to inquire; it was better not to know. And as to what would happen when they reached the city…that was in the hands of the gods.

The day was warm but not oppressive, with a pleasant breeze from the sea. There were few travelers on the road. In better times he would have enjoyed walking along this road with Palta. He had always liked her. To be honest, he had loved her, a little bit. She, too, loved books. And she had been to so many places—Roma! Gallia! And far into Barbarica! But she was entirely mysterious to him. She never really explained what she had been doing in these places. She talked more freely to the director, of course. Well, he was no one. If he could help to make her happy, he would be satisfied.

They stopped at mid-day to drink water and eat bread in the shade of a tree. Palta lowered her close-fitting hood. "How much farther?" she asked.

"We are about halfway, I think," Menander replied. "It is a long journey on foot."

"What is Alexandria like nowadays?" she asked. "We hear little about it."

"It is much the same, Palta."

"Are there many soldiers on the streets?"

"Not so many as there used to be. Or perhaps I have gotten used to seeing them."

"Are you happy under the Gallians, Menander?" she asked.

"As long as they don't conscript me into their army, Palta, or take me away from the library. They say that Ploterus is doing good things. We were all so tired of the war."

"How is Olef-Nan?"

"She, too, is much the same. She misses you."

"Olef-Nan was like a mother to me," Palta said. She said nothing after that, and she wept a little more.

Menander wanted to make her feel better, but of course he didn't know how, since he understood nothing. So he stayed silent too. And eventually they arose and continued their journey back to the great city.

———

Olef-Nan

The man who called himself Larry Barnes showed up as instructed on the second day. He sat down in her office and refused refreshment. "My lady, I have followed your instructions," he said. "I have stayed away from the library and asked no one about my friend Palta. Now I have returned to learn if you have any information about her."

He was really quite a handsome fellow, she thought, although he looked rather disheveled and smelled rather bad. If he were a spy, they weren't paying him enough to own more than a single robe.

She nodded. "Here is what I can tell you," she said. "Go to the bazaar in the Bafelni district. It is not far, and anyone can direct you. I cannot be sure, but you may find information there."

"*May find information*?" he repeated. "Is there someone I should ask?"

She shook her head. "Ask no one. Find a bench. Sit. Wait."

"Someone will find me?"

"I cannot say. Perhaps."

"And if no one does?"

"Then return there tomorrow."

"My lady, I do not understand," the man said. "I think perhaps you are simply trying to get rid of me."

"Think what you like. But if you want information about this woman Palta, I suggest that you go to the bazaar in the Bafelni district and talk to no one."

The man stared at her, and his stare had some power in it. Olef-

Nan thought he might be quite interesting to know. Then he shrugged, stood up, and bowed to her. "My lady, I thank you for your assistance," he said, and then he left her office.

Olef-Nan watched him go. *Palta, I have done what I could,* she thought. And then she said a prayer to the gods.

———

Larry

Larry made his way to the bazaar.

What was the director up to? Maybe it was worse than he had thought at first. Maybe she wasn't just getting rid of him; maybe she had sent him to this place so he could be arrested or beaten. But arrested for what? For trying to find a woman he once knew?

Wasn't it more likely that the director knew Palta, and just wanted to be careful? More likely, perhaps, but Larry forced himself not to feel optimistic. The disappointment if he were wrong would be too crushing.

The bazaar, when he finally found it, was large and crowded, filled with stalls selling food, clothing, jewelry, little statues, and many other things he couldn't even identify. He bought a roll, found an open spot on a bench, ate the roll, and looked at the passing crowds. None of the people looked remotely like Palta. The women were all dark-skinned, and most of them wore the dark, hooded robe that covered their body and obscured most of their face. Occasionally soldiers strode past, but they paid no attention to him.

He waited.

He was tired and hungry and dirty, and now he was sitting on a bench next to a very fat woman in an alien city in an alien world. And what would he do if he didn't find Palta in this bazaar? Where would he look next? How would he find her? Perhaps it was time to give up, to return to Elysium. He missed Lucia's cooking. He missed talking to Rigol and Hieron and the others. He missed so much.

He stayed where he was.

The hours passed. The daylight waned. Torches were lit. Some stalls closed, and others opened. Fast music began to play—pipes and lyre and drum. Strange high-pitched voices began to sing. Was there going to be a dance? He went to pee finally, and he bought another roll, and when he returned his spot on the bench had been taken, and he had to find another bench, another weary fat woman to sit next to.

This was better than returning to his hot room in his dirty inn, he supposed. Would he even be able to find the inn? Perhaps he would sleep outdoors tonight; he had done that often enough on Terra. The fat woman heaved herself up and waddled off, and another woman took her place.

Perhaps he should buy himself something to drink. He probably had enough money. He sighed. If he stayed any longer in Egypt, he would have to find work. He would have to make a life for himself. Could he stand that?

He started to rise, but a hand suddenly covered his. He looked at the woman next to him on the bench, and she looked at him.

"Welcome home, my love," Palta said.

FORTY-FIVE

Palta

She took down her hood. He reached out to touch her face. "I just want to make sure you're real," he said.

"I'm real," she replied. "I'm here." And so was he. After all these years. After all that had happened. He was next to her, touching her, gazing into her eyes.

She didn't know how long they sat there until finally Menander murmured, "We must go, Palta. I don't know if you are safe here."

Larry looked up at Menander, standing in front of them. "What's happening?" he asked.

"This is my friend Menander," Palta said. "I'll explain more on the way. Come."

They rose from the bench, and Menander bowed to Larry. "I am very pleased you are here, Larry Barnes. But we must hurry. The streets will be dark and travel difficult."

Menander led them out of the bazaar. Palta and Larry followed, holding hands. She put her hood up once again. Larry's hand felt warm and rough and strong. He was taller now, of course, and he had the beginnings of a beard—perhaps he hadn't been able to shave lately. But he had the same curly brown hair and deep-set eyes. His robe was grimy. So was hers, she noticed, after she had walked along

272

dusty roads all day. She couldn't wait to change her clothes. But that didn't matter.

"We are going to the house of Olef-Nan, whom you have met," she explained.

"From the library? Yes. I hoped she was your friend, but I couldn't be sure."

"She is my friend—more than that, really. She was trying to protect me—I shouldn't be in Alexandria. It is ruled by Ploterus—do you remember him from Massalia?—and he has asked Olef-Nan about me. Do you know any of this?"

"Some of it. Valleia and Carmody showed me your letter. I visited them first when I…came back. That's how I knew you were here."

Ah, there was so much to talk about, so much to learn. "How are they?" she asked.

"They are happy. They have two children—a boy and a baby girl. They wish you happiness, too."

"That's wonderful. And you traveled here from Scotia?"

"I did," he said.

She squeezed his hand. He was here. He was real.

They fell silent as they walked through the darkening streets towards Olef-Nan's villa. How many nights she had spent there, talking, learning!

When they finally reached the villa, it was dark except for a flickering light in the entrance hall. Menander knocked, and Olef-Nan herself opened the door. Palta fell into her arms, weeping with joy. "This is very good," the director murmured. "Very good. Come inside, all of you."

They went in. Olef-Nan bowed deeply to Larry. "I am sorry for the mystery and the subterfuge," she said. "But Palta is very dear to me, and I could not risk harm coming to her."

"I am glad she has such friends," Larry replied.

They walked into the open, airy atrium. "I have dismissed all my servants for the night except Filomena, whom I would trust with my life," Olef-Nan explained. "Menander, you are welcome to stay. You must be very weary."

"No, my lady, I will go to my home," he said. "It is possible you will speak of things I should not hear."

Olef-Nan smiled. "Menander, you are becoming a very wise young man."

Menander grinned at that. Palta hugged him. "I am so grateful to you," she said, and his grin widened.

When he left, Filomena appeared, standing shyly by the door to the kitchen. And of course Palta had to run and hug her as well; she seemed older and frailer than when Palta had last seen her. "You are a mess, my dear," Filomena pointed out.

"Yes, I know."

"I will find a robe for you after you dine."

"I love you, Filomena." The old servant face lit up and she went back into the kitchen. Palta could smell the aroma of broiling fish. Delightful!

She returned to Olef-Nan and Larry.

"Now I will leave you," Olef-Nan said. "Filomena will bring you dinner. Here is a jug of wine, and your know where your room is."

"No, please stay," Palta begged her. She turned to Larry. "If that's all right?"

"Of course it's all right."

Olef-Nan smiled, and they all sat down. She poured the wine, and Palta took a sip. She hadn't had any wine since she left Alexandria. The priests couldn't afford it; they couldn't afford much of anything.

Filomena brought out the fish on a platter, and Palta ate ravenously, in silence. Then she said, "Larry knows a bit about my story. Now can you tell us yours, Larry? Olef-Nan knows everything I know—up to the moment when you disappeared on that hill in Scotia."

"Well, then," he replied, "My story starts to get interesting at that point."

And he told it.

Palta had thought constantly over the years about what had happened to Larry—was he alive? Was he happy? But she hadn't imagined this. How could she imagine this?

"You can build your own portal," she said, as if saying the words aloud would make them easier to believe.

Larry nodded. "I don't know why I have this ability, but it seems that I do."

"And Affron is alive and happy."

"That's right. And he will be pleased to know you are doing so well."

This was better than Palta could have dreamed.

"The most remarkable part of your remarkable story," Olef-Nan added, "is that Hieron is still alive."

"He is. And not very long ago he visited Terra to learn what was happening here. It troubled him greatly."

"Amazing," she murmured. "And he created our Via? That is not the story we learned."

"No, he didn't want people to know."

"So, people who build portals can live forever?" Palta asked. She found this idea disconcerting, even frightening. She didn't want Larry to be so different from her.

"It's not like that," Larry replied. "There's something about the world where he lives—the place called Elysium—that slows down aging, at least for some people. I don't quite understand how it works, and Hieron can't really explain it."

"But you chose to leave Elysium. And come here."

He reached over and took her hand. "Elysium is a wonderful place," he said, "and Affron is happy there. But I needed to find you."

"And now you must decide what to do next," Olef-Nan said to Palta. "You are welcome here tonight, but it would be dangerous to stay longer in Alexandria. I have learned that Ploterus is returning to Roma. He is a Gallian, but as a ruler he has been fair enough. His successor is likely to be far worse, and far more interested in the rumors about you."

Palta realized that it was time to explain her situation to Larry. "Perhaps I should have left with Decius and the others as the rebels advanced on the city. But I couldn't. I loved the library—I loved Olef-Nan—too much. So I stayed. It was a mistake, I suppose—too many people knew me. Finally Olef-Nan convinced me to leave with some priests, who had been living here and were also in danger. We went to a compound south of the city, where they spend their time writing down everything they could remember from the schola. They were the ones who burned down the schola, Larry, to keep the Gallians from possessing all that knowledge. Someday, they thought, the Gallians would be defeated and their knowledge would be needed once again."

"They've been at it a long time," Larry said.

"Too long, I think. Many priests have given up and left—I don't know where they've gone. Even the ones who remain are discouraged. We thought the Gallians might be overthrown when their gants ran out of power, but that hasn't happened. Even so, I have been happy there.

275

Menander went to the compound yesterday to tell me about your arrival. Today we walked back to the city. And here we are."

"And now you must decided what to do next," Olef-Nan said.

"I would like to meet those priests," Larry said.

Palta was delighted to hear him say that. "Oh yes, Larry. I would love that. And so would they."

"Whatever you do, you must be careful," Olef-Nan said.

"We will."

———

The evening grew late, and Olef-Nan retired. Palta went to her room, splashed water from the basin onto herself and put on the turquoise robe that Filomena had laid out for her. Now Larry could see her the way she wanted to be seen. She returned to the atrium, and to Larry. He put his arm around her, and she laid her head against his chest. "I still can't believe this," she murmured. "Does it feel like a dream to you?"

"I worked too hard to get here, to be with you. It's not a dream."

"What will happen next, after we visit the priests?" she asked.

Larry was silent for a while. "I'm not sure," he said finally, "but I think I need to save Terra."

Astonished and hopeful, she gazed up at him. "Do you think you can?"

"Not by myself. But perhaps I won't be alone."

Palta had never been happier. They kissed then, alone in the fragrant night.

And in the morning they made the journey south to the compound of the priests.

FORTY-SIX

Larry

It was a long journey. Larry wasn't used to walking such a distance, but he wasn't going to complain. Palta was beside him, and that was what mattered.

He thought about the priests at their destination, spending their lives trying to preserve the knowledge once stored in the schola. It seemed like a thankless task, but what else could they do? Larry vaguely remembered studying the Dark Ages in history. Wasn't that what the monks had done back then? After the class where they learned about this, his friend Kevin had told him about a science fiction novel he'd read where some sort of monks in the future were doing the same thing. That was the kind of book Kevin liked to read. What was its name? He couldn't remember. Ah, Kevin. He would be in college now, wouldn't he? Larry himself should have been in college, back on Earth.

His thoughts returned to Terra. Could he save it from the Gallians? It seemed possible, with the help of the priests he was about to meet. But what if he failed? What if the result was something far worse than Feslund and his mother?

They stopped at mid-day to rest and eat the food that Filomena had prepared for them, and then they trudged on. They talked more about their lives. Larry finally mentioned his visit to Earth, to his home in Glanbury. "That must have been awful for you," Palta murmured.

"It felt awful," he admitted. "But looking back on it, I think it was okay. It told me something I needed to know."

"What's that?"

"That none of this is going to be easy. That every choice has consequences, good and bad. And there's nothing I can do to change that."

Palta seemed to ponder this. And then she said, "Whenever I thought about what had happened to you, I liked to think: he finally made it home. And now he's safe."

"Elysium is safe," he replied. "Everywhere else is full of danger and confusion. And reward."

"I would like to be safe, for once in my life," she said. And he couldn't argue with that.

It was late in the day when they finally reached the priests' compound. Palta had described everyone who lived there during the journey, so it was easy to recognize them—from the viator Lamathe to the little girl Cetonia and her mother, Uduon. And they all knew his name and were delighted to see him. Everyone, it was clear, loved Palta. "Nothing could make us happier than your arrival," Lamathe said to him.

Larry bowed to him. "Nothing could make me happier than to be here."

Their compound was bigger than Olef-Nan's villa, with a courtyard just inside its outer wall rather than an atrium in the center. After the introductions in the courtyard, Palta led him to an airy room where he washed and changed into a robe he found there. He was tired, but he knew another night of talking lay ahead of him. Palta had warned him: they had no guests here, no diversions. His arrival would be the most exciting thing that had happened to them since they had left Alexandria.

So finally at dusk they all sat in the courtyard and ate and drank weak beer. And Larry told his story once again.

The priests were mostly silent at first. Did they believe him? One of them, Samos, looked skeptical. When Larry told of how he had met Hieron on Elysium; the black-haired priest named Theodosius began to sob. "Hieron must save us," the priest managed to say.

His wife, Karellia, put her arm around his shoulders and drew him to her. But Samos shook his head. "How can you expect us to believe such things?" he demanded.

Larry shrugged. "I find it hard to believe these things myself sometimes."

Palta reached out and grabbed his hand. "If you trust me," she said to the others, "you will trust Larry."

"Would it help," Larry asked, "if I were to build my own Via right here in your compound?"

The priests looked at each other. "You can do that?" the leader, who was called Lamathe, asked.

"It's not easy, but yes, I can."

"Can you bring us to Elysium, to meet Hieron?"

"I can't do that—only those who can build Vias can enter Elysium. But you can see what I'm capable of."

"Can you go to Palta's world?" Samos asked. "Can you bring us gants from Gaia?"

Everyone fell silent. Larry glanced at Palta; she looked frightened.

"Isn't it obvious?" Samos persisted. "Isn't this the solution to defeating the Gallians? Apparently their gants don't work anymore, and they haven't found a viator who will go to Gaia and obtain more for them. So if we obtain these weapons, we can destroy the Gallians; we can take over the empire once again. No more wasting our lives in this ghastly country."

"Gants brought nothing but pain to Gaia," Lamathe replied. "And they surely didn't work as we had hoped when we used them here on Terra."

"I believe," Larry said, "that we won't need gants to defeat the Gallians."

"You have a plan?" Lamathe asked.

"Perhaps. But first I need to build my Via."

———

Palta

Palta sat with Larry in his room. She was exhausted and confused. "I just found you," she said. "I don't want you to leave again so soon."

"Building a portal will take a while," Larry replied. "And I don't want to start right away—it requires strength and concentration. But the sooner I get started, the sooner I can return to Elysium, and we can figure out if we can defeat the Gallians."

"But what is your idea? You wouldn't tell it to Lamathe and the others."

"I want to convince Hieron to help us. I don't think that by itself will be sufficient, but it's a start."

"Will he agree?"

"I think so. He saw what was happening on Terra, and he feels guilty about it. He left this world to fend for itself, and he realizes now that he probably shouldn't have."

"What about Affron? Do you think he will help?"

"I'm not as sure about Affron. In any case, we need something more. Something that will convince Ploterus to join us."

"Ploterus? What makes you think he'd fight against Feslund? He's a Gallian himself."

"We only met him that one time in Massalia, but he seemed reasonable and competent, didn't he? I like to think that if Arminius were still alive, he would join us. Perhaps Ploterus will be the same."

"Olef-Nan thought he ruled Alexandria fairly," Palta recalled.

"I don't know if he will help. I don't know if anyone will help, and I don't know if any of this will work. But we have to try."

"What about your...power? The one you used in the temple of Via."

"Ah, I need to avoid that." And he told her what happened when people used that power. She shivered, thinking about what could have happened that day in the temple of Via.

"Promise me that you'll never do that again," she said, holding him close.

"That's an easy promise to make," he replied. "Don't worry. I'll be all right."

————

Larry

Days passed. They were wonderful days, safe here with Palta at long last. Larry could tell that Palta fretted, though, and the priests, especially Samos, seemed increasingly dubious as time went by and Larry didn't start creating his portal. And then one morning at breakfast, he decided that it was time. "I'll begin today," he told them.

"How does it happen?" Lamathe asked.

"Come and watch if you want. It won't be finished in an hour or a day. But it will happen."

He went to the small garden behind the compound. He liked being outdoors, as he had been in Elysium. The rest of them followed.

"This will do," Larry said.

He sat on the ground. The others stood in a semi-circle behind him. He smiled at Palta, who looked nervous. A marmalade-colored cat from the compound came up and lay down next to him. He petted her.

Then he raised his arms in the air, closed his eyes, and began to dream a portal.

FORTY-SEVEN

Hieron

Life went on as it always had on Elysium, except that Hieron missed Larry. He had been gone a long time, and Hieron worried about him. What if he never returned? Such things happened, and they became a permanent layer of sadness in your memory.

"I feel old," he said to Lucia at the café one day.

"You *are* old," she pointed out.

"Perhaps I should go back to Terra."

"To look for Larry? It's a big world."

"No. To go back and fix it."

"Fix Terra? Without Larry? How?"

Hieron spread his hands. "I don't know. I had energy once. I had ideas. Now I spend my days playing chess and reading books and gardening."

"And talking to me. And eating my food." Lucia poured him a cup of wine and wiped Veronique's face. "Wait," she said to him. "Larry will come back. Even if he found the girl he was searching for, he will come back, if only to tell you what happened. He's a good lad."

"I suppose you're right."

"I'm always right."

And Lucia was right.

He arrived a few days later, knocking quietly on Hieron's door. They looked at each for a long moment before embracing. "I knew you'd return," Hieron lied. "Come, sit, and tell me all that has happened to you. Did you find Palta?"

"I did. It took me a long while, but I found her. She is living with some priests outside Alexandria."

"Alexandria? In Egypt?"

"That's right."

"What are they are doing there?"

"It's a long story. The priests burned down the schola so that its books wouldn't be available to the Gallians. They've spent the years since then secretly writing down all the wisdom and knowledge they could remember from those books, so it wouldn't be lost when the Gallians were finally defeated. Palta is helping them."

"Oh," Hieron replied. "Oh." This news moved him deeply. He had devoted so much of his life to securing that wisdom and knowledge. To think of those priests spending years of their lives trying to recreate it…"Ah, Larry, this is bad."

"I know."

They were silent.

"You want me to help," Hieron said finally.

"I think you want to help," Larry replied.

"I do. But how? I'm old. Lucia pointed this out to me just a few days ago."

"Well, you wouldn't have to fight in a battle," Larry said. "You would just have to be you. You're pretty good at that."

"What do you have in mind?"

Larry told him.

It seemed…plausible. What would Lucia think? "Will Affron help?" Hieron asked. "You could use him, too."

"I don't know. He's so happy here. And he's always been troubled by how much people expected from him on Terra."

Hieron pondered this. "You need to ask him," he replied.

"Yes, of course."

"And give me some time. Old people find it difficult to make up their minds."

Larry smiled and stood up. "You'll do it. I'll go see Lucia. She'll talk you into it."

"Ah, you are a dangerous man, Larry."

Larry left, and Hieron watched from the window as he strode off down the street.

Hieron felt younger already.

———

Affron

Affron was working with Amelia in the garden behind their home when he spotted Larry. They both dropped their tools and ran up to him. Larry hugged Amelia and shook hands with Affron. "I'm back," he said, "and Palta is fine."

"This is wonderful news," Affron said. Palta had been a quick-witted, resourceful girl, and now he supposed she was a quick-witted, resourceful woman. It was good that she was still alive—and that Larry had found her.

"Larry, I'm so happy for you," Amelia added. "And now what?"

Yes, now what? Affron thought. Palta couldn't live in Elysium. Could Larry live without Palta?

"Now," Larry replied, "I need to convince Affron to help me save Terra from the Gallians."

Ah, Affron thought. There was that, too. "Why would you think I'd leave Elysium—leave Amelia—to help you save Terra?" he asked Larry.

"Amelia can help me save Terra, too," Larry replied. "By the way, Lamathe says hello. He hopes you are well, and he says that he too would like your assistance."

"You met Lamathe as well? He is a good man."

"I met several priests. They are desperate and need your help. And Hieron's."

"Hieron? Will he agree to this?"

"Of course he will. Things are bad on Terra. He has been there. He knows it. And so do you."

Amelia looked at Affron. "We should talk more about this," she said.

He sighed. "I suppose we should."

"Let's go to the café," Larry suggested. "Apparently Lucia's opinion will be important."

"Lucia's opinion is always important."

———

Larry

They went to the café and talked. They had concerns, of course. Hieron was too old, Affron was too happy, too in love. Larry understood, but he was confident that they'd agree. Terra was their home; they would help save it.

And if they didn't agree, he would figure out a way to defeat the Gallians on his own.

There was one more thing he had to do while they pondered their decision. And he supposed this would be harder than anything else he had done.

First, he had to pay a visit to Rigol.

FORTY-EIGHT

Kevin

I was walking with Emily through the Yard, heading for the physics lab. The day was chilly and overcast, and I was a bit worried about the lab; still, I was happy. Who wouldn't be happy, walking with Emily?

We were just passing the statue of John Harvard when I heard someone say my name. "Kevin?"

I stopped and turned.

He was sitting behind the statue, on the steps to University Hall. He wore a woolen cap and a ratty parka that was too small for him. He needed a shave, but he looked lean and fit. He was smiling at me.

"Kevin," he went on, "I was trying to remember: what was the name of that science fiction book—the one where monks spent their time writing up knowledge from the past? After a nuclear war or something."

I barely recognized him—but, you know, I did recognize him. My oldest and best friend. My companion during the biggest adventure of my life. The one who had stopped existing when we were in middle school.

"*A Canticle for Leibowitz*," I managed to say.

"Yeah," he said. "That's the one. Strange title. It sounded interesting. Never read it, though. Haven't read much of anything in a long time, to tell you the truth."

"It's you," I whispered.

"It's me," Larry replied.

Tears filled my eyes. I think I turned to Emily, who I think was staring at me, puzzled. "Kev? You okay, Kev?" I think she said. I have no idea what I said to her, or if I managed to say anything. But Emily must have gotten the message, because finally she laid a hand on my arm as if to say *It's OK*, and she walked away.

I turned back to Larry. He had come over to me. We embraced. I was still having difficulty speaking. He said, "You look great, Kevin. And you got into Harvard. I'm impressed. My dad wanted me to go to Harvard, like he did, but that was never going to happen. Even before —you know. I didn't have the grades."

I finally found my voice. "Your family thinks you're dead," I said. "Everyone thinks you're dead—or maybe kidnapped by some pervert. I tried to tell your parents about the portal, but they just thought I was crazy. I tried to show them the portal but of course it was gone, like the first time. You went into it again, didn't you? To help the preacher."

He nodded. "I did. And then complications ensued. I suppose complications always ensue when it comes to the portal. Can we go somewhere and get something to eat? I've been sitting here for a while hoping you'd come by, and I'm cold and hungry."

"Sure. Of course."

We walked over to Bartley's Burger Cottage on Mass. Ave. Larry had a trace of an odd accent now. I thought I knew why. "You haven't been speaking English," I said.

"No, not much. Latin, mostly."

"Latin?"

"Yeah. It's a long story."

"I've got time."

"First tell me about my family," Larry said. "I went back to Glanbury once before, and they were gone. It was snowing, and the only person I saw that I knew was Stinky Glover, but he didn't recognize me and I didn't really say anything to him. When I came back this time, I went to the Glanbury library and found out about you from the high school yearbook."

"Wait—you came back before? Are you back for good now?"

Larry shook his head. "I can't stay. I'll explain, but first, you know, my family. Are they all right?"

"They moved away after you disappeared, Larry. To Acton—closer to your dad's job. They couldn't stand living in Glanbury, with every-thing reminding them of you. Cassie went to college, although I guess she's graduated by now. Matthew must be in high school, I think. I don't really keep in touch—it's too painful for everyone. But I'm friends with your mom on Facebook—do you even know what Face-book is?"

Larry shook his head.

"Doesn't matter. Anyway, your dad is mad at me for putting this crazy idea about the portal in your mom's head. And, like you said, he probably thinks you should be the one going to Harvard. But, you know, I got kind of obsessed after you left. Well, even more obsessed, if that's possible—trying to understand about the multiverse, about how we can travel from one universe to another. You know what it was like after we got back. This was all stuff that I knew was real, was true—it had actually happened to us—but on Earth, scientists would think I was crazy. I wanted to figure it out. There's got to be an explanation—we just don't know what it is. So I studied pretty hard. I'm still studying hard."

"I'm sorry I put you in that position, Kevin. I've thought about that a lot. I got stuck on this other world—it's called Terra—and couldn't get home. It must have been awful for everyone."

"Wasn't great," I agreed, which was the biggest understatement of my life. "Anyway, here's Bartley's."

Larry ordered a burger and fries. He ate the burger like he'd never had one before. "I'm not really used to meat," he explained. "Not beef, anyway. There's nothing like this where I've been living."

Meanwhile Emily texted me to ask if I was all right. I texted her back. Told her an old friend had shown up. I'd never mentioned Larry or our adventure to her. I didn't want her thinking I was crazy too.

I couldn't wait to hear Larry's story. And I felt a little envious. My life is awesome—Emily is amazing, I'm going to a great college and studying what I want to study. But I think every day about our adven-ture. It had been awful in many ways—I got sick and almost died, for starters—but in my memory I didn't bother with the awful parts and concentrated on the wonder of what we'd experienced. Living in a totally different world, learning how to do things on our own, helping to win a war—and most of all, seeing the different path that history could take.

"Okay, Larry," I said when I couldn't stand it anymore. "You've gotta tell me. What's going on? Where have you been?"

"Fine," he replied. "Here goes. I've been rehearsing this, because the story is pretty complicated. I'll do my best."

I tried not to interrupt. But finally he reached the heart of his story, and I had to learn more.

"Wait," I said, "you learned how to build your own portal? How did you do that? Can anyone do that?"

"I don't think so. Kevin, I seem to have a…talent. A power. Don't know why, don't know how. It took me years to develop it, but the preacher—Affron—helped. I was kind of obsessed—like you, maybe."

And I suppose my envy grew then. My friend from middle school had a freaking superpower. But the envy was overwhelmed by my gratitude that he was alive. That he was here, talking to me. Like the old days.

"That's amazing, Larry. I've got a ton of questions, but keep going. Tell me the rest of your story."

He continued, talking about living in a place that sounded like heaven and returning to Terra to search for this girl he was in love with. He told me of his plan to rescue the Roman empire from the bad guys. And, finally, he told me why he was back here on Earth.

"That's it?" I said. "That's why you came back? You need a gun?"

Larry shrugged. "That's it. Doesn't need to be a good one. It just has to work."

"Why do you need it?"

"To impress someone—a general who can help us. Remember the calculator we showed the guards at the refugee camp in Boston? It's like that."

I considered. "Well, I don't know how to buy a gun. They make it hard in Massachusetts. You need a license, and I don't have one."

"Well, what about your cousin Brendan in Quincy? I remember you talking about him."

"Oh geez, Brendan." My cousin was kind of a creep. "He's not just going to give us a gun, Larry. We'd have to buy it from him."

"Of course," Larry said. "I have money." He reached into the pocket of his parka and threw a wad of hundred-dollar bills onto the table.

I stared at them. "How did you get that much money?" I asked.

"I got some gold from a guy on Elysium who collects stuff." Larry took out some gold coins and added them to the pile of money on the table. "You can't use gold to buy stuff on Earth, but you can sell it at a jewelry store, which is what I did with a couple of these coins. The coins are weird-looking because they're from another world, but they're still gold. Kind of freaked out the person at the jewelry store. I had to make up a story about where they were from."

I picked up one of the coins and stared at it. It had indecipherable writing on it, and a likeness of a woman wearing a strange triangular hat—some kind of crown?

"Keep it," Larry said. "The jewelry store gave me plenty of cash. It might help pay your tuition or something."

I wasn't going to sell the coin, but I put it in my pocket. "Thanks," I said. "Let me see if I have Brendan's number." I looked through the contacts on my phone. His number was there, though I couldn't remember the last time I had called him.

I tapped Call, and he answered after a couple of rings. "Hey, Brendan, it's Kev," I said. "I've got kind of an unusual request."

It was a difficult conversation. Brendan and I aren't close. He's older than me, and pretty much a complete loser—dropped out of high school, in and out of trouble, always working on some get-rich-quick scheme that never works out. At family gatherings he likes to make fun of me for going to Harvard. *What do you want to spend all that time studying physics for?* he'd say. *That's never gonna make you any money.* I'm pretty sure he doesn't know what physics is.

But he liked the idea that I was asking him for a favor. *Smart college kid needs help!* And he especially liked the idea of making a lot of money for no work.

"Okay," I said to Larry when I'd finished negotiating with Brendan. "He'll sell you a gun. It's totally illegal, but he doesn't care. Let's go to Quincy."

"Thanks, Kev. Sorry to be such a bother."

I laughed. "Larry, don't be silly. This is the best day of my life."

We took an Uber. Larry, of course, had no idea what an Uber was. He'd missed so much. Not just Uber and Facebook but high school. Summer jobs. Learning how to drive. Taking the SATs. College visits. Senior prom. Normal life for a normal suburban kid. Did he regret it? Maybe he did. But you can't have everything.

As much as I envied Larry, I'd had all those things.

Brendan lived on the second floor of a run-down two-family house in a rough neighborhood. I had never been there before. A mangy dog chained in the yard growled and lunged at us as we opened the rusted gate in the chain-link fence. We made our way up onto a porch that was lined with dead potted plants. Brendan's doorbell was broken, so I rapped on the door. After a minute he let us in. He had greasy black hair, a scrawny beard, and bloodshot eyes. He was wearing sweat pants and a stained sleeveless t-shirt. His heavily muscled arms were covered with elaborate tattoos. He was very proud of his muscles and his tattoos.

"Hey, Brendan," I said.

"What's up, Kev." He nodded to Larry.

We followed him upstairs into his living room, which was filled with empty beer cans and pizza boxes and dominated by a huge TV. The place stank of weed and stale beer.

"So, you want a gun," Brendan said. "Gonna rob a bank to pay your tuition?"

"I told you—my friend needs it."

Brendan turned to Larry. "You robbin' a bank?" he asked.

Larry looked at him. "Don't ask me what the gun is for," he said. And then I noticed something about Larry that hadn't quite struck me before—a presence, a hidden strength. *My friend has a freaking superpower,* I thought again.

Brendan seemed to sense it too. Something in his expression changed; the smug cockiness seemed to fade. And I thought: *Oh my God, Brendan is afraid of him.* What did he think Larry was going to do to him?

"Look," Brendan said to Larry, "they can trace this gun to me. You really can't be using it to do anything illegal. That was just a joke. Just for protection and stuff."

Larry shrugged and took the wad of hundreds out of his pocket. "Don't worry about it. I also need some ammunition." He handed Brendan a bunch of the hundreds. "This should be enough, right?"

Brendan quickly checked the bills to make sure he wasn't dreaming. "Yeah, sure," he said, "that'll be fine."

"All right, let's finish the deal. I'm in a hurry."

"Okay, lemme just get the piece."

Brendan hurried out of the room. "You terrify him," I murmured to Larry.

"I have that effect on some people," he replied. "It's stupid."

Except, I thought, it wasn't.

Brendan returned a few minutes later with a gun and a small box of ammunition. "This is a Glock nine-millimeter," he explained to Larry. "It's really sweet. You know how to use it?"

"Show me."

He gave Larry a quick demonstration. Then Larry put the gun and ammunition in the pocket of his parka and zipped it up. "Okay," he said. "We're done."

"If you want to do any more business," Brendan said, "I'm happy to—"

"That won't be necessary," Larry replied. "And never mention this to anyone. Ever."

"Okay. Sure. Of course."

Larry nodded. "Let's go, Kevin," he said, and he turned and walked back downstairs. "Jesus," Brendan whispered to me at the top of the stairs. "That guy is something." I ignored him and followed Larry. Outside, we made our way past the barking dog and back out onto the sidewalk.

"Thanks, Kev," Larry said. "Brendan should go back to high school, I think."

"No chance of that. So, what happens now?"

"Now I return to Elysium."

"Where's the portal?" I asked. "Where it was before—in the conservation land behind your house?"

He shrugged. "More or less. Here, take the rest of this money. I don't need it."

He shoved more hundreds at me. I thought about refusing them, but why would I do that? I put them into my pocket. "Thanks, Larry," I said.

And here's what I wanted to say: *Take me with you, Larry. Let me see Elysium, let me see Terra. Let me experience these other worlds. Just for an hour, a day. Let me see their people, eat their food, smell their smells.*

But I didn't. Emily had sent two texts that I hadn't responded to yet. *I'm worried about you. Let me know you're OK.* I had missed a lab; I had a quiz to study for. I had a life here. I had no time for Elysium or Terra or the multiverse. So instead I said: "You'll come back, right? After all this is done on Terra. Come back to your family and friends."

Larry looked like he didn't want to talk about it. "I'm not sure," he said.

"You've got to. You know you do. This is your home."

"It's actually kind of hard to say where my home is now."

I decided to ignore his indecision. "When you come back, can we test you? Like, put you in an fMRI or something?"

"What's that?"

"It's a machine that looks at your brain. Maybe it'll explain why you have this power."

Larry laughed. "No, it won't," he replied. "Other people have done that sort of thing, on other worlds. Machines never show anything. Whatever is going on, it's down at a level that machines can't reach."

"Okay, fine. Larry, never mind that. *I* want you back. I've missed you every day since you disappeared. We've both changed, but we're both still the same, you know?"

"I know," Larry murmured. "I know, Kevin." We were both tearing up. We embraced, there on the cold Quincy street, and then he walked away.

I watched him turn the corner, and I thought for a moment about all the lives I would never live, and then I took out my phone to text Emily that I'd be back in Cambridge soon.

FORTY-NINE

Larry

Everyone was at the café when Larry returned. He had told them where he was going and why. Now he took the gun out of his pocket and placed it on the table. People stared at it for a while in silence. He could tell that they didn't like the look of it. He didn't blame them.

"You were successful, then," Hieron said finally.

"Yes," he replied. He sat down, and Lucia brought him a plate of food. He wasn't hungry after the meal he'd eaten on Earth, but he wasn't going to tell her that.

"That is good, then." Hieron didn't sound thrilled.

"Was it painful, going back there again?" Amelia asked.

Of course it had been painful. And leaving had been almost unbearable. But he didn't want to talk about it. "A bit," was all that he said.

"Did you visit your family?"

He shook his head. "Just my friend Kevin. That was all I needed to do to get this gun. I did it, and I came back."

Lucia squeezed his hand. She seemed to understand.

"Going home is never a good idea," M'Nasi observed.

"If I went back to my home world I'd be burned at the stake," Rigol said.

It was time to change the subject, Larry decided. "What's been happening here?" he asked. "Have people made up their minds about helping me?"

"They'll do it," Lucia responded. "All of them. Including Amelia."

Larry smiled and turned to Amelia. "You don't need to help," he said. "It's not your battle."

"It's Affron's battle," she replied, "and so it's mine as well."

"When do we start?" Affron asked.

Larry considered. "Do you have any plans for tomorrow?"

Samos

Samos couldn't stay away from the Via in the garden. He would sit and stare for hours at the spot where it stood. Did he detect a shimmering at times? The faintest blue light? Or was that just his imagination? Occasionally he would approach it and diffidently place his hand inside, watching in wonder as his hand disappeared. His hand was still there, of course, but where? And what would happen if he strode into Via and out the other side? Where would he end up? Could he return?

The others—Lamathe, Theodosius, Karellia, even Palta—were less interested in it, he supposed, because they had actually used Via. But Samos had never had the chance. He'd been too young; he was just in the early stages of his training in Urbis when the Gallians arrived. So Via had just been a luminous, beckoning shape in the temple—something to gaze at in awe, but not to use. Someday, always someday.

And then the someday turned to never. Oh, at first Lamathe and the others thought: surely it would all change when the Gallians' gants lose their power and the people rise up against them...But their gants had failed, and the people had risen, yet still the Gallians clung to power.

And now?

Samos had been angry and despairing for a long time. When Palta's friend arrived, Samos had been happy for her, but who could really believe that this fellow had built his own Via? And then he sat on the ground in the garden and built one before their eyes, in some baffling way that Samos could not hope to understand. And when finally it existed, when finally Larry Barnes walked into it and disappeared, Samos had felt a strange, unexpected, unfamiliar emotion: hope.

And then the agonizing wait began. And every day that passed, Samos felt his hope slipping away. Soon, he thought, the anger and despair would return, only redoubled to make up for the time he had allowed himself to think that perhaps something good would finally happen.

But not yet, not just yet. Still he could sit in the garden and stare at the nothingness, and ponder the incomprehensible mystery that this nothingness represented, and imagine Larry Barnes walking out of that nothingness to save Terra.

Then, finally, it happened. As Samos watched, Larry Barnes walked out of his Via and into the garden.

And Larry Barnes was not alone.

———

Lamathe

Lamathe could not stop weeping. Usually it was Theodosius who wept, and probably he was doing so as well; Lamathe didn't notice, didn't really care. He only cared that Hieron was here, alive, standing in front of them. Lamathe could now see the end of all their struggles, all their doubts and fears. Hieron would be their guide, their savior. With him, anything was possible.

Affron was here, too, and his presence by itself would have been enough to buoy their spirits. He brought with him a woman named Amelia who also had the power to create her own Via. They were all here to help them defeat the Gallians.

It was too much to take in.

Everyone went to the courtyard and sat. Uduon and Cetonia brought them food and beer. Lamathe regained control of his emotions soon enough; the other priests depended on him, and he couldn't let them down. Larry presented his plan, and everyone discussed it. Disagreements were resolved; refinements were proposed. It seemed that no one had told Larry about Hibernia. They would need the priests who lived there, would they not? The plan would take time, they all agreed; it would entail risk. But Lamathe thought: how could it fail? Here was Hieron; here was Affron; here was a weapon from another world.

Larry showed them the weapon, let them hold it. Lamathe had seen such things on other worlds, of course—dangerous worlds that viators often avoided. It was far less lethal than a gant, but in some ways it would be better for their purposes.

When the plan was settled, they talked of other things in the cool evening air. He and the other priests asked questions of Hieron. There was so much they wanted to know. They had spent their lives in the service of Hieron's ideas, and now he was here, sitting with them, happy to explain himself.

And what did Lamathe learn? There was so much, but mostly this: though he and his fellow priests tended to think of Hieron as like a god, someone whose opinions and beliefs were to be treated as sacred, he was just a man like any other, a person who had tried to do his best with the gift that had been given him. "I made many mistakes, I'm sure," Hieron said. "I saw so many worlds, so many ways of living. You have seen them, too. What was best for our world? I was overwhelmed with knowledge, overwhelmed with choices. What worked in one world seemed not to work in another. Many improvements were impossible for Terra; others would take lifetimes to implement, and in the mean-time many people would suffer. Others people would have made different choices, I know; other people would certainly have done better."

Lamathe did not think that this was possible.

And at last the meeting was over. Larry was staying; the others were returning to Elysium. Hieron hugged each of the priests. Then he, Affron, and Amelia returned to the garden, stepped into Larry's Via, and disappeared.

Those who remained on Terra stood in silence for a moment. And then Theodosius said what Lamathe himself had been thinking: "With Hieron on our side, we cannot fail."

Lamathe looked at Samos, the anger-filled cynic. "What do you think, Samos?" he asked.

"This is the first time I have ever agreed with Theodosius," the young priest replied.

Lamathe smiled. "Well, then," he said, "I am going to bed. There is much to be done, and there is no time to waste."

———

Palta

"Thank you," Palta whispered to Larry. They sat alone in his room. His arm was around her shoulders; her head was on his chest.

She had worried every moment since he left. The last time he had left her it had taken him years to return. She did not think she could have survived if that had happened again.

"Affron was very pleased to see you again," Larry noted.

"He looks well," she replied. "Older—there's gray in his hair."

"I hadn't noticed. But you're right."

"And Amelia is lovely."

"Yes," Larry agreed. "And she has been good for Affron. Elysium has been good for him, too. I wasn't sure if he would help us. I think she convinced him."

They fell silent. Palta listened to the wind in the palm trees. "You went home," she said finally.

"Yes," Larry said. "That was the plan—I knew how to obtain a weapon on Earth, more or less. And the gun will be sufficient, I think."

"How was it, being on Earth? How did it feel this time?"

He was silent for a moment. "It was better than the first time," he said finally. "I didn't feel so scared, so alone, so out of place. Things had changed in ways I didn't quite understand, but that was all right. I'm used to not quite understanding things. But I still didn't visit my family. I saw my friend Kevin, and that was hard enough."

Then Palta asked him the question she had been waiting to ask. "Do you want to go back again?"

"I don't know. Not right now, anyway. We've got a job to do. We should focus on that."

"Yes. Of course."

She burrowed deeper into his embrace. She never wanted to leave it. Soon enough more decisions would have to be made. But not now, not now.

Now they had to go on a journey together.

FIFTY

Ploterus

Ploterus arrived at the newly built palace in the morning. Gretyx was in the ornate meeting room, of course, along with Feslund, now king after the death of his father, and a man named Liber, the governor of the Roman province. He supposed that Liber's presence told him what he needed to know.

"Welcome, General!" Gretyx said, actually bowing to him. "We glory in your achievements. Come, sit with us."

Ploterus sat and listened to a few minutes of their praise. It all seemed forced, perfunctory. He didn't care. He had done his duty. They understood what he had accomplished, and if they didn't understand, he did.

"We have read your dispatches, of course, but tell us what is left to be done in Egypt," Gretyx said.

"The rebel army no longer exists as a cohesive fighting force," Ploterus replied. "But there is still scattered resistance. Memmilon is a very competent general; he will take care of the situation."

"And the government of the province?"

"Things will proceed as they have been, I'm sure. The grain will continue to be shipped. The Egyptians are happy enough—they just want peace after years of conflict. I don't foresee any problems."

"What about Decius?" Liber asked. "He has not been captured, I take it?"

Ploterus recalled that Decius was Liber's predecessor as Roman governor. "Decius is still at large," he said. "But he isn't a problem. He has no troops, no support among the people. He ruled Alexandria well enough, it seems, but he was an outsider—like me. They had no particular affection for him."

"And what about priests?" Gretyx asked. "Did you find any?"

"None, my lady. There have been rumors, as I mentioned in my dispatches, but nothing we could ever track down."

"That is troubling."

Ploterus said nothing. The priests, too, were not a problem, except apparently to Gretyx.

"We will instruct Memmilon to pursue the search more vigorously," Gretyx said.

"As you wish, my lady." He didn't care what she instructed Memmilon to do.

"I expect you want to know why you've been recalled to Roma," Gretyx went on.

"I am hoping you have another assignment for me in which I can serve the king and the empire," he responded.

"Of course. Well said. As you may know, General Gregorius, the leader of our armies in the Roman province, has died. He was a worthy man, but far advanced in years. We would like you to replace him."

As Ploterus had feared and expected. "I am honored, my lady, but would not my skills be better used elsewhere? Roma is safe at the moment, is it not?"

"Protecting the city and the province is our most vital task," Liber pointed out. "I fear that Gregorius was somewhat lax in his leadership. The Roman legions need discipline; they need a new sense of purpose."

Their main purpose in recent years had been to kidnap peasant boys and send them to fight in Egypt, Ploterus recalled. And, of course, searching for priests, whom they never found. But he said nothing of that. "Roma is quiet," he pointed out, "but I'm told there are problems elsewhere—incursions from Parthia, the Caucasus…"

"There are always incursions," Gretyx said, waving away the problem. "We know your capabilities, General. We know that, in another crisis, you would be able to assist us as you have in the past."

"Why not enjoy the city while you are here?" Feslund asked. "The citizens of Roma love you—see how they turned out for your arrival yesterday. How did they know you were coming, I wonder?"

Was Feslund jealous of him? Of course he was. And afraid of him, as well. "I didn't try to hide my plans," Ploterus replied. "I wrote ahead to friends and colleagues, so many people knew the date of my arrival. I apologize if what happened yesterday was not appropriate."

"Of course it was appropriate," Feslund replied. "You are our greatest general. You have saved the empire. Why wouldn't the people show their gratitude to you?"

Ploterus inclined his head. "You are very kind, my lord."

"Well then, will you accept the appointment?" Gretyx asked. "We too would be grateful to you."

And what choice did he have? "Yes, my lady, of course I will. I am at your service."

"Excellent! You and Liber can work out the details. Saturnalia is coming before long, and we are planning special celebrations. We cannot allow any disturbances."

"Of course, my lady."

He arose, bowed deeply, and left the room; Liber followed him. Liber was a short, unprepossessing fellow, but his eyes were intelligent. They walked along a hallway lined with tapestries depicting the glories of the Gallians. "You saw this coming, I assume," Liber said.

Ploterus shrugged.

"Gretyx and Feslund are afraid of you," Liber went on.

They have reason to be afraid of me, Ploterus thought. "They have no reason to be afraid of me," he said. "I am merely here to do my duty."

"Of course," Liber replied.

They walked down the grand marble staircase, across the vast entrance hall, past a pair of guards, and out of the palace, where Cymbian and three other soldiers awaited. He had felt the need for bodyguards upon his return to Roma, and Cymbian had been eager to lead them. It had occurred to Ploterus, of course, that Cymbian could be a spy planted by Gretyx or Feslund, but Ploterus felt that he could trust the man. One needed to make such judgments every day in his position. And he needed people who understood what was going on in Roma.

"Gretyx has revived the ancient Praetorian Guard," Liber said, noticing Ploterus's soldiers. "They report only to her and Feslund. They are sworn to protect the lives of the imperial family."

"Why are you telling me these things?"

"Because I would like to be your friend. And I want you to know the situation here."

You are not going to be my friend, Ploterus thought. And he already knew about the Praetorian Guard. "That is very kind of you," he said.

"Life is not bad for people like us," Liber went on, "if we give Gretyx what she wants."

"I have always striven to do so."

They walked across the Forum, past the temple of Via, a replica of the one in Urbis. Outside it was a statue of Hieron with his arms stretched held forward, palms up, as if presenting Romans with the future. Why was that statue still there?

"They are going to tear down the temple during Saturnalia," Liber said, as if reading his mind. "We are going to build a senate house, just like the one that stood there in the old days. And the senators will name Feslund emperor, as they did in the old days. It will be as if the priests never existed."

"Won't people object to having an emperor?" Ploterus asked.

"What does it matter to the people? They know who their rulers are. Why should they care about their titles? They certainly won't complain if we distribute enough denarii to them."

"Where will all the denarii come from?"

"Ah, that is a problem. Gretyx's palace has emptied the royal treasury. I suppose the people of Egypt will be paying higher taxes before long. As well as everyone else in the empire. Come, here is the provincial government's building. Not nearly as glorious as the royal palace, but that is at it should be. Let's go inside and discuss your important new role. I am very pleased you are here."

Ploterus followed the governor into his building. No, this man would not be his friend, he thought. He would look out only for himself.

Perhaps it had been a mistake, he thought, to return to Roma without an army.

───

Gretyx

"I do not trust Ploterus," Feslund said.

"Of course not," Gretyx replied.

"He has hired Cymbian to be on his personal staff," her son continued. "That is unacceptable."

Gretyx didn't bother to respond; Cymbian didn't matter in the slightest. She stared out the window at the Forum below. Ploterus and Liber were walking past the temple, deep in conversation, surrounded by soldiers.

In moments of weakness, she regretted everything that had happened since Siglind returned from Roma with her two friends and their gant. Now Gretyx was the most powerful woman on Terra, but her family was all but gone. Siglind was dead. As was Carolus, victim of a wasting disease that even Feslund's magic medicine could not cure. And Feslund was a drunk who could scarcely be trusted to give a speech, never mind lead an empire. She had longed for a grandchild, but that fool Bathanala had failed to give her one, miscarrying time after time until finally she produced a sickly creature who died within a month. Now she scarcely left her rooms, unwilling to speak to anyone, unwilling to let Feslund touch her. And this, of course, did not bother Feslund at all.

So it was all up to Gretyx. Regret was unacceptable, a weakness she could not allow herself. The only way to succeed was to ignore the past and refuse to admit the possibility of failure.

"If we don't trust Ploterus, why is he here?" Feslund demanded. "Why not leave him in Egypt, or send him to win the war with the Parthians?"

"We have discussed this," Gretyx responded with all the patience she could muster. "We can keep our eyes on him here. Do you remember the history of the empire? Before the priests, armies regularly proclaimed their generals to be emperor. Their loyalty was to their general, not to some far-off ruler they had never seen. He could promise them whatever he liked—land, treasure—and they would follow him. Do you think we could have withstood an invasion by battle-hardened legionaries led by Ploterus?"

"He will command legions here," Feslund pointed out.

"They owe no loyalty to him—at least not yet. The people love him because he has been victorious, but the people have no swords. And

303

they are fickle. They will love us when we shower them with gifts at Saturnalia."

"We should murder him."

"He has surrounded himself with bodyguards. He is too clever to let himself be murdered."

"We should have had him killed in Egypt."

"Perhaps. But what if the assassin was captured and told Ploterus that we sent him? Then he would surely have attacked us."

Feslund slouched in his chair, brooding. "I need a new wife," he blurted out finally.

Gretyx didn't respond.

"Don't you agree?" he went on. "This isn't working. I can barely stand to look at Bathanala. And she certainly isn't interested in me. I have done my duty by her, but she hasn't produced an heir. Let's find someone else."

"You know the problem," Gretyx responded wearily. "Her father—"

"I don't care about her father!" Feslund roared.

Gretyx glared at him. He fell silent. "We do not need any more internal rebellions," she said, explaining to him what she had already explained to him a dozen times. "We cannot risk losing Aquitania. If the king decides to sever ties to the empire because we have treated his daughter badly, we lack the soldiers to stop him. As it stands, there's little reason for him to continue supporting us."

"But Bathanala doesn't want to be here. She hates us all."

"I am well aware of that. And so is her father. He doesn't care, and neither do I. He wants a grandson who will rule the empire. He won't get that if he accedes to her wishes—or yours. So both of you will continue to do your duty. You don't need to like it. But we have no choice."

"What if we find a baby and pass it off as hers?"

"Will she agree to that?"

He shrugged. "We could find another bride with a rich father," he suggested.

"Do you think I haven't tried?"

And Gretyx thought: what if she had Feslund adopt Ploterus as his "son" and successor? The Roman emperors had done such things in the past. It had worked after a fashion. It might be better than waiting for Feslund to sire an heir.

304

It wouldn't happen, though. Ploterus would be foolish to agree—and Ploterus wasn't foolish. Why wait decades for Feslund to die when he could seize power now? Or he could let himself be adopted and then poison Feslund. And her.

It was difficult, always difficult. If only they could find a viator who could bring them more gants. They thought they had found one recently. He was married, and they had kept his wife as a hostage. He had walked into Via—and didn't return. It seemed that the wife had agreed to this with her husband, knowing she would be killed as a result. Better that than help the Gallians.

Sometimes Gretyx thought: could they have done something else along the way? Used the gants more wisely, perhaps, or been more merciful, as Carolus had forever been urging? But it didn't matter. This was the path they had chosen. There were other worlds where other decisions had been made, apparently—where Siglind was still alive, and they were all happy back in Gallia. But she didn't care about those worlds, and she didn't care about the past. They were here, now. Nothing else mattered.

And she would defeat anyone in this world who challenged her.

FIFTY-ONE

Decius

He lived in Judea now, in a small port town called Joppa, sharing a cramped flat with Corscius, who refused to leave him. The flat was in a building on a hillside overlooking the harbor, and every day he looked out at the harbor and wondered if this would be the day when they would board a ship that would take them far away from this place. Or, more likely, if this would be the day that soldiers would arrive to arrest them and lead them off to their deaths. He had governed the province of Roma; he had governed Egypt. Now he eked out a living as a scribe for a local merchant. Corscius was better at this sort of thing, and earned more than he did as a secretary to the owner of an orange grove.

Did anyone suspect that they had been rebels—that he had been one of the leaders of the rebellion? It seemed possible. But no one here cared much whether the Gallians or the rebels or the priests ruled the empire, as long as the harvest was good and there were markets for what they produced. Most people probably saw them for what they were—two foreigners among many who had washed ashore here, victims of a world in ferment. And they were left alone.

Until, finally, a knock came on the door.

No one ever knocked on their door. Corscius looked at Decius. "Shall I open it, my lord?" his aide whispered.

Decius shrugged and nodded. What was the alternative?

Corscius rose from his chair, crossed the room, and opened the door. And their lives changed.

Palta was standing there next to a brown-haired man wearing a gray robe. She embraced Corscius. "It's so good to see you again, Corscius," she said.

Corscius seemed to be too overcome with emotion to reply. Palta smiled past him at Decius. "And it's good to see you too, my lord," she said. "This is Larry Barnes. You may remember him from a hot changing room beneath the Circus Maximus many years ago."

Ah, he did remember a younger version of the man standing in the doorway. Palta had spoken a great deal about Larry Barnes. And somehow they had found each other. And then they had both found him and Corscius. How astonishing.

"Come in, then," he said. "Let Palta go, Corscius. She needs to hug me, as well."

The two guests entered the flat. Seeing them in the small main room, separated from the sleeping area by a dingy curtain, Decius was acutely aware of how low he had fallen.

"But how did you know we were here?" he asked as they settled themselves around the table. Corscius had produced a jug of the local wine, which was far better than anything to be had in Egypt, and poured them each a cup. Then he set out a plate of olives and dates.

"Olef-Nan knew," Palta replied.

"But how? I didn't tell her."

"My lord, when we arrived here I wrote to the director to let her know where we were," Corscius said. "Forgive my presumption, but no one knows who I am, so I thought it would be safer than a communication from you."

"Ah, thank you, Corscius. And stop addressing me as 'my lord'. It will get us in trouble someday."

"Of course," Corscius replied. But he wouldn't do it, Decius knew. Not for long, anyway.

But that didn't matter. And neither did the size of their flat, or the quality of their wine. Here was Palta, sitting at his table, still alive, still lovely—and happy, it seemed, now that she had found her friend.

"Our story is easy to tell," Decius said. "We are here. We are alive.

And we worry every day that we will be discovered and arrested. But I expect that what you have to tell us will be far more interesting."

"I believe that you are right," Palta replied.

Then she and Larry told their story. It lasted long into the night. And when they were done, Decius felt as if he had been reborn.

"And so you want us to come with you to Roma," he said at the end.

"More than that," Larry replied. "We *need* you to come with us. We will defeat the Gallians, but then we will have to rule the empire. We will have priests, but they won't be enough. The people of Roma loved you. You can gain their support, and you can make sure they are on our side."

Decius looked at Corscius. "What do you think?" he asked.

"We cannot do otherwise, my lord," Corscius replied. He was already using "my lord" again.

"Then we shall do it," Decius said. "And gladly. When do we leave? We will have to book passage on a ship."

"A ship awaits, my lord," Palta replied. "We leave when you are ready."

———

Borafin

Borafin awoke before dawn, as usual. The room was cold, as usual. Outside, the wind howled, as usual.

He lit the stub of a candle by his bedside, used the chamber pot, gnawed at a hard roll left over from the previous night, and brought the candle over to the table. He rubbed his eyes and stared at the stack of paper on the table. He read the page on top. Was there anything more to be said? Did his words even make sense? Often he didn't know anymore. He found his ideas and his memories fading and shifting. Had he ever lived in Urbis? Had he ever traveled to other worlds? All that was real was the wind and the sea and the relentless passing of time.

After sunrise, he snuffed out the candle and went downstairs. Livia and Clovis were already there. A large but smoky fire blazed in the stone fireplace, yet the room was still cold. Livia and Clovis were young. They had been lovers once, but no longer, he thought, though they were still friendly enough to each other. They would leave before long, he was sure. Like the others. They wouldn't want to end up like poor old Metius, wasting away in his room, unable to get warm no matter how they built up the fire for him, raving about ancient grudges.

Now his body lay buried on the headland, overlooking the sea he had come to hate.

Honoria came down in a few moments, and they all made breakfast together. "It will be warmer today, I think," Honoria said. It was odd, but often she actually seemed to like it here—the silence, the isolation. She still had much to write, long after the rest of them had run out of things to say. He had read it all, of course, and it was good, if wordy— long disquisitions on the structure of government under the priests; biographies of pontifexes, many of whom he scarcely remember from his studies; and, of course, descriptions of the worlds she had visited— how could she remember so much?

"Perhaps we could boil a chicken for dinner," Clovis suggested.

"Yes, I suppose so," Honoria said. "That would be good, for a change."

She too was worried about Clovis and Livia leaving. Clovis in particular was hungry all the time, and he had grown to hate the fish they ate meal after meal. Borafin couldn't blame him.

After breakfast they set about their daily chores. It was good to have something to do, even if it was as simple as feeding the chickens. By mid-day they were done. Then Borafin tried writing some more, but no words would come.

For Borafin this was the hardest time. This was when the dark thoughts came.

He donned his cloak and went outside, stood on the headland, and stared out to sea. Behind him their home loomed, dark and forbidding. It had once been a fortress of some kind, guarding the western coast of Hibernia, but it had long been abandoned by the time they arrived. They had done what they could to make it habitable, but it would never be anything other than drafty and damp and ill-suited for human habitation.

When the four of them were gone, there would be no one left. Borafin imagined the last of them—it would be Borafin himself, perhaps—sitting by himself, scratching away on his dwindling supply of parchment day after day, knowing that his words would never be read, that his life had been wasted.

Or, afterwards, the fortress standing empty on the windswept headland once again, facing out onto the deserted ocean. Would anyone ever venture into it, someday in the distant future, and find his words—written, perhaps, in a language long forgotten? Would they try to decipher them?

More likely they would use the parchment to feed the fire. A couple of days' worth of warmth against the bitter winds. What else would they be good for?

And that was when he spotted the ship.

At first he wasn't sure. He had been mistaken before. His eyes weren't what they used to be. But he stayed there on the headland, staring out at the dot on the horizon, and it grew and gained form, until finally he raced inside and brought the others out to share his excitement, or tell him he had gone mad.

"It is a ship," Clovis agreed.

"What does it mean?" Livia asked. "We thought that soldiers, if they ever came for us, would arrive overland. Why would someone come here by ship?"

"Perhaps it is heading elsewhere," Clovis suggested.

But no, the dot on the horizon grew steadily larger. It was coming towards them.

"What do you think?" Borafin asked Honoria.

Honoria said nothing. She was afraid, he knew—and not just by the prospect of soldiers finally arriving. She had long ago stopped taking her turn walking to the distant village for supplies, claiming her joints were too sore. It had been two years or more since she had seen another human being besides the three of them.

"They will have to anchor offshore and row a boat to shore," Livia said.

"Should we do anything with the manuscripts?" Clovis asked.

That was always the question. The manuscripts were why they were here. What would they do with them if the soldiers came? They had discussed this. They had a plan. "I will burn them if we need to," Honoria said. "Just give the signal."

"We can't burn them," Livia said, tears in her eyes. "We just can't."

"Of course we can," Honoria replied. "We burned the schola. We can burn these few books."

"Surely it won't come to that," Borafin said.

"Let us hope not," Honoria said. "But we must prepare."

Along with Clovis and Livia, Borafin made his way down the winding rutted path that led to the narrow beach where a boat would have to land. Honoria stayed at the top of the path, awaiting their signal.

The three of them stood there, looking out to sea. Time passed. The ship came to anchor a few hundred paces off shore and stayed there, bobbing on the waves. "What now?" Clovis demanded. Borafin didn't respond. Finally they saw a boat being lowered into the water, then people clambering down a rope ladder into it.

Who would come here, Borafin thought, except soldiers in search of priests? Surely someone in the village had made a guess—it wouldn't be so hard. They were not natives; they kept to themselves; they seemed not to do any work. They were priests who were hiding from the Gallians. And that person had told someone, who had told someone else…

But why were the soldiers coming by sea?

Perhaps other soldiers were coming by land, leaving them no escape—not that they had anywhere to escape to.

They had been here so long, it was hard to imagine being anywhere else. It was home, he thought. As strange as it seemed, it was where they belonged.

"Can you make out anything?" he asked the others.

"Not yet," Clovis said.

"I don't see sunlight glinting off metal," Livia said. "Wouldn't they have swords?"

Of course they'd have swords.

Whoever they were, they were making good progress. Rowing with the tide, he realized. It would be over soon. He turned and looked up the path. Honoria was standing there, ready for his signal.

"I think these are not soldiers," Clovis said quietly.

"It is Lamathe!" Livia shouted. "I see Lamathe! And Samos!"

She rushed out into the frigid water, and Clovis followed. Borafin walked up to the edge of the water and stared at the men waving to him from the boat. Yes, yes, yes! Borafin's spirit soared as he realized that there would be no soldiers, no imprisonment, no torture. Only old, dear friends whom he never expected to see again.

"Come, Honoria! Come!" he shouted. "It's all right! Everything is all right!"

Lamathe and Samos stumbled out of the boat as it slid to a halt on the rocky beach. "Oh my friends, it's good to see you!" Lamathe said as they all embraced. "We arrive with amazing news. Are the others in the fortress?"

"Ah, there is only Honoria," Borafin said. "The others have died or gone away. It has been a long time."

Lamathe shook his head sadly. "Yes, it was much the same in Alexandria. But it is all going to change. I cannot wait to tell you."

They pulled the boat up onto the beach and made their way up to the fortress. Honoria met them on the path, weeping. "Oh, I did not expect this," she gasped. "Oh, Lamathe. And Samos. Come, come."

They went inside. Clovis put more wood on the fire, and Livia got out the jug of whiskey they hadn't touched since the death of Metius. If ever there was a cause for celebration, this was it. Then they sat in front of the fire, and Lamathe and Samos told their story.

It could not have been stranger, or more welcome. Lamathe and Samos had met Hieron? Someone had built a Via in their garden? They thought they could bring down the Gallians by themselves, without soldiers, without gants? They had come all this way to bring their fellow priests to Roma with them? Perhaps the long years of isolation and tedium had driven the two of them mad.

Borafin had not known Samos well, but he had attended the schola with Lamathe. Lamathe was not mad. And Borafin believed him.

But did he believe this plan would work?

Honoria put his doubts into words. "I fear that you have deluded yourselves," she said to them. "These are wondrous events, surely, but how can you expect to bring down the Gallians, even with Hieron and Affron? Why did you not use this Via you possess to obtain gants? Perhaps then you would have a chance."

Lamathe shrugged. "Hieron and Affron both refused to use gants. They will not do this with violence."

"But you said the other one—what is his name?—has a weapon."

"Larry is his name," Lamathe replied. "And yes, he has brought a weapon from his home world. But he does not intend to harm anyone with it. It will simply demonstrate our powers."

Honoria looked as if she was going to weep again. "You are asking all of us to trust you, to travel to Roma with you," she said. "But if we fail, our cause is doomed. Everything we have been working for—here and in Egypt—will have been wasted, because there will be no one left to carry it on."

"If we do not try, we may not *have* another chance," Samos pointed out. "Terra may not have another chance."

"But what are you doing with your manuscripts? Surely you are not leaving them unattended, for others to find and read."

"We left Theodosius and Karellia behind in Alexandria," Lamathe said. "They will bury the most important of them. After they leave for Roma, we have friends in Alexandria who will make sure the rest of them are safe."

Honoria merely shook her head, as if these precautions seemed far from sufficient.

"Well, I'm going," Clovis said. "How can we stay here? How can we not return to Roma?"

"I will go too," Livia added. "Perhaps the plan will fail, but we must attempt it. We have done all we can here. The time has come."

Honoria looked at Borafin. As did Lamathe and the others. Borafin gazed back at Honoria. *She is afraid to leave,* he thought. Not because the plan might fail, but because *she* might fail. She was too used to her life here. She would not know what to do in Roma, how to act, how to live. Borafin grasped her hand. "I too will go," he said. "Please come with us."

She shook her head, her eyes filled with tears. "Someone must stay here and guard our manuscripts," she said. "If you are successful, come back for me."

"You will be alone, Honoria," Lamathe pointed out.

"Others can stay with me if they choose."

"What if you become ill?" Livia asked.

"Then I will die. We all die someday."

The room fell silent.

"Very well," Lamathe said. "We have no time to waste—we have a long voyage ahead of us. We will leave tomorrow."

So it was decided.

Borafin wanted to try one more time to change Honoria's mind, but instead she tried to change his. "They will fail, you know," she said to him the next day, as the others prepared to leave. "We can be happy here, whether they succeed or fail."

"I won't be happy here," Borafin replied. "Not if I know I could be helping them. In any case, I want to see Roma and Urbis again before I die. I want to use Via. I want to help Terra. Do you not want these things?"

She did not respond for a while, and then she shook her head. "It seems that I no longer care. You go, Borafin. I will be fine. And if I'm not fine, I have only myself to blame."

And as he left her there and went down to the beach and got in the boat with the others. As they rowed away he looked up and saw Honoria, alone on the headland, raising her hand in a final salute. He raised his hand as well, and then he watched as she turned her back on them and disappeared into the fortress.

FIFTY-TWO

Affron

Affron began building his own portal.

It wasn't easy. Perhaps it would never be easy. But now, in particular, it was difficult, because he wasn't sure he wanted to do this.

He didn't want to leave Elysium, but he knew that he had to.

He had promised to help the others save Terra, but he didn't think he, or they, would succeed. More likely they would all be captured or killed. Or he would be forced to use that strange power he and Larry possessed, and end up like Jubal and Veronique. The power was still inside him, he knew, and it might come out in spite of himself in a moment of danger or anger. That had happened before, and those had not been happy moments. Now that he had seen Jubal and Veronique and the others, those moments seemed terrifying.

No one had to worry about such things on Elysium.

He complained to Amelia every night. She comforted him every night. "We are more powerful than our enemies," she said. "And far smarter."

"Perhaps you are right," Affron replied. "Or perhaps the others are deluding themselves. Lamathe and the priests need to do something or their lives will have been wasted. Larry needs to make up for handing

315

the empire to the Gallians. And Hieron—his life's work has been destroyed. He has to set things right. But what is any of this to me?"

"They are your friends. It is your home. You must try."

"There are other versions of my home."

"But this is the version that you lived. This is the one that brought you here, to me."

Affron could not argue with that. So he went into the woods and built his portal. He had time, of course. The others back on Terra had vast distances to travel to get the people they needed and bring them to Roma. And if they arrived before him, they would wait for him; they had nothing better to do.

Eventually the portal was done, and it was time to leave. Amelia was there, along with Hieron and Lucia and Rigol, who gave him a purse filled with gold for the expenses he would incur on Terra. He embraced them all. "I'll be back when we're ready," he said.

"We'll be here," Amelia said, smiling. She kissed him, and then pushed him into the portal. He took a step, and then another step, and he was standing in an alley. It was cold out. The alley smelled of garbage. A black cat stared at him; he stared at the cat. "Am I in Roma?" he asked.

The cat ignored his question and sauntered away. Affron followed him. Out on the street, he recognized where he was—in Trastevere, a neighborhood on the west bank of the river. Close enough to where he needed to be.

He bought a woolen cape to keep him warm. Then he made his way to the waterfront tavern they'd agreed would be their meeting place. As he'd expected, none of them were there. They would arrive eventually, he hoped. Then he wandered through the city—watching, listening. Most of what he saw and heard was just the stuff of everyday life, of course—gossip, work, idle chatter. But he could sense what Hieron had sensed in his short visit to a rural village—the despair, the fear, the sense of futility. In his experience Romans had always resented the priests and expected more from them than they received—it was the Roman people who had created the empire in the first place, after all. But that had been an argument between equals, of a sort. And they had a champion in Decius. This was different. Now they were ruled by foreigners, and they had no champion, and no hope.

Affron had enjoyed visiting new worlds and trying to understand them, trying to speak to the natives and perhaps to help them in some small way. He thought he had wisdom to share. But what wisdom could he share with these people—his own people? They didn't need wisdom; they needed to overthrow their rulers.

As night fell he ended up in the Forum, where he stared at the Gallians' garish new palace, right next to the temple of Via. Then his attention was caught by activity in front of the temple. He joined a crowd watching as workmen tore down the statue of Hieron that had stood there ever since the temple had been built—Hieron, his arms outstretched to the people, guiding them, inspiring them.

Affron felt distraught, even though he had left the real, living Hieron only hours before.

"What are they doing?" he asked a group of men.

"Getting ready to replace the temple," one of them said.

"Shouldn't be doing that," another man said. "It's not right."

"They don't care. Why should they care? They need their senate house."

"What's the point of a senate house?" Affron asked.

"Someplace for the rich folks to play, I suppose. They give the king money, he makes them senators. They make him emperor, they get to wear old-fashioned togas and lord it over the likes of us."

"Why does the king need the money, is what I want to know," a third man said. "The war in Egypt's over. That'll save him money."

"He and his mother have to pay for that palace, don't they?" the second man replied.

"I hear they'll use the money for their Saturnalia gift to the people," the first man said. "A hundred denarii to every citizen, is what I heard."

"Bah," the second man scoffed. "Any money they come up with, they'll spend on themselves. We'll be lucky if we get an increase in the bread ration."

Saturnalia, Affron thought. When servants could mock masters, when for a few days the world was turned upside down before grim reality took over once again. What strange things could happen during Saturnalia?

Suddenly Affron could not wait for the others to arrive.

He bought an empty insula from an owner shocked that someone was willing to take it off his hands. "You'll have a hard time finding tenants," the man felt obliged to point out. "Ones who'll pay their rent, anyway."

"I'm sure things will get better," Affron replied.

"Can't get any worse."

The owner threw in some beds and chairs, and Affron found other furnishings in the neighborhood. And every day he went to the tavern, sipping a cup of wine and listening to Romans bemoan the state of the world.

And then finally Theodosius and Karellia arrived on a ship from Alexandria. It was good to have company. But he was relieved when Larry and Palta showed up from Joppa a week later, bringing with them Decius and his aide. The others would be useful, but the plan could not succeed without Larry.

Larry liked the new version of the plan that Affron proposed as they discussed it in the insula. "We'll have to convince Hieron," he pointed out.

"Don't worry," Affron replied. "Hieron will agree to it. Now that you're here, I can go back to Elysium and make sure."

"Go, then. There's no time to waste."

And that's what he did.

It was good to be home again in Elysium, sitting in Lucia's café with Amelia and Hieron and the others. He longed to stay, but he knew he couldn't. He described to Hieron and Amelia what he wanted them to do. And, as he expected, Hieron didn't hesitate. "I will do it," he said. "It will be…interesting."

"You'll need to practice," Lucia pointed out. "I'll help you."

"You will do nothing but criticize me."

"Only if you need criticism."

Amelia smiled and squeezed Affron's hand. "You don't need to return to Terra right away, do you?" she whispered. "I have missed you."

He smiled back. "I can spare some time for you," he said.

He and Amelia walked back to their home through the moonlit night. And it was hard to leave her the next morning. But he did. In the meantime, Lamathe and Samos had arrived in Roma with the priests from Hibernia. It was delightful to see them again, especially Borafin. At last they were all together, and not a moment too soon.

"We're ready to begin," he said to them, as they sat in a chilly room on the second floor of the insula. "And now we will reclaim the empire that we lost."

FIFTY-THREE

Ploterus

Ploterus had quickly come to despise everything about Roma, except for its public baths. Feslund had built a spectacular one outside the Forum, and Ploterus had taken to going there every day. He was there now, relaxing in the heated caldarium, eyes closed, thinking.

It was absurd that Feslund and his mother considered these baths an expenditure worth making, along with their absurd palace. Why not increase pay for the legionaries? Why not buy off some of the tribes who continued to pour across the empire's borders from the north? But this was what Roman emperors did, he supposed. Invading tribes were a problem, but they were far away; the people of Roma were right outside your palace gates. You needed to keep them happy—and above all you needed to keep yourselves happy.

The baths kept Ploterus happy, even if his new assignment did not. Of course, he understood why Gretyx wanted to keep him close, rather than giving him command of distant legions that he could use to march on Roma and seize power from her. Would he do such a thing? Possibly. He was a Gallian, so he felt some loyalty to the royal family. King Carolus had been beloved. But Feslund had turned out to be a drunkard and a fool; Gretyx was neither of those things, but she was cruel and greedy. And the combination of the two of them had created immense suffering for the empire.

Anyway, here he was, commanding the army of the Roman province—a useful but undemanding task for someone who had defeated German tribes and a rebel army and had governed Egypt. The more demanding task was ensuring that Gretyx didn't kill him.

But right now that wasn't worth thinking about. Instead he thought about moving back to the tepidarium and completing his bath.

"My lord," Cymbian murmured.

Ploterus opened his eyes, tensing at the possibility of danger. But Cymbian didn't look concerned. He held out a piece of paper. "A man asked us to give you this message, my lord."

"Did you recognize him?"

"No. He said you knew his master in Egypt. He doesn't look dangerous."

Ploterus often received messages asking for favors, though rarely in the baths. He sighed, took the paper, and read it. Then he frowned and read it again. "The man is alone?" he asked Cymbian.

"Yes, my lord. You can see him over there."

The man was standing by the door to the caldarium. He was middle-aged, stout, and gray-haired, with a long scar on his shoulder— a sword wound? He didn't look like a soldier—at least, not a legionary. Could've been retired, though. He was sweating profusely. The baths would do him good.

Ploterus looked around; there were others in the caldarium, of course, but his guards always made sure he had a private corner. "Bring him to me," he said to Cymbian. "Then don't let anyone else near us."

Cymbian nodded and motioned to the guard at the door to let the man approach.

The man sat down next to him. "*Governor Decius wishes to speak to you,*" Ploterus said, reading the message aloud. "But you are not Decius."

The man nodded. "My name is Corscius. I am his aide."

Ploterus vaguely remembered the name. "Decius is in Roma?"

"He is, my lord."

That was strange. "Does he want to surrender, to plead for mercy?"

"No, my lord."

"What else do we have to speak about, then?"

Corscius glanced around, evidently to ensure that they weren't being overheard. "My lord, there are priests in Roma as well," he replied. "They will soon be reclaiming the empire as their own. Decius has joined them; he would like you to join them too."

This was not a message that Ploterus expected to hear. He considered ordering Cymbian to haul the man away; but he didn't. "That is absurd," he scoffed. "What do you mean, priests are in Roma? How can they reclaim the empire? They have no power."

"My lord, they do."

"What sort of power? The rebels have been destroyed. We have our legions; we have Via."

Corscius shook his head. "The priests have created another Via."

"What?" Ploterus noticed that the man had omitted his obsequious *my lord*.

"Another Via," Corscius repeated. "Which gives them access to weapons beyond human understanding."

"I don't believe it."

Corscius shrugged. "We do not expect you to believe anything on my word. Or on anyone's word. Come to the cemetery outside the north gate of the city at the sixth hour."

"If they have such weapons, why haven't they already seized power? What do they want with me?"

"They want you on their side."

"Why?"

Corscius stood. "You will learn more at the cemetery. Come alone. They will find you."

"Wait!" Ploterus demanded.

But Corscius was already leaving the caldarium. Ploterus considered going after him and demanding he explain himself further. Have him arrested. Tortured.

But Ploterus did nothing. The aide was nobody. Was this a trick, a trap? If so, what was the point of it? If the priests had weapons like the gants, then what need did they have of Ploterus? He had never believed the story that it was the gods who had given the priests those weapons. He didn't pretend to know the true story, and really, the truth didn't matter. The priests either had the weapons or they didn't.

So what should he do? Follow the man's instructions? Find out if there actually were priests waiting for him in the cemetery, if they actually had an offer to make?

One thing was clear: he wasn't going to the cemetery without his bodyguards. He got up and signaled to Cymbian. They had much to discuss.

———

He arrived at the cemetery at the prescribed time with Cymbian and two others. The weather was cold and gray—a fitting afternoon to visit the dead. He dismounted and waited for something to happen. A procession of mourners walked past him, heading back to Roma; a couple of them glanced at him with a mixture of curiosity and fear. What were these soldiers doing here?

He wondered that himself as time passed and no one else appeared. If Decius or priests were in fact here, they could be observing him from behind some monument. Perhaps they wouldn't show themselves because he wasn't alone.

"Not a fit place for a meeting," Cymbian said.

"No, probably not."

"We should leave."

But Ploterus decided to wait a while longer. Finally he spotted a woman approaching along the cemetery's main path. She was young and pretty, with blonde hair and gray eyes. She wore a dark blue cloak over her robe.

"General, you have not obeyed your instructions, I fear," she said as he came near. She spoke Latin with a trace of an accent.

"Who are you?" Ploterus replied.

She shrugged. "Come with me—alone—and we can talk."

"I will come, but I won't come alone."

"Palta?" Cymbian said suddenly.

Palta looked at him and smiled. "Cymbian? It's been a long time."

"It has indeed. We always wondered what happened to you and Larry. We thought you'd gone off in Via after we left you in the temple."

"Ah," Ploterus said. "I should have recognized you as well. We searched for you in Alexandria."

"Yes, I'm aware of that, my lord. Cymbian can accompany you. Send your other men away. You are in no danger. We just need to speak to you in private."

Ploterus turned to Cymbian, who nodded. "Very well," Ploterus said to Palta. He told his bodyguards to wait for him at the north gate.

Then he and Cymbian tied their horses to a tree and followed Palta into the cemetery.

The dismal road was lined with large mausoleums—fine places for brigands to lie in wait. If there were enough of them, he and Cymbian wouldn't survive the fight. Ploterus thought he was safe—but really, he had no idea. Better to be ready for a fight, just in case. He kept a hand on his sword.

Palta took a turn, and then another. The path narrowed. They were now among smaller, less ornate mausoleums. They walked past stunted, leafless trees. A wind sprang up. Damn, he was not used to this cold.

Finally he spotted three men seated on a bench. They stood as he approached. One of them was older than the others—lean, bald, with deeply tanned skin; that would be Decius, Ploterus thought. He didn't recognize the other two—one was young, with brown hair; the other older, stocky, and black-haired.

"We finally meet, General Ploterus," the bald man said. "I am Decius."

Ploterus nodded to him. "I thought as much."

"My lord—and Cymbian," the younger man said, bowing to both of them, "do you remember me from Massalia? My name is Larry Barnes. Palta and I were with Feslund and the others as they set out for Urbis."

"Salve, Larry," Cymbian said. "I recognized Palta but not you. You have changed greatly."

Like Cymbian, Ploterus remembered Palta well enough, but he couldn't summon up any memory of this fellow. Larry Barnes was an odd name. He also spoke Latin with an accent that Ploterus couldn't place. He nodded to the man.

"And I am Lamathe," the third man said. "I am a viator. You perhaps heard rumors of my presence in Alexandria."

Ploterus nodded to him as well. He had never heard of the man by name. "Very well," he said. "I have come. Someone tell me the offer you want to make me—why I should believe it's real, and why I should accept it. And why I shouldn't arrest all of you as traitors to the empire."

Larry reached into the pocket of his cape and pulled something out. It seemed to be made of hard, dark metal. A weapon, Ploterus supposed. It looked like nothing found on Terra. Except..."You have seen a gant?" Larry asked him. "Cymbian certainly has."

"Yes," Ploterus replied. "This is shaped something like it. But not quite the same."

"It is not a gant. But it is a weapon. Its power is different from a gant's, but just as destructive. Would you like a demonstration?"

"What do you mean?" Ploterus demanded, reaching for his sword.

"Don't worry. Do you see that wall over there?" The man gestured at a crumbling brick wall about thirty paces distant.

"Of course I see it," Ploterus said.

"Watch. And listen."

Larry turned to the wall. He raised the weapon.

And then Ploterus heard a sound like the crack of thunder, except much louder, much closer—so loud it was painful. And he saw pieces of brick fly away, and part of the wall collapse in on itself.

Larry waited until the sound died away before speaking again. "This is called a *gun*," he went on. "Use it on a soldier, and it will kill him instantly from a hundred paces away. Other soldiers will drop their swords and flee in terror at the sound. A dozen of these will defeat an army." He put the gun back in his pocket.

Plotus's ears were still ringing. He could feel his hands shake. *Gun*, *gant*. The same short, ugly sound. "You obtained this thing through your Via?"

"That's right," Palta said. "The gods have sent us another Via as a sign of their blessing."

"Gods are for children," Ploterus scoffed. "Don't talk to me about the gods."

"As you wish," Lamathe said. "You are an intelligent man, general. We understand this. And here is what you need to understand. The Gallians have captured a few priests, but none of them have helped them, and many more remain. And we have been waiting for this moment. We have our own Via, as you say. We can obtain weapons like these, and even more powerful ones. The Gallians cannot. The Gallians are doomed."

Ploterus and Cymbian exchanged a glance. He could tell what Cymbian was thinking: this was just what he had been hoping for. At long last. "If the Gallians are doomed, why do you need me?" Ploterus asked Lamathe. "What is your offer to me?"

"We do not wish to use these weapons," Lamathe replied. "We do not want to repeat the mistake the priests made with King Harald's army. Too many people have died already fighting the Gallians. We want to return to the old days, when the empire was ruled with wisdom and fairness. We realize the priests have made mistakes—Governor Decius here is happy to point them out to us. We can do better. We will surely do better than Feslund and Gretyx, in any case. But we need your help."

"What kind of help?"

"You command the soldiers in Roma. When the time comes, we want you to issue certain orders to your men. We want them to be on our side."

"When is this happening?"

"Soon. During Saturnalia."

"What we ask of you will be neither difficult nor dishonorable," Palta added. "And it will spare the empire much bloodshed."

"And what is your offer to me?"

"First," Lamathe said, "you have probably considered seizing power for yourself. You would certainly be a better ruler than Feslund and Gretyx, but you must understand that this is not going to happen. When the priests return to power, however, we will need people like you. We will have to keep the peace, by force if necessary. There will still be wars to be fought with sword and shield. You have demonstrated your competence as a general. Your reputation is high, even among the rebels. You have won many great battles. You governed Egypt fairly. So the priests want you to lead their legions."

"And what of Decius? Why is he here?"

"Decius, too, is competent and respected," Lamathe replied. "He will resume his role as governor of the Roman province."

"We can and must work together," Decius said to him. "The time has come to rid the world of Feslund and Gretyx. You know it, Ploterus. And you know that, really, you have no choice. Join us, or you will not survive the coming battle. As Lamathe said, we do not want to use weapons like this one, but we will if we have to, to defeat the Gallians. You must understand this."

Ploterus pondered the viator's words. Then he turned to Cymbian. "What do you think?" he asked.

Cymbian was silent for a moment before he spoke. "You don't want to be a traitor," he replied at last. "I understand that. And you have no love for the priests. Neither do I. But nothing matters more than defeating Feslund and Gretyx."

"They will not leave without a fight," Ploterus pointed out.

"Then we can give them a fight."

"I cannot be sure of my troops."

"They will follow you, my lord. You can count on them."

Everyone fell silent then in the cold cemetery, waiting for his response. Ploterus's ears still rang from the noise of the gun. How could such a small object make a noise that loud? Finally he turned back to Lamathe. "Tell me what you want me to do," he said.

———

Liber

Liber walked home from the government building in the Forum, his servants lighting the way with torches. The Forum was usually deserted at this hour, but some people were already getting a head start on Saturnalia, drunkenly shouting out songs as they swayed through the plaza. In a couple of days the Forum would be filled for the official start of the festival. It would be a success—it would have to be a success.

He recalled the night many years ago when he walked through the crowds of Saturnalia having lost his last pupil, wanting only to drink away his sorrow and fear. So much had changed. Now servants lit his way! Now he was in charge of Saturnalia, and all of Roma!

Was he any happier than he had been back then?

He could not say that he was. Now he was consumed by fear—fear that Gretyx would not be satisfied with him, fear that she would rid herself of him as she had rid herself of so many others. A moment of irritation, a passing suspicion of disloyalty. Then arrest, torture, and death.

If he was lucky, she would skip the torture.

But for today he was safe. Everyone felt good during Saturnalia—if things didn't get out of control. He would not let things get out of control. In the end Gretyx would be happy, the people would be happy, and Liber would be safe for a while longer.

He reached the governor's residence on the Capitoline Hill. Again, he recalled that night during Saturnalia when he had been brought to this same house, in a drunken stupor, to meet Decius. Decius was gone, but somehow Liber had survived.

The servants escorted him inside. Barascus brought him a cup of wine. "My lord..." he began.

"Not now," Liber interrupted, swallowing the wine in a single gulp. He held the cup out to be refilled. It was good to be inside, in the warmth.

"My lord, in your study…"

"What about my study?"

"Visitors, my lord."

"Who let them in? Send them away. I am not available."

Barascus almost seemed to writhe with discomfort. "My lord, I cannot."

"What do you mean, you 'cannot'?" Liber was tired. He had no wish to see anyone. He wished only to sit by the fire and have another cup of wine.

"You had better see them, my lord."

Liber made a disgusted noise and marched off to his study. If Barascus wouldn't do his job, Liber would do it for him.

He opened the door, and then he felt his world collapse.

There, seated at his table, were Decius and Affron.

"Governor Liber," Decius said. "I see you've bought new tapestries for the room."

Liber tried to respond: a cold nod, a call to his servants for assistance…but he could do nothing.

"I remember Barascus. He was always fond of me, I think," Decius went on, "but not fond enough join me in rebelling against the empire. I have put him in an awkward position, but you shouldn't blame him. Please, sit down. You recall Affron from your days in the schola, of course."

Yes, Liber remembered Affron. Affron still haunted his dreams. He sat. "What do you want?" he managed to say.

"First, let me reassure you that we mean you no harm," Decius replied. "You're not a bad fellow, I think—and Affron agrees with me about that. And I'm told that you've not been a bad governor either, given the constraints placed on you by your masters."

The brazier in the corner was pouring out heat, but still Liber felt cold. He could barely make sense of the words Decius was speaking. Decius was supposed to be on the run in the wastelands of Africa. And Affron—oh, Affron! Liber had tried so hard to track him down and have him killed. Did Affron know about Harmalo? Perhaps Affron knew everything.

"What do you want?" he repeated. His voice was shaking. He could not stop it from shaking.

Affron spoke finally. "The priests have returned to Roma to reclaim power from the Gallians," he said. "You will help us."

"What? How will the priests do this? Where is your army?"

"We don't need an army," Affron replied. "You know that, Liber."

Liber shivered, recalling Affron's power, which had all but destroyed him. Was that what he was talking about? Could he defeat the Gallians with it? Of course he could. He could do whatever he wanted. "I don't see how I can help you," he said.

"We do not ask much," Affron said. "But we require your help at the beginning of Saturnalia."

"What? Why?"

"Because that is when it will happen."

Saturnalia? "There will be troops throughout the city during Saturnalia," he pointed out. "I do not control the troops. General Ploterus does. He reports to me, in theory, but he won't obey orders that threaten Feslund and Gretyx."

"Do not worry about Ploterus," Decius replied. "He will be assisting us as well."

Ploterus too? "Who else?" Liber asked. "What is your plan?"

"None of that is your concern," Decius said. "You need to know only this: you must do what we say. We are going to be victorious, and after our victory, we will remember who helped us, and who refused."

"If I help you, will I remain governor after your victory?"

Decius shook his head. "No, but you will remain alive. That is all we promise. And that is the most you deserve."

Liber looked from one man to the other. Their faces were calm, relentless.

It is over, he thought. Not in one of the ways he had imagined—not a sudden summons from Gretyx, not legionaries running him through with their swords as he lay in bed. But whether the priests won or lost, it was over for him nevertheless.

It was a wonder he had survived as long as he had.

And with that realization came a sense of relief. He had done what he could. He was still alive. And perhaps the gods would allow him to live a while longer.

"Tell me what you need," he said.

FIFTY-FOUR

Larry

The priests sat at the table on the second floor of the insula. Darkness was falling; the moment approached. Affron spoke, then Lamathe, then Borafin. They talked of their love for Terra, for the priests' empire, for Urbis. Now, finally, they were going to take back what had been stolen from them. If anyone had doubts, they weren't spoken. But Larry could tell they were all nervous. The next couple of hours would determine whether they succeeded or failed.

Larry stood with Palta in a corner of the room. He felt left out. There would be little for him to do tonight, if all went well. And that was fine with him.

And afterward? He forced himself not to think about what would happen afterward; he just wanted to get through tonight. The priests and Decius had talked endlessly about their plans—how they would set up the government, how they would win over the people, how they would defeat the Gallians if they chose to resist. But he had mostly stayed silent; they knew how to run an empire better than he did.

Finally he went downstairs and outside. Palta followed. The night was cold but clear. He could hear music and shouting in the distance. "It will be fine," Palta said, grasping his hand. "Affron's idea is brilliant. Your ideas have been brilliant. How can we fail?"

Larry could think of many ways in which they could fail, but then, so could Palta. "Yes," he agreed. "It will be fine."

"Do you have your gun?"

"Of course. But I hope I won't need it."

"You shouldn't have to. But just in case…"

They stood there in silence, holding hands. Finally the others joined them, and it was time to begin.

As they walked to the Forum, Larry clicked the side of the gun to put a bullet in the chamber, the way Brendan had taught him. Just in case.

———

Feslund

In the palace, Feslund practiced the speech in front of Gretyx, Bathanala, and Liber.

"You need to be loud," his mother reminded him yet again. "The crowd will be large and festive. You must make them pay attention."

Liber nodded his agreement. Bathanala, as usual, said nothing. They were both useless.

"No one cares about the new Senate House," Feslund argued. "Especially not during Saturnalia. We should just re-dedicate the temple to the old gods. People still remember them fondly."

Gretyx looked annoyed with him, as she so often did; he had made this argument before. "We can build such a temple somewhere else," she replied. "Right now we need senators. We need to make you emperor."

What she meant was: we need wealthy men to pay us for the privilege of becoming senators. Because there wasn't enough money; there was never enough money.

"But I don't like speaking in front of the temple," he said. "It will remind people of the priests."

"But that is the point, my lord," Liber replied. "The old days of the priests are gone. The temple has stood empty for too long. You have defeated the rebels. We must celebrate. We must change."

Feslund wasn't stupid. He knew that he hadn't defeated the rebels; Ploterus had. But it didn't matter, he supposed. In any event, Gretyx was agreeing with Liber. "Yes, it is time to celebrate," she said. "In any case, it is all arranged."

"Must I go?" Bathanala asked.

Now Gretyx looked annoyed with *her*. As she should be. "Of course you must," his mother snapped. "Don't be stupid. The people love you, and they expect to see you. I think it wiser if I stay in the palace, however."

This was fine with Feslund—he had no wish to have his mother standing behind him as he spoke, judging his performance.

"Your people will miss you, my lady," Liber protested. "I think you should accompany your son."

"They will not miss me," she replied. "They will be delighted that I am not there. I will stay here and watch from the balcony. Is it time?"

"Almost, my lady," Liber said. "But I really think--"

The queen waved him silent and turned to Feslund. "You will do well, my son. I am very proud of you."

She was not proud of him, Feslund knew. But in any case he was grateful for the praise. He went over the speech one last time.

———

Palta

The Forum was filled with people and torchlight. A band played; people sang and chanted and swigged wine from jugs. Palta and Larry stopped a hundred paces from the royal palace. Its huge doors were heavily guarded, and a line of soldiers kept open a path from the palace to the temple.

The soldiers guarding the palace doors wore purple capes. They were members of the Praetorian Guard and were led by Escondo, another one of Feslund's mates; unlike Cymbian, he had remained loyal to Feslund. The soldiers in the Forum wore red capes; they were regular legionaries: Ploterus's men. The existence of the Praetorian Guard made Palta nervous; their plan had not accounted for it. They were sworn to protect Feslund and Gretyx; they were not likely to surrender without a fight.

Everything made her nervous, actually. She wished there was something for her to do.

"There's Amelia," Larry pointed out. "By the temple doors. Next to Ploterus."

"Ah, that's good."

Everyone had something to do, now or later. Amelia was there at the temple. Larry had his gun to use if needed. Decius would be governor; Lamathe would be pontifex; Borafin would be vice-pontifex. The other priests would have their parts to play.

Everyone had something to do except Palta.

For years she had longed for this moment to arrive. Now it was finally at hand, and she could do nothing but watch.

She shivered in the cold night air.

———

Ploterus

"Now," the woman murmured to Ploterus.

So it was beginning. He turned to the soldiers guarding the temple doors. "Open them," he ordered.

They did what they were told. He grabbed a torch from a bracket next to the doors and walked inside, followed by the woman. The light flickered. The temple was immense and deserted. The place smelled musty; no one used it anymore. Furniture was piled up in corners; the frescoes on the ceiling were faded and water-stained; someone seemed to have taken an ax to the altar. He watched the woman stride to a spot in the middle of the marble floor and reach out her hand. She murmured something to herself in what sounded like a foreign language. Then she turned back to Ploterus. "Mane hic," she said to him. *Stay here.*

He stayed where he was. The woman turned away. She took a few steps.

And she disappeared.

Ploterus shook his head in disbelief. He knew that if he went to look for her, he would not find her. Via was in Urbis, so what was this nothingness that she had stepped into? The priests' new Via, it seemed. He knew what was happening, but still it was strange and terrifying, like the gun.

And these strange and terrifying things convinced him that he had picked the right side.

Amelia

Amelia walked out of the portal and into the woods of Elysium; the woods were magical in the starlight.

Hieron was waiting for her. He looked nervous. He had been nervous ever since he had agreed to the plan. Nervous but excited. Alive. "Are we ready?" he asked.

She nodded. "Almost. You will need to find exactly the right spot."

"I can do that."

"I know you can."

"It's the rest of it," he added.

She put a hand on his arm. "You are a god," she said. "Don't forget that."

Hieron smiled. "I am not," he replied. "But thank you for the compliment."

She smiled back at him. "A few more minutes," she said.

Liber

They left the palace. Feslund smiled and waved to the crowd. Liber heard the usual mixture of cheers and boos. He looked around to see if he could spot Affron or any other priests, but there were too many people to make out individual faces. He knew they were out there, though. He could *feel* them.

Feslund descended the palace steps, followed by Bathanala and Liber. A few Praetorian guards accompanied them. Legionaries had kept a path clear to the temple. Liber looked over at the temple entrance where Feslund was to speak. It seemed so bare to him since they had removed the statue of Hieron with his hands outstretched. Removing the statue before the speech had been Gretyx's idea, but it had not been wise. The people may not have liked the priests, but they had always loved Hieron. Liber had tried to explain this to her, but of course she paid no attention to him.

Meanwhile, things had already gone wrong. Affron and Decius had told him to make sure Gretyx accompanied Feslund, and he had failed to do so. They would be upset with him, he knew. They would think he hadn't upheld his part of the bargain. But surely they would understand—no one could control Gretyx!

He had done his best.

And what if their plan failed because of his failure? And what if Gretyx found out about his treason? That would be the worst outcome of all, of course.

They made their way across the Forum to the temple, then up its steps. The band stopped playing. The crowd began to quiet. One of his aides had told him the people would be upset if Feslund promised them anything less than ten silver denarii. The people were fools. They should have stormed the palace long ago. They should have joined the rebellion, instead of being satisfied with scraps from the royal treasury.

He should have joined the rebellion, like Decius.

But it was all about to end. Wasn't it?

Ploterus and a woman he didn't recognize came out of the temple. What were they doing in there?

"Where should I stand?" Feslund asked Liber. He hadn't noticed the woman.

Liber pointed to the spot. "Right there, my lord." Right next to where the statue of Hieron had stood.

Liber motioned to Bathanala to step back a few paces. He went and stood next to her.

Feslund raised his arms to acknowledge the scattered cheers, and finally he began to speak.

————

Affron

"Io Saturnalia!" Feslund roared the ancient greeting.

The crowd shouted the greeting back. Some of them, anyway.

He paused for a few moments, evidently waiting for the crowed to be quiet, but silence never came, and so at last he simply began his speech.

He was not a good speaker, Affron thought. He thought he was cleverer than he actually was, and he did not understand the mood of the crowd. They didn't want to hear about the brave soldiers fighting in Egypt. And they didn't want to hear about his plans to tear down the temple and build a new Senate House. That was not what they were here for.

But Feslund's speech didn't matter. The timing mattered; where Feslund stood mattered. The Praetorian Guard mattered. Affron didn't see Gretyx with her son. That was bad. The fool Liber was supposed to make sure she was there.

He kept his eyes on Amelia up by the temple doors, standing next to Ploterus with her arms crossed. She didn't look worried; nothing seemed to worry her. He was so lucky that she loved him. Now they just needed to accomplish this.

"The priests have finally been defeated," Feslund orated. "They will trouble us no more. The old gods have risen again, stronger than ever, to make Terra a better world for all of us."

Modest cheers from the crowd. Somebody shouted out a demand for denarii.

And then it began.

In the midst of the boisterous, drunken crowd, Affron finally smiled.

Lamathe

It was barely visible at first—just a shimmering in the air. It could have been caused by the smoke from the torches. But then the shimmering turned the lightest shade of blue, and it revealed its shape—it was a large sphere, floating a couple of paces to Feslund's right.

The crowd around Lamathe began shouting and point as they noticed what was happening.

To get things started, Lamathe shouted: "Via! It is Via!"

From somewhere else in the crowd he heard Borafin's voice: "Via!"

And then Samos, and Karellia, and all the others.

And Lamathe's heart soared as others in the crowd began to shout. "Via! Look, it's Via!"

Feslund

The speech had been going fairly well, Feslund thought. And then…

From the crowd came screams and pointing and confusion. He didn't understand.

He turned and saw a shimmering blue sphere, just paces away from him. He heard voices shouting "Via!"

He fell silent and stared helplessly, uncomprehendingly at the sphere. One of his guards came up to him. "I think you are not safe here, my lord," the guard said. He look frightened himself.

Ploterus came over. "Take him into the temple," he ordered the Praetorian guards. "And the wife with him."

They looked doubtful. He was not their general

"Go, you fools!" Ploterus shouted. "Before it is too late. Do you not see this thing? It is Via. The priests have returned."

Feslund stared at Ploterus. He stared at the sphere. Via. Here.

He felt hands on him, pulling him backwards, into the temple.

———

Ploterus

"What is happening?" Bathanala asked when they were in the temple.

Ploterus ignored her. They were supposed to grab Gretyx along with Feslund, but Gretyx hadn't been with Feslund. Liber had failed, and now the plan had become more complicated.

Ploterus motioned to his own soldiers, who were standing behind the Praetorian guards. In an instant their daggers were out and they had slit the guards' throats.

Good men.

Bathanala screamed. Feslund saw what had happened and wheeled around, seeking escape. There was no escape. He reached for his sword, but he was not wearing a sword. Why would he need a sword to give a speech? Two of the soldiers grabbed him; another grabbed Bathanala.

"You're a traitor!" Feslund shouted at Ploterus.

Ploterus shrugged and took out his dagger. "It is over, my lord," he said to Feslund. "And I have no time to waste."

"What do you mean?" Bathanala cried.

Feslund stared at Ploterus. Understanding seemed to dawn on him. "Spare my wife," he said. "She is nothing to you."

Ploterus considered, and then said, "As you wish. Avert your eyes, my lady."

Bathanala began to howl. Not out of grief for her husband, Ploterus thought. Out of fear for her own life. Without Feslund, what protection did she have? Ploterus could give her none. But no matter.

"Are you ready, my lord?" he asked Feslund.

Feslund looked as though he wanted to argue, to plead. But then, once again, he understood. Now it was not about saving his life; it was about leaving this world properly. "I am ready," he said. His voice was shaking, but he didn't flinch. That was good. He would die like a Gallian soldier.

It would have been easier to use a gun, Ploterus thought. But no matter. He took out his dagger and did what needed to be done.

———

Hieron

Hieron waited, as Affron had told him to do. Let the crowd see and understand what was happening. Finally he stepped out of his Via and out onto the broad entrance to the temple. He wore an ancient toga— the kind depicted on his statues; he hadn't put on such a toga since he'd left Terra. He put his left hand on his breast and raised his right arm into the air—a gesture of greeting and of triumph.

"Hieron!" a voice shouted. "It is Hieron!"

"Save us, Hieron!" someone else shouted.

The crowd roared. They were confused. They were drunk. Perhaps they thought it was a spectacle like those they witnessed in the Circus Maximus. He waited for them to understand. It didn't take long. The priests in the crowd helped. "He has returned!" someone shouted. "Let him speak!" shouted another.

And then people started to kneel. Soon all were kneeling—even the soldiers; some were weeping. Just as Affron had predicted.

Wait, Affron had instructed him. *Make sure you have their attention. Then step forward.*

And that is what he did. "I am Hieron," he said, "and I have returned to save Terra. You have not deserved the suffering you have undergone at the hands of those who have ruled you these past few years. With your help, I will change all this. And the change begins now. The rule of the Gallians has ended. Peace and justice have returned."

He looked to his right, and Amelia was there, smiling at him. A general, who must have been Ploterus, came out of the temple with a few soldiers.

And then he heard a voice.

————

Gretyx

Gretyx watched Feslund speak from her balcony in the palace. She could make out little of what he said. She heard occasional cheers, and that was good.

And then she saw a blue sphere forming next to him. What was it? It could not be Via.

She saw Feslund and Bathanala hurry into the temple with Ploterus and some guards.

She saw a man wearing an ancient toga step out of the sphere.

She saw the crowd fall to its knees.

What was happening? What was Feslund doing in the temple? Who was the man in the toga?

It was Hieron, she realized.

She was terrified, but she would not give in. She would not be defeated.

————

Larry

Everything seemed to be working beautifully. Here was Hieron, exactly where he was supposed to be. And the crowd reacted exactly as they had hoped. His voice was strong and clear, his words inspiring.

And then Palta grasped his arm and pointed. Larry looked up to see Gretyx on the palace balcony. Hieron fell silent as her voice rang out.

"My fellow citizens," she said. "Pay no attention to this magic

339

conjured up by evil priests. Their only purpose is to enslave you once again. My son has set you free. My son has brought you peace. My son—"

"Kill her," Palta urged Larry.

Kill her? Yes, he supposed that this was his job. He and Palta had been kneeling like all the rest of the crowd. He got to his feet and took out the gun. His hand was shaking. His whole body was shaking.

"...We have worked tirelessly to make your lives better. In this festive season, we have promised to give every citizen—"

He raised the gun and tried to aim. Finally he pulled the trigger.

And there was the deafening sound again.

Gretyx spun backward against the door to the balcony. Larry tried to shoot again, but she staggered back into the palace and out of sight.

In the Forum, chaos erupted. People rose to their feet and started running, holding their hands over their ears. Children wept. Women screamed.

Had he hit her? Had he seen her clutch her shoulder? He thought so.

Palta was tugging at his sleeve. "We need to get into the palace," she shouted into his ear. "We can't let her escape."

They pushed through the crowd. Cymbian stood next to the palace doors with a few of his men. Two purple-caped guards lay dead next to them. "We need to capture the queen," Larry said.

Cymbian nodded and gestured to his soldiers. "Don't worry," he said to Larry. "We have posted soldiers at all the doors to the palace. She is trapped inside."

The doors were locked, so the soldiers put their shoulders to them till they opened with a crack, and then rushed inside. A few Praetorian guards met them in the huge, gilt entrance hall, swords drawn. Escondo was there with them, shouting orders. Larry aimed the gun at Escondo and shot him; he fell with a thud onto the marble floor. The rest of the guards turned and ran.

"Go after them," Cymbian instructed his men, who were now staring in terror at Larry. "Kill anyone who doesn't surrender. Disarm anyone who does. Find the queen and bring her back here."

Ploterus and several soldiers entered behind them, escorting Hieron. Hieron looked shaken. "It'll be fine," Larry told him. "Gretyx has been wounded, but we'll capture her."

"This is not what I'd hoped," Hieron said, shaking his head.

"Plans never go as smoothly as one would like, my lord," Ploterus replied. "But Feslund is dead, and Gretyx can't have gone far. Come, sit in this room," he said, gesturing to a large, frescoed chamber just off the entrance hall. "You'll be well guarded, and the other priests will show up soon. Someone will find wine for you."

As they took care of Hieron, soldiers started returning from their search. A few of them brought prisoners with them, but none of them had found Gretyx.

"She's not in the palace," Palta insisted. "She would've given herself a way to escape."

Cymbian shook his head. "All the doors are—"

"There'll be an exit we don't know about. Like the tunnel in Urbis."

"Bring me the servants," Ploterus ordered. "One of them will have to know."

Soldiers left and soon returned, herding frightened servants into the entrance hall. "Come then," Ploterus said to them, "we must find the queen. You have heard our magical weapon." He pointed to Larry's gun. "We don't want to kill you with it, but we will. If there is a secret passage or other means of escape from the palace, we need to know about it. Right now."

The servants stared at the gun, glanced at one another. Women clutched each other, weeping. Finally a wizened old man wearing a green tunic and dirty trousers stepped forward. "There's a door just off the kitchen, my lord," he rasped. "Always locked. We were told never to open it. I thought I heard footsteps on the stairs a while ago, before the soldiers came for us. People in a hurry, I thought. And the door was open."

Ploterus grabbed the man. "Show us," he demanded.

Larry and Palta followed Ploterus with a couple of soldiers as the man led them down into the bowels of the palace. Gretyx couldn't have gone far with a gunshot wound, Larry thought. But of course she'd have guards with her; perhaps they carried her.

"There, my lord," the old man said, pointing at a door with a trembling finger. "It's open, you see. Never been open before."

Ploterus grabbed a torch and shone it into the darkness beyond the door. Stone steps descended to a passageway.

They went down the steps, then along the damp cobblestones of the passage. Larry remembered making his way through the tunnel in

Urbis with Palta and the others. That seemed like a lifetime ago. He could barely speak to Palta then—he knew no Latin, and she knew no English. He had been young and terrified. He had only wanted to go home, and everything he did seemed to take him further away from his home.

"Up ahead," Ploterus muttered after a while.

Larry saw a wooden staircase. When they reached it they clambered up the steps. Ploterus pushed open the door at the top and rushed through it with Larry, Palta, and the soldiers following.

They were in a stable. Horses snickered. A frightened boy stared at them in astonishment.

"Is the queen here?" Ploterus demanded, drawing his sword.

"No, my lord," the boy answered. "She *was* here. I think it was the queen, anyway. No one has ever come through that door before. Septimus says—"

"How long ago?"

"Not long, my lord."

"Do you know where she went?"

"No, my lord. She demanded a carriage and a driver. And horses for her guards. She was hurt, I think—holding onto her shoulder, like so. And in a hurry. She threatened to have us whipped if we went too slow. We're not used to—"

Ploterus waved the boy silent and turned to Larry and Palta. "Now what?"

"She'll head north," Larry said. "Back to Gallia. She'll have support there. We need to stop her."

"She could be going to the port," Palta suggested. "She might have a ship waiting for her."

Ploterus pondered for a moment, and then gave orders to his soldiers. "Return to Cymbian and tell him to send troops to the waterfront in case the queen is headed there." He handed one of them the torch. They bowed and headed back through the door and down into the passage.

Then Ploterus turned back to the boy. "Saddle three horses for us —the best you have. Quickly, now."

"Yes, my lord. I'll need Septimus to help. I'll just go and—"

"Yes, yes."

The boy hurried off to get Septimus.

"She can't get far," Larry said to Ploterus. "The streets are too crowded."

"They'll be crowded for us as well," Ploterus replied. "And her guards wielding swords can scatter people in short order. Once she makes it through the north gate, the Via Flaminia will be clear."

"But dark and dangerous," Palta pointed out.

Ploterus nodded. "True enough." No one traveled at night if it could be avoided.

They walked out into the stable yard. Their breath made clouds in the cold night air. Palta grasped Larry's hand. "We're so close to victory!" she murmured as she waited. "We just need to catch her."

"Gretyx must die," Ploterus said in response. "There is no victory while she is alive."

Finally their horses were ready. Larry chose one and mounted it. He knew it would be hard for him to keep up with Palta and Ploterus. But he'd have to try.

The boy opened the gates of the stable yard for them, and they headed out into the city.

Palta knew the way to the north gate, of course; she always knew the way. Even with Ploterus roaring at people to get out of his way and whipping them if they refused, they made slow progress through the streets for a while. But finally the crowds thinned and they sped up.

Larry wondered what would happen if they didn't find Gretyx. She could gather loyal troops, he supposed. She could raise an army, especially if she made it back to Gallia. And with an army to fight for her, perhaps she could defeat the priests. Why not?

But really, he had no idea—about that or anything. No idea what the future would bring here on Terra. No idea if the priests would succeed, or if they would rule wisely. So many versions of Terra; so many possible outcomes.

Finally they reached the north gate. "Queen Gretyx!" Ploterus shouted at the guards. "Did she pass through here in a carriage?"

The guards looked confused. "A carriage did pass through, my lord," one of them said. "There was a woman in it. Don't know who it was."

"With soldiers on horseback," a second guard pointed out.

"Praetorians," another guard added. "Wearing the purple cloaks."

"When?"

"I don't know, my lord—not long ago, I suppose. They were in a hurry, it seemed."

"Let us through, then," Ploterus ordered. "We're in a hurry, too."

The guards hastened to obey. When the gates were open the three of them rode out of the city and onto the Via Flaminia.

The night had turned overcast, and as expected it was difficult to make their way along the road. Larry looked over at Palta; he couldn't see much of her face, but as always, she rode easily and well. Horses loved her, and she loved them back.

Yet another adventure for the two of them, he thought. He was getting tired of adventures.

And he thought about all that Kevin had missed, staying behind on Earth. And all that Carmody and Valleia had missed, raising their children in Scotia. But each of them was happy. There were so many ways to be happy.

They rode for a while and encountered no one. Then suddenly Ploterus slowed his horse and raised a hand. Palta and Larry came up beside him. He pointed to a light bobbing up and down ahead on their left. A torch. But it was low to the ground—whoever was holding it was not on a horse. And not moving away from them.

Larry heard curses, a horse's whinny, indistinct voices.

"Something's wrong with the carriage," Palta whispered.

"Get out your gun," Ploterus ordered Larry.

He did as he was told. How many bullets did he have left? Enough, he supposed. Would whoever was up ahead be able to see them in the darkness? It would be difficult.

Ploterus dismounted and started to move forward. Palta and Larry followed him.

Now Larry could make out Gretyx's voice—impatient, imperious. And he could see that the carriage was tilted. It had veered into a ditch, perhaps, or a wheel had come off. She was angry about it, he assumed.

She knew that her life was at stake.

Larry realized that they were walking alongside the cemetery where they had met Ploterus. And suddenly, weirdly, he could feel the Roman dead all around him. The thought made him dizzy, as if he were experiencing the multiverse. So many people had lived their lives in Roma —working, loving, suffering…And so many of them had ended up here —cold, silent, uninterested in this little drama playing out on a cold

December night. They had been as real as Larry himself was, and now they were gone.

The gun was heavy in his hand.

Up ahead, the torch stopped moving. Gretyx said something—a question, a command.

And then Ploterus spoke. "I am General Ploterus," he called out. "Men, come out into the roadway and bring Queen Gretyx with you. I need to speak to her."

A sharp command from Gretyx. No response from the soldiers.

"You are soldiers, and it is important that you obey me," Ploterus went on. "No harm will come to you or the queen."

The torch didn't move. Gretyx spoke. Larry thought he could make out her words: "You are Praetorian guards, and you are sworn to defend me with your lives."

Ploterus stopped. "It is time to use the gun," he told Larry.

"I can't make out Gretyx," Larry responded. "I won't be able to hit anyone from this far away in the dark."

"It doesn't matter if you miss," Ploterus said. "The noise will be sufficient. Aim for the coach." He stepped forward. "You are about to experience the magic of the priests," he called out. "Again, we do not mean to harm you, but you must understand how important it is to obey my command. You must let me speak to the queen."

He turned and nodded to Larry. "Now."

"Cover your ears," Larry murmured. He raised the gun, aimed at the coach, and pulled the trigger.

The night exploded with sound. Larry's ears rang; the horses went crazy with fright. Up ahead, the torch dropped to the ground.

Ploterus took out his sword and walked swiftly forward. "Come then," he announced. "The next time we use the magic, it will kill you. Give us the queen."

They reached the carriage. Next to it stood three frightened men— two purple-caped soldiers and a driver wearing a short jacket. Palta picked up the sputtering torch.

"Where is she?" Ploterus demanded.

"My lord, we don't know," one of the soldiers said, his voice quavering.

"Must've run off into the graveyard, my lord," the gruff, bearded driver said.

"Can't be far, my lord," the second soldier said.

Ploterus nodded. "All of you, stay here. You have done nothing wrong—you will not be punished. But you must not interfere. Do you understand?"

"Yes, my lord."

"Let's go," Ploterus said to Palta and Larry.

The three of them made their way into the cemetery. Larry's ears were still ringing. Amid the ringing he thought he could hear the ghosts of the Roman dead whispering to him as he walked among them. *Join us*, they seemed to say. *Stay here with us.*

His knees wobbled. What was going on?

"You go over there," Ploterus ordered Larry, gesturing to his right. "You take the center," he said to Palta. "I'll take the left."

Larry didn't reply. He held the gun tightly in front of him and started walking among the mausoleums, across the graves. He walked around each mausoleum to ensure that Gretyx wasn't hiding behind it. She was lurking here somewhere, he supposed, hoping they'd give up and go away, and she'd find a way to reach Gallia and continue the fight. It seemed like an absurd hope, but in some universe it would come true, and she would defeat the priests and rule the empire again, finally dying triumphant and beloved in bed.

But not in this universe. Not if he could help it.

How far could she run in the darkness with a bullet wound? How far did she want to run? Would she risk tripping on a root, a rock, a gravestone? Call attention to herself and she was doomed.

He moved slowly, carefully, among the dead. The cemetery was huge. It would be easy to let her get away. They were so close to victory. They couldn't let her escape.

And then Larry heard the noise. To his left: a scuffle, a cry. The light from Palta's torch faded. He ran towards the noise.

He reached it in moments. Ploterus came from the other direction. The torch was on the ground by a mausoleum. Behind the torch Gretyx was holding Palta, a dagger pointing at her neck. Palta was struggling fiercely but couldn't escape the queen's grasp.

In the flickering light Gretyx looked wild-eyed, haggard. A cornered beast. A blood-soaked bandage was wrapped around her left shoulder. "No closer," she ordered the two of them.

They stopped. Larry stared at Palta. She looked angry as she struggled, as if she blamed herself.

"Put down your weapons, back away, and bring me a horse," Gretyx said. "Do you understand?"

"We will not do that," Ploterus responded, his voice calm, unconcerned.

"The girl will die," Gretyx responded. "I will enjoy killing her."

"As you wish. Larry, use your gun. Kill the queen."

Larry shook his head. He wasn't a good enough shot, even at close range. He would miss, and Gretyx would cut Palta's throat. Or the bullet would kill Palta.

"Go ahead, Larry," Ploterus insisted. "This is why you have the weapon, is it not?"

It wasn't. It was just supposed to be a way of convincing Ploterus to join them. But of course if you have a weapon, it will get used, just as the gants had been used on Terra. Just as he had shot Gretyx in the Forum. But he couldn't shoot it now—he couldn't risk Palta's life for this awful woman. Let her ride to Gallia. Let her take over the empire. Let her die beloved in her bed. It didn't matter. None of it mattered.

But it did matter, just as all these dead Romans had mattered as they lived out their lives. Everything and everyone matters.

And he knew what he had to do. He had always known, he supposed. One last time, here among the dead. Perhaps he would join them. But Palta would live.

He lowered the gun, and he opened his mind to the multiverse. It rushed in, and he sent it out towards the woman with the dagger at Palta's neck. As he had promised himself he'd never do again. One last time, sending a human being out among the stars and the galaxies and the dark matter and beyond, into the infinite profusion of the living and the lifeless and the dead, knowing that it would destroy her and probably himself, because how can any one being survive such immensity?

The multiverse exploded around him and in him, and he felt himself falling, falling, down to a place where he never wanted to go, and taking the evil queen with him.

And then there was blackness, and utter silence.

———

Ploterus

The queen lay on the ground.

Larry, too, lay on the ground. Palta knelt over him, sobbing.

Ploterus felt unsteady, dizzy, short of breath. Something had happened inside his mind, and he had no idea what it had been. More priestly magic, it seemed.

It had been awful, but he was strong. He could overcome it. He walked over to Larry and Palta and took the gun from Larry's hand. It was a strange, terrifying weapon—so much power in such a small object. All magic was terrifying. He had watched Larry use it; he thought he knew what to do.

He went over to Gretyx. She wasn't moving, but he couldn't be sure she was dead. He needed to be sure, so he aimed the gun at her chest, and he fired. The body jerked from the impact, and then lay utterly still.

Now at last it was truly over.

EPILOGUE

Helen

The hardest time is after Christmas is over. If it were up to me I wouldn't celebrate Christmas at all, but Bob and the kids insist. I go along without complaining, because I don't want to hear any more pep talks about how you need to move on and how living a normal life is the best way to get over it.

I'm not getting over it, ever. And why exactly must I move on? Where should I move *to*? The kids are grown, mostly. And Bob shouldn't have to deal with me, day after day, year after year. So why am I here? Why am I making life unbearable for everyone?

I have these thoughts every hour of every day. But I never do anything about them. The pull of the ordinary is too strong: brushing your teeth, making out the shopping list, getting the oil changed. And today, taking the ornaments down from the Christmas tree.

There was a time when Bob was afraid to leave me alone. And he was right to be afraid. But he couldn't quit his job to be with me every second. Life must go on, right? And so there are days like this—too many of them. He's at work, Cassie has gone back to her apartment in the city, Matthew is at school. And here I am, alone in this awful house, with nothing to live for but my memories.

But to be honest, I like being alone. There's no one to stop me, no one to reason with me, if I want to sit down and wallow in those memories. I try to do the right thing—I'll clean up the kitchen and put in a wash, I'll exercise, I'll pretend to read a book. But eventually I crack, and I return to the past. When I was happy.

Today, after the ornaments are packed up, I go upstairs, open a drawer, and find a piece of paper from Larry's first day of kindergarten. It is a red handprint next to a printed poem:

> Here is my hand so tiny and small
> For you to hang up on your wall
> For you to watch as the years go by
> How fast they grow, my hand and I

Oh, how I loved that handprint, that poem. I left the paper taped to the refrigerator for years, until everyone, and especially Larry, was sick of it.

I look at a stick-figure drawing he made of "Mumma and Me" from later that year. I study the way he printed his name in the bottom right corner. He had trouble with his R's for a while.

And he never liked his name. *Lawrence. Larry.* No one was named Lawrence anymore, he informed me one day when he was in the fourth grade or so. I explained that it was a lovely name, his grandfather's name, and so what if you have a different name from everyone else? It makes you special. But he never softened. Somebody had made fun of it, I suppose.

When Bob catches me looking at drawings like this I say: At least I'm not still consulting psychics. At least I'm not still pestering the police with theories and suggestions. At least I'm not still sending money to random cranks who send us tips.

I think I have made my peace with everything and everyone. Except, I suppose, Kevin Albright.

Bob forbids me to talk to him about Kevin. I understand that. Bob his own limits, and having to hear about Kevin's crazy story is one of them. I want to say: *Does Kevin sound crazy to you? He's a smart kid. He and Larry were so close...*

We don't talk about Kevin anymore. But I think about him. I allow myself to think about him now, even though it makes things worse. Because he is here and Larry isn't, and why is that? *Why is that?*

Thinking about Kevin, I go into one of my states where I'm just not *here*. In a way these are good states, because time passes and I'm not aware of it. I shut out reality and I'm in the past. Larry's a baby, or a toddler, or riding his bike. I am watching him, and strangely, I'm not worried. I was always worried in real life. I had reason to be worried.

I don't hear the knocking on the door at first. Usually I don't answer those knocks. It will be a reporter, or a creep, or just someone trying to be kind. I don't want to deal with any of them.

But the knocking doesn't stop, so finally I wipe my eyes and go downstairs and open the door.

And I gaze into the eyes of my missing son.

———

We sit together on the couch in the living room by the cartons of Christmas tree ornaments. He is trying to explain things—so many things—but my brain doesn't make sense of his words. There will be time enough to understand. For now I just look at him, touch him, stroke him. My baby. My boy. A young man, home at last.

"How do you know? How do you know for sure?" Cassie will demand when I finally call her. Of course she doesn't believe me. She is sure that I have finally gone crazy, finally fallen for a scam.

But I know. At some point I show him his handprint from kindergarten and he laughs. "How long did we have that thing taped to the refrigerator? Probably till you got Matthew's handprint and replaced it."

Do you see?

His laugh restores my life.

I call my family, and one by one they return home, worried, disbelieving: Matthew from school, Bob from work, Cassie from her apartment. They have probably texted each other: *She needs help. She may do something dangerous.*

And even when they see him they are all dubious at first. There have been imposters before, especially as the years went by. Children's faces change; memories fade. Bob was always worried that I'd fall for one of them. I never did.

But Larry knows what he has to do. He tells them things that only he could know—late-night conversations with Matthew in the room they shared. Dinner-table arguments with Cassie. Going shopping for a Mother's Day gift with Bob when he was seven. Oh, I still have the coffee mug he bought me that Mother's Day! *World's Greatest Mom.*

And so they finally believe. And eventually Larry tells his story, and it starts the way Kevin's story did, and then it gets stranger, more incomprehensible. Larry is apologetic: *I know this is all hard to believe, but…*

Bob and Matthew are excited and curious, of course. They have many questions that he tries to answer. I don't really care about those answers. I know something that perhaps they don't: his story is even stranger than the one he is telling them. Things have happened to him, and he has changed, but he doesn't want to talk about all of it. But that's all right. I understand.

Cassie is angry with him, of course. "Do you have any idea what you put us all through?" she demands.

He nods. "I do," he said. "And I'm so sorry."

And then of course Cassie begins to list all the things Larry has put us through: the police interrogations, the endless searches of woods and rivers, the candlelight vigils, the tearful TV interviews…Finally I put my hand on her arm and she stops. She has gotten better over the years.

"Let's tell Larry about *us*," Bob said. "He needs to catch up."

And that's fine. But what can I tell Larry about me? My life has been a blank. I don't want him to feel bad. He is smart and wise and he has experienced things unlike any we can possibly imagine. He can imagine me.

I get up to make supper, but Cassie pushes me back down into my chair and makes supper herself. We talk about food. We talk about his odd accent, the way his sentences sometimes come out wrong. We talk about clothing. Unexpectedly he takes out gold coins and tosses them onto the kitchen table. A present for us from some other world.

We don't talk about what's going to happen tomorrow, or the day after. Today is enough.

We eat and we talk, and finally we're all sleepy. Cassie and I make up the bed for him in the guest room. He hugs us all. When he goes to turn out the light, he can't figure out how to do it. He's out of practice with light switches.

I get into bed with Bob. He holds me tight, but he knows not to say anything, he knows that there is nothing he can possibly say to make this moment any better, or to make up for all the time that has been lost. I feel like I can breathe again, for the first time in years. I feel like life makes sense, even though what happened is impossible to believe. My son has come back to me.

I can't sleep. I gently extricate myself from Bob and make my way into the guest room. I pull up a chair and stare down at Larry. I listen to him breathe. I watch him in the dim starlight. I could watch him forever. He's handsome and strong. He's a man.

Eventually he senses me sitting there and opens his eyes.

"I've been wearing a beard," he says. "But I shaved it off. I thought that might make it easier for you to recognize me."

"I would have recognized you anyway," I reply.

He reaches out and takes my hand. I squeeze it. We are silent for a while.

"There is a girl," he says finally.

I hadn't thought about girls. "All the better," I reply.

That seems to be enough. I don't ask him anything more, and he doesn't say anything more. Finally he falls back to sleep. I stay sitting beside him all night long.

———

Palta

I am in my room in the royal palace, waiting.

Larry told me his plan as we walked through the empty streets of Urbis, remembering our brief time there. The place felt cold and alien. The priests have plans to move back to Urbis and return it to what it had once been, but what did those plans have to do with Larry and me?

He felt better, he said as we walked. He had survived that terrible moment in the cemetery when he saved my life once again. It had been awful, but now it was in the past. And he felt satisfied. We had done what we wanted to do. The Gallians were gone; the priests had recovered their empire. They would control the future of Terra—this Terra, anyway.

It was time.

And so he walked into his portal and left me. He had left me before, of course, on that hill in Scotia. In Scotia he promised to come back, and he did. But it was long years later that he returned. Could I live through that again?

And now he is gone, and I cannot think; I can scarcely breathe. This can't keep happening, I tell myself. We must figure this out.

I feel helpless. Why should I feel that way? I have fought in battles; I have survived kidnapping and shipwreck and war and every kind of outrage. I should be strong. Invincible. But I'm not.

I want to be happy. Can't I be happy, at long last?

I can't be happy without him.

He has been gone for days. How long will this take him?

What if he doesn't come back? That is impossible, he told me before he left. But I have seen many impossible things take place in my life.

There is no need to stay here in this room. He knows where he can find me. There are meetings I can attend. People listen to me in these meetings—Affron and Hieron and the rest. They want my opinion, although they often don't agree with it. They are glad I'm here. I can help. They will let me help.

But I don't want to leave my room. I don't want to speak to anyone, do anything. The others understand.

And then I hear a knock on the door. It isn't Larry. He wouldn't knock, would he? It would be Corscius, or Clovis, or Karellia, or any of a hundred people.

"Come in," I say.

But it is Larry, wearing his odd Earth clothing. He is smiling. It's so good to see him smile! I race into his arms.

"It's all right," he murmurs. "Everything will be all right."

When we have finished embracing he explains a little. There will be complications. He disappeared, and that made him famous. Now that he has returned, he will become famous again. He will have to find a way to explain to his world what happened without really explaining. This sounds hard, but I don't care. His family is fine. His family is lovely. I will love them, even the sister he never got along with.

"Thank you," I say to him. "Thank you for coming back."

He nods. "And now it's time to leave. Together."

We find the others and say our good-byes. The good-byes are hard, but everyone understands. Hieron gives his blessing. Affron says, "Perhaps I'll return to Earth someday. I've always liked your world."

Larry says, "I can't wait." I think perhaps he is joking.

Lamathe and the rest of the priests from Alexandria hug me so hard I think my ribs will crack. I will miss them. I will miss everyone and everything.

But this is what I must do.

Finally we leave the palace and make our way to where Larry has left the portal. *His* portal. In a forgotten alley of a forgotten part of the city.

"Are you ready?" he asks me.

"Of course I'm ready."

He takes my hand, and we walk into the portal.

We are going home.

The End

ALSO BY RICHARD BOWKER

The Portal Series

PORTAL

TERRA

HOME

The Last P.I. Series

Dover Beach

The Distance Beacons

Where All The Ladders Start

The Psychic Thrillers Series

Summit

Marlborough Street

Other Titles

Pontiff (A Thriller)

Replica (A Techno-thriller)

Senator

Forbidden Sanctuary

ABOUT THE AUTHOR

Richard Bowker is the author of many highly regarded science fiction novels, including *Replica*, the Portal series, and the Last P.I. series. His novel *Dover Beach* was a finalist for the Philip K. Dick award as Best Paperback Original Novel. He lives with his wife near Boston.

www.ingramcontent.com/pod-product-compliance
Lightning Source LLC
Chambersburg PA
CBHW072310020726
47501CB00002B/466